WHEN THE MOON WHISPERS

FIRST CHRONICLE

Rebecca Lochlann

ERINYES PRESS

To the readers who stuck with me

And to girls everywhere.
May the world evolve into what it should be,
For you and everyone.

Book Seven

The Child of the Erinyes Series

Crone

A Note to Readers

The physical version of *When the Moon Whispers* is told in two books: the First Chronicle, and the Second Chronicle.

The book you are holding or considering is the first part to the story.

The digital version contains both chronicles in one file.

A list of all the various life names can be found at the end of the Second Chronicle.

Readers Weigh In

"These books, while historical fiction/mythic fantasy/dystopian future, seem to encompass so much of the pain and fear experienced by women in our society. This has been a stunning series that I've enjoyed unfolding. The current edition leaves you wondering about how to galvanize our society in the here and now."

"This, the seventh and final labyrinth the triad must traverse, is a shocking glimpse into a dystopian future where women are stripped of their autonomy and brutally subjugated. Cruelty, a uniquely human trait that can be taught through example as easily as selflessness, is fast becoming societal norm in a stark reflection of humanity's grim past, as well as a projection of what could conceivably come to pass yet again - if the world's oligarchs succeed in manipulating society through selective elimination of current fact and falsely sentimental rewriting of history."

"This book traverses into more of a sci-fi feel than the previous books that were in a historical setting, but Lochlann still manages to keep a lyrical prose. I recommend this series to anyone who enjoyed *Circe* by Madeline Miller, or *The Witches Heart*," (by Genevieve Gornichec).

"Through joy tempered by suffering, and trust undermined by betrayal, Athene's objective, the purpose behind the triad's odyssey, is ultimately revealed. The mystical, enigmatic threads of prophecy interspersed throughout the previous books are woven together seamlessly, revealing their nuanced significance as they come to fruition in an earth-shattering finale."

WHEN THE
MOON
WHISPERS
FIRST CHRONICLE
REBECCA LOCHLANN

The Story so Far

The saga that began in the Bronze Age returns to a dark, dystopian future.

Two brothers topple a society that flourished for thousands of years. Goddess Athene resurrects them, along with the Cretan princess both men love but betray, forcing all three to live seven distinctly different incarnations.

Athene's Resolve (as told to Aridela):
I have lived many lives since the beginning, and so shall thee. I have been given many names and many faces. So shall thee, and thou wilt follow me from reverence and worship into obscurity. In an unbroken line wilt thee return, my daughter. Thou shall be called Eamhair of the sea, who brings them closer, and Shashi, sacrificed to deify man. Thy names are Caparina, Lilith and the sorrowful Morrigan, who drives them far apart. Thou wilt step upon the earth seven times, far into the veiled future; seven labyrinths shall thee wander, lost, and thou too wilt forget me. Suffering and despair shall be thy nourishment. Misery shall poison thy blood; thou wilt breathe the air of slavery, for as long as thou art blinded. For thou art the earth, blessed and eternal, yet thou shall be pierced, defiled, broken and wounded, even as I have been. Thou wilt generate inexhaustible adoration and contempt; until these opposites are united, all will strangle within the void.

Each incarnation has inched these mortals closer, ever closer, to this one.

The Seventh Labyrinth

"She will betray all people everywhere, and her Holy Mother, and all she loves, and all who love her."

Damasen of Crete

"Remember the ladies and be more generous and favorable to them than your ancestors. Do not put such unlimited power into the hands of the husbands. Remember, all men would be tyrants if they could. If particular care and attention is not paid to the ladies, we are determined to foment a rebellion, and will not hold ourselves bound by any laws in which we have no voice or representation."

Abigail Adams, in a letter to her husband, John

The Erinys Archives

Archive One

May, 2049

UTAH

In the Time of Stolen Women

Chapter 1

The first time I stepped into Ramandu's Dawn, I was blindfolded. But I could smell, and I could hear. I heard the kind of expensive silence that lifts one far above the endless noise, stench, and misery of crowded cities. I smelled sage and jasmine, and as Rafe guided me through a door and sunlight struck my face, I smelled the cold, wise scent of timeworn mountains, and billowy cumulus clouds. My ears caught the iconic hoarse *screeer* of a red-tailed hawk, giving voice to joy as it soared on magic carpets of air.

I heard and smelled *home*.

My mother never trusted Rafe, and looking back, I get it. Skipping college, getting pregnant, marrying a rich boy from the part of the city that proudly excluded us? That was not how she envisioned her daughter's foray into adulthood.

This is a story I was told to write. It hasn't been easy. I wasn't sure where to begin, then it came to me. Mine is a record of betrayals. The kind that are right in front of your face. Once you realize, you feel kind of stupid for never seeing them creep up on you. There's a lot of *I should have known* thoughts. Then you realize with a certain twist of the gut that you've betrayed, too. Betrayals run in circles, around and around and around like an ouroboros feeding on itself.

The kind of betrayals I'm talking about devour happy lives. But consuming individual lives isn't enough. They're ravenous. Still unsatisfied, they set out to swallow the world.

Our driver halted at a red light.

"Look," I said. "It's Doctor Provost."

He was sitting in the driver's seat of a van parked against the opposite curb. It was an unexpected but welcome surprise, giving me the opportunity to ask a question that had come to me during the night. My comfort level with the information being transmitted made our interviews on live TV go much more smoothly, not to mention I didn't like asking stupid questions on camera.

I opened the car door and jumped out. "I'll be right back," I said to the driver.

"It's raining." Rafe reached out quickly but I evaded him. Rafe was always reaching for me. I had become rather good at evasion.

"Doctor," I called, hurrying across the empty street. "Hello, Doctor Provost!"

He looked up, his face expressing surprise then annoyance. His gaze traveled beyond me, to Rafe, no doubt. Since his window was open, I clearly saw all this. My steps slowed. "Doctor?"

Glancing over my shoulder, I saw that Rafe was indeed advancing. His scowl didn't bode well.

The doctor ordered his vehicle to start; the VSP warning whistle sang and without speaking a word to me he sent his van careening away, leaving me standing in the middle of the street like a rejected teenager, wondering what she had done wrong.

Now I could see what the van had blocked—four mud-splattered men grouped around a large rectangular hole in the ground. All four held shovels. Another man sat at the controls of an idling backhoe.

Gravestones stretched to the horizon. It was one of the biggest of the city cemeteries, but that hole was too wide and long for a single coffin.

Were we burying people en masse now? What about the law of cremation?

Rafe gripped my upper arm and returned me to the car as drizzle hardened into a downpour.

"Did you see that?" I asked.

He shrugged. "Maybe he was late for an appointment."

"It was rude."

"What can I say? Men are rude."

Our driver politely held the car door for me and we continued to our destination in damp silence.

Doctor Provost didn't show up for the interview. Another man did, one I had never seen before. He was sweaty. His hands trembled and he refused to smile or even look me in the eye.

This was intolerable. While I wouldn't go so far as to say Doctor Provost and I were friends, we had developed a genial pattern of bantering that received positive reviews in nearly every poll.

Now here I was, stuck on live TV trying to draw out this stranger, whose answers to my questions were stilted and vague. He was about as witty as a drugged turtle.

The instant I finished and said thank you, he unclipped his microdot, dropped it into the script supervisor's hand, and stalked away, shrugging out of the white lab coat and flinging it to the floor.

I broke the magnet on my microdot and handed it, with a smile, to the technician, but he kept his gaze averted and didn't see it. What was wrong with everyone today?

"That was perfect." Rafe entered the circle of hot bright light, squinting as he kissed my cheek. The technician switched off the lights and we were plunged into restless shadows.

"It was not perfect. It was awful. Who was that guy? What's his problem? What happened to Doctor Provost?"

"Who knows? Who cares. Come on and get changed. It's pouring rain."

Although I hated it, Rafe insisted on his personal security accompanying me everywhere, even to the bathroom.

Next, he'll be telling them to come in with me. Well, maybe not. Rafe was too jealously possessive to consider something like that, so I could continue to enjoy the luxury of a locked steel door between me and the terse, ex-military stereotype in a black suit that was slightly too small for his muscles. He even had a buzz cut.

I loved the dress I'd worn for the interview, with its elbow length sleeves and sweetheart neckline. It fit close through the bodice and belled out at the waist, a romantic throwback to the nineteen-fifties. Very feminine, covered in tropical hibiscus and plumeria, a nice touch to offset this dreary, wet spring. In the old days, it would be reproduced and flying off the shelves within hours.

I might put it back on for fun when we got home, but right now I had to be dressed like a man, complete with a felt fedora worn low to hide my face. Another of Rafe's paranoid directives.

Folding the dress into a bag, I left the bathroom. The guard escorted me to the auditorium's foyer, where Rafe waited, none too patiently.

Outside, rain fell in sheets. It looked cold and miserable through the fogged glass doors. Four more security guards joined the first. One propped an umbrella over my head; they hustled me down the steps and into the armored SUV.

As I waited for the guards and Rafe to bundle in, I glanced across the street at a gloomy, deserted park, and my heart started missing beats.

He was standing beneath the branches of an oak tree.

The man. Or, more correctly, the hallucination.

Even as I took in the form, which appeared as solid as Rafe and the guards, it melted, leaving nothing but a cloud of copper-colored dust swiftly dispersed by the rain.

There is light water and heavy water. Light water leaps and laughs, dancing sunlight, seeking clouds. Heavy water is weary, its reflection pewter, its sheen hard and impenetrable. It glances into the eye, blinding yet revealing the way.

The slamming of the SUV doors, the smell of wet wool from Rafe's overcoat, the whine of the electric engine—all faded into insignificance next to the bright copper of that apparition and the water images it placed in my brain.

"You hungry?" Rafe asked.

I hardly heard him. "Hmm."

"Take us to Le Melon d'eau, Luka."

"Yes, sir." The driver flipped on the ADAS, cloaking our vehicle in techno-logical shields, and pulled away from the curb. Rafe preferred a human driver to the level 5 fully-automated car systems. He said it was to give men jobs, but I knew it was more of a status thing. Only the wealthiest and most influential had human drivers anymore.

I had never been threatened by anyone since Rafe became President Montague's senior advisor. As far as I knew, neither had he. All this role-playing seemed a bit overblown, but I never said anything. It wasn't my place.

I blinked, but there was nothing under the tree. I knew better than to ask if anyone else had seen it. I'd given that up long ago.

An automated utility transport passed, going the other way. Emblazoned on the side was an ad for a new type of archery set. A laughing boy aimed at a bullseye shaped like a woman's bare buttocks, although that had to be my own weird imagination. "What's with the transports? None of them have my face on the side anymore. Is everyone bored with me?"

"It's not that, sweetheart. Women trust you. Almost all have entered quar-antine. We removed your image so it's not being rubbed in the faces of the men left behind. A gorgeous woman like you? That would be cruel."

He leaned in. "I wouldn't mind if you rubbed it in my face later, though." He laughed as I shoved him.

"I hope I told the truth when I promised it wouldn't last long."

"The best and brightest minds in the world are working twenty-four hours a day on a solution," he reassured me. "Let's get your pill taken care of." He removed a dispenser from his inner coat pocket and shook one out. "Here you go."

Per our set routine, I obediently opened my mouth and he placed the pill on my tongue. They weren't round or oval-shaped but complex icosahedrons, providing interesting textures. Each one imparted a different flavor as it dissolved.

"What was this one?" he asked as he put the dispenser away.

I scowled. "Licorice."

"Ugh. Can't win them all." He leaned in to give me a kiss and laughed again as I turned my face away. I didn't like public displays of affection, as he well knew. The men in the rear of the SUV couldn't hear us, but they could see us through the glass.

I felt their resentful stares bombarding the back of my head like waves of radiation.

They had no women to kiss.

WHEN WE GOT HOME, OUR AI ALERTED ME TO A TRANSMISSION FROM THE President.

"Read it to me, Samson," I said, removing my jacket and tossing the fedora on the counter.

A perfect imitation of Henry Montague's voice spoke as though he was in the room.

"Congratulations, Erin!

"I want to send a heartfelt thank you for all you have done. Do you know how invaluable you've been? I state without reservation that you have played a key part in saving the very future of humankind! Without you, most women would never commit themselves to a quarantine. Though they know it's for their own good, even with the enticement of a generous stipend, it's a long-held matter of pride among Americans to be suspicious of anything the government asks of them.

"It is because of you, my dear, that this was accomplished in such a smooth, secure manner."

I glanced at Rafe, who had arguably done more than I to pull off these difficult goals. He shrugged, giving me a magnanimous smile.

Samson continued. "I look forward to the day when lunacy is a thing of the past and we can have our lives back. I don't have to tell you how much I miss my wife.

"In the meantime, I am happy to report that after today, except for televising you and your daughter joining the others in quarantine, we are suspending your interviews and video chats. The few women who continue to resist will be gently rounded up and brought in.

"Rafe is lucky to have you, Erin.

"God bless,

"Henry Montague."

Samson displayed a hologram of the official presidential seal and several scrawled initials.

"That's so nice," I said.

Rafe wasn't surprised. He must have known about Henry's plan to contact me. They were like brothers. After Henry made Rafe his official aide-de-camp and Senior Policy Advisor, Rafe became his go-to in everything, large and small, though he was only twenty-nine to Henry's sixty-six.

"Don't be long," he said as I left the kitchen. "I want you."

Deep inside, I tingled. I couldn't pinpoint the exact moment I'd started enjoying sex as much as he did, but I wasn't complaining. We were intimately synced in a way I rarely saw in other couples.

McKenna bounced up and down on her bed as I came into her room. "Mommy!"

Dismissing the nanny—I struggled with the presence of a male nanny, but there was no other choice these days—I picked her up and she wrapped her arms around my neck. I dropped into the rocking chair, tucked her beside me, and we talked about her day.

Eventually, she fell asleep, her cheek on my chest. As I sat and rocked, nearly asleep myself, it hit me. My role as the public face, the spokesperson of the Protective Quarantine, was over. I'd liked being so important, and at only twenty-six, leading the world's women, old and young, to healing and health.

Rafe and I lived luxuriously, both in DC and, when we could get away, Deer Valley, a resort village tucked into the mountains east of Salt Lake City. Yet I could honestly say I was not afraid to enter into the confines of quarantine. I wanted to do my part and had publicly eschewed the monthly reimbursement promised to women who voluntarily committed themselves, so that someone more deserving could have it.

Maybe I would be the patient who ultimately received the cure. I had as much chance as anyone.

The time had really come. We would have to go. Though McKenna and I were lucky enough to have no symptoms, it was one of my promises to the women of America, that we would join them as soon as my message was complete. Our housekeeper, Naomi, and Emilia, McKenna's original nanny, had already gone.

Henry Montague's email was more than a thank you. It was farewell.

I couldn't tell my daughter when life would return to normal. I couldn't give her a date when we would come home, or when she would see her father. No one knew how long it would take the doctors and scientists to find an effective treatment or cure, and visitations were forbidden, because they hadn't figured out exactly how the disease spread. No men were infected as of yet, but strict precautions made sense as so little was understood about this deadly illness.

My sight blurred. I felt fresh empathy for the women who had already said goodbye to their loved ones. I pressed my nose to my daughter's hair and breathed in her wonderful scent, of powdery baby shampoo and something else, something irresistible and ephemeral. A scent, I suspected, specifically shared between mothers and their children.

Rafe would continue to shine, but I would be quickly forgotten, since I would no longer be on the news, in the tabloids, or smiling on transports and in subpod concourses.

Fame and fortune were fickle playmates.

I would be absorbed into quarantine, one of the many faceless female patients, some of whom had active lunacy—an ugly name that stuck for its supposed connection to the second moon—and others, like me, who remained completely normal.

There was no escape. I would contract it at some point. I wasn't afraid, though. Somehow, I knew I wouldn't die. I was never afraid for myself, only for McKenna.

"There's Henry." Rafe donned his famed public smile, full of confidence, white teeth, and hints of seduction. The way he brought that smile into his eyes was what made the magic. Women melted and men sought to please. Only I knew the other Rafe, the one who thrashed in his sleep, muttering strange names, shouting. On occasion he woke with tears streaming down his face. His nightmares could get so bad I would have to intervene, and then endure him not knowing me and calling for someone else. He never remembered doing that after he fully woke, and used to accuse me of making it up, so I quit asking who that other woman was, the one he dreamed of so often.

I suffered from repetitive nightmares too, ghastly dreams of being bitten by snakes and carved with a knife. I didn't tell Rafe about them. They were too disturbing to share with someone who would only laugh. I wished I could laugh, but since I had slightly raised, crescent-shaped scars of unknown origin over every one of my pulse points, it was impossible.

I had a habit of running my fingers over the scars when I was worried or concentrating. There was a different kind of mark on the inside of my left wrist, a reddish birthmark shaped rather like the head of a bull. The crescent-shaped scar nestled between the horns like a crown. In times past, when I suffered from uncontrolled anxiety, those diminutive scars made themselves known. The first time I ever saw Rafe, as our eyes met through a chain link fence, they all throbbed simultaneously. That was many years ago, but I remembered.

A black luxury pod, dotted with antennas and probes that masked it from spy drones, pulled in beneath the massive stone porte-cochère; our man rushed to open the door as the security switched off. Henry Montague, president of the United States, smiled suavely and straightened his lapels as he strode to us. Armed guards followed, fanning around him.

He shook Rafe's hand. "Am I the first?"

"Yes, but look, here comes one of the others now."

As Henry moved from Rafe to me, literally picking me up and twirling me in a circle, an identical pod pulled into the spot vacated by the first.

"It's been too long since I've seen you, sweet thing." He gave my cheek a smacking kiss, and I pleased him with a giggle.

He didn't ask how I was feeling. Nobody ever asked anybody that question anymore.

Our other two guests had apparently decided to come together. I wasn't sure I liked that, and glanced at Rafe, but his face revealed nothing, so I let my suspicion go. First to exit the pod was Grigory Andreiovich Novikov, like a ramrod and taller than any of his security detail. He called himself the president of Ukrus, but in truth he was its dictator. He was followed by the short and paunchy Soung Jae-jin, also officially titled president of North Korea, also a dictator. A man and woman followed. I pegged the man as a scientist, due to his distracted air and the leather portfolio clutched in his arms. His hair was unkempt and so was his beard. Scientists and astronomers were rock stars in this world dominated by mystery, fear, and violence, but they didn't always dress the part. The woman was immaculate and glamorous. Maybe she was a wife, maybe a concubine.

An SUV pulled in behind the second pod. SFUV, I amended, once I saw the full array of technology, one of the rare and elite Special Forces Utility Vehicles. It had quite the menacing air, with its silver armor and blinkers that gave warning; when activated, the slightest touch would result in a lethal shock. The blinkers cut off and about twenty armed men disgorged from both sides. More male paranoia. Our house was already inundated with security. Over the last week every nook and cranny had been scanned, every electronic device examined, and a thermal infrared tower erected, cloaking the property under an invisible screen to prevent eavesdropping by drones, for this meeting was taking place at night, in utmost secrecy.

Rafe was tight-lipped, but I'd gathered tonight's affair was at the request of Novikov, a long overdue follow-up to their classified one-on-one meeting in Moscow about a year and a half ago. Rafe had missed Christmas, and after he got home, he was moody and preoccupied. For the next six months his nightmares exploded in frequency. I tried not to harass him, as he was overwhelmed with the responsibility of setting up the Protective Quarantine, as well as finding the right words to bring the American people on board.

My unverified theory was that Novikov hoped to persuade Henry to abandon the Western Alliance and throw the United States into the ever-expanding pot with Ukrus—Novikov's reimagined name for Mother Russia and the many countries it had absorbed. I could think of no other reason for this meeting.

If so, it was a waste of time. Henry wouldn't do that, not even if Novikov got down and kissed his bare ass. America would never relinquish its independence and we hated Ukrus, not because of the barbarity it exhibited towards its inhabitants but for the fact that it had grown so bloated, arrogant, and threatening. Ukrus was the only true competition to the US in terms of sheer size and military power. War between us would result in extermination of the human race, or at least a dystopia of epic proportions.

I'd never met these foreign leaders, and I was nervous. The things I'd heard…

The approaching visitors were not our friends. They weren't America's friends.

But I had these two men, one on each side, towering over me. I felt categorically bulwarked.

Novikov's eyes were glacial. He didn't smile. He looked like a man who never smiled. I stared, nonplussed. How could he appear so *young*? Twenty-seven maybe, thirty at most. How could that be? This man had murdered the

Russian president in 2030, nineteen years ago. True, plastic surgery had made impressive advances, but this was beyond anything I'd ever seen.

The damnable little scars throbbed and burned like they were on fire.

I tried to rally, reminding myself that Henry and Rafe were ready to defend me like knights of old. I would show no fear.

Rafe held out his hand and spoke a flawless Russian greeting. Novikov replied in kind. Rafe duplicated the greeting to Soung Jae-jin, in Korean.

It wasn't necessary. Both men spoke English. It was a gesture of respect, though. It made me angry how neither one showed the slightest appreciation.

The anger almost, but not quite, overshadowed the sense of impending doom that swept over me, as if something horrible was catapulting at me with the velocity of a rocket.

There is a saying about blood running cold. As Novikov's gaze landed on me, I knew what a mouse feels as it stares into the eyes of a hawk. I couldn't move.

Rafe had draped his arm around my shoulders as the two men approached. His embrace now tightened. Perhaps he sensed my unease.

Novikov kissed my knuckles, but his lips mocked with a slight sneer. Why? Did he not like my dress? My hair? Perhaps he simply hated women, as so many men did, blaming us for every bad thing that had ever happened or was happening in this world. Since the second moon came, blame had become a tiresome diversion for many. Thanks to the lunacy, much of it fell on women.

Soung Jae-jin gave an almost imperceptible nod, as if acknowledging my presence was a waste of his precious time.

After the greeting to Henry was completed, Rafe and I escorted our guests inside.

I was proud of our Utah home. Modeled after the fanciest of French country houses, it had once been a ritzy gathering spot for wealthy skiers, but was abandoned after the financial debacle of 2028, when so many lost their livelihoods, including the owner of the resort. Rafe bought the chateau and the entire mountain upon which it sat as a wedding gift, and I spent nearly eight years on the renovation.

It had an open, expansive design, with enormous flagstone fireplaces, impossibly high ceilings of golden oak, formal and informal rooms that catered to every occasion, and a chef's delight of a fully computerized kitchen. We had created areas to accommodate any mood, a music room and dance studio with two pianos on a dais—it was a dream of mine that McKenna learn how to play, but I was putting off instruction until the end of this crisis—a connected ballroom for our once-a-year holiday parties—also on hold—a sunroom designed to resemble the Amazon Rainforest, twin libraries, numerous studies, and a movie theater. There were three swimming pools, two outdoors and one inside, hot tubs, and sumptuous bath suites that provided everything one could desire in the way of pampering. The master bedroom was a two-story affair, encompassing the entire third floor and part of the fourth. We'd added an observatory; it was completely glassed in, both ceiling and walls, for stargazing, which we both loved to do, and with the clearer air here, we could often see the Milky Way. We would stare at Saturn and Jupiter through the telescope and wonder when humans would move into space and leave this ruined Earth behind.

It was too late for a formal meal but I'd arranged for an array of elegant snacks to be served in a prepared conference room on the first floor, along with a well-stocked wet bar.

Once the men entered the conference room, I was no longer needed. Arm candy, that was me. A subtle, or not-so-subtle message of affluence. Since the lunacy struck, walking, talking, visible women had become as rare as tanzanite, and Rafe knew how to make an impression.

I smiled, inclined my head, and asked if there was anything else I could do. Novikov's lips quirked; in response a scowl so menacing passed over Rafe's face that I feared what might happen. Henry cleared his throat. I excused myself before my presence could cause more harm, thanking the universe that my blushes were not readily visible.

My obligations were complete. I poured a large glass of wine and went out to the main terrace. It didn't matter if I drank too much. I wouldn't see any of them again tonight.

Moonlight turned the snow-capped summits a mystical kind of bluish-white, almost violet. Setting the glass on a table, I shook my arms, stretched from side to side, and bent at the waist, pressing my palms to the flagstones in an effort to excise the tension of the last few days. Whatever happened now, I had done my best. My duty.

"Are you feeling well, Mrs. Konstantinou?" Samson spoke as softly as a breath. "Can I help?"

"Just releasing some stress." Our interface had sensors that could detect things like an elevated heart rate and spiking adrenaline caused from electro-pulses between the dACC and the hypothalamus. Or the amygdala. Those were the only terms I could remember from Samson's patient attempts to explain the workings of a human brain, and I always mixed them up. "This wine will do the trick."

"I could ask someone to bring you a pill."

"No, I don't like mixing those with alcohol. I'm not feeling anxious. This is fine, Samson."

"As you wish, Mrs. Konstantinou," came the reply, and I was alone again.

I always knew Rafe would make his mark, though I never could have predicted that he and the most powerful leaders in the world would be sitting in my house finagling the course of the planet over cigars and Scotch whisky.

Out of nowhere, alone on the terrace with a glass of wine, loneliness washed over me. I wished like hell I could call Maya and vent.

But my main worries centered around state secrets that couldn't be shared, even if I knew what they were beyond my own conjectures. Not to mention the other dilemma, that my best friend didn't like my husband. My husband didn't like her. I realized as I contemplated the shadowy mountains and blazing central swath of the Milky Way, that I hadn't seen her but once since McKenna was born.

It wasn't all my fault. She was busy too. She'd probably finished medical school by now and started her residency. Her vow was to turn the institutionalized world of psychiatry inside out and remake it from scratch.

Dropping onto a chaise lounge, I covered myself in a warm, fleecy blanket and sipped wine.

Sudden searing pain in every one of the small crescent scars brought me erupting out of a deep sleep. The moons were in a different position. It was colder.

Before I could react beyond a small indrawn breath, I heard the men's voices.

And life, as I knew it, was destroyed.

Archive Two

April, 2072

TWENTY-THREE YEARS LATER

SNEFFELS

A Jerry Garcia Tie

Chapter 1

The cake landed with a thud and slid halfway off its bioplastic plate.

Will sighed. "Is cake illegal now?"

"And this coat." The interrogator held it up. "Were you planning on losing more than half your weight and shortening your arms so it would fit?"

"My father is smaller than me. I want to give it to him for Christmas, unless you confiscate it."

"Why were you shopping in Montrose?"

"I like full strength beer. I don't like shopping so I come over to Montrose to get all the non-perishables I'll need for a month or two, including beer. Maybe you could tell me what I've done wrong. I have a dog that isn't getting fed."

"Your passport says you live in Monticello. Moab would be much closer."

"I don't like Moab. It's crowded with bikers and tourists and there's no liquor store anymore, only breweries. When I come to Montrose, I get a scenic drive and I can buy everything I want in one place. Look, I've been doing this for years, and there's never been a problem. I have a valid passport and my face is scanned every time I go through the roadblocks."

"What was your exact route? Step by step."

Drawing in a breath and blowing it out again so the officer would understand just how bored and annoyed he was, Will recited. "491 to 141 and up to 145. I take 145 east to 62 till I get to Ridgeway, where I catch 550 to Montrose." Did they really think he could be tripped up that easily?

The detective tapped his wrist and studied the holo that popped up. It was backwards to Will, but he could see it was a list, probably a record of his jaunts through the Utah-Colorado checkpoint.

Now he would find out if his elaborate methods to throw the government off his trail had been worthwhile.

"You can't see why that's suspicious?"

"No. It's a two-hour drive and I only do it once a month. We're allowed two cross-state trips a month, or has that changed?" Had they found his tech? Had a drone spotted him on the century-old ruts he used when he wanted to sneak undetected from one state to the other?

"Are you Indian?"

"You think I look like I'm from India?"

The man blinked and amended. "American Indian."

"You have my passport. No doubt you know more about me than I do."

There was a knock on the door and a man peeked in. "A minute, Kendall?"

Will's interrogator nodded and left, closing the door behind him.

Will stared at the cake. If these men had five brain cells between them, they would find the tech on the Jeep. Even if they didn't realize the paint was heat-absorbing, they would take note of the switch that activated the adaptive camouflage, though he'd made it look archaic, a metal lever that clicked up and down and also started the windshield wipers. He hadn't even tried to hide the water tanks, mounting them on the rear bumper to keep the dust down when he went off road. He'd thought he could come up with a reason for that, if necessary.

Then there was the radar jammer, but it was small and hidden.

If they didn't buy his story…if they found the illegal tech…if some random drone pinged him crossing the border on those backcountry desert trails…

They could potentially track him right back to the cabin.

And Erin.

Hold on, Erin. Don't be afraid. I won't let them find us.

He tapped the surface of the table, eight fingers, one after the other in a rolling pattern that helped dissipate his worry. Like everyone else, he'd heard of methods used to get the truth. People didn't have the rights they'd taken for granted in times past. If this detective wanted to, he could pull out Will's fingernails, or teeth, or burn him, or any number of unpleasant things. All was allowed these days in a government official's quest for truth.

The detective returned. Something was different. He came in, leaving the door open, and looked at the wall behind Will's head rather than belligerently into Will's eyes.

"We've finished the background check." He tossed Will's old leather wallet on the table, followed by the holographic passport giving him permission to travel between Utah and Colorado. "You're free to go."

Will picked up the wallet and passport, keeping his smug triumph hidden, though inside he lifted his middle finger.

He knew what had happened. All his life, he'd hated and begrudged his name, until now.

"Everything you had with you is by your Jeep."

Erin was safe…for the moment.

Will shoved the wallet and passport into his back pocket. "Keep the cake," he said, but he took the coat.

The detective's lips tensed.

Outside, he threw the supply boxes into the Jeep's rear seat. He could still feel the silent, suspicious stares of the policemen he'd walked past inside. No surprise, the beer was gone.

He ordered the engine to engage and did his best to peal out, remembering wishfully the days when one could slam a heavy foot on the gas pedal and leave the sound and smell of burning rubber, not to mention a cloud of noxious gasoline fumes. Nowadays, with everything being solar-powered, gunning vehicles just didn't make the same kind of statement.

His tech was undisturbed. Maybe they'd been too interested in the boxes to spend any time on a rusty vehicle that appeared to be held together with popsicle sticks and glue. They'd fallen for the illusion. Thank providence.

His overwhelming instinct was to drive directly and swiftly to the cabin. Erin must be out of her mind. He'd already been gone too long, and she didn't handle changes in routine very well.

But those assholes could have affixed a GPS on the Jeep, or sent a drone to follow him, disguised as a dragonfly or something even smaller.

He would have to abandon the Jeep he'd worked so hard on. He'd need a ghillie suit, so he could bushwhack through heavy forest until he threw off any possible tracking. Then he'd have to acquire another vehicle, one that could make it up the astoundingly horrible roads to the cabin.

Chapter 2

From her eyrie, the eagle inspected the forests, mountains, and valleys, the pure cerulean lakes and wild, foamy rivers that made up her world. She plucked at something in her nest, trying three times before she hooked it securely in her beak. Spreading her wings, she took off, soaring over an ever-changing landscape before spiraling downward and gliding above a stream swollen with snowmelt. Picking her spot, she released what she held in her beak, circled a few times, then flew away.

The morning was clear and crisp, the sky a bottomless pool of blue—the best time for wandering.

This path used to be popular among those who wanted to get out and enjoy nature. Yet today, even with aspen leaves sprouting and tender new tips forming on spruce trees, even though the snow was retreating, I hadn't encountered a single hiker. While it did seem strange, I had noticed a steady decline in human visitors over the past several years, something for which I was not sorry.

Movement drew my eye to the middle of Dallas Creek. As I watched, transfixed, a large golden eagle swooped down and dropped something. It circled then lifted high, higher, making a few of those peculiarly whistling eagle cries, *yip yip yip*. The object it dropped fell only a meter or so before getting caught in a tangle of branches from a fallen tree. Rushing water caused the branches to twitch and jerk, which in turn caused the object to catch and reflect sunlight like a beacon. Shading my eyes with one hand, I tried to determine what it was, but the movement and ever-changing reflections made it impossible.

I started to go on then stopped. Voices. At least two males were coming up the path. They would be upon me any second.

Right after thinking how I hadn't seen anyone in so long. Go figure.

Through sheer luck, one of my many hiding places was nearby. I turned off the path and crouched beside the trunk of a huge old ponderosa pine that had been struck by lightning or burned in a fire long ago. Over the years the damaged trunk developed a triangle-shaped opening and an eroded, hollow space underneath that I could, and had, fit into on occasion. I slipped through and dropped onto damp earth at the tree's core.

I'd had the most vivid daydreams in this secret space. Once, I dreamed I was chained by the wrist to the inner wall. As I struggled to escape, an invisible female told me I was the betrayer as well as the promise. I never forgot the seductive scent of decaying wood and earth, or the soft, sorrowful voice.

The tree trunk wrapped protectively around me. Standing inside, my head a little higher than ground level, I could see through the weeds and across the path. I even caught glimpses of the object hanging in the debris over Dallas Creek. This lower angle changed its reflections from bright white to infinite colors, like leaping rainbows.

The men were close, climbing the upward slope of the path. I heard every word of their exchange.

"I don't see the problem."

"Of course you don't. You've never known anything else, but damn it, there are things I miss. The challenge. I always thought that's what gave a man his spirit. Hell, it'd be nice if a woman chose me, on her own. There's nothing like the sparkle in a woman's eye when she likes you, when you know that at the end of the night, you're gonna get in there and she's gonna respond. There was a secret sort of invisible wavelength, I guess you could call it, and when two people were tuned in, it was magic. You're too young, but I remember what that felt like. I remember a lot of things."

"I couldn't care less what a woman thinks or whether she likes me. The only thing that pisses me off is what I have to do to get what I want."

"You've been pissed as hell ever since Carnevale."

"I worked damn hard to get into that. I spent almost everything I had while I was there, and ended up with nothing."

"I tried to teach you how to track when you were a kid."

"Rub it in, damn it. Rub it in."

"Don't you ever miss your mom? What about Heidi? We never even got to bury them."

"That was a long time ago, Uncle David. Life goes on."

The surge of Dallas Creek was drowning them out now. "You need to… man, and quit…things…you killed."

This was followed by silence. They were passing beyond the tree, their voices no longer coming at me, but away.

I thought I heard "a reckoning," but I wasn't sure. "I wonder..." His next words were lost. Then, "Germans said when Hitler..."

They hiked on and I heard no more. What the hell? That might be the strangest conversation I'd ever eavesdropped on.

We will make ourselves barren. No more children. No more love. Not until they all lie dead. Then we will begin again.

This extraordinary declaration had resided deep in my psyche for longer than I could pin down. Every now and then it floated to the surface as it did now, drifting from behind my eyelids and through the triangle-shaped opening in the trunk of the pine tree. I watched pale ghosts of each word glide and waver over the wild tumble of white diamonds and sapphire crystals that formed the essence of Dallas Creek in early spring. Frenzied spray reared up and dispersed them, leaving nothing but inscrutable forest on the far side.

A beetle crawled over the back of my hand, its scratchy little feet bringing me out of reverie and chasing away the shroud of silence that came with that perplexing vow.

The object in the branches glimmered. *I wonder how deep it is there? That water will be damn cold if it gets in my boots.*

I listened but couldn't hear the men or anyone else. Nothing but the warbling of a bluebird above me and the eternal gush of water. I crawled out, brushed dirt from my hair, and returned to the pebbly bank.

Two moons hung in the sky, one close and gloriously white with the rising sun shining on it, the other farther away, bluish and hazy, like a lamp through veils of fog, which was why everyone started calling it *L'ombre Moon*. I kept my gaze on them as I took deep breaths, preparing myself for wading into this mad flow of water.

I often lay outside the cabin at dusk to watch our moons rise. I thought of them as pearls set into the heavens by an invisible god-hand, shy or sly, depending on how light struck the craters. In the cities, pollution blurred them into mere smudges, but here in the San Juan Mountains, at an altitude of 3800 meters, every expression in the nearer moon was clearly etched, barring clouds.

I stepped in. My boots were waterproof, so there was only a chilly sensation. I took several more steps, fighting the frenetic current. I was almost there and could tell that the object was metal. It looked like jewelry. My next step dropped off; I sank to mid-calf and nearly lost my footing as the creek bed shifted under my boot. Water flooded in. *Damn it's cold!*

But I'd come this far. I took two more steps, working to keep upright as water penetrated both boots.

Brilliant quicksilver embracing a cobalt blue bead.

Lapis lazuli.

Where the hell did that come from? I had no idea what lapis lazuli was. I'd heard of it, of course, but I wouldn't know lapis lazuli from an opal.

I untangled the chain and squelched back to shore, shivering as I held the beautiful ornament up to the light.

Will would be interested in this. I wonder if he's home yet?

The sound of flowing water diminished. I fell into a spell created by the mesmerizing depth of a swaying blue stone crisscrossed with filaments of white and specks of gold.

Movement out of the corner of my eye brought my gaze up. *The hallucination.*

I hadn't seen it in a very long time, not since before I came to Will's cabin over twenty years ago.

It was standing closer to me than it ever had. I saw new details, like the dark, rich, coppery shade of hair and glowing blue eyes. For the first time, the hallucination's mouth moved, though I heard nothing; its arm stretched forward, fingers spread, and I saw something that made me stop breathing.

A replica of my birthmark on its wrist.

It vanished into glittering dust as every crescent scar on my body burst into violent throbbing.

Not until they all lie dead. Then we will begin again.

That voice. It was mine. My own voice.

When had I said that?

Why had I said it?

What did it mean?

I lost the spell when I was seized from behind.

"A WOMAN!"

"I don't believe it. Is this our lucky day or what?"

"Wait a minute—"

"No way! A tiger, too. Thinks she can win. News flash, little girl. There's two of us, and we're a lot stronger than you."

"Wait a minute. Who is she? Why is she here?"

"You think it's a trap? Right now, I'm inclined to believe those rumors about phantoms."

I'd always concealed myself from strangers, even before Will advised me to. I never really examined why I was so afraid of encountering people on hiking trails. It was wholly instinctual.

No matter how hard I struggled, I could not break free. My shoulder joints threatened to come apart. I would chew off my own hand to get away. Not getting away might mean death, or worse.

One of them had my wrists smashed together right in front of my face.

Wait. Chew!

Bite!

"Who are you?"

"Who cares who she is? We can keep her, Uncle David! I'll build a bunker. We'll tie her up and gag her, put her in that old gun cabinet in the garage till it's done. No one will ever know." The man threw back his head and laughed. "After all I've gone through to get a woman, and one falls into my lap on a damn hike! I now officially believe in serendipity."

I sank my teeth into his thumb, harder than I had ever bitten anything in my life. I think I even growled as I imagined ripping it clear off.

"Ow, goddamn it, you bitch!"

The thumb was yanked free. I saw blood. The hand doubled up and slugged me on the cheekbone.

"John—"

"Stop it. Don't try to ruin this. I'm willing to share, but if you don't want it, fine. Leave. You're not going to change my mind. This is a once in a lifetime opportunity. I can fuck her whenever I feel like it, without having to kiss some guy's ass first. You're goddamn right I'm going for this."

"You know what happens to men who hide women."

A shadow fell across the sun and one of the men shouted *Fuck what's that!*

There was a trilling, yipping sound and a steady beating, somewhat like old-fashioned helicopter blades. No. A bird's wings. A large bird by the sound of it. *That eagle.*

The hands fell away. I didn't waste time trying to figure out what was going on. I ran. I raced through the forest, gasping, searching for anything that would offer hiding. The necklace was torn from my fingers as I shoved between two pine trees, but I didn't pause.

One of them caught my upper arm, jerking me hard then throwing me to the ground.

Only one. Maybe I could—

He flung himself over me, holding me with his superior weight. He lowered his face. I thought he was going to kiss me, but he put his nose close to my head and smelled my hair. He did the same thing under my ear. When he raised his head, his eyes were gleaming.

I knew that look. Every woman is born knowing that look. Triumphant. Hungry. Pitiless.

Something struck him. He fell away and the other man was there, pushing him off me with one foot. There was a thick branch in his hand. "You can come with me on your own or I can carry you. Either way. Doesn't matter to me."

I spat at him and kicked, catching him near the groin.

"Fine," he gasped. Grimacing, he raised the branch and swung.

There was a white, blinding shock of pain. Then, nothing.

Chapter 3

RAFE IMAGINED BEATING HIS BROTHER'S FACE UNTIL THERE WAS NOTHING LEFT BUT bloody pulp. He breathed shallowly, deliberately, trying to maintain restraint, at least until he'd heard everything.

Twenty—no, thirty, hell, maybe thirty-five years since they'd last seen each other. Will's face was lined, stubbled, his hair threaded with gray, his hands dry and weathered. Thanks to the length of his dark hair and prominent cheekbones, the faded jeans, worn boots, and tee shirt that had seen better days, he was a perfect stereotype of the aging half-breed from an old Western. All he needed was a cigarette dangling from the corner of his mouth.

He was thin. Miserable, tormented, at the end of his unraveling rope. The old scar that slashed through his left eyebrow and circled his eye stood out, white and wicked. Rafe didn't often see scars, except on punished women. Most men had them fixed if they could afford it, along with wrinkles, sunspots, and hair loss. If he'd learned anything in his fifty-two years, it was that men were intrinsically as vain as their female counterparts. Even with no women to impress, men did everything they could to hold the signs of aging at bay. He'd heard that the remedy for erectile dysfunction was as popular as ever, though one had to wonder who these men were having sex with. Each other, no doubt, though the penalty was death.

As he stared, taking in the changes, he glimpsed translucent color roiling around Will's head. The vividness of the blue, the way it churned, signaled emotion barely held in check. As a child, the phenomenon around his baby brother had frightened Rafe. He didn't know what it was or if it would hurt him. Eventually it vanished. He'd almost forgotten it had ever been there.

Erin, his beloved Erin, had run away and hooked up with this. Not only hooked up with, but she'd chosen Will over him all this time. *Will.* It would hurt less if she plunged a knife into his heart.

Apparently, she didn't even have a tracking tattoo, which explained why the best operatives search-crypto could buy, not to mention official government investigators, had never been able to get a hit on her.

His wife was a True Phantom.

"I didn't know what else to do," Will said.

"That's obvious."

"Are you going help or not? Maybe you don't care about her anymore."

"Oh, I care. I'm trying to get my head around the fact that my wife is not dead. She's been with *you* for twenty-three years."

Will said nothing.

"And you never once thought to let me know."

"Water under the bridge. Look, I tracked her to about six kilometers east of the cabin. There was blood on the ground, a tree limb, and signs of a fight. Someone—actually more than one person—was dragged off, and I found this."

Rafe didn't know he'd risen until he found himself ripping the necklace from Will's hand.

Twenty years ago. That was the last time he'd seen this bit of silver. Three years after Erin disappeared, he ran across it at the back of his safe and took it onto the terrace to examine it under a jeweler's loupe.

"I gave this to her." He felt like his bones were dissolving. That wasn't true. He had intended to give it to her, but she vanished before he had a chance.

"You did?" One of Will's brows lifted. "I've never seen it."

"Maybe you don't know her as well as you think you do."

Hatred ignited between them like one of those summer blazes that start out of nowhere and ravage entire states. They were equally tall, but Will was thinner. Worry was burning every calorie. That or Erin's cooking. She'd never been very good at putting a meal together.

"Give it back." Will held out his hand.

Rafe hesitated. He didn't want to, but in the end, he shrugged and tossed it. Will caught it and stuffed it in his jeans pocket. What did it matter, anyway?

"Mr. Konstantinou." Rafe's secretary rose from the chair by the door, where he'd been alternately scribbling and searching his holo for any careless scrap of information, rumor, or gossip that might help. "We should take this as good news. Your wife has been found at last. Surely she's not dead. If her attacker had killed her, he would have left her body where it lay. If anyone can find out where she is and what happened, it's you, sir."

"That's why I'm here." Will pressed the heels of his hands against his eyelids. "The *only* reason I'm here. Because I know you can find her."

True Phantoms, the both of them. As rare as…as declarations of *till death do us part*, these days. "How did she come to you? Did she know you before? Did the two of you plan it? Don't even think of lying to me."

"No. None of that is important now. It was happenstance. Fate. I don't know. Fucking kismet."

Rafe forced himself to return to his chair, using the shining expanse of his desktop as a buffer between them. "I thought you lived in Monticello."

Will's head jerked slightly. "Checking up on me?"

"Father wanted to know once, a long time ago."

"I have a place in Monticello."

"Thaddeus."

"Yes sir?" The secretary looked up from his holo.

"Anything?"

"No, sir. Not yet."

"Get Flannery. Tell him to start an investigation. Tell him I want it underway within the next two hours, and I'll expect an initial report tomorrow morning. Tell him no hint of this gets out. Understand?"

"Immediately, sir."

Glaring at his brother, he added, "Tell him to start around Ouray and cover the whole area from Ridgeway to Telluride. He won't find anything in Utah."

Will flushed.

"Yes, sir." Thaddeus left, closing the door behind him.

Rafe leveled Will with his coldest, most threatening stare, the kind that sent underlings into panic, but it had no visible effect on his brother.

"I will find her. She had better be alive, damn you. I hold you responsible—"

"I hold myself responsible. Does that make you feel better? Do whatever you want to me. Just help her. Find her."

Will's hands were shaking.

Oh, don't tempt me. If I did whatever I wanted, you would never see the light of day again. I would lock you so far down you would feel the heat of the earth's core. "The only reason I don't have you arrested for kidnapping is because of our mother, and I'm pretty sure I'll regret it in another five minutes."

"She'd bake you a cake," Will said indifferently.

Rafe's vocal cords burned with tension. When he spoke, his voice was hoarse. "I have conditions. You will never attempt to contact her. Never see her again. Ever. If you do, you'll find yourself in a maximum-security prison for the rest of your sorry life and I'll stop protecting her. I won't lift a finger for either of you."

"Why am I not surprised? Not even saving Erin comes without a price. Yes, all right. As long as you let me know when you find her. Let me know she's alive. If you do that, I'll stay away."

Rafe nodded. "Not a problem."

"No wonder they call you the Cannibal."

Chapter 4

EVEN IN THE DEAD OF WINTER, WHEN SNOW DRIFTED HIGHER THAN MY HEAD, THE rising sun blasted the east-facing veranda at the cabin with warmth. I quickly grew to love waking up, snuggling under a blanket on a chaise lounge Will had carved from a fallen ponderosa pine, sipping coffee, and being introspective. Mostly thinking of McKenna, though I never said so. I usually had one of my hands upon Duke's massive skull, scratching his ears while he rested his heavy head on my thighs.

Chickadees and sparrows were always happy to greet another new day on the mountain, and we had a doe who came to visit nearly every morning, thanks to the alfalfa bale Will provided. In spring and summer, she brought along a fawn.

Duke never threatened them. A Norwegian Elkhound and hunter by nature, he seemed to sense our affection for these wary guests. Maybe he considered them our pets, since we put out food for them.

The only creatures I loved as much as deer were dolphins. If reincarnation was the truth of the universe and I had to return as an animal, I hoped I could be a dolphin. I'd swim in tropical waters, chatter in dolphin-language, and race my brethren through foamy spindrift.

Dolphins would never muddle things up the way humans did. They were too smart.

Will was going to teach me how to kill with a bow, flesh the hide, and carve the meat. Even if I never had to kill anything, he said, it was a good skill to master. Me, the city girl, who never left the house without perfume and mascara. He'd already given me riding lessons and I was learning how to cook on a wood stove. My rabbit stew was actually becoming edible, or it would be if I could remember to add salt and pepper.

I watched the doe and her fawn step timidly into the meadow and cross to the alfalfa. The fawn kicked up its heels and galloped around its mother, prompting a breathy *woof* from Duke.

Will sat in his creaky rocker with a cup of steaming coffee. The old jeans he wore had holes in the knees. So did the straw cowboy hat he'd pushed back on his head. Pale, deep squint lines fanned from the corners of his eyes, and his hands, resting on the armrests of the rocker, looked tough enough to wrestle grizzlies.

Halos of color formed around him, bewitching blue and violet curling into hints of indigo. I'd first seen this the night we met. It was vivid that night, but had grown fainter every day since. Soon, I feared, I would no longer see it at all.

"Will…"

He didn't respond. "Will?"

Nothing. He watched the deer, ignoring both his coffee and me. He was motionless, like a painting or a statue. He didn't even blink. "Will!"

My voice echoed. A tunnel, round and close and dark, wrenched me off the veranda and thrust me into a square of white light.

He never turned, even when my calls escalated to screams.

I FELT WALLS CLOSING IN AROUND ME. IT SMELLED LIKE THE HOLLOWED-OUT PINE tree near Dallas Creek.

A low, menacing growl exhaled from the darkness. A lion. In Colorado, in the Uncompahgre National Forest, it would be a cougar.

Then I heard the breathing. Quiet, calm breathing, and the warmth of a body beside me.

"Velchanos must defeat the lion. Yet he must also submit, and be consumed. Each one fights to escape his fate."

Iphiboë. What was that word? A name, surely. I tried it out loud. "Iphiboë." Whatever it was, it filled me with a balm of trust and comfort.

The growl amplified into a roar. The tree quivered. Terrified, I shrank, trying to make myself as small as possible within this confined space.

The person beside me was gone but for a soft echo. *You are the betrayer as well as the promise.*

Jerking wildly, I flung my arms out before opening my eyes and realizing I wasn't actually falling. There was a sharp metallic *clank* then silence.

The only light came from some kind of rectangular opening to my right. Whatever I was in, it was scarcely big enough to accommodate me. The flooring was hard and smooth. Too smooth to be the ground.

The episode on the veranda hadn't happened. I hadn't seen deer. Duke had been dead these last six years, killed in his old age by a mama bear. Will hadn't been sitting beside me in his squeaky rocker, nor had I heard a lion. I'd been dreaming.

I'll build a bunker, one of my attackers said, and something about tying me up and gagging me.

I lifted my hands to my mouth. I wasn't gagged, my hands were free, and if I were in a bunker, wouldn't it be dark?

The space where light came in was barred with chain links. Reaching out one hand, I touched them. They didn't move. I pushed. They remained secure.

Through waves of dizziness and dull pain, I turned my head to examine the rest of this place. There was not enough room to straighten my legs, not while lying down. I could sit up, but I couldn't stand. I touched the wall. It felt like...heavy plastic.

Plastic walls on every side except the one, which had the steel links. There was a hole cut through the plastic in the floor beside the links, stained all around with what must be dried excrement, from the smell.

I moved my legs and heard that clanking sound; one leg felt weighted with something hard. I sat up, suffering another wave of dizziness and a sharper throb through the temples.

A chain ran from an iron ring around my ankle to the wall, where it was anchored. It had rubbed my ankle raw.

I searched for a way to explain this, but could only come up with flashes, glimpses, a feeling of emerging from stupor, a sensation of jolting as if I were lying in a moving vehicle, and a man's eyes peering into mine. Another dark place. Men arguing.

Now I saw that I was no longer wearing my clothes. When I went for the morning walk by Dallas Creek, I'd had on hiking boots, jeans, a flannel shirt and a jacket. Now all I wore was a thin, mud colored smock of coarse burlap. It covered my torso from throat to knees.

I fought to control rising panic. Those men had kidnapped me and chained me in a...a...dog kennel.

Gradually, I realized how hot it was. I was sweating, and somehow, even though the light outside the kennel was muted, it was intense, like a humid tropical place in the middle of the day.

The next thing I noticed were the flies. I brushed and swatted to no avail. There were too many. They kept trying to get in my mouth and eyes and ears; they were very interested in the raw spots at my ankle and the shit hole.

As I tugged on the chain to see if it could be broken, I heard moaning. The roof of my enclosure grated.

There was some living thing above me, on the other side of the plastic. I wanted to call out but I didn't know what was up there. What if it was one of those men?

I scooted closer to the link-covered opening and put my fingers through. There was a broad strip of bare earth with a depression running down the middle. The flies were thick over that depression, and the stink rising from it was horrible, like an overfilled, long neglected outhouse.

On the other side of the open area, about fifteen meters away, a line of kennels, stacked two high, reached both directions as far as the steel barrier allowed me to see. Not far above all this, an elaborate roof of leafy green-brown camouflage waved gently like the upper ceiling of a forest, rendering the sky nearly invisible. It kept the sunlight from beating down unchecked, but I had a feeling its purpose wasn't to provide comfort. This kind of basic, inexpensive camouflage was meant to keep things hidden from spying eyes.

There was no grass or any growing thing that I could see.

Now I heard more moaning, some nearby, some distant, and once, a bark of laughter that sent shivers through me.

Catching brief movement, I returned my gaze to the kennel directly opposite me on the other side of the bare space. I glimpsed a woman's face, pale behind the chain links, with patchy red sores around her mouth and dark smudges under her eyes.

It disappeared. I stared, but the face didn't return.

The iron ring chafed my ankle. I pulled it higher.

I'd held off panic by studying my surroundings, but it was hard. Fear swelled. I was breathing so shallowly I was almost gasping.

Where was I? What were those men going to do to me?

Stupid question. I knew damn well what they meant to do. They would either rape me or sell me to someone who would rape me. Probably both.

What were all these other containers, though? Who, or what, was in them? Surely two men couldn't kidnap and imprison so many victims. They'd acted like they hadn't seen a female in years.

I started counting. Just as I reached fifty-seven kennels a woman's low voice interrupted. "You awake over there?"

I was so surprised that when I tried to respond, I choked and coughed. My eyes watered. "Who are you?" I croaked.

Skeletal fingers came from the left and pushed between the wires. "You're alive. I wondered, when they brought you in. I expect they had you drugged."

I stared at those grimy fingers and couldn't help touching them with my own. A woman. A woman with a soft, kind voice, probably in a kennel next to mine.

"Where are we?"

"I don't know for sure. Someone said Georgia."

"What is this place? What's going on?"

"I was dumped by my owner." Her voice hardened. "He used me for years, from the time he bought me, when I was just a little kid, then all of a sudden he was calling me a worthless old skank. How about you? We're all dying to know."

"Two men kidnapped me. Are we prisoners?"

"What two men? Police? Sentinels?"

"I don't know what they were. They were hiking. I didn't hear them come up behind me."

"You didn't have your owner or a sentinel with you? Were you trying to escape? They must have turned you in for the reward."

"Owner? What the hell does that mean?"

There was a long pause. "Who *are* you? Where have you been?"

At that moment, shadows fell across the screen and the woman's hand was struck with a wooden cudgel. She shrieked and jerked her fingers away.

"What are you doing, Seven-seventy-six? You know better."

She sobbed. The club had hit her so hard I could easily believe bones were broken. I scrambled backward until my spine pressed against the rear of the kennel and I could go no farther.

Two men in dark uniforms with fringed epaulets and shiny brass buttons squatted and stared at me. "Look here," said one. His grin framed broken front teeth. "Seven-seventy-seven is awake."

"You're the talk of the town," said the other, through an auburn beard that hadn't seen scissors or a trimmer in months, if ever. The hair around his face was drenched in sweat.

I didn't think they were the same two men who had attacked me, though my memories were vague, other than the moment when one of them pressed me to the ground and smelled my hair.

"Who are you?" I hated the tremble in my voice. I'd heard that in a kidnapping situation, it was often helpful to humanize yourself. "I'm Erin."

They laughed. "How cute," said the first man. "She thinks she has a name."

"That tells us all we need to know. She really has been off the grid. Man. That's impressive. A True Phantom. I guess those guys weren't lying."

"Where you been hiding all this time, little lady?"

A horrible idea came to me. Did this have something to do with Rafe? Had he found me? Was I locked in a dog kennel to satisfy his brutal sense of vengeance? It was just the kind of cruel punishment that would appeal to a man who hated betrayal more than anything. An eye for an eye.

Oh Will. Where are you? I want to wake up from this nightmare and sit beside you on the veranda.

Deep inside, before I could stop it, I thought *I'll never see Will again.* I choked on a sob and shoved the thought far, far down.

"Won't do you any good to clam up. We have ways of getting the truth out of you bitches. Come on. Was a man hiding you? Did you get away from your owner? You don't have a tracker or even a scar where one would have been."

"If you tell us who your owner is, we might let him know we've got you. Maybe he'll pay the ransom. Have you made yourself worth a ransom, Seven-seventy-seven?"

"She seems well fed. Healthy. That won't last long in here."

"No kidding. I've forgotten what a woman with any fat looks like."

They waited. I said nothing.

"We'll just let you think about it awhile."

They rose and strolled away. I heard one of them say something about the effectiveness of hunger and the other mention how much fun they were going to have "breaking her in."

I put my face against the links and my fingers through as far as I could. "Are you okay?"

"My hand is broken. If it gets infected, I'll die."

"Try not to move it."

"I can't move it. It's busted up bad. Swelling so fast."

"I'm sorry."

"Not your fault. What's your name? Erin? Don't trust anybody. Not me, not anybody. Don't tell me or anyone where they caught you, or how. They'll torture it out of us. Some will give it up for an extra cup of water. No secret is safe here."

As I turned this over in my mind, two different uniformed men and a barely controlled German shepherd passed my enclosure, hauling a dead woman by the arms. Her face was gray and stiff, her mouth open, eyes staring. Runnels of dried vomit smeared her chin and the filthy burlap rag. The flies were thick upon it, and her eyes, lips, and genitals.

I shuddered and looked away, but I would never forget that frozen grimace.

For the first time I noticed the crudely scrawled number on the front of my smock.

777.

RAFE INSISTED ON BEING INFORMED OF EVERY LEAD, NO MATTER HOW SLIGHT, AND traveled all over the country so he could see for himself if the woman his investigators unearthed from some remote cage farm or rich man's house was Erin. It was the longest two weeks of his life.

By the end, hope had degenerated into angry cynicism every time he heard, *We think we've found something, sir.* So far, nothing had come close. One was a corpse, murdered by her owner. Through every drawn-out moment of the flight to Minnesota, Erin's face, as youthful as it had been twenty-three years ago, wavered before his eyes, colorless and stiff, death taking her beyond his reach.

He remained angry even after finding out the dead woman was not Erin. He was about to fire the whole lot. Flannery especially. Dragging his employer across the US of U on one wild goose chase after another. He was stuck with the Secret Service, though. Dismissing them would offend the president.

What if she'd been shipped to another country, or was being held by some backwoods redneck? An imaginative and circumspect kidnapper could hide a woman for years. She might be kept, and used, until she got too old to be of interest. Then her body would be dumped in some lake, landfill, or shallow grave. A greedy man could collect a reward by turning her over to the Cages with some bullshit lie. The Cage guards were notorious for getting rid of bodies if they were offered enough untraceable crypto.

The Cages brought up a whole new set of worries. If she was in one, she would be vulnerable, not only to the diseases that rampaged through them, but the guards, who were a law unto themselves. By the time his people investigated all the anonymous women who came in without any formal history, it might be too late.

At which point his thoughts grew too dark to tolerate and he had to wipe them out with alcohol or drugs.

The worst was what this had done to McKenna. He shouldn't have told her, but she'd seen it all over him. After Will came to his office, he'd been close to bursting, imagining wonderful scenarios of Erin being restored to him, loving him again. He wanted their daughter to feel that joy. Her mother was *alive!* Probably.

Possibly.

Maybe.

A LINE OF BAREFOOT FIGURES SHAMBLED BETWEEN THE KENNELS, CHAINED ONE TO the next. Each was shrouded in a full-length mud-colored garment that reminded me of a burqa, heads covered but for a circular opening at the mouth and eyeholes. The guards used whips on whomever lagged, laughingly giving each other points for the cries of pain they elicited.

"They're off to the Glory Wall," my neighbor, Gemma, told me. "We're taken in shifts."

"What is that?"

"For the soldiers. To keep up their morale, among other things."

"Oh."

"It's a wall with holes—"

"You don't need to tell me. I know what it is."

"You do? That's the first thing you've known since you got here."

"I don't really. I mean, I know what a glory hole is, so I can connect the dots."

"Oh."

We were silent until the women were gone.

"The world has gone mad." I was so hungry and weak it was hard to speak coherently. Forget thinking.

"Someday, I hope I get to hear your story," Gemma said. "I bet it's a good one."

"Just ordinary." I laughed bitterly. "What used to be ordinary."

We were quiet again, until I said, "It's so damn hot."

"Wait till winter. The blankets they give us are so thin you can see through them."

The two guards who had first spoken to me after I woke up approached and squatted. "Past time for your shaving," the one with the scraggly red beard said. "Sorry to leave it so long, Seven-seventy-seven. Unforgivable of us. You itchy?"

I was, as a matter of fact, but I made no reply. I'd tried to mark lines in my kennel so I could keep track of the days, but my fingernail wasn't strong enough to scratch the plastic. Every day we were taken out in small groups to shuffle around in circles, guarded by men with guns and growling dogs. Gemma said it was to keep our spines from becoming deformed and our legs from atrophying. I could sit up in my kennel and stretch out my legs, but I had to keep them bent when lying down. Once, so far, I'd been "showered" with about twenty others, all of us naked, hosed down like cars in an old-fashioned carwash, the first spray soapy, the next a tepid rinse. My eyes burned for two days after.

The other guard bent so his pupil was in line with the padlock and I heard it click. He swung open the steel door. "Come on." He reached in and released the chain from the wall with a small silver wrench.

My heart rose, blocking my throat. These men had more than a shave on their minds. I hung back until I heard Gemma.

"Go on. It'll be worse if you fight, believe me."

The men gave me no time to get my bearings once I crawled out of the kennel. They pushed me. I stumbled, but managed a backward glance.

The guards never took out adjoining women at the same time, so I hadn't ever seen her. She was scary thin. Her head had been shaved at some point, leaving her nearly bald, but her eyes were large, as dark as the night sky. She was in no way "an old skank." When she gave me a tremulous smile, I saw that her teeth were brown and rotted. Two at least were missing. My own teeth ached, and were covered in fuzz.

I smiled back before being shoved away.

In the Quonset hut that served as a guardhouse, I was handed over to a dull-eyed female with a buzz cut of dirty hair. A ring around her ankle and a long chain kept her tethered. I was told to sit and the woman turned on her shaver. She ordered me to pull up the smock so she could shave my genital area. The men lounged in chairs, smoking. Watching.

"No. No way."

The woman struck me in the face with the razor. "Do it."

Blood trickled over my cheek. I complied, reeling from the pain and trying not to break down.

"Open your legs."

The men watched without any particular fascination. They must have seen it all many times.

When I was bare, nicked, and bleeding, the woman squinted and turned her attention to my scalp. Quaking with fear and rage, I pressed the burlap tightly over my thighs.

One of the men stood, stubbing his cigarette in an ashtray. "Hold on."

The woman immediately stopped, turning her face down in a servile attitude. She clicked off the razor and waited.

"Lice or not, a man needs something to hold, don't you think?"

He glanced at his companion, who nodded and rose. "I agree. It really helps with those fine adjustments."

The prisoner tossed the razor on a table and retreated as far as her chain would allow. Dropping into a foul, greasy looking plastic chair, she thumbed through an ancient magazine.

My skin burned where she had shaved me. She hadn't even tried to be careful.

"Didn't anybody tell you?" The redhead with the beard grinned. "There's a price for all this maintenance. Every woman here has paid it."

"Some come back for seconds."

"Or thirds."

They unfastened their belts, then their trousers, and dropped them. My heart pounded so hard I felt like I might faint. Both were more than ready to be serviced.

"If you milk me really good," the bearded man said, "I might bring you an extra slice of bread. Maybe butter, but you'll have to go beyond good for that."

"See if you can make that mouth useful for the first time in your life." The broken-toothed guard came forward and grasped my hair.

I jerked, wincing as my hair tore. "Fuck off, asshole! You slimy disgusting shits!"

I heard a shocked snort and glanced behind me. The girl's mouth hung open. Had everyone before me caved without protest?

A shrill whine brought me twisting back around just as the sharpened end of a steel chain struck my right upper arm.

I screamed.

The guard yanked his arm and the chain dug in, slicing back to front, leaving behind a broad furrow. I glimpsed white bone before it was covered in gouts of blood.

I gaped. Blood and bone. I couldn't breathe yet guttural sounds escaped, then a high, animal shrieking such as I had never heard in my life.

The other guard, the one closest to me, grabbed my chin. He pulled my face around and up. "Suck it. Now."

I sobbed and choked through his rancid pumping. The pain in my arm was agony, like it had been doused in gasoline and ignited. The man's sex assault happened at a distance, through a fog. I hardly knew when the first one stepped away and the second man took his place.

A voice echoed. I didn't know which one it was. "Now, seven-seventy-seven, I don't feel like you gave that your all. She wasn't enthusiastic, was she, and I felt teeth. Teeth! That is inexcusable."

"I did, too. What a bitch move."

"Do you want to try again?"

"No." I bent over, retching. "No."

Out came the chain. I recoiled, blocking the wound on my arm with my left hand, but he had another target in mind. This time the sharpened point gouged into my forehead. The rest cleaved around my left eye and across my cheek.

Blood flooded everywhere. There was an instant of numb shock before pain flared. Dimly, I heard my own helpless screaming as I fell and hit the floor. I writhed away from them, blood gushing between my fingers. *I'm going to die here.*

"All you had to do was suck it, you dumb cunt! It's so easy!"

"What the hell happened? That powder should have tamed her."

"She ate it. I watched."

"It didn't work."

"Maybe we got an old batch."

Then I fell into a dream, or maybe a nightmare. I heard Rafe. It had been twenty-three years, but I knew that voice even through searing, hammering torment.

"What the *fuck!*"

I couldn't think. I couldn't see. I could only moan and send my mind into a dimension where one survived second by second.

Two deafening blasts in quick succession caused the air to vibrate. My ears rang. Was someone else screaming, or was it still me?

Strong arms scooped me up and cradled me like a baby. A voice echoed through bestial moaning. "Shh, shh. Don't be afraid, Erin. I'm here. I have you."

Archive Three

May & June, 2072

RAMANDU'S DAWN

Now is the Time for Courage

Chapter 1

WILL LOST TRACK OF HOW MANY TIMES HE FOLLOWED THE TRAIL WHERE ERIN disappeared, hoping to discover some valuable new clue.

Broken branches. Scuff marks. Torn up grass. Dried bloodstains. Every time it rained, more evidence vanished.

He lifted the branch that had probably been used to subdue her. A smear of dried blood stained the thicker end. Was it Erin's? Had this branch killed her? If only Duke were alive. He would have been with her and he would have killed her attacker. If Duke were alive, Will would never have had to go to Rafe. Duke would have tracked Erin to the ends of the earth.

He stared for hours at the mysterious necklace. Had Rafe given it to her, as he claimed? Will felt certain that was a lie. Had her attacker or attackers dropped it as they chased her? He closed his fist around the pendant, noticing that it was strangely hot.

Come back to me, Erin.

He guided Rafe's investigators and their dogs to the attack site, but they didn't find anything, or if they did, they didn't share the information with him. After collecting samples of the bloodstains, they moved on. He hadn't seen them since.

Every evening, he drove to the highway, parked under a tree in a spot with satellite coverage, and brought out the flat, round, palm-sized device Thaddeus had given him. It was an expensive looking gadget. He had to speak a certain code to turn it on. He could tell it wasn't connecting to *Ticolo*, the pathetically generic and meager public search engine. This had a smooth sophistication and layers of security he'd never seen before. It read his iris and verified his voice.

I knew the web was there, he thought as a pale blue background bloomed above the disk along with the words, "Welcome, William Konstantinou." *Things that big don't just vanish.*

Every day, the blue background and greeting. Nothing else, though he stared without blinking until his eyes watered.

Rafe had promised to post a picture of Erin when he found her, but the screen remained blank. No message. No photo, and the device restricted him to that one background. He couldn't figure out how to escape its boundaries, though he knew the web was there, gigantic and all-encompassing, just out of reach, accessible to members of the Reformation Brotherhood and their cronies. Rafe had him locked out.

Will had a reputation as a decent hacker in his military days, but this sleek, stylish instrument defied every trick he knew.

The drive home was long, dusty, and tough, and he always feared her photo would display the moment he left so he put off leaving, instead walking along the empty highway for a half hour then checking the device again. By that time the moons, one small, one large, were sending their pale, unfathomable light over the mountain summits.

A niggling corner of his mind suggested that since he'd turned his back on all that was happening in the world, he'd grown stupidly complacent. Outwitting the government had become a gratifying sport, but here was proof that they were stronger, smarter, and crueler. That was why nothing remained of Erin but dried blood and a necklace. The damned thing seemed familiar, but Erin had come to him without any jewelry, not even a wedding ring. She'd had but one thing clutched in her hand—a green crayon, from which she would not be parted.

What did the necklace witness the day Erin was taken or killed? If only it could talk.

In a way, it was. It seemed to plead. *Don't give up. Keep searching.*

I should have told her what was going on around us. Warned her, prepared her, taught her the things she needed to know, instead of pretending we weren't a part of the world, that it was not a part of us.

She was high-strung. Afraid of everything outside their cocoon. He enabled that fear. He silently encouraged her desire to abandon the world and everything except him. To help her feel secure, he'd even quit cutting back the trees around the cabin. Nowadays it and the barn were camouflaged from drones and satellites by a screen of thick, leafy branches.

Misery tapped down his spine like skeletal fingers.

Because of my selfish need to protect her from the truth of this world, I might well wonder for the rest of my life what happened to the woman I love.

I DREAMED OF FLOWERS. PENSTEMON, COLUMBINE, AND TINY PURPLE STIFF-STALKED things I never could remember the name of. They were too small for thistle.

Lupine, maybe. The grass was long and green and the air smelled fresh, like pine and spruce. Another few steps and I would emerge from the forest into the clearing at Will's cabin. My heart was happy.

But the sound of singing birds slowly warped into an incessant *beep... beep...beep*, like water torture, bringing an end to any hope of rest.

Eyes unwillingly opening, I took in a room lit only by the cold flare of a drone beacon sifting through the half-open blinds at the window.

There was a soft drum of rain, then the wind changed; raindrops pelted the window in a sharp staccato.

A green dot pulsed at the edge of my vision, in time with the beating of my heart. I gradually identified it as a monitor, and another narrow shadow as an IV drip.

I was in a hospital. Now that pine scent made sense.

Breathing emanated from the darkness like the trailer for a horror movie, then, as though to reassure me, it broke, wheezed, and huffed into a decidedly non-menacing snore.

I discerned the outline of a form huddled in a chair. A delicate aura of color floated around it, clearly visible, perhaps because it was so dark. The colors were reddish, mixed with orange, and hints of something darker.

Maybe it *was* an aura, perhaps the same marvel I remembered seeing around Will long ago. That had been several shades of blue and violet merging to white.

My mind returned to practicalities. If I woke this person, perhaps he or she could explain what was going on, but I resisted, wanting to remember on my own.

Think. What happened?

I closed my eyes. *It will be done before they can even begin to realize what a mistake they made, and by then it will be too late. People are sheep, and we've been herding them into this pasture for years.*

The voice was male. The words flashed and were gone too quickly to make sense of.

That's the only car you have left? Not a single Toyota?

Another snippet cleared, giving me a glimpse of an annoyed older man behind a counter. *Take it or leave it. And why aren't you in quarantine?*

Without warning a whole mudflow of images dumped through my memory. Tires screeching. A blinding glare of headlights bouncing off a tree trunk, followed by the sickening crunch of metal.

Breaking glass. Terrifying blankness.

This had to be the worst headache I'd ever experienced. Any minute and my skull would explode. I couldn't see out of my left eye. My right arm throbbed, syncing painfully with the throb in my head.

What I wouldn't give for a healthy dose of synthetic endorphins. Or even antiquated morphine. Anything.

"Will? Is that you?"

The mass on the chair moved. The breathing faltered. "Erin?"

The form sprang up and bent over the bed. "You're awake." The voice was male, husky and sleepy, the tone relieved. I watched that peculiar drift of color rise and vanish into the ceiling.

He didn't sound right. Maybe it was the pain in my head, but I couldn't put a face to this voice. He gathered me in, kissing my throat, which made me shudder with alarm.

"How do you feel?"

I didn't know what to say. It would be impolite at this point to demand his identity. He obviously knew me. Bristles from an unshaven face rasped against my throat. Maybe it was Will after all, and he just sounded weird. Will didn't shave all that often. Too much trouble, and I liked his stubble. I liked rubbing my fingers over it, or sometimes my cheek.

I breathed in a scent that seemed vaguely familiar and suddenly I wasn't seeing Will but a distant image of Rafe, laughing as he said, *Hell, it's like this stuff makes my dick grow ten centimeters.*

Tiny bolts of electricity tickled along my skin where the man touched me, but I hardly noticed through the distinct thuds of pain carving my brain to pieces. "My head hurts. Everything hurts."

"I'll get you something." With a kiss to the forehead, he withdrew. Bright white light blinded me. This was it. Angels, coming to carry me off to wherever my life's actions dictated. I had a feeling it wasn't the good place. Then I realized it was only a door opening. It slid closed and the room returned to darkness.

A man in scrubs soon entered and spoke a command. A light at the top of the bed flickered on.

"Awake at last." His voice reverberated, causing psychedelic colors to bounce across my vision. I winced and blinked, trying to see.

"Feeling better?" He checked the drip and with the swift ease of an expert turned up my right wrist and slapped on an illuminated tape. It flashed dots and lines, some green, some red. "Let's just see." He brought out a neurological translator and studied the numbers it displayed.

As my eyes grew accustomed to the light, I noticed someone standing behind him. A tall man with a pale, tired face and two-or-three-day growth of stubble. His hair was lighter than the stubble, and tousled, perhaps from sleeping in the chair.

Chrysaleon, I wanted to say, then shook my head to clear out the cobwebs. I was hallucinating. But shaking my head made everything worse.

His shirtsleeves were rolled up, the shirt unbuttoned at the top, his elaborate tie skewed to the side.

"Ninety over fifty," the nurse said in mock horror. "You're dead, Mrs. Konstantinou." He laughed. The sound was loud, like a donkey braying. "Just kidding. You say you have a headache?"

I nodded, biting back a rude comment.

Mrs. Konstantinou. No one had called me that in over twenty years.

My gaze shot to the man in the shadows.

For an instant, I would have sworn Will stood there, hair pouring like black rain over his chest, lean and motionless as a panther, but when I blinked, he was gone.

"We'll fix you right up. Back in a jiffy."

The nurse left. The man and I stared at each other.

"Rafe," I said finally.

He came closer.

"God, Erin, you had me so scared."

His voice was the same. Perfectly modulated and smooth as butter rum. A professional voice. I'd often wondered if it played a part in his meteoric rise to fame and power at such a young age.

"What happened?" I lifted my hand and felt the bandages on the left side of my face, then the one on my upper right arm. Both felt strangely numb yet at the same time exquisitely sensitive.

"You don't know?"

"This headache…it's like a thousand drums. With rainbows."

He sat on the edge of the bed and took my hand, running the tips of his fingers across my knuckles, which renewed the tingling sensation. "Don't worry about it now, sweetheart."

The nurse reappeared. He held a syringe under the light and shook it once. "Fenyl number three," he said. "It will knock out any headache, even a cluster, and induce a nice, calming euphoria." He pressed the tube against my left arm. "There you go."

While the idea of euphoria sounded wonderful, it scared me too. There was something beyond my ability to pin down. I didn't want to be manipulated, or lose one iota of my ability to think.

"Could I have a glass of water? Room temperature."

"Sure." He went off to the corner and wheeled back an overbed table, then brought a pitcher of water flavored with fresh lemon slices. He poured a glass and handed it to me with a straw. It was the most delicious liquid I'd ever tasted. I couldn't remember the last water I'd had that didn't taste like human excrement.

"You okay in here, Mr. Konstantinou? There's a portable bed in the wall if you want. just push that button. She'll be asleep in a minute."

"I'm fine," Rafe said.

"Call me if you need anything." The nurse left, the legs of his cotton scrubs swishing.

I stared. It took me a minute to add it up. Twenty-three years. That's how long it had been since I'd seen my husband. My mouth went dry. I didn't know if it was from the shot or fear.

After a moment he drew my hand to his mouth and kissed my knuckles. It lessened my fear—a little. Once again, that could have been the shot.

His face melted into two fierce green stars, like a hunting jaguar taking stock of his next meal.

I blinked, but it didn't help. "Are you going to eat me?" My voice came from far away. It sounded high and small, like the voice of a tiny winged fairy.

As darkness crashed, I saw his mouth curve into a smile.

In an odd, slow-motion voice like a vintage 78 vinyl record being played at 33, I heard him say, "Not just yet, Erin."

Everything faded away.

WILL'S SLEEP WAS HAUNTED BY NIGHTMARES.

He saw awful things in grisly detail. Erin, her neck broken, falling to the ground. Grass withering around her body. Decay spreading, mountains crumbling, crops dying. The sky above turning from blue to yellow, thick with something he could not name.

When he brushed his teeth, the mirror revealed sharp dark grooves under his eyes and around his mouth. While forking hay, checking traps, or feeding the chickens, he would jump, certain he'd heard Erin's voice. The first few times he searched, saddling Daisy and circling his property, calling and calling until he was hoarse.

Like a grizzly rudely awakened from hibernation, he wanted to rear up on his hind legs and use his twelve-centimeter claws to slice his tormentors to ribbons. Whenever he imagined this scenario, Rafe's was the face swiped into a mask of blood and gore. Eyeballs flying, nose ripped off. All that arrogance and confidence destroyed in an instant.

Hurry.

The pitchfork clattered loudly against the stable floor. He retrieved it and turned a resolute back to the open barn door.

Dusty pricked his ears, snorted, and sidestepped. Daisy drew away into the shadows.

"Cowards." Unlatching Daisy's stall door, he entered and began mucking soiled straw into a wheelbarrow. "You gonna let some ghost scare you?"

Daisy nickered as though ashamed of herself.

"What I want to know is, how can you hear something that's in my head?"

He lies.

Flippantly, he tossed the next forkful of dung and wet straw through the door instead of into the wheelbarrow. "Have a face full of that."

When he'd finished, he saddled Dusty and sent him galloping, following a negligible path through the forest.

His cheeks burned in the morning chill. He rubbed a hand across his jaw, thinking he ought to shave. He was becoming quite grubby. But what was the point?

Something stirred in the scrub oaks. Way too large for a rabbit, but not as large as a bear.

He pulled Dusty up. "Who's there? This is private property."

A tall man stepped out, eyes scattering light, white-blue then cobalt. Slightly slanted brows, reflective hair and skin.

Will's ears hummed. "W-who are you?"

The man took another step. Was that the tree behind him? Yes. He could see through the figure. Whatever this was, it wasn't real.

Will had never noticed the beauty of a man's smile before. The specter appeared to be genuinely happy to see him.

"Father," it said, not in a normal way but directly into Will's mind. "I have missed you."

Insanity.

Prodding Dusty, Will reached out, but before he could touch it, the apparition diffused into whorls of mist.

Come to think of it, that's exactly what the damned thing looked like. Mist turned to flesh.

For several moments he remained, breathing heavily. Then he shook his head and laughed. Cabin fever. Lack of sleep.

But the gelding had seen something too. He snorted and backed away, his eyes rimmed in white.

"Easy, boy." Will urged him on. When the Paint cleared the trees, he reined in and dismounted, replacing the bridle with a halter.

Brushing a film of water off a flat rock, he settled in. From here, he could admire the heavens, the endless expanse of cumulus cloud shadows drifting across Old Man Sneffels, and all the aspen groves in between.

The summit's stony profile had gazed into the starry universe for several million years. How many comets and meteors had it seen? How many galaxies birthed and stars dying? He had coaxed Erin into climbing to the very tip of the Old Man's eagle-like nose. It was a difficult ascent. He wasn't sure she would make it, but she did. She made it that time, and four times more.

One could picture all sorts of things in those clouds. They looked like heads of cauliflower.

As he watched, one cloud separated from another and drifted closer. He decided it resembled a woman with wild flowing hair and big round breasts. A tendril lifted to the side and became rather like an arm wielding a spear.

He could swear the thing was flying closer. Closer yet. Too close.

Will stood and stepped off the rock. Now he saw a face, a female with sharp cheekbones and two arms, stretched out like she meant to draw in the four elements and blast him to bits.

"What the hell," he muttered.

A gust of wind hit him so hard it threatened to knock him over. He braced one leg behind the other.

The cloud was a banshee, open mouth screaming.

Will lifted a hand to shield his eyes.

The wind died. The cloud swirled, so close he could touch it, if a cloud were touchable.

Tresses flew, alive with wind, the very picture of Medusa, but the enraged face remained constant.

Will closed his eyes and opened them again. She was still there. He backed up. Over by the trees, his horse neighed frantically.

A menacing rumble of thunder came out of nowhere.

Go!

Slipping in a patch of snow, Will's shoulder struck the ground, but he didn't pause to nurse the pain. Stumbling to his feet, he ran, calling, "Dusty!"

The big Paint cowered by the trees. Will caught him, leaped into the saddle, and kicked, hard, sending the horse through the forest at a dangerous run. Snow slid off a pine branch and landed on his back. He gasped but never slowed his pace until he reached his own clearing and saw the reassuring sight of smoke rising from his chimney. Sliding off the horse, he ran inside and searched everywhere, for what, he didn't know.

Had a young man with copper hair and spectral eyes formed out of mist? Had a cloud come to life and commanded him to go? Go where?

Four abysmal weeks since Erin had vanished, and he was losing his mind.

Chapter 2

"Will, take me home before someone sees me."

"Erin?"

"Leave me alone. I'm not a number."

"Erin, can you wake up? You slept through the night."

When I opened my eyes, my lashes scraped against a wad of gauze. The sense of disorientation slowly faded as I withdrew from nightmares and entered perilous reality.

There was that face. Very, very real.

He sat by the bed, rubbing my knuckles. "Feel better?" He looked tired.

"Headache's gone." Cautiously stretching, I pushed myself into a sitting position.

I'm so hungry.

This was new. In the kennels, we were lucky to get a bean in the watery broth they gave us twice a day. *Just enough to keep your heart beating,* the guards liked to joke. Only women who gave head or whatnot got bread with the broth. At first the hunger had been agonizing, but later, it dwindled to almost nothing. "I'm starving."

"You can thank the IV for that. It's been replenishing you. Can I get you another pillow?"

"No. You don't look so good."

"That chair's not the most comfortable, but Erin, I've never been happier." He presented me with his dazzling smile.

I could almost convince myself I was twenty-two, recovering from McKenna's birth. Rafe had filled the hospital room with lilies, camellias, peonies, and hyacinths. Nurses dropped in to inhale, one after another assuring me of my luck in meeting and catching such a successful, handsome man. Young and old, they adored him. Their smiles grew flirtatious and their hips swayed when he was around. Several who hadn't bothered before started wearing lipstick and fixed their hair.

"Where am I?"

"UCLA Med. The head of plastic surgery is a friend of mine. I want the best for you, Erin."

An orderly opened the door and carried in a tray. He plopped it on the overbed table, mumbled at his holo, and left.

I wrinkled my nose. The eggs weren't real, I could tell by the grayish color and watery residue. There was no seasoning—not even a sprinkle of cheese. The toast was burned. Starvation is a powerful motivator, however. The survival instinct took over and I shoveled through three large bites without tasting anything.

"Stop," Rafe said. "Don't eat that." The severe frown I saw when I glanced at him caused my heart to flutter and various depictions of punishment to sweep through my imagination.

He got up, went to the door, and spoke to someone. Then he took the tray and set it on a table near the door. I stared hungrily.

It took ten endless minutes for another tray to arrive. This time the plate held real scrambled eggs, so light and fluffy, so perfectly seasoned, that I wanted to hold them on my tongue forever. There was sourdough toast, my favorite, dripping with butter, and at the edge of the plate were slices of kiwi, strawberries, and a square of chocolate. I sipped the coffee and nearly moaned, it was so delicious.

My mind wanted more, much more, but my stomach rebelled. "I feel a little sick." Regretfully, I put down the fork after consuming less than half the feast.

"You're dangerously undernourished. It will take time to recover."

"What happened?"

"What do you remember?"

"I..." What could I say? I'd abandoned this man and our daughter. I'd spent the last twenty-three years in hiding. With his brother.

My brain lurched to life. Because of Rafe, I was no longer in the kennels. I was free.

"Hardly anything," I said, and rubbed my unbandaged temple. I needed time to think. What would he do to me in retaliation for what I'd done to him?

"You were attacked, but you'll be fine, Erin. The doctor will tell you more."

He actually came in a moment later and introduced himself as Doctor Cohn. He peeled back the bandages on my face, taking his time to examine the wound with a small bright light, every now and then pushing with his gloved index finger. He was so close I smelled hints of bergamot in his aftershave, which brought vivid memories of better times with Rafe and caused a stream of confused emotions. After a few seconds I stretched out my left hand, hoping for what, I wasn't sure. Rafe instantly sandwiched it between both of his, and I wanted to weep. A tear did escape from my right eye, trickling over my temple.

"Good, very good." Doctor Cohn went around the bed to the other side, where he inspected my right arm in the same meticulous fashion. "You'll be just fine, Mrs. Konstantinou. I don't want you to worry. Everything is sutured underneath the skin, both because your wounds were deep, and to limit scarring. There will be no need for removal of the stitches. Your body will absorb them." He ran a penetrating gaze over my face. "In the meantime, we can be grateful that your brachial artery wasn't nicked. If it had been, we wouldn't be speaking to each other. Now, I warn you, some nerves were severed. You'll experience numbness at both sites. There's really nothing we can do about that. It will take time, and everyone is different, but the feeling will probably come back. It could take weeks, months, or years."

"All right. I understand." I did. Once I'd cut my pinkie finger pretty badly, and it was numb for ten years.

We wouldn't be speaking to each other. Goosebumps rose across my arms. If Rafe hadn't come at that moment…

"I want you to limit your movements for a couple of weeks. It's easy for patients to forget they have sutures because they can't see them, but they can tear. Don't lift anything over two kilograms with your right arm, and try not to overuse the muscles in your face. I know that will be hard, but do the best you can. Small movements are fine."

"No smiling. No crying. No frowning. Got it."

He snickered appreciatively then sobered as he met Rafe's gaze. "What I'd like to do is give the sutures about three weeks, I think, to really knit the layers together. Timing is everything with scars. You have to let the wound heal and bond, but you cannot wait too long, or the scar will set in and be difficult to erase. This one will be easy. When I'm done, it will be like it never happened. You'll be as beautiful as ever, maybe more. If you like, we can freshen things at the same time. Smooth the lines around your eyes, plump your lips, lift your eyelids and firm up your jaw. I'd be happy to do it."

I stared at him, wondering what I'd done to make him think I was so frivolous. What about the men who attacked and kidnapped me? Those kennels? The other prisoners?

Glancing at Rafe, I caught a brief, satisfied smile.

Where was Will? How had Rafe found me? Did he know where I was before the kennel?

"Your husband tells me you're having a problem remembering things."

"Yeah." It was true. Some things I remembered, but there were blank spots. Completely blank. Like why I left him to begin with.

"Hmm." He checked my ears, my throat, and listened to my heart. "Can you tell me what you do remember?"

"Bits and pieces. A car wreck, and…everything from before." I added hastily, "With Rafe."

"I'm going to set up a brain scan," he said to Rafe. "Depending on the results, we may need an SEPM as well."

"What the hell is that?" I asked.

He frowned at me and I fought an urge to apologize for using the word *hell.*

"A synapse electropulse magnifier. It measures in detail how your brain's working." The doctor walked to the door and it slid open. "Don't worry. Everything's under control. You rest and get back your strength. We're all so very glad you've been found, Mrs. Konstantinou. Nurse!" He waved at someone and left.

I searched for a sign on Rafe's face, a signal, some warning of my fate.

He sat on the bed. "Beautiful Erin. Elfin Erin." He leaned forward and kissed me tenderly on the lips then pulled me to his chest. "I feel like I'm alive again. All I care about is that you're here, in my arms. Alive. I may never let go of you again."

Memories surfaced. Love words against my throat in the night. *We'll always be together, you and I. For as long as the pyramids stand in Egypt.* Rafe had a way of starting at my earlobes and working his way down to my toes. I couldn't get enough of him in those days. Sometimes I made him leave his office, break his appointments to come home and make love.

As long as the pyramids stand in Egypt. Unending. Invincible. That's what he always said.

No, he didn't know where I'd been. He couldn't. It would kill him if he knew. But not before he killed me.

I FELT WOOZY. MAYBE IT WAS SOMETHING TO DO WITH HAVING A FULL STOMACH. Everything seemed too much of an effort, even thinking. I sank into the fog and could not fight my way back.

When I woke, the room was dim and I was alone. Everything was a blank after Doctor Cohn left. For the first time, I drew an easy breath, but within five minutes the door opened and there was Rafe, filling me with confusion, disquiet, and questions I was too afraid to ask.

He held a bouquet of tulips. "You're awake!" His voice was eager, impatient. He turned, gesturing.

Another person paused in the doorway.

"Your daughter, Madam." Rafe bowed theatrically.

Shock froze my reaction for a second or two.

What was that in her face and eyes? It screamed without making a sound. *Don't hurt me again. Do you love me? Why did you leave?*

"You're all grown up," I said shakily, fighting tears. For a moment I thought such overwhelming emotion might break me like an eggshell smacked against the edge of a skillet.

Rafe pulled on her wrist. "Every time I looked at her, I knew you'd come home someday. She kept me sane."

His words were distant. Unimportant.

"I remember your first smile," I said. *I remember when you were inside of me, and holding you when you were a baby. How did I live without you all these years?*

McKenna's lips curved upward, but the half-smile disappeared at once into a pinched frown. She hunched as though she wanted to close in on herself and hide. I had a sense that but for Rafe's presence, she might start screaming. Maybe throwing things.

I did this. I hurt you in ways I can never fix. In that moment, I welcomed Rafe's punishment, whatever it might be.

Slowly, afraid to push, I held out my hand.

"Welcome back." She stepped closer and took my hand, shook it politely like one does when meeting someone for the first time, then let go.

"Grandmama!"

A small, skinny girl stood in the doorway, one auburn braid falling to her waist. Her long-lashed eyes were dark brown, only slightly lighter than mine or McKenna's. Freckles covered her face. She had bony elbows and a scab on one knee.

"I'm Brianne," she announced. "Granddaddy wanted me to be a surprise, but I'm tired of waiting. Can I come in?"

"Brianne?" I glanced at McKenna.

"My daughter." McKenna's cheeks flushed and her luminous eyes darkened.

I held out my arms.

Brianne needed no urging. Giggling, she ran forward and threw herself into my embrace. With cold, small hands, she patted my cheeks. "Don't cry, Grandmama. Everything will be all right. I promise."

WILL BREWED COFFEE AND WATCHED FROM THE WINDOW AS THE WEATHER worsened. If he got snowed in, he wouldn't be able to drive down and check Rafe's satellite device. By about five, he could hardly make out the barn. This was a bona fide late season blizzard.

What he did catch sight of was something under the old leather couch he'd picked up years ago at a garage sale in Ouray. A sliver of curled blue ribbon, shining in the firelight. He bent and slid out a box wrapped in yellow paper, which he tore off. A silver filigree cigarette case. He hadn't seen one of these since he was small. His father had carried one around, thinking it made him debonair.

He pressed the tab on the side and it popped open. Another band of ribbon, this time scarlet, tied around two locks of hair braided together, both so dark one could scarcely be separated from the other.

He cradled it in his palm. She must have saved his hair when she'd given him a trim. She'd become quite good at it over the years. He laughed softly as he remembered the first time. That could only be called a butchering. Had she forgotten to give it to him for his birthday, or had she been saving it for another occasion?

Loneliness and worry wiped away the laughter. Was she alive? Would he sense it if she wasn't? What if she was alive, and Rafe did find her? Would she want to stay with him? Try again, for her daughter's sake if nothing else?

That might be preferable to the visions he could not quite eradicate of her being kept as some man's plaything.

The Erinyes tear the skin from my bones.

Perhaps he was getting used to the voice. He hardly reacted when it came out of nowhere, a woman's desolate whisper winding through the deepest currents of his mind.

He sat in front of the fire tracing the braid with one finger. His coffee grew cold. The fire subsided and the room fell into darkness. Returning the hair to the cigarette case, he placed it inside his shirt and rested his head on the back of the chair, closing his eyes.

Bright fires on a black horizon. Women chanting. Ripened barley whooshing in night breezes.

Something prevented him from moving. He strained to no avail. Flowing robes, hands stretched out, palms down, over his torso. The chanting died away.

Erin's voice. *Alcmene, anathema.*

A shadow loomed into a man who resembled Rafe. He held a curved white knife. Will struggled, wanting to call out, to warn Erin, but he couldn't. His body remained frozen.

The blade flashed. He could no longer feel anything but paralyzing cold that spread through his legs and arms as it stole his life away.

He heard himself say, "Selene. My child."

The woman bending over him wasn't Erin after all. Her hair was black like Erin's, but she was younger. *I will take care of them.*

Pain faded into numbness. "Aridela!"

Could she hear? She stared down at the man's face while he drifted above. Surely that wasn't him lying there, so bloody and limp? "Aridela!" he cried again.

She never turned. She pressed her forehead to the corpse's cheek and sobbed.

THE BRAIN SCAN SHOWED NOTHING OF CONCERN. DOCTOR COHN BROUGHT IN ONE of the country's top psychiatrists who happened to be based at UCLA. He carried out an evaluation designed to test Erin's memory and triumphantly announced that she had a simple case of dissociative amnesia. He assured them the attack had caused her memory lapse. With time, rest, good food, and normalcy, all would soon heal.

Rafe sat patiently through these unnecessary exams, noting the covert glances Erin sent his way. He could have told the doctors they would find nothing.

Erin was lying. Lying to the doctors, lying to him. She'd abandoned him, abandoned McKenna, and hooked up with Will. That was the bare, unvarnished truth.

For twenty-three years he hadn't once considered the idea that she would leave of her own volition. Especially not after becoming a mother. Nothing tied a woman to a man more staunchly than a child, even in those days, when women spat out children like sturgeons laid eggs.

Nowadays, of course, sturgeons, like children, were quite rare.

He'd told himself so often that someone had broken in and taken her that he'd convinced himself it was true. Everyone around him agreed. *She loved you,* they affirmed, never seeming to realize they always spoke of her in the past tense, even in those early days. After a year, their condolences changed. *She's dead, Rafe. Accept it. Some criminal got in and kidnapped her. If she were alive, we would have received a ransom demand. It's time to get on with things. Find someone else. We need your offspring for the next generation. We need your sons to carry on the Reformation Brotherhood.*

Henry's vice president, Redmond Warwick, took a different approach. He brought women to the chateau in Deer Valley, gorgeous females conditioned to give pleasure, to do and be whatever was asked of them. Rafe thanked him and played the game, but only to keep the whores from being punished. In those early days, he recognized the fear lurking in women's eyes and felt pity. That was Erin's lingering influence. Now, after so long, women's fear made no impression on him at all.

Raphael Konstantinou was described as a "warrior of men," "merciless," "the Cannibal." Through the years, innumerable women, always as physically close to Erin as could be found, were brought for his pleasure. Most tried to break through his wall and become a favorite, fully realizing that if they succeeded, they would eat. They would drink. They would live another day. Another week. Not one had ever come close. When he was done, he waved and they were taken away.

Erin spent six days in the hospital. Rest and good food, antibiotics and euphoria drugs, time spent with McKenna and Brianne, all these things returned a healthy tint to her cheeks, renewed energy to her movements, even hints of the old sparkle to her eyes. The initial fear receded, as did the color that eddied around her, the same pale purple and gold he'd first seen when she was a child in elementary school. In the Quonset hut, the colors had roiled like angry fireworks. Every day since they'd grown more muted.

He wasn't sure why he allowed her to relax, to tell herself he didn't know the truth. Sometimes he wanted to scream in her face. *You've been fucking my brother!*

But he didn't.

Now that the lies he'd told himself for so long were shattered, the old, never-answered conundrum returned.

Such a coincidence, her leaving me that night. Could she have heard something? Did she eavesdrop on us? Even if she did hear us, the pills should have kept her from thinking it through or having the will to run away.

If she did hear something, and did manage to think it through, why did she never betray us to the Western Alliance or the insurgents?

He tried to recall the things he, Henry, Novikov, and Soung Jae-jin had discussed. He thought about the conference room, how it was soundproofed and wired to set off an alarm if anyone came near the door. The only other place they'd talked was the terrace, but that was very late. She was probably already gone.

There's no memory loss. She's pulling the wool over this idiot's eyes and trying to fool me, too. If she had heard our plans that night, she would not be looking at me now with anything less than terror. She's lying because she's afraid to confess she's been with Will.

He smiled, kissed her, and held her hand. Little by little, she relaxed. He would keep up this charade until he won back her trust and discovered the truth. Then he would see.

Chapter 3

Screwing on the back of a diamond earring, I hurried down the staircase, praying to the universe that I wouldn't trip on the hem of the red velvet gown.

I could hardly believe the holes in my earlobes hadn't closed after so many years of neglect, but I'd managed to push the posts through without much trouble. The dress was new, but these were my own earrings. He'd kept them all these years.

Before we left the hospital, the heavy bandages on my face and arm were replaced with pale pink butterfly strips. I could now see out of my left eye without obstruction. Rafe and his bodyguards whisked me through oddly deserted hospital corridors up to the roof and into a quietly humming personal aerozepp, which transported us in record time to a private airport in Utah, where a luxury limo pod waited, the passenger doors open and two uniformed men standing at attention. There was no human driver; at some point during our separation, Rafe had given in to technology and bought an automated hover car that ran on a cushion of air a meter or so above the ground. I could barely see anything through the tinted windows as it followed the sensors on either side of the winding roads to the chateau.

Rafe and his parents watched intently from the foot of the stairs. McKenna and Brianne hung back near the massive front door.

You want me to trip, don't you, Cordelia? Fall flat on my face? Take a tumble?

My mother-in-law's gaze never wavered, nor did she make any attempt to mask her disapproval.

She isn't happy about my resurrection.

"Did I keep everyone waiting?"

"Of course not." Rafe sounded too cheerful. He'd been getting the third degree plus disparaging comments, no doubt, about the wisdom of returning his wayward wife to the fold.

"Erin." Cordelia gave me one of those movie-star air kisses, careful to avoid touching me.

"You don't look a day older," I said. Age was probably too fearful to attempt a takeover in such well-guarded enemy territory. My mother-in-law had intimidated me when I was seventeen and newly married. Cordelia was as formidable as ever at seventy-four.

My father-in-law, Dillon, gave me a kiss on my right cheek. "This is a happy surprise, Erin."

"It's good to see you again." My smile was forced. Dillon had cut his second son out of his life like a cancer. I had no respect for him, and that would be hard to hide.

Oh, boy. A night full of lies.

McKenna looked apprehensive. She must be feeling the tension. Brianne, dressed up in a pretty knee-length frock of emerald green, white leggings, and shiny black shoes, held her mother's hand and stood protectively close.

Taking my arm, Rafe led the way to the dining room. I felt the charge zipping from his hand into mine, fainter than it had been when he touched me in the hospital, but still noticeable.

Speaking softly, I said, "It's my first night. Couldn't this have waited a day or two?"

"I told them not to come, that you needed rest. You see how well they listened. Sorry."

Things hadn't changed much. The chateau sprawled flamboyantly across the summit of its lofty mountain. I used to think it magnificent. Now all these rooms, piled one on top of the next, seemed a waste, with only Rafe, McKenna, and Brianne living here. These days, my idea of a welcoming and happy home was Will's cozy cabin in the San Juan wilderness, where you didn't need a com system to find your housemates.

What was Will doing? What was he thinking? If only I could ask.

Rafe's chef, a fiftyish man dressed in a traditional snowy white jacket, inclined his head and gestured. "There's caviar and champagne on the terrace, sir, and the fireplace is lit."

Cordelia's lips turned up in an avaricious smile. I remembered her devotion to caviar from the old days, and how Rafe and I laughed behind her back because she never failed to have a glass of champagne with her caviar, though she called herself a rigid teetotaler.

"Thanks, Dale." Rafe herded us outdoors.

The terrace had always been one of my favorite spots, winter or summer, but now, for some reason I couldn't define, fear ran through me as I stepped onto the flagstones.

Someone had placed a glass-topped bar table and chairs near the fire. Rafe held out a chair for me, as Dillon did for Cordelia. The evening was chilly, especially as my shoulders were bare, but the roaring fire helped.

Various caviars sat on ice in a silver serving dish ringed by vodka glasses. Almas, Sevruga, and, best of all, Beluga.

Dale had gone above and beyond traditional folded blinis, crackers, eggs, and canapés with fancy dishes of scallops balanced on crunchy potato pancakes, topped with caviar, diced shallots, and crème fraiche.

The champagne was close by, buried in ice, along with a bottle of Eye of the Dragon vodka. Rafe must really want to impress someone. Me? Surely not, but who else? Was he hoping, as so many rich men throughout history had hoped, to buy the love of a woman through grandiose display?

I bypassed the pairings to savor my first taste of Beluga in twenty-three years on its own, using a tiny mother-of-pearl spoon which I turned upside down on my tongue as I'd been taught.

Guilt crept through my thoughts. What would Will think if he could see me sitting here in velvet and diamonds, relishing costly fish eggs like a spoiled, decadent socialite?

"I guess the world found a way to save the Caspian Sea," I said.

"Afraid not." Rafe picked up one of the scallops and had a bite. "Oil spills, chemicals, sewage, trash. Nobody wanted to take on the cost or responsibility for the cleanup. Far-sighted Iranians saved a few sturgeons, and now they're kept in harvesting farms. The eggs are removed without killing the fish."

"They control the market and love bleeding us for their fish eggs," Dillon said.

He poured Cordelia a modest flute of champagne and she sipped before placing a spoonful of the Sevruga on toast and topping it with crumbled egg yolks. It was her third since we'd sat down.

How would she have fared in the kennels, with a cup of broth that was mostly dirty water, dotted with dead flies? I couldn't imagine, but knowing her love of caviar was the only thing keeping her attention off me, I sent out silent thanks.

"I wish we could come up with a solution so neat for everything else," Rafe said. "Unfortunately, our best minds have so far failed us."

"What do you mean?"

"Droughts. Hurricanes. Glaciers melting. Gigantic tornadoes. Sea water rising and fresh water drying up. You name it, we're dealing with it. Crops the world over are failing. The fresh fruits and vegetables of our childhood are almost impossible to come by these days."

He poured us each a shot of vodka and quirked his brow. I knew what he wanted. We picked up the glasses, tapped them, and drank, slamming them down and laughing as we acknowledged one more remembered detail of our past. For a few seconds, it felt as though I'd never left, and there was no betrayal to be punished or forgiven.

McKenna had only a little caviar but she managed to gulp several shots of vodka before I caught Rafe sending her a warning frown.

Brianne said fish eggs were gross. It wasn't my place, but I dipped a spoon in the glass bowl and scooped out a smidgen of the smoother Almas. "Try a tiny bite," I said. "Don't chew. Press with your tongue and the roof of your mouth. See what you think."

She nodded and trustingly allowed me to place the spoon upside down on her tongue. She closed her eyes and pursed her lips; I could see her moving things around. Her eyes flew open and she cried, "They're popping!"

I laughed, and she giggled. "That is better, a little," was all she would admit.

I was able to steal a few clandestine glances at McKenna. Every now and then, I saw something in her expression that reminded me poignantly of my baby.

Then there was my granddaughter, whose face contained so many freckles that they'd even invaded her lips. Her eyes and brows were darkest brown, a perfect complement to her auburn hair. I had never seen anyone quite like her. She looked nothing like me, or Rafe, or Cordelia, or Dillon, and only superficially like McKenna, in the shape of her lips and bone structure. I had no redheads in my ancestry and I doubted Rafe did either, so that hair color and complexion must have come from the father, whom I had yet to hear a word about.

Dale fetched us to supper.

Someone had drawn the drapes over the stained-glass windows and lit a fire in the fireplace on the north wall. Crystal and silver twinkled in the candlelight.

I designed this room. "It looks like a bordello," Cordelia had said, which made me shrink with humiliation, but I managed to stand my ground and now, as a mature woman, I knew the warm dark red walls invited one to enter, to be comfortable, to enjoy good food, laughter, and companionship.

Rafe seated me on his right. No one spoke until the formally suited footman poured the wine and slipped out.

"Will you ever hire a man who is capable of remembering that I do not drink, Raphael? We're here often enough that I shouldn't have to keep reminding him." Cordelia unfolded her linen napkin and placed it in her lap.

I, like most married women, and certainly everyone at this table, knew better than to defend the footman for being understandably confused, or to call her out on her hypocrisy.

"I'll speak to him." Rafe dabbed his forehead with a corner of his napkin. His gaze flickered over everyone, lingering on me last. His hand briefly clenched the napkin into a ball.

He's nervous.

So was I.

Lifting his glass, he said, "To lovely Erin. To my answered prayers."

Dillon and McKenna raised their glasses, but Cordelia cut in with, "It isn't proper to drink to an answered prayer. Toast Erin's return, by all means, but keep alcohol in its proper place, as far removed from God and prayer as can be."

Without losing a beat, Rafe said, "As you wish. To lovely Erin. To my answered dreams."

"Yay, Granddaddy!" Brianne picked up her glass of milk to join in the toast.

We sipped. Everyone except Cordelia and McKenna pasted on pleasant smiles.

With a proud flourish, Dale carried in an enormous serving dish of seared mahi mahi, topped with sprigs of shallots, capers, and lemon slices.

Mahi mahi!

World governments had declared the oceans empty of edible fish more than a decade ago. Will told me when I expressed a longing for sea bass. Scientists had been predicting it since before I was born, so I wasn't surprised. Over-fishing was the main culprit. The oceans couldn't keep up with the ever-expanding human population. Then there were the red tides, trash, plastic, and pollution.

Perhaps far-seeing entrepreneurs had set up mahi mahi fish farms. I gave our meal the proper humble admiration and praised the caviar. Satisfied, Dale retreated, leaving us to enjoy his efforts. The footmen brought in course after course of fragrant dishes.

Too bad for Cordelia; my first bite revealed that the lemon-garlic sauce also contained a generous helping of wine.

I was getting used to food again, but the memory of starvation endured. I ate slowly, appreciating the flavors of an exceptional meal, and spared a few heavy thoughts for the women in the kennels.

To fill the awkward silence, I asked, "What are you doing these days, Rafe?"

He nodded at Dillon. "I get in to the office with Dad once in a while—"

"Tell her," Cordelia interrupted. "Don't be modest." To me, she said, "You don't know?" Her icy gaze and voice were irritatingly antagonistic.

I shrugged to indicate my ignorance, then wished I hadn't as the stitches in my arm tugged unpleasantly. What hornet's nest had I unwittingly poked now?

"Raphael has very little free time to spend with his father," she said with unadulterated pride. "He is head of Jasper Simonson's equal rights group, Aquilo. He is their Lion. Their Lion of God."

I knew I failed to mold my face into an expressionless mask quickly enough. "Really?" Good. The word came out sounding polite, nothing more.

"Mother, please." Rafe turned to me. "It happened right after I lost you. I'm not sure if I ever told you that Jasper got lung cancer. It worsened and he had to go into the hospital. They were in need of an attorney, and Jasper sent them to me as our firm is Christian-based and we'd met. I don't suppose you remember him?"

I cleared my throat. "Yes. Yes, I do." The president had introduced Rafe to Jasper Simonson shortly after Rafe started law school in Washington. Jasper was a favorite of Henry's; they held numerous prayer fests in the Oval Office.

Like everyone else, Simonson was impressed with Rafe and invited him to attend his famous rallies. His group hadn't been called Aquilo, though. It was something else, I couldn't remember what.

The man nabbed headlines with his far-right evangelical stance, misogyny, and conspiracy theories. He raged constantly against homosexuals, transgenders, and especially women. Women, he thundered, were created to serve men's needs and bear children. Period. He claimed the Bible spelled it out—the destiny of womankind was to be a helpmate to man, and that was literally the only reason for her existence. It was of no matter if a woman didn't happen to be an evangelical Christian. In Jasper's world, all women had to comply with evangelical Christian values anyway. On the question of wives who refused to follow his puritan mandates, they were first to be reprimanded lovingly, beaten if necessary, and finally abandoned without succor, stripped of everything, home, clothing, currency, and children, if they would not mend their ways. I remembered him avowing that heaven was closed to all but submissive women who worshipped their husbands as the earthly representatives of God.

The symbol for his organization was as controversial as the man himself, a lightning bolt that ended in a sharply pointed arrowhead. It always made me think of a penis as a weapon, and I did not believe that was coincidence. There had been rumors suggesting that the group possessed a secret arsenal, and at one of the few rallies I attended, I heard Jasper promise his righteous followers that in the longed-for final days, they would have permission to massacre disbelievers and those who opposed him.

The demented fanaticism in Jasper's eyes remained with me over the years, that and his wife's face of dead stone. She never spoke or smiled. I wasn't sure she could.

"I just…didn't realize you had…"

Everyone was staring at me. I shrugged helplessly.

In the hospital, I had watched Rafe as he slept in the chair by my bed. The lines around his eyes were smoothed. Asleep, he seemed a lot more vulnerable. His closed eyelids and fans of dark blond lashes were like an innocent boy's.

Not once had he blamed me, accused me of anything, or shown any sign of anger. I had dared allow a fragile hope to form that we might go forward on friendly terms. I imagined him forgiving me for Will. I pictured being allowed to see McKenna and Brianne.

But if Rafe was an acolyte of Jasper Simonson, if he believed the things Simonson preached, and was now preaching that same drivel, such kindnesses seemed impossible.

The Rafe I remembered had made fun of Jasper, mimicking the way he sprayed spittle that hung in his beard every time he went into one of his rants about corrupt society and what men of courage needed to do. Jasper had denied accusations that he hated every country where the native population elevated women to equal status with men, but hate he did. It was clear in his speeches, in his exhortations, and the way he looked at me when Rafe wasn't paying attention.

Dillon interrupted my depressing reminiscences. "Jasper trusted Raphael so much he put him in charge of the legal department for the entire organization. People sued them right and left in those days. Disgruntled liberals, you know. When Jasper was told he only had a short time left to live, he hand-picked Raphael to take over."

I couldn't be sorry that Jasper Simonson was dead. The only problem was that my husband was keeping his legacy alive instead of letting it fade into obscurity where it belonged. "You conduct rallies like he did?" I asked, picturing him on a stage blaring at crowds of thousands.

"That and much more," Cordelia snapped. "Raphael is a very important man, Erin. He accompanied the president on his last summit to Israel. Grigory Novikov has threatened three times to bomb Jerusalem out of existence if they don't stop fighting. The peace talks Raphael initiated have accomplished more than any other effort in the last fifty years." She paused for emphasis. "My son —your husband—was the architect of the Ukrus-US coalition."

"The—the Ukrus US...." No, it couldn't be. Rafe had ripped the US out of the Western Alliance? The final bulwark of freedom in the world? He'd given us to that totalitarian regime? I must be misunderstanding. He would never do such a thing.

America, the land of my birth. My home. The world's finest, most successful democracy. America no longer, but simply another of Novikov's conquered territories? It took a moment for the full implication to set in.

I recalled the night I'd met Grigory Novikov, right up until the moment my memories stopped as though blocked by a stone wall. Rafe and I waited outside our front door to greet our guests. My flesh had crawled at the way Novikov looked at me. It crawled again in remembrance.

The rich food I'd enjoyed turned to wet cement in my stomach.

Henry Montague had not done that alone. My gaze lifted to Rafe. *Your husband was the architect.*

I remembered Henry as a patriot, the countless criminal investigations, impeachment probes, and other attempts to gouge him out of the White House notwithstanding. He'd engineered a way to usurp the Twenty-Second Amendment to the Constitution, and had served as America's president twenty-five years by the time of that fateful meeting at the chateau. He often used Franklin Roosevelt as his inspiration, and hummed *America the Beautiful* as he strode the White House corridors. I'd heard it. I'd also observed him touch Alexander Hamilton's foot every time he passed the bronze statue. More than once, he claimed that Rafe was his Alexander Hamilton.

"Henry—I mean, President Montague," I said unevenly. "Is he alive?"

"No. He had a stroke and died in '53. You didn't know?"

I shook my head.

"You never were one for politics. President Warwick asked me to stay on in the same capacity. Do you remember Redmond Warwick, the vice president? Henry's nephew? Their goals meshed. It's been a long and fruitful collaboration."

"He's actually president?"

Hints of a frown appeared around Rafe's mouth and between his eyes. "The US is still a power to reckon with, Erin. There used to be hundreds of world leaders, none of whom ever agreed on anything. Now there are two, Grigory Novikov and Redmond Warwick. There would be three, but Soung Jae-jin was murdered. North Korea was absorbed by China, which was later absorbed by Ukrus. Novikov and Warwick run things pretty much equally, for the benefit and future of the planet. Things are much more streamlined."

I hadn't misunderstood. "What about Canada, Europe, the UK? Mexico? South and Central America?" They had been our partners, the core members of the Western Alliance, the brave countries holding off Ukrus and its threat of world domination.

"You really haven't been paying attention, have you? Most of the world willingly joined with Ukrus, but there are a few holdouts. Germany, Norway, Sweden, and Greece. Their defiance caused the disintegration of the New European Confederation. Scotland, Greenland, and Mexico also refuse to join. 'Independent Territories,' they call themselves. In our own country, California, Oregon, Vermont, Connecticut, and Illinois seceded, and renamed themselves the 'Unified Free States.' UFS for short. Our borders are closed to them."

His upper lip curled ever so slightly, making clear what he thought of the Unified Free States.

There are a few left with balls. A very goddamned few. Good going, UFS.

I sipped wine as my mind worked through this information. *Why did Henry give in? Why did my country allow it? What did Ukrus do to make it possible?*

Cordelia may have answered the question when she said Ukrus threatened to bomb Jerusalem. That had to be the answer. Ukrus grew strong enough to make everyone cower, even America.

"Advisor to the president, world ambassador, social agitator…when do you find time to sleep?"

"It's only that grand in Mother's mind." Rafe sent Cordelia a resigned frown. "Aquilo simply tries to steer men in a biblical direction. Mostly I contribute a monthly column to their digital newsletter. There aren't that many rallies anymore. Usually once a year, just enough to…"

His expression darkened. What was he thinking? I waited, but he changed the subject.

"The unification has been a fait accompli almost as long as you've been gone," he said. "Mother wouldn't agree, but my biggest complaint will always be the freeze of technological innovation. The minute the US joined Ukrus, everything stagnated. America was on the verge of developments that would save the oceans, get rid of pollution, grow healthy vegetables in smaller spaces, eradicate viruses, explore and colonize space—the moon at least. Maybe because so much of it was being developed in California, it all stopped. They threw a tantrum and refused to work with us."

"Why didn't other states take up the slack?" I asked. "No scientists or engineers anywhere but California?" I tried not to sound snarky, but Rafe's piercing glance told me I hadn't quite succeeded.

Cordelia answered before he could. "The rest of the country wanted a return to traditional, wholesome living. We no longer wished for godless technology over simple human life. It was completely out of hand. Especially the internet. Evil run amok."

Rafe had fulfilled his mother's most ardent desire. He'd become an evangelist. Though he physically resembled my Rafe, he must have undergone a complete mental and emotional transformation and abandoned the cocky, privately irreverent, sexy husband of my memories.

Would it have happened, if I hadn't left? Had I unknowingly kept him out of that pit of vipers?

My anxiety spiked. I glanced at the doorway, wishing I could excuse myself. Then my gaze landed on McKenna and I stiffened my spine. She'd lived with this her entire life without any help.

"Why Aquilo?" I asked. "I don't remember that name. Wasn't it called something else?"

"Ah, you do remember," Rafe said. "Yes, it used to be called *Men for Right*. That name lacked the kind of spark that catches on and generates passion. When I took over, I changed it. Aquilo is Latin for the north wind."

"How does the north wind generate passion? Makes me think of snowstorms and freezing."

"You're not the only one. I had to educate men on that score. In ancient times, people considered the north wind to be one of the most powerful, unstoppable forces on earth. They believed it could impregnate women, among other things. I incorporated a cyclone into our new logo to represent the power of wind."

"I didn't approve of a pagan name for a Christian organization," Cordelia said, "but I must admit it caught on."

"Mother." Rafe's voice hardened. "Rome was the seat of Christianity. You don't object to other Roman symbols, like the fish."

"Congratulations, Rafe," I said quickly. "It sounds like you've been doing something that...makes you happy." I had started to say *something important*, but those words would strangle me.

"Sometimes I thought I was happy. Rare, fleeting moments. Now I know how wrong I was." He ran his fingers over the back of my hand. "I was busy. That is very different from happy."

He hadn't lost his legendary charm. Dinner and its revelations had turned my blood into polar sludge, but that smile brought me exploding back to life.

We'd been happy together. I didn't like his politics, but I kept it to myself. There were things about me he probably didn't care for, and he kept those to himself. That's how successful marriages work. Our initial passion, both for sex and fighting, settled into a steadier routine after McKenna was born. At least, I realized as I sat there thinking, Rafe's fingertips grazing mine, until the second moon came. That moon changed everything. I didn't fall victim to the lunacy, but I did struggle. Every thought I tried to construct was an effort. The fog refused to lift, no matter how many vitamins I took or cups of coffee I drank. My anxiety escalated, too. At first, I tried various sleep aids, thinking I was exhausted. Nothing helped. Sexually, though, things improved. I was always ready for a little one on one naked time, no matter how tired I felt.

I'd actually been with Will six years longer than Rafe, but those memories were completely different. Will and I had passion in plenty and it never waned, but it was tempered with friendship, laughter, and respect. We rarely fought and never held grudges. Anxiety never troubled me.

Dillon snuffed the invisible threads of fire zinging between Rafe's hand and mine with a blunt question. "Erin, you disappeared in the middle of the night without explanation, except for that note, which was obviously a lie. Did you write it? Were you kidnapped? Where have you been? Is there a reason you never let us know you were alive?"

Here it comes.

There was no way I would admit the truth in this setting. Confess out loud that I'd been with Rafe's brother, their youngest son, for twenty-three years? That was a conversation I would reserve for a better moment, when Rafe and I were alone. *I will tell him the truth, but not here. Not tonight.*

The heat from the fireplace was suddenly miserable. Twice I had to clear my throat before I could speak a partial, convoluted truth. "Note? I don't remember a note. I don't remember anything. I've tried and tried. It's just not there. Two men attacked me. I think they drugged me because I have no memory until I woke up and I was in a kennel. Like a plastic kennel for a large dog." My breathing quickened. The memory of what those two guards did was unbearable. Forcing me to relive it in this place of safety and real food, on my very first night home, was cruel. I dropped my hands onto my lap, using the table to hide the sudden, uncontrollable shaking.

A glance passed between Rafe and Dillon. I wondered what unspoken message they were exchanging.

Unmoved and no less acerbic, Cordelia asked, "Are you saying that you cannot remember *anything* from the last twenty some years? Not your husband or your own child? You have *no idea* where you were?"

McKenna's gaze was riveted on me. Rafe shifted uneasily. Cordelia's Norwegian blue eyes made me think of a cold, staring fish.

I stuck to my story, sensing it was the safest for now. "I—yes. That's what

I'm saying. I'm sure it will come. Won't it? With time, and distance from the attack?" I glanced at Rafe. "That's what the doctor said."

His frown eased. "I'm sure it will. You need to heal."

Of all the unexpected supporters. Not only had he not demanded an explanation for my long absence, he had given me the most exquisite gift I could imagine—our daughter, McKenna, and her daughter, Brianne.

I would confess the truth, but I would not be dragged into it by Cordelia. I would not succumb to her interrogation.

I have to lie. They won't only hate me, they'll hate Will. Rafe might kill him or something. McKenna would never forgive me. She would think I left her for a love affair. I know I didn't do that. I know it.

"Believe me," I said, "no one feels worse than I do about what's happened."

"Can you at least tell us if you were faithful to your husband?"

I resisted the urge to fan myself with my napkin. The old witch. I wasn't sure how much longer I could keep my temper in check.

"This is dinner, Mother, not the Spanish Inquisition," Rafe said.

"We have a right to know. You, especially."

"There are better times to ask." Rafe sent a subtle nod towards Brianne.

Cordelia glanced at her great-granddaughter. "Very well." She bent her head and concentrated on the mahi mahi. Another awkward silence commenced.

Dillon coughed. "Speaking of not changing, you haven't either. Well, you have, but even that wound on your face doesn't take away from your beauty, Erin."

Cordelia sent him a narrowed glare. I almost laughed. She didn't like her husband giving me compliments.

Dillon blinked and changed the subject. "Has Raphael told you that your scars can be removed?"

"Yes. A plastic surgeon saw me at the hospital. His opinion was different than yours, Dillon. He said he could make me look like a teenager again. Apparently in his eyes, I look horrible and need fixing."

"That's not true," Rafe said soothingly. "He mostly works on men, Erin. He didn't mean it like that."

Dillon bravely, or rashly, returned to compliments, of a sort. "Whenever I think of you that night at the hospital when you had the miscarriage, I'm grateful the doctors didn't report us to the juvenile authorities."

Truth to tell, I didn't like getting compliments from Dillon either. It turned my stomach. Nor did I like being reminded of the loss of our son. The miscarriage was late-term, and devastating. The pain only lessened when McKenna appeared, five years later.

To this day, I imagined him, a boy like his father, with wild tawny hair and eyes greener than absinthe.

"It's hard to believe so much time has passed," I said, forcing a light tone. "Here's McKenna, a grown woman and a mother herself."

McKenna made no reply. She drained her wineglass and regarded it wistfully.

I shouldn't have brought her into the limelight. In this setting, with these people, she seemed insecure, ill-at-ease, less a woman of twenty-seven with her own child and more like an adolescent. Why was she living here? Who and where was Brianne's father?

I pictured Rafe and Dillon throttling the guy and dumping his body in Emigration Canyon.

The atmosphere in this dining room was fraught with instability. I felt like I was tiptoeing the narrowest of precipices.

Dale and two footmen brought out individual plates of chocolate cheesecake garnished with strawberries and coffee-flavored curls of chocolate.

"Delicious," I said when we finished. "I am positively stuffed. Thank you, Dale." I was also glad that the end was in sight.

"Shall we have coffee by the infinity pool?" Rafe asked. "I know, Mother. None for you. Perhaps an eggnog?"

Brianne tugged on my hand in the hallway. "Night night, Grandmama."

I gave her a hug. "I'll come in and kiss you as soon as I'm allowed." I lifted a brow, and Brianne giggled.

"I called my grandmother *Meemah*. It would mean a lot to me if you would call me that."

"Meemah." She patted my cheek as she seemed to like to do, an endearing gesture that showed her innate kindness. "Everybody calls me Brie."

"I love that, and it fits you," I said. "Night, Brie."

McKenna said she wanted to retire as well. I watched them climb the stairs, feeling like the covered wagons were abandoning me to a storm of deadly arrows.

Not giving me time to dwell, Rafe twined his fingers through mine. "Let's get it over with."

"Isn't it our business?" I returned, but the question was rhetorical. Cordelia and Dillon made Rafe's business their own. They always had, and always would. He replied with a shrug.

The fire in the stone fireplace was bright and inviting. We crossed to the pool and settled into deeply cushioned chairs, each with its own fleece blanket. Rafe poured coffee from the silver pot and passed out cups. Mmmm. Gourmet coffee. I'd never got the hang of making good coffee at Will's, no matter what brand I asked him to get on his monthly shopping excursions. It was bitter, and we often ended up spitting out grounds.

The urge to be alone with Rafe was growing stronger. My heartbeat was shallow and rapid, and my skin tingled. I could hardly take my eyes off him. What was happening? I hadn't had that much alcohol, had I?

Cordelia stirred a pinch of nutmeg into her eggnog. "We must understand exactly what you've done. Only then can we prepare for the media onslaught. Brianne and McKenna have gone to bed, so, Raphael, would you agree this is a better time?"

"Just keep it short, Mother. We're tired." He sent me an intimate smile.

Did he think…no, he couldn't possibly be thinking I would sleep with him as though we'd never separated.

"Erin? Are you going to answer me?"

"Sorry?"

"I asked if you remained faithful to Raphael while you lived…who knows where?"

"Mother, do you see her face? If only you could have seen her arm that day. It was sliced open to the bone. Yet the way you talk, she's been off somewhere drinking tequila and dancing on tables."

"It's a logical question. You may be unwilling to ask, but I'm certain you want to know the answer."

"You know she wasn't."

I watched Rafe's hands clench reflexively and inwardly shuddered.

"She didn't remember us. I've already told her I don't care."

Christ, now he was lying for me. I never said that. I'd implied in the hospital that I didn't remember the last twenty-three years. I'd stated that I *did* remember Rafe and McKenna.

Hadn't I? My subterfuges were getting mixed up along with my ability to think clearly.

Inside, my spirit screamed, and I wanted to let that scream out. *It's none of your business you bitch!* "My memories are confused right now," I said. "I can't answer any of your questions." She was making everything harder, if not impossible. "I'm sure I never meant to hurt anyone."

"How can you be sure? By your own admission, you don't remember. Not why you left, where you were, or who you were with. So perhaps that *was* your intent. Why else would you lie to him about where you were going?" I could almost feel Cordelia's insinuations strike my face like sharp stones. "Why else would you allow your family to live so long not knowing if you were dead or alive?"

"Is this about the note you mentioned? I swear I have no memory of that night." I glanced at Rafe, hoping for help. "I do remember greeting Henry and the other—others. I remember that very well, but nothing after. Nothing."

Damn this horrible woman. *You're lucky to be away from her, Will.*

"It comes down to one thing." Dillon cupped a hand around his wife's forearm, in restraint or comfort, I couldn't tell which. "Are you coming back to your family? If so, you must ask for God's forgiveness. I've talked to Raphael. I know he wants you. Do you realize how fortunate you are? You left your husband and child, not for a week but a quarter century. It ripped a hole in their lives that never healed. Yet here they are, willing to accept you into their hearts again. I'm not so sure I could be as forgiving. Are you back, Erin?"

"I-I can't answer that either," I said. "I only got out of the hospital today. Rafe and I haven't had time to discuss anything yet."

When he found out about Will…not to mention there was Will to think of… my love for him, the years we'd spent together…

A surge of grief-stricken yearning passed through me. If only I hadn't gone out hiking that day!

Cordelia snorted. I had never heard my mother-in-law make such an indelicate sound. Two red splotches appeared on her cheeks and her hands moved restlessly.

She'd like to replace the water in this pool with my blood.

I glanced at Rafe, who was staring fixedly at his shoes. His hair was thick and wavy, brushing over the back of his high, stiff collar. The style suited him. I always thought of it as a mane, and it struck me that he did actually resemble the human equivalent of a lion. I used to mess it up as he was going out the door to work. The only thing that had changed were the paler strands threading through his sideburns and temples.

I loved you.

As though I'd spoken aloud, his head lifted and he gazed squarely into my eyes.

Silence stretched. Rafe's gaze held mine like pins holding a butterfly to a sheet of cardboard. Ah, I remembered that look. It was the one he'd used to get me to agree to sex the first time, and many times after. An ardent stare, set off by those long, oh-so-long eyelashes. Captivated like a princess in a fairy tale, my fifteen-year-old self hadn't felt him slip his hands under my shirt and unhook my bra.

Funny how men never seem to lose sight of the goal during seduction.

Caught up in bittersweet memories, I heard myself say, "You have another son, right? William, isn't it? Is he here in Utah?"

Rafe blinked and looked away.

"We don't know where he is," Cordelia said shortly. "He left us, long ago, before you did. We have no communication with him."

"Oh," I said. "That's sad. Your own son."

"He abandoned God, and thus his family. It was Will's choice to leave, not ours to send him away."

"Really? He was never here. I never once met him, not even when we were young. Are you saying he made the choice to leave when he was a child?"

"He was rebellious," Dillon said. "We sent him to one of New York City's finest private evangelical schools. They tried everything." He shrugged. "Nothing worked. Not even military school."

An image flashed through my mind of Will as a little boy having the rebellion beaten out. "So, I guess you don't know if he's alive or dead."

"Will found fault with the Scriptures," Dillon said. "He argued that they couldn't be right or real. He called God a fantasy. That was something we couldn't tolerate."

"He turned his back on us," Cordelia said coldly.

"Before or after you turned your back on him?"

Cordelia rose and threw down her blanket. "How dare you show up after twenty-three years and preach to us! I know what you're trying to do. Distraction, pure and simple. It won't work. Are you going to stay with my son? He wants you, for some reason. If you stay, the family will pardon your adultery. Your abandonment. But nothing like this can ever happen again. *Ever*. You will accept your ordained place and role upon this earth."

It was always about control with these people. Power and submission.

I stood as well, refusing to allow her to loom over me. "I don't know what will happen. There's been a lot of water under the bridge."

Rafe made a soft choking sound. I glanced at him, puzzled.

He avoided looking at me as he rose. "Is it any wonder she ran away? In her shoes I would have left too. Said to hell with all of us."

Without another word he turned and was gone.

Cordelia sounded almost triumphant. "Now see what you've done."

"What I've done? You had nothing to do with it?" I started to follow Rafe, but Dillon grabbed my forearm.

"Pray for God's grace and wisdom, Erin. You know where your place is in this life. By Raphael's side. Don't destroy your heavenly resurrection."

I wrenched my arm free and ran after Rafe, muttering, "Damn you and my heavenly resurrection."

Chapter 4

"SAMSON," I SAID. "I'M LOOKING FOR RAFE'S BEDROOM. IS IT STILL ON THE THIRD floor?"

Needles of pain radiated through my sutures. I needed meds—boy, how I needed meds—but this was more important.

"Nothing has changed, Erin," the AI replied. "You can take the elevator or the stairs to the second floor. Turn right, and when you come to the window alcove, head up the staircase."

"It's the entire third floor?"

"Yes, Erin, and part of the fourth. Just as it used to be."

"Yeah," I muttered. Rafe's bedroom could hold two or three of Will's cabin. Maybe more.

"Rafe said you're no longer an interface, Samson. He said you have a form."

"I do." The air before me billowed. At first the face, more male than female though it would not be wrong to call it androgynous, stared at the ceiling, but it gradually swiveled until it observed me directly. Its eyes were open but the effect was a bit creepy, as there were no pupils or irises, no eyebrows. Just finely carved blank orbs, like an ancient Greek statue. The lips and nose were perfectly detailed, but Samson was missing an actual head. He was nothing more than facial features. Nor was he opaque. I saw the wall behind him. The effect was more like a holograph than a live being.

What was I thinking? Samson was not a live being. The representation was sound. "Very nice, Samson. Very handsome. Do you like it?"

"I would enjoy having more expressions. I actually could have an entire body, much like a human being, but Mr. Konstantinou says he prefers me this way. Here is his door." He might not be able to mimic a human's varied expressions, but he did sound pleased at my compliment.

"Thanks." I knocked, opened the door, and stepped in. Samson evaporated behind me.

Light from the old moon reflected off the skylights and windows.

"Rafi?" My tentative query disappeared in the cavernous depths. Perhaps he'd gone to the office, his male refuge next to the observatory on the fourth floor. I turned to leave but paused when I heard a rustle.

"I'm here."

He stepped into the ghostly moonlight, loosening his tie. He unfastened the top two buttons on his shirt and pulled off his jacket, tossing it over the back of a wing chair by the fireplace.

"Funny, isn't it," I said, "how some things never change?" I entered fully and closed the door.

"What do you mean?"

"We're on the downside of the twenty-first century, yet men haven't given up looping nooses around their throats."

"Maybe we're masochists."

I crossed to him, put my fingers under the tie, and lifted it off the pearl-buttoned waistcoat. The waistcoat had drawn my admiration in the dining room. It was a beautiful shade of violet that went well with his tawny hair. Since I'd awakened in the hospital, I'd observed the latest in male fashion on Rafe, Dillon, and Doctor Cohn. They wore their ties in elaborate knots with many complicated twists and turns which made the top rather bulky. Fancy pins secured the center of the twists and kept everything in place. The pin on Rafe's tie was a gold lion's head. He'd paired the tie with a dark gold shirt that had an underlying paisley pattern and a stiff Edwardian-style collar. The violet waistcoat also contained a shimmering gold pattern invisible but for when it caught the light a certain way. "No. There's some other reason why men go on wearing ties year after year. Maybe they really are phallic symbols."

He gave me an achingly gentle smile.

"Rafe…"

"It's all right. I was an idiot to think you'd want to come back to this."

I pulled on the tie, drawing his face close. Kissing his cheek, I breathed in bergamot, musk, a touch of cloves, a fleeting hint of mango. It brought our history flooding over me as though no more than an hour had passed.

I closed my eyes to better experience one of my favorite scent combinations. "That aftershave. What memories it brings."

"They haven't made it for…I don't know…ten, fifteen years, but I never put it on again after you left." With the softest of laughs, he added, "I tore this place apart searching for it."

I startled as I realized his hand had slipped from my arm to the side of my breast, and retreated hastily to the safety of the door. "I guess I've given you the wrong idea."

He ran a hand through his hair, leaving behind a tousled, seductive mess of waves and cowlicks, like he'd just gotten out of bed. "I thought maybe…"

My face burned. "No, Rafe, but seeing you again is good. It's very good."

He moved in, probably hearing some hidden invitation in my voice, no matter what my words conveyed. I fought to breathe normally. What was it about him that made the primal, basest parts of me want to throw a beloved history with Will into oblivion?

And where had my fear of his retribution gone? The Rafe I knew did not forgive easily.

It had been a score of years though. He could have changed. I certainly had.

Hoping to create a polite barrier between us, I said, "I have so many questions. I'd like to know about McKenna's life. More of yours too, if you want to tell me."

For a moment he remained there, caressing my hair and ear. Then he drew in a breath, turned, and walked away, speaking a command. Soft light illuminated stuffed chairs and a loveseat grouped around a fireplace, leaving the rest of the room in shadow.

I released my pent-up breath. I wasn't seventeen anymore, or even twenty-six, and like I'd said downstairs—there was a lot of water under the bridge.

Wading through my nervousness, I crossed to one of the chairs and perched on the edge, my legs pressed together, my arms stiff, my hands interlocked on my lap.

"Want a drink?" Rafe asked.

"What've you got?"

"Champagne on ice."

My chin snapped up. "What?"

"Hope springs eternal. I've missed you, Erin."

I bit my lower lip and rose. "I'd better go."

"I won't take advantage. Promise."

Was he aware of how he was affecting me? Rafe had a way with women. I had never fully pinned the quality down. His long-lashed bedroom eyes? The intimate smile? The way he made a woman feel he was completely involved in the moment with her? Whatever it was, he had it turned up full blast. Even so, was I this easily seduced? I'd always considered myself pretty damn faithful, and Will had been a near constant ache since the moment I woke up in that kennel.

It would have been wiser to seek him out in the bright light of day, maybe in a crowded restaurant.

Unwelcome recollections of the things we'd done in restaurants brought another round of heat to my face. "Can we just talk?"

My mind whirled, whether from the alcohol I'd already had or suggestion, I wasn't sure. The thought that he found me attractive and could want me after so long…

Logic told me it couldn't be true, but it was tantalizing. My girlish psyche wanted to believe.

Why did he never remarry? Has he had lovers? I scolded myself. *Don't be a moron. As soon as he finds out where you've really been all these years, he'll throw you out of here so fast and hard it'll probably break your neck.*

Was it wrong to want to postpone that inevitable moment?

WILL HAD NO DUPLICITY. HE WAS A QUIET, PLAIN-SPOKEN, DOWN-TO-EARTH MAN who avoided attention like others avoided rattlesnake bites. Rafe, the slick attorney, loved being in the spotlight. He used duplicity like a musical instrument to create the response he wanted. Jasper Simonson must have valued such talent.

I'd best not forget that.

Rafe spoke another command. The fire blazed to life and burned cheerfully. He poured two fluted glasses of champagne, handed one to me, then dropped onto the loveseat. I sipped, only remembering after I finished and he gave me a refill that I should not be drinking any more alcohol, especially in this setting.

What the hell. I could control this situation, and the champagne tasted like a cool summer's twilight. Will and I rarely had alcohol, other than beer. I'd missed it as much as the coffee and caviar.

"Before you came in, I was thinking," he said.

I waited.

"About the day I brought you here blindfolded."

I knew I shouldn't play into this, but I couldn't help myself. "To present me with my wedding gift in Rafe fashion. Splendidly."

He grinned.

"You timed it so we'd be on the terrace at sunrise," I said.

"And you knew immediately what to call the place."

"Ramandu's Dawn." I hoped he didn't notice the tears stinging my eyes.

"You had to explain what that meant," Rafe said softly. "Tell me again, Erin."

"Why?"

"Humor me."

"I made fun of you for having multiple degrees and not knowing a simple thing like Ramandu. You were pissed."

"I got pissed over stupid things in those days. Tell me again about Ramandu."

As I began, he leaned back and closed his eyes.

"He was an old man who used to be a star. He lived on Ramandu's Island with his daughter. Every day at dawn, white birds flew out of the sun and one placed a fire berry in his mouth. Each fire berry made him a little younger. At some point, he would be young enough to be a star again. Ramandu's Island was the last island the *Dawn Treader* visited on its epic voyage across the seas of Narnia in *The Voyage of the Dawn Treader*, by C.S. Lewis."

He opened his eyes. "You loved those books."

"I love those books. Present tense."

"McKenna loved them too." He fell silent and stared at the fire. I sensed him remembering.

"I brought in a nanny for her when she was young," he said. "Swedish fellow. Lots of experience. McKenna seemed to like him, but she was lonely. I didn't do a very good job with her, Erin. After you left I…worked. Often till two or three o'clock in the morning. Then, after a couple hours of sleep, I'd get up and work again. I didn't want to be here. There was no spark, nothing to come home to. I shouldn't say that, but that's how I felt. Too many memories. The place depressed me. It probably had the same effect on her."

Desperate to change the subject before losing control, I asked, "How did you find me?"

His lids dropped over his eyes and he rubbed his jaw. "I never stopped looking for you. Never. I've used private investigators, the FBI, the Secret Service. The finest intelligence and spying tech the country could muster. This last guy I hired, Flannery, he did it. He came through. Just in time, from what I saw."

"Yes." I was almost choking on tears. "You saved my life. Like a knight in shining armor. Literally." I could only hope he'd entered the Quonset hut after those men finished using me. I couldn't bear the thought that he'd seen my degradation.

Those men. The flies. The stench. The shackled prisoners being whipped away to the Glory Wall. The shaving, and what was done to me afterwards. Had I remained there, things would have gone from bad to worse. Much worse, I had no doubt.

He regarded me as if reading my mind. Then he finished his champagne, got himself more, and topped off my glass.

"What about whoever was running that thing?" I wished I could control my emotions better, but it was hard, with the irritation of bandages, intermittent pain, the memory of those men, and my helplessness—the helplessness of every woman trapped in that place. "What about the guards? Everything is foggy after the chain hit me."

I saw his shallow breathing. He was angry. Maybe as moved as me. "I shot them. They're dead."

A fierce hot jolt of satisfaction seared me. "What about the others?"

He gave a one-sided shrug. "The other prisoners? I don't know. We sent in the police. I'm sure they sorted it out. I was concerned about you. I had to get you to the hospital."

"Ah. Okay. Good. You can't imagine what they've been going through. The woman next to me said she'd been there for *years*. She was all that kept me going. Thank you, Rafe."

The police would have freed those poor women. No doubt they would have figured out by now who was behind that horrible place and arrested him, or them. I would definitely follow up in the coming days. It would be wonderful if I could find Gemma and thank her properly. Maybe find her a home, help her get on her feet. It was the least I could do for the strength she'd given me.

I discarded circumspection and spoke my true feelings. They were too potent to suppress. "What I did. Walking out on you that way. Never once sending a letter, or calling, or anything. I put you both through hell, Rafe. The last thing I deserve is forgiveness."

He searched for me for over twenty years. Twenty years! Then, when he found me, he asked no questions. Made no accusations.

It was not what I expected.

If only I could remember why I left. Why did that part and no other remain blank? What could he have possibly done that would make fleeing from him and my child in the middle of the night, hooking up with Will, and staying gone for over two decades, my only choice?

Rafe studied the bubbles in his glass then he turned to me. No accusatory glare. No blame or frowning anger. His gaze was serious, but kind.

No matter what he'd done, if he'd done anything at all, I should have stayed and dealt with it instead of taking off like a petulant child. Now here I sat in a mess so tangled it seemed beyond any hope of unraveling.

Cordelia was right to be angry. She had every reason to suspect my motives.

"I'm so ashamed," I said brokenly.

"Erin, tell me the truth. You can't remember what happened that night? The night you left?"

"No, I can't. Honestly."

"Then you can't say, nor can anyone else, that you walked out on us. Maybe you were kidnapped. That's what we believed. That someone broke in and took you, and left a note to throw us off. If you can't remember, then that's a possibility."

He had a point. After all, I was kidnapped from the Dallas Creek trail.

He leaned forward and grasped my hand. "The note said you were going to Brown, to see Maya. You didn't say why. When you never showed up in Rhode Island and I brought in the police, they discovered you hired a pilot and a jet and flew to Denver. One of the facial recognition cameras at the airport pinged you. They found the rental place where you acquired a car, and eventually they found the car. The driver assists and safety systems were disconnected and the seat bands were tucked away like they were never employed. The car had collided with a tree, and you were launched into the windshield. That couldn't have happened if the survival mechanism had worked, but it didn't. It was inert, probably had been for years. There was blood all over the glass, the steering wheel, the dash, the seat. Skin and hair in the windshield. More than enough DNA to identify you."

His mouth tensed and whitened.

"You thought I was dead."

"A shoe. That's all they found, Erin. I couldn't stand to think that you'd wandered off bleeding, that maybe a cougar found you. Or a bear."

Or your brother.

"How could I have been kidnapped if I was alone when I did all this?"

Giving a one-sided shrug, he said, "Threats. Bribery. Brainwashing. The kidnapper could have been hiding outside the camera angle, unseen but still controlling you."

The champagne had wormed clear to the center of my brain. The edges of my vision were unfocused. I opened my mouth, wanting to bare my soul, *in vino veritas* in full effect. But some shred of sense warned me. *Not while you're tipsy.* All that came out was, "Rafi."

"Do you know how long it's been since anyone called me that?" He pulled relentlessly until I got up and floated to his lap.

I shouldn't have drunk the champagne, but every sip sent the guilt drifting farther away, and along with guilt went the twinging from my wounds.

It would be easy, so easy, to shut off doubts, suspicions, and fears. To fall into the moment. I sat on his lap like a mannikin, my legs and arms rigidly immobile, but he made no overtures. He merely watched the fire and sipped his champagne.

The wood crackled, giving off the scent of apples. Shadows danced. Rafe sat in undemanding silence.

There were more questions I wanted to ask. Why hadn't he remarried? Who was Brianne's father?

Then his hand pressed my head to his shoulder. "I've missed this."

I dropped hazily into a place where there was nothing but the intoxicating glamour of his aftershave.

Will, where are you?

I deliberately envisioned him chopping wood by the barn, shirtless and sweaty, but quickly realized that wasn't a good idea.

The day had been long and exhausting, but at this moment I felt safe, protected, almost anesthetized, for the first time since that fateful day I waded into Dallas Creek and retrieved a silver necklace.

His magic spell engulfed me.

He found me when I was nine years old and latched himself to me like a second skin. I never dated any other boys. We discussed marriage when I was twelve. Rafe was nearly as much a part of me as my bones, and this moment brought home our past as if it had never been interrupted. I'd loved him almost to obsession. He was like the best euphoria drugs, but addictive like the old-time stuff, heroin and cocaine.

I determinedly brought up Will's face. He was alone, and I knew in my heart he hadn't given up on me. He just wouldn't. He had to be out of his mind with fear and worry. No way would I betray him, not with his brother…

…who I slowly came to realize was kissing me. He tasted of sparkling champagne; I couldn't help reaching my tongue out for more. I gripped his upper arm then ran my fingers down his chest, where the beat of his heart was heavy and rapid.

"I've never been with another woman, Erin," he said. "You wondered, didn't you? I've tried for twenty-three years to let you go. I never could. Not for one second."

Will ebbed into gauzy fantasy, a particularly beautiful dream, and Rafe, the reality, took over. How could I have forgotten the way he spoke to my nerve-endings and heartbeat? How he sent me shivering and caused those damnable little pulse scars to throb? Denying him was refusing to breathe.

Big mistake, Erin, coming in here.

He touched the fastener at the back of the red velvet gown. It parted with a hiss, all the way, and gaped in front. His mouth moved to my throat, then lower. His other hand slipped beneath the velvet at my ankles and crept upward, along my thigh to the scrap of silk he'd thoughtfully provided with the dress. He nudged it out of his way.

I woke up. Almost too late, but not quite.

"No!" I shoved his hand and jumped off his lap, pressing the loosened velvet to my chest. "No!" I backed away, thinking he would come after me, force himself upon me in his usual demanding fashion, but he didn't. He remained on the loveseat, breathing hard, watching me go.

This, too, was different.

I reached the door. With escape assured, I looked back.

He had his fingers pressed to his nose. His eyes were closed. He looked like a man who had just received something beyond imagining.

He looked like a man who had not been with a woman in twenty-three years.

I fled.

Chapter 5

ALL MY LIFE I'D SUFFERED FROM ANXIETY. IT GOT MUCH WORSE WHEN THE SECOND moon became visible in 2046, before the lunacy took hold.

I struggled with Rafe's ascent into fame. It chucked me, an introvert, under the media microscope, but the arrival of the second moon made those battles with anxiety seem like scrimmages. Full-blown panic attacks, plus hallucinations, joined my more familiar adrenaline rushes.

I tried various treatments, but none helped, and I didn't like the side effects. I was resigned to living with the syndrome.

Once, during a visit with my doctor, I asked if the moon could be the cause. He'd barely bothered to keep from rolling his eyes, and told me I was being influenced by mass hysteria, but I went on wondering. Could I have contracted a different form of lunacy? An early strain, maybe, before it mutated into such horrific violence and insanity that a quarantine became necessary?

In late December of 2047, a few days after Rafe returned from the Henry-ordered conference with Grigory Andreiovich Novikov in Moscow, the doctor called, excited to offer an experimental once-a-day pill that treated multiple unrelated issues. The one he wanted to try on me was newly minted for my exact array of symptoms, plus he'd found another that would prevent McKenna's recurring ear infections. His enthusiasm transferred to me and I had him messenger them over. I chose the same type of oral formulation as McKenna was prescribed so she would feel more comfortable about taking hers. As it turned out, she loved the icosahedron shapes and guessing the flavor. For her, it was a game, but we were happy that her ear infections improved.

Rafe insisted on being in charge of the pills. Every day, he would place one on my tongue and one on McKenna's. At first, I thought it ridiculously controlling, but he claimed he wouldn't be able to sleep or concentrate if he wasn't certain his girls had taken their pills.

I didn't notice much difference in McKenna's energy or curiosity, but unfortunately, one of the side effects of my pill was a decline in cognitive function. When I brought it up, the doctor claimed it wasn't possible. He patronizingly asked me if I could be imagining things.

I really missed female doctors.

The pills didn't get rid of the hallucination, either. In fact, I saw it more often. I also experienced a near-insatiable desire for sex. I didn't know whether to blame the pills or the moon. Maybe it was just me. I was too embarrassed to ask the doctor about these problems, knowing he would once again dismiss me as a hysterical female. The pills did alleviate the anxiety and panic attacks, so I kept on using them.

The strange thing was that it all went away at Will's cabin. I'd left the pills behind—why, I didn't know—and for a week or two I had mild symptoms of withdrawal, but as time passed and I recovered from my injuries, I realized my lifelong anxiety was gone. So was the mental fuzziness. I no longer saw that coppery phantom, and sex became enjoyable rather than frenzied.

From time to time during my years away, I wondered about that. Could there have been a contaminant or allergen in the water or the air, in both Utah and DC, that aggravated my disorder? It seemed unlikely, but there had to be an explanation for why every one of my symptoms vanished while I lived with Will in the Uncompahgre wilderness.

The shower in the guest bathroom massaged, polished, and bedewed me until my senses reeled. I stood in a cloud of scented steam, feeling smooth as silk and ten years younger.

"Doesn't mean anything. Doesn't change anything. He got me drunk. Rafe and his tricks."

I've never been with another woman, Erin, haunted me, unabated.

As I wiped the fog from the mirror, I saw I'd been marked with two small bruises beneath my ear. "I hope he put a rollneck in here somewhere," I muttered. It would not do for McKenna to see such things.

Shoveling through the drawers in the closet, I actually found one. Red, like the dress. *Thoughtful Rafe, providing a way to hide what he did. Almost like he knew it would happen.*

"Samson? Is McKenna's room still in the same place or has it changed?"

The AI's amused tone sounded quite authentic. "It, too, is unchanged, Erin, although it's been remodeled. You can find it at the north end of the second floor. Brie's room is across the hall."

"I see you call Brianne 'Brie,' too."

"She requested that I do so four years, three months, and six days ago."

I set off for the other side of the house. "Why do you think he bought this place, Samson?"

"If I were to hazard a guess, I would say it was to impress you, Erin."

"Huh. To keep me from getting fat."

"I can extrapolate from your metabolism and genetic profile that your weight has remained stable since you gave birth. There, Erin. McKenna's door is to the right."

"McKenna?" I knocked.

"Come in," I heard, and entered. My daughter was lounging at a dressing table, brushing her hair.

"Just wanted to say good morning." I closed the door.

McKenna's eyes met mine in the mirror. "Have you been crying?"

I blushed. "It's a bit overwhelming. You, Brianne. Your father. I imagine you feel something similar."

"Maybe. I don't know how I feel. Doesn't matter, anyway."

What does that mean? "I would love to spend time with you, if you don't have plans."

"All right," McKenna said without any warmth.

I glanced around. They'd knocked out a couple of walls while I was gone. This newer version of her bedroom was nearly as large as Rafe's. I glimpsed a theater screen stretching across the far wall beyond a half-moon doorway. Off to the right was a reading nook, snack bar, and coffee maker, and on the south wall, a waterfall trickled over a surface of stones. Oddly, there were stuffed animals strewn over the unmade bed. Tubes and bottles of cheap makeup cluttered the dressing table. Jewelry was heaped on top of a lovely cherry-wood chiffonier.

My throat tightened when I spotted the hobbit door in the east wall. A secret garden room lay on the other side. We'd hired a master artisan to build the room, and an artist to create a forest on one wall and a meadow on the other, painted in such a way that you would feel you were in the forest or in the meadow. It had its own window alcove with a padded seat, and built-in bookshelves. McKenna had kept her tea set, her baking set, her favorite books and dolls, all her treasures in there. No one was allowed in without permission.

"I'm surprised you still live here," I said, to get my mind off the past. "I couldn't wait to get out on my own when I graduated." I didn't add that I'd made a beeline from my parents' home to Rafe's.

"Which you did early because you were so smart." McKenna sent me a frosty glance before turning her attention to the mirror and clipping false lashes above and below her eyes. While they did add length, it was a bit of overkill. "You could've become something great if you'd gone to college. Maybe save-the-world great, but instead, you got pregnant. The world was left to survive on its own."

I was shocked. Rafe had told her about Matthias, the son we lost.

"I-I see you know things."

"Oh, yes. You're all Daddy could talk about whenever he was here, which wasn't often."

"That must have been boring."

McKenna glanced at me in the mirror, another measured stare that chilled me.

"I'd really like to know about you, if you want to tell me."

McKenna shrugged and picked up a clay pot. She dipped her middle finger in and rubbed color on her lips. Too much color, I thought. It was garish.

"Are you going to college?"

She released a short, incredulous laugh. "Not even Daddy has that much clout." She examined her lips in the mirror.

I hesitated to ask what she meant. I felt like we were speaking different languages. One thing was certain; my girl was prickly as thistle. Any misspoken word could send this brittle chill into open hostility.

"Brianne is a sweetheart," I said at last. "Smart. Outgoing. Beautiful smile. The way she talks makes me think she's ten going on sixty."

"She must take after you."

This roundabout conversation would get us nowhere. In fact, I was sure McKenna was relegating me to that sphere of tedious elders who had nothing to say worth listening to. As a teenager, I would have called this older version of myself a "bourgeois."

Clenching my hands, I asked straight out. "Where is her father?"

McKenna faced me, her expression one of scornful amusement. One brow lifted, drawing attention to the little mole on her temple I remembered kissing when she was a baby.

"Gone."

"He left you?"

"You know what? I never told Daddy or Grandpa about him, and they interrogated me for years. Are you sure you want to waste your time this way?"

"I'm just trying to learn about you. I don't mean to be annoying or intrusive."

"I'll tell you something I never told Daddy. Brie's father never knew about her. I broke up with him and he left. Haven't seen him since. Don't know if he's alive or dead. Don't care. I had what I wanted."

"You wanted to have a baby alone?"

"Alone?" She scoffed. "I'm never alone."

"Being a parent is hard work."

"Is that why you took off?"

I chewed my lower lip. We needed a reset. "I'm sorry," I said. "I didn't mean to preach, really, McKenna."

"Speaking of preaching, you might want to change. It's Sunday, you know."

A groan slipped out. Church was something I hadn't missed, but as long as I stayed in this house, I'd be expected to attend each and every Sunday and Wednesday.

My daughter's lips slid into a smirk.

"Okay. I'll get dressed in a minute." I dropped into the deep leather chair in the corner. How did Rafe, evangelical leader of the ultra-conservative Aquilo movement, react when his unwed daughter gave birth at what...I mentally calculated. Holy moly. Seventeen. The same age as me when I got pregnant with Matthias.

By now I knew better than to point out the similarities. "How about a job? Do you work?"

McKenna gave me a look of disbelief. "Are you serious?"

"I'm sure there's plenty you could do, including college. It isn't too late. You're young."

Her gaze drilled into me with frowning speculation. She rose, shrugging out of her robe and leaving it where it fell. Completely naked, she opened her closet doors and brought out a short black dress with three-quarter length sleeves, which she stepped into and pulled up, not bothering with underwear. I saw the outline of her nipples as she reached behind her head and touched the fastener that sealed the dress in back. There was a round hole in the upper right sleeve, lined up with a tattoo I'd noted when she disrobed. I'd seen the same oddity when I met her at the hospital, but had been too overwhelmed to ask what it was. I tried to remember the dress she wore to dinner last night. I didn't think there had been a hole in that one. I was sure I would have noticed. "What—" I started, but she interrupted.

"It's pretty obvious you think I should move out." She slipped into black high-heeled pumps. "Why is that, I wonder? So you can take off again without feeling guilty?"

"I'm just trying to get to know you, McKenna. I realize I don't deserve anything from you, but I hope we can get past this."

"Believe me, if it weren't for my kid, I'd have found a way. I do admire how you managed it for so long. You were free, and not even Daddy's connections could find you or force you back. It was smart to tell them you don't remember where you were. Don't ever tell them. If you do, they'll always know how to find you, if you ever get the chance to get out of here again, which, head's up, you probably won't. And for sure, whoever helped you stay hidden will disappear. You'll be screwed. Just like the rest of us."

Which one of those statements should I try to decipher first?

McKenna peered into the mirror and fluffed her hair. "You'd better get changed. Daddy doesn't like to be kept waiting, and he hates being late for church."

With a smile that was pure contempt, she went into her bathroom and closed the door.

I RETURNED TO MY ROOM AND OPENED THE CLOSET. THE DRESSES THAT CONFRONTED me were beautiful floaty things, too fancy for the woman who'd spent the last two decades mucking out stalls, chopping wood, riding horses, and scouring sticky pine sap off her clothing and palms. They reminded me of the outfits I wore in my twenties, my trendsetting days.

Some of the dresses had that round hole in the right upper sleeve and some didn't. I chose one that didn't. It was too clingy and short for me, but they all were. This one at least was a pretty dark purple, with abstract designs of silver. The neckline was cut in a plunging vee. Next, I inspected the drawers and found a bra that seemed made for the dress, providing just a hint of visible lace in the same colors. It fit me perfectly. I had to laugh. How, when, had he done this? How had he known?

Other than last night's dinner, this would be the first time I'd worn a bra in many years. No need, really, at the cabin. After the one I'd been wearing when I met Will wore out, I never asked for another.

The dress wasn't made for a woman bearing down on fifty, but at least the sleeves extended to my elbows. Rafe must have been picturing me as I looked before I left—a twenty-six-year-old. Not this woman with crow's feet, silver at the temples, and the inevitable loss of elasticity.

I needed something more comfortable to wear, preferably sweats. There was nothing like that in the closet. I should go shopping, but I had no way to pay for anything.

Speaking sternly to my reflection as I brushed my hair, I said, "It's a waste to shop for clothing when you're going back to Will, plus it would give Rafe the wrong idea."

How was I going to go back to Will, though? I couldn't vanish from McKenna's life again. Or Brianne's. If I were honest, there was something about Rafe, too.

What an unholy mess.

One thing I had to do, soon, was contact Will. Perhaps I could call the bar in Ouray where he liked to have lunch. Maybe the bartender would pass along a message. The only other thing I could think of was writing him an old-fashioned letter, but I wasn't sure he would appreciate that, not to mention he had no address. He was a man off the grid. A letter could draw attention to him. So could a call, for that matter.

Once more, everyone was waiting for me at the bottom of the stairs. Rafe smiled in a way that was embarrassing. Cordelia looked impatient. Dillon, annoyed.

"You've made us late," Cordelia said.

"I'm sorry."

"Put this on. I didn't know what you were wearing, so I chose white. It goes with everything."

She held out a mask and a hat. When I didn't immediately take them, she shook them warningly.

"What is this?"

She shook them again, harder. "Just put them on, Erin! We're late!"

Rafe's gaze was unblinking, like he was trying to see into my brain. He said nothing.

The mask was striking. Snow white, carefully crafted papier-mâché, the eyeholes were lined in black and ringed with what looked like diamonds. The lips were pouty red, crusted with sugar-like crystals, or again, maybe diamonds. It reminded me of a Venice carnival mask. A filmy black scarf was attached, voluminous enough to cover my hair. The hat was also white, a jaunty thing covered in black lace and little pearls.

McKenna and Brianne came out of the receiving room by the front door. Their faces were covered from the bridge of the nose to the throat with Bedouin type veils. While not exactly sheer, they were gauzy, weighted along the bottom with disks that looked like a mix of platinum and rose gold. Brianne's was blue, a complimentary color to her dress, and McKenna's was black. Her eyes above the mask were seductively, mysteriously beautiful; the color I had thought garish on her lips was diffused by the veil into perfection. On Brianne, the effect of a veil was different. It looked absurd.

But nobody was laughing.

"Oh, I almost forgot," Rafe said. "I had the doctor give me some of your pills when we left the hospital." He brought a container from his jacket. "I imagine you've had a bad time, being without them for so long."

I looked at the small, perfectly-shaped icosahedron sitting innocuously on his palm. This pill was green. Probably lime flavored. I experienced a brief yen, then suspicion. "I don't need those anymore, Rafe." I caught myself before revealing that I hadn't had anxiety in years and giving away that I did, indeed, remember my time apart from him.

He shrugged and closed his fist over the pill. "Okay. We'll talk about it later."

McKenna watched this exchange as keenly as her father had studied me moments earlier.

"What is there to talk about? I don't need them."

"We are getting later by the moment," Cordelia said. "Do you have to argue with everything?"

Before I could demand to know the reason for wearing a mask, Rafe explained. "These full-face masks are for new women. In a month or so, you'll be wearing a veil like Mother's and McKenna's, but for now, this mask alerts people to be patient with any mistakes you might make."

"Erin, *please*." Cordelia's cheeks flushed. "No expense was spared. The mask is beautiful. Everyone will see how valued you are."

"All right. All right." I would go along with this idiocy for now, and find out what it really meant later. Perhaps it was a way to maintain our privacy from the "media" that Cordelia was going on about last night. I put the mask over my face and snapped the elastic band around the back of my head. I arranged the black drapery and hat as best I could without a mirror.

While I aligned the mask, Cordelia donned one of her own, a veil of gold glinting with little spangles and sequins.

Next were elegant gilded chains, hooked around our wrists—Cordelia's, mine, McKenna's, and Brianne's. Dillon held the other end of Cordelia's and Brianne's. Rafe held mine and McKenna's.

While I thought my head might explode, the chain was in no way strong enough to be considered a restraint, and they were decorated at each end with what looked like real gems. Perhaps this was a status thing, or even a fashion thing. I had been gone a long time. Whatever it was, I had to bite the inside of my cheek to keep from refusing outright.

"Let's go." Dillon herded us to the front door where we were met by no less than six steely men in olive drab jodhpurs and skin-tight tee shirts, buckled boots, baldrics supporting pistol holsters, and opaque round sunglasses. The front of their tee shirts displayed a red lion prowling beneath two black sabers that crossed over the barest outline of a female torso drawn in just four abstract strokes, two creating a nipped waist, one suggesting breasts, and one more, a V, hinting at the pubic area. I had to look twice to make sure I was seeing what I thought I was seeing. The men were heavily armed, not only with pistols, but also knives and rifles.

"Hurry, please." The apparent leader urged us females down the front steps, keeping us hemmed in on both sides.

Another batch of men marched in from either side, creating a second layer of protection. Their rifles were held in a ready position across their chests, which made it possible for me to see the identical crossed saber tattoos on the backs of their left hands.

The door on the extra-long hover limo was already open. Cordelia gestured impatiently. "Hurry up. Get in," she ordered curtly.

What the hell was going on here? Were we living in a war zone? It reminded me of Rafe's requirements back when I was serving as spokesperson for the Protective Quarantine. He claimed we were always in danger. That's why I had to dress like a man when we went into public, and have a guard accompany me everywhere.

I stifled my uneasiness, determined not to fall into a full-blown panic attack.

After blithely assuring Rafe I no longer had those, I didn't want to be proven wrong in ten short minutes.

Chapter 6

At the church, we women were enclosed by a blockade of armed men. They whisked us inside and down a poorly lit corridor smelling of mildew. The leader rapped on a nondescript door; another man in the same olive-green uniform let us in.

This felt far too much like the dog kennel place. I half expected to see the leering faces of the guards who attacked me. Starting to hyperventilate, unaccustomed to wearing heels, and with my peripheral vision hampered by the mask, I stumbled, and at once earned warning glares from two of the men.

"Come *on*," Cordelia hissed. A man whose rifle was slung across his back unhooked a velvet rope from four chairs in the front row.

The room was dim. It was hard to tell how many other people were seated behind us. All that I could see had their faces turned down. None looked up as we took our seats.

The men patrolled the boundaries of this stuffy room, some holding their assault rifles ready to shoot.

Where had Rafe and Dillon gone? "What's—" I began, but Cordelia pinched me. "You're not allowed to talk. Shut up and listen."

Three of the men scowled at me.

Brianne gave me a smile before turning her face down like the others.

After a few minutes, the sermon began. Slightly echoing, it came from everywhere, like the voice of God in an old-time movie. I clandestinely peeked from side to side without moving my head, but saw no human speaking.

The voice, which struck me as familiar, chastised us, telling us how fortunate we were to be under the protection of men who cared about us, how we should be grateful and do everything in our power to please them.

When he started talking about how our men were our earthly gods, I nearly gasped. The voice belonged to Jasper Simonson, the dead prophet of Aquilo.

"There is only one place for you if your gods are displeased," he intoned. He didn't say what that place was. Hell, no doubt. He added casually that things could be much worse for us if we didn't cultivate constant, instant obedience.

I pictured him as he had been, fiery-eyed, long, unkempt beard, screaming and spitting from his pulpit, and I had to bite my lip to keep from releasing the loudest, most disgusted snort of my life. Nobody in the room was laughing, or talking, or smiling, or snorting.

This was…it was…*crazy!*

Forty-five minutes into the sermon, if that's what it could be called, I caught McKenna flashing one of the guards. It was subtle, and I was the only one who knew she wasn't wearing underwear.

The man stared. He swiped his forehead with his sleeve.

How was Cordelia missing this? She never missed anything.

Stealing a glance at my mother-in-law, I saw that her eyes were shut. Her lips moved in prayer.

McKenna's left hand wandered to the hem of her dress. She pushed it up, centimeter by centimeter. Teasing. Would she lift it more? He didn't move. She placed her hand on her lap and briefly picked up the material then let it fall again. Her legs opened wider then shut like they were spring-loaded.

The man's breathing was shallow, his stare fixed. His forehead and sideburns were sweaty. I was afraid he would lose control and do something everyone would regret. Maybe that's what McKenna wanted. She had her face turned down, but no doubt was glancing up enough to gauge the results of whatever she was trying to accomplish.

Finally, the sermon wound to a finish, with the command to "do better," to "improve," so we could be "worthy."

"I have to pee," McKenna said as we stood.

"You always do this," Cordelia complained. "Sentinel." She gestured to the very one, who had moved closer. "Take my granddaughter to the restroom."

"Uh-um," I stammered. "Alone?"

"Your ignorance is mind-boggling, Erin. See that mark on the back of his hand? These men are completely trustworthy. Otherwise, they would not be anywhere near the Konstantinou family."

The new eunuchs, then, I wanted to reply as snidely as she, but I figured I ought to keep my mouth shut, especially around these weapons. Cordelia might order one of the guards to shoot me.

McKenna and the man left.

Could he be Brianne's father?

Something struck me as I waited for Cordelia to gather her things. Watching the attendees line up to leave, I saw that every single one was female. Though the veils made it difficult to be certain, a couple of them were about Brianne's height and build, and their neatly braided hair, small, smooth hands, and youthful foreheads told me they were young. A few others were taller; they could be fourteen or fifteen, but the majority appeared to be in their late teens or early twenties. There were no gray-haired women other than Cordelia. None of those I watched filing out looked older than McKenna, and there were no babies. I was the only one wearing a full-face mask.

I saw the round holes too, always on the right sleeve, always outlining black tattoos, which reminded me of Celtic knots. No one chatted, smiled, or laughed.

I felt like I had been gone multiple lifetimes or had been stuck in outer space for generations.

This civilization was unrecognizable.

WE WERE TAKEN TO THE LIMO POD TO WAIT FOR MCKENNA, RAFE, AND DILLON. Heavy curtains were drawn over the windows so no one could see in and we couldn't see out. Cordelia and Brianne removed their veils, and I was happy to be given permission to remove the mask. It was hot and claustrophobic.

McKenna arrived. The guard escorting her veered away before I could get a glimpse of his face, but her chin was slightly red, her hair messy. Not so much that the breeze couldn't be blamed, but I knew better.

She settled into the corner and kept her gaze fixed on the curtain as she took off her veil and dropped it onto her lap. An enigmatic smile came and went.

My mother had often stated, especially after I started seeing Rafe, that I came out of the womb defiant.

No doubt about it. This girl had my blood in her veins.

WE WAITED A GOOD FIFTEEN MINUTES FOR RAFE AND DILLON. I FINALLY HEARD them laughing. One of the uniformed men opened the door and they slipped into a spacious area in front of our more cramped back seat, where my knees almost hit Cordelia's.

I fumed inwardly. The limo pod was comfortable, just the right temperature, but sitting here, minute after ticking minute, with Cordelia's judgmental frown and McKenna's secretive distant expression got old quickly. Brianne showed me the holographic Bible Rafe had given her for her tenth birthday, made from white leather so soft it felt like velvet, and embossed with her name. One could choose different characters to read out loud as they floated, dressed like the ancients, above the pages. It was impressive, but I was distracted.

I caught a whiff of brandy. Dillon's eyes were shiny, his expression mellow. Rafe had his back to me, but to all appearances, their time at church had been rather more pleasant than ours.

I looked. Sure enough, neither man had any kind of hole in the upper sleeve of his suit jacket. Why only the women? For that matter, only women wore veils, or had their wrists chained.

The curtains folded away as the autonomous driver lifted the pod and crept forward, careful to avoid the stragglers walking from the building to their vehicles.

I glanced out the window and my gaze latched onto a peculiar sight. Two women were being led by men garbed in the olive drab uniforms and opaque glasses. While Rafe and Dillon held the chains around our wrists in an unobtrusive way, this was very different. One woman's chain was attached to a leather collar around her neck. Her wrists were bound to each other in front and her chain was heavy, not like ours, that I would call mere decorations. It ran from the collar to her wrists and out to the man's hand. An ornate mask covered her face. Not fancy like mine, but a caricature of a witch with a long, hooked nose, frowning black holes for eyes, and thin, downturned lips. There were even two large moles, one on her nose, the other on her chin, both sprouting coarse black hair. Perhaps the woman was having a hard time seeing or dealing with her high heels, for she stumbled several times and when she did, the man holding the chain jerked it violently, once sending her to her knees. I saw blood when she struggled to her feet.

In overt opposition to the mask, the woman's body was young and voluptuous. Her outfit did more to accent than hide her large breasts, rounded butt, and long, shapely legs. It was more revealing than any other woman's I'd seen that day, and that was saying something. Other than Cordelia and the youngest girls, all the females wore suggestive attire.

The second woman, walking next to the first, was also being led by a chain, but hers was ornamental like ours, and fastened around one wrist. Her face veil was a flimsy bit of decoration much like McKenna's, Brianne's, and Cordelia's. She wore long earrings and gem-studded bracelets.

I didn't remember seeing these two in the stuffy room. I wouldn't have forgotten that mask.

"What the fu—" I said without thinking, but I caught myself in time to keep from finishing that ugly word in front of Brianne. It had been ages since I'd had to watch my language around children.

The interior of the pod fell into abrupt silence. Brianne turned fearful eyes to me. The men behind us, who had been talking quietly among themselves, stopped. Cordelia leveled a glare upon me so venomous it sent a shiver across the back of my neck.

Dillon scowled furiously.

It had been wrong to speak so crudely in the company of these fundamentalists and Brianne. Even I, the square peg trying to fit into a round hole, knew that. "I'm sorry," I said, knowing it wouldn't be that easy to earn their forgiveness.

Only now did Rafe face me. He moved slowly, almost reluctantly, his jaw clenched and his eyes enraged. What the hell was he so angry about? He used to say that word and worse, but, I conceded, never in front of his mother or children. I opened my mouth to make a second apology.

Without warning, his hand came up and he slapped me. His palm landed on my left cheekbone, perhaps not full force, but hard enough. Two fingers struck the healing wound. Pain blazed and I cried out, shocked and humiliated to my core.

Without a word, he turned away, but not before I saw swift, sadistic pleasure flit across his face.

Frustration, bewilderment, and anger had been steadily building since I descended the staircase at the chateau. Everything now erupted into sizzling hot, primal haze. My sight focused on the back of his head; my hearing disintegrated into buzzing. I knew and saw very little until I realized both arms were caught in some kind of vise. I was being pressed against the leather seat, held there by brute strength. Another vise wrapped around my throat so ruthlessly I had to gasp to draw in any air.

My sight cleared. My arms and throat were restrained by the men behind me. I could kick the back of Rafe's seat, but that seemed like something a child would do, so I just stared at him, breathing hard.

"Feel better?" he asked. Two long red scratches ran down the right side of his face, bleeding in three spots. Had I done that? I must have. I felt what must be skin under my fingernails.

"Not quite," I managed to hiss.

Rafe shook his head with an impatient sigh. "Let her go," he ordered, and his guards released me, their hands hovering at the edge of my vision, ready to constrain me again if necessary.

"You'll learn," he said, turning away, dismissing me.

Disbelief and anger were written all over Dillon's face.

Cordelia, who never could resist making things worse, said, "Yes, you will learn, if you want to survive."

What kind of threat is that? My hands shook so hard I had to clench them. I wanted to lash out, to fight, but for Brianne's sake—*only* for Brianne—I would not.

McKenna watched from her corner. Gradually, her expression changed from shock to puzzlement.

Tears spilled from Brianne's eyes. I wanted to reassure her, but I couldn't. I didn't yet have enough control.

The men in the rear started conversing again. I heard a suppressed chuckle.

Rafe had never lifted his hand to me. Not ever, not in the worst of our hotheaded fights.

He'd just destroyed any chance of reconciliation, if that had truly been his hope.

When the limo pod stopped outside the chateau, Cordelia stormed inside right behind me and shoved me into the receiving room.

McKenna took Brianne's hand and tugged her upstairs, despite the child's reluctance.

"You've been in a Unified Free State or an Independent Territory, haven't you?" Her voice could cut icicles. "I can think of nowhere else you could speak in that filthy manner, or any other explanation for why you're acting like you've never seen a mask or tether. Was it California?" She made a rude scoffing sound. "You had better change your ways, Erin Ophelia *Aragon*. If you don't, you will wish you had."

Was she threatening me?

"You are Raphael Konstantinou's wife, his soiled, despicable, unworthy wife. That makes you news. The snakes will dig until they turn up every sordid detail of what you have been up to. I won't allow you to tarnish his glory. Do you hear me? Do you understand? Answer me!"

My cheekbone felt tender, hot to the touch, maybe even slightly swollen. "All of you are overreacting. It was a word. Just a word. I didn't even finish it. I don't think Brianne had any idea what I was saying."

"You stupid fool!"

Dillon and Rafe came in. "Mother, would you and Dad go now please?"

"I frankly cannot believe she is worth it to you, Raphael. In fact, I—"

"Yes, we'll go." Dillon took Cordelia's arm and propelled her out of the room.

Rafe poured himself a cognac, saying nothing until the front door closed. He didn't offer me one. I could have used it, after the morning I'd had.

"I hope you understand what you've done," I said. "You claim to want me back. That chance is gone, now."

He sighed, drank, and slammed the glass on the table beside the couch. I wouldn't have been surprised if it shattered, but it was heavy crystal, and survived.

"I'm sorry, Erin," he said, but he didn't look or sound sorry. "You had to push me. You pushed me to the point where there was nothing else I could do. Too many heard you."

"I don't give a shit who heard me."

He scuffed his hair with both hands, the gesture relaying his frustration, but something else, too. Something about it sent alarms ringing, but he didn't give me time to work it out.

"I had to show everyone that I am the leader of this family. Your leader. Otherwise, it would get out. Things always get out. You have to be careful what you say and do outside this house. You put your own life in danger when you defy the rules, and McKenna's, and Brianne's. I should have warned you, but I forgot what a potty mouth you have. I don't care what you say when we're alone, but outside? You cannot do that. If I hadn't been there, the sentinels might have really hurt you."

"What the hell is a sentinel?"

He drew in a sharp breath. "Specialized, highly-trained soldiers assigned to guard females, keep them safe. Mothers, wives, and daughters. Cherished women, like you."

I put aside the question of why we had to be guarded for the moment. "Why was that woman being led around like a dog, with that horrible mask? Why did you put chains on us? What the *fuck fuck fuck* is going on here?"

His jaw clenched. I looked down; his hands were clenched too, his knuckles white. "Maybe you'd better kill me this time."

"Where have you *been?* You act like you've never seen any of these things before." His mouth worked. "I've been patient. Don't you think it's time to let me in on the secret?"

No way was I going to confess my sins at this inopportune moment. "I don't remember. I've already told you."

His brow lifted in the old, familiar way, conveying skepticism. "One of the seceded states, an Independent Territory, or that hellhole I dug you out of. Those are the only places that could conceivably have kept you from being exposed to the world as it is. I'm thinking one of the UFS states, because there's no way you could have survived twenty-three years where I found you. Where was it?"

"I'm not falling for your distractions. You hit me. I'm leaving. We're done. We'll work out some kind of schedule so I can see McKenna and Brianne."

Instead of the worry, fear, or rage I might have expected, he simply looked puzzled. "You aren't leaving me, Erin," he said. "As you ought to know, women aren't allowed in public without a mask, a tether, and a sentinel. If you were to leave our home without a mask, a tether, and a sentinel, not to mention my permission, you would be caught within fifteen minutes, frankly, before you left the property. But let's say you did manage to get off the property. You'd be hauled away to jail, or worse. There are men out there—" He stopped, the only outward sign of his emotion the frown that formed between his eyes and the rise of color in his cheeks. Then he spoke, and I heard the emotion. "I can't go through that again, wondering if one of them got you. As much as you might hate me right now, you don't want that either, believe me."

"Since when are women not allowed in public?"

"It's been more than twenty years. You helped set it up. The documentaries, the advertisements, the quarantine. God*damn* it, I really need to understand *where you have been.* I don't like having to explain our society as though you're some kind of alien."

Goosebumps flared. "Are you telling me there's still a quarantine? After twenty years?"

"No, but things evolved because of it. Because of the second moon."

Slowly, that fact sank in. Somehow, by encouraging women to turn themselves in, I had condemned them to this. Through my actions, at least partly, women were now leashed and masked, subject to armed control. It made no damn sense.

"Explain this to me," I said shakily.

"These laws have been in place for a generation. They protect women. That's why you don't see them fighting the constraints. If you had been here, with me, you wouldn't have those bandages on your face, or any need of a plastic surgeon. You wouldn't have the memory of what those men did to you."

He had my attention. "What about the lunacy? It was never cured?"

His penetrating gaze ran over me, suspicious as hell until it came to the cheekbone he'd struck. There it lingered and his frown deepened. "Nobody knows what happened. It burned itself out or women developed natural immunity. Those who were cleared went back home, but by that time the men were uncontrollable. Women were attacked in horrible ways. Many were literally torn to pieces. Women themselves demanded the government do something. They were fed up with being victimized and men getting away with violence. Fed up with being prisoners in their own homes. Quite often, their homes became their graves. We took the necessary steps. We did what had to be done. The important thing is this: there is peace now, and has been for a very long time. Women don't have to support themselves. There are no unwanted babies, no single mothers needing government assistance. There are no more female drug addicts, and precious few male addicts, now that men have access to meaningful work that rewards their efforts. Everyone is happier. Men are calmer. Women are cared for, either by the government or male relatives. Inside the house, if it's just the family, you don't need to wear a mask or anything else, but if you want to go out, you have to have a tether, a veil, and either me or a sentinel escorting you. Be thankful that I have access to them. It means you, McKenna, and Brianne will always be safe. I'll feel much better once we get you tattooed."

"Tattoo? What's that?"

"Trackers. All women have them. They're to protect you. There are a few stubborn pockets of subversives who would *love* to kidnap and ransom Raphael Konstantinou's wife. That's what I thought had happened for years, and I'm not about to give them the chance to do it now."

"Like a microchip in a dog or cat?"

"If you want to put it that way. People microchip their pets because they want to protect them. To never lose them, like I lost you, but you're far more important than a dog or cat."

He made it sound reasonable and rational, like he was a professor and I, the student. It pissed me off royally. "I've returned to a country where women are forced to accept a role as slaves or pets, literally leashed, to make men happy and less violent. My country, my America, decided that was a worthwhile tradeoff. That's the route my country chose. I'm guessing we lost our voting rights somewhere along the way, didn't we?"

"I'm sure you know it's more complicated than that. You're only seeing the outward shape. It's men who are really being controlled. Men are always the underlying problem. Men are like animals. You can't reason with them like you can women, like I'm doing with you. You have to deal with men on the basest level. You have to make them feel the consequences of their actions. That's what we did. Men understand now what they can lose, what can happen if they break the law."

He picked up his glass and finished off the cognac. "All of this aside, I can't believe you're talking of leaving me already. I accepted your explanation and I forgave you, but I won't again. Leaving me is one thing. Leaving McKenna… *again?* It would destroy her. Not to mention how Brianne feels about you. Are you that selfish, Erin?"

He was right, damn him. That exact thought had hounded me constantly since the moment my daughter and granddaughter walked through the door at the hospital.

A man is a man is a man, but a child is forever.

I also knew he was shamelessly using them to control me.

If only I could talk to Maya. Rafe had agendas, and I knew how adept he was at lying when it suited his purpose. But for the present, I was defeated.

"I'm sorry for what I said and did in the car," I said stiffly. "From now on, I'll try to avoid doing things that force you to physically abuse me in front of our daughter and granddaughter."

Asshole hung, unsaid, at the end of that sentence.

I saw again in memory that instant of grim pleasure after he struck me. Perhaps anger, not love, was the true inspiration behind his actions. That would make more sense. The Rafe I knew could be coldly, savagely vindictive.

He poured another cognac and offered it to me. As I took the glass, he ran the back of his hand over my hair and his expression softened. "I wish you could see inside my mind. Then you would know beyond any doubt how much I love you. I am sorry, Erin. I want you to be happy. I will spend the rest of my life making you believe that." He paused. "Once you understand the rules, there will never be any need for violence."

Glad he could not see into my mind, I lowered my gaze and swirled the amber liquor, breathing in the scent of caramel edged with vanilla.

We took the necessary steps. We. Not "they." Did he realize what he'd let slip?

I doubted it. He'd had so much power for so long it was probably just an invisible part of his everyday outlook.

When I was in the kennel, every moment was perfumed with the smell of human waste, death, and disease. I constantly heard moaning and the shuffling of bare feet as women were sent to service unseen men with their mouths like they were no more or less than a convenient utensil.

I was still waking up in that damned kennel. The chateau was a different size and shape, that's all. Rafe was handsome, subtle, and rich, but he was no different in raw substance from those two guards.

Chapter 7

WILL BUILT HIS CABIN WITH HIS OWN TWO HANDS, ADDING ON LITTLE BY LITTLE. HE quickly grew accustomed to being alone, and soon evolved into the stereotypical mountain man, hunting game with his bow, fishing, netting, and corralling small animals in cage traps. He made his own furniture and prepared his own pelts. Over the course of time, he reduced his supply trips to once a month, sometimes less.

He had scant knowledge of what was going on in the world and he liked it that way.

The night he met Erin, he'd stayed out late hunting a buck, following it sixteen kilometers from the cabin. An earlier rain had lightened into drizzle; everything was drenched, nixing hopes of a fire. He set up his tent and was getting ready to turn in when he heard the unmistakable crunch of heavy metal hitting a tree and the obnoxious squeal of a car alarm.

He hiked into the dripping forest and came upon a woman, wandering alone, sobbing. Blood covered one side of her face. He couldn't now remember which side.

Christ Almighty, he'd never before seen such a female. Even soaking wet and bloody. She took his breath away. He wasn't sure why; she had two eyes, two ears, a nose and a mouth just like anyone else, but his reaction was immediate and staggering.

Convinced she was about to crumple, he gently put his arm around her, surprised to feel shocks run through his flesh like static electricity. She gasped and tried to pull away as though she felt it too, but it could have just been her reaction to being manhandled by a complete stranger. He guided her to a rock, sitting her down and speaking softly, explaining what he was doing while he examined her head. A gash on her scalp kept pumping blood no matter how hard he pressed. He ripped his flannel shirt into strips, securing several around her head. He created a crude stretcher from his tent and two sturdy pine branches, tying the whole thing to his gelding's saddle.

Her left hand was clenched, her knuckles white. He carefully pried her fingers open to find a green crayon. She instantly closed her hand over it again, and he let it be.

He set off, walking behind the stretcher, holding the branches so they wouldn't bounce on the ground and cause more harm.

Color came off her, easy to see in the dark. Lavender and hints of gold coiling like cigarette smoke. No matter how many times he wiped his eyes and squinted, the colors remained.

Once they reached the cabin, he cleaned and bandaged the gash and the other cuts he found, trying to ignore the distinct, sizzling shocks whenever he touched her. After she fell asleep, he watched her, his gaze roving from her face to that vague, nearly transparent mist of color. Was she really as gorgeous as his mind was telling him? More likely, his reaction was due to three years of solitude.

When she crawled out of his bed the next morning, quick to accept his offer of coffee, she confessed she didn't remember the wreck or where she was going or even who she was. His fingers brushed against hers when he handed her the cup and that odd tingling shot up his arm. She twitched and spilled a few drops of coffee, but said nothing, so he wasn't sure if she felt it too.

Without much medical knowledge to back up his claim, he reassured her that her head injury was probably causing the amnesia, and he'd wager every-thing would be fine in a few days when the swelling subsided, but he'd be glad to take her to a doctor.

Her dark eyes reflected the light coming in through the window. Her hair, of the same color, was snarled and messy from sleeping on it wet. "Where are we?" she asked.

"My cabin in the San Juan Mountains, near Mount Sneffels."

"Sneffels? Sounds like a cold."

"She's a fourteener, not far from Ouray."

"Fourteener?"

"An old American term for mountains over 14,000 feet high. Forty-two hundred meters."

She nodded. When he repeated that she ought to see a doctor and offered to take her, she put him off. He remembered being glad she felt safe with him and spent a lot of time surreptitiously studying her gestures and expressions. He brought her a comb and a leather cord, which just made things worse. With her hair pulled back every exquisite centimeter of her face was revealed, culmi-nating in those eyes. He couldn't tell where the pupil ended and the iris began, and there was a hint of Asian heritage in the shape. Her skin, with its warm, olive undertones, also suggested a mix of ethnicities. She was, he suddenly realized, his childhood fantasy of an ancient Middle Eastern queen, but for the fact that she was not very tall.

A week later, when he drove to Montrose for supplies and stopped at his favorite pub for a shredded ham sandwich and a beer, he saw the breaking news alert on the TV suspended near the ceiling. The image of his brother, bombarded by reporters, the ribbon at the bottom displaying the text *missing wife of presidential advisor Raphael Konstantinou*. The screen cut away to a photo of *her*, the woman at his cabin, and her name, *Erin Konstantinou, née Aragon*.

Erin Aragon! That was the girl Rafe got himself involved with years and years ago. Erin Aragon, the girl his parents hated, mostly because she was a *child* when Rafe first brought her home, a kid in elementary school. Of course, they blamed her instead of their perfect Rafe. She'd done something to him, cast some kind of evil spell, seduced him somehow. They dismissed the fact that she hadn't even entered puberty.

Plus, she was multiethnic, an unforgivable dereliction on her part, never mind that what they considered pure was pretty much defunct. He and Rafe were also multiethnic, since Dillon was Greek-American and Cordelia Norwegian-American, but they always found a way to excuse that, something about superior and inferior bloodlines and cultures.

They had argued and threatened. They called her a "half-breed," along with other slurs, but nothing could separate Rafe from that girl.

Will had never met her. He heard about the scandal from Doris, his parents' cook, on one of his infrequent visits from the New York boarding school that had been his home for most of his life.

Driving back to the cabin with his usual purchases plus a few treats he hoped she might like, he pondered what to do.

Something had happened while he was gone. She'd had her own revelation. He saw it in those magnetic eyes. She remembered who she was. He waited for her to say something, but she didn't. She just kept fiddling with that green crayon. He waited three days; she never said a word and showed no sign that she wanted to leave.

"Maybe I should take you to the police," he said finally. "Someone is probably very worried about you."

Tears ran down her face. "I need time to think."

He couldn't argue. He didn't want to. He was already lost in love.

He walked to the window. It was snowing again. Big, thick, soundless flakes.

There was an odd shadow by the barn. A man shaped shadow. He squinted. It *was* a man. He ran to the door, ripping the deadly Bowie knife from its hook, and raced across the veranda.

The shadow-figure was there, but as Will leaped down the steps and waded through the snow, it vanished like sparks flying off a fire.

He stopped, wondering if he'd really seen anything. Snow brushed against his eyelashes and collected in his hair.

"All right," he said. "Are you listening, damn it?" Yes, he'd gone mad, but he might as well follow his madness to the end. What did it matter? He had no woman, no child. Nothing but the animals. Rafe was never going to let him know one way or the other about Erin.

Returning to the cabin, he packed saddlebags with matches, water, a flashlight and an emergency blanket. He'd become friendly with Brian, the owner of the bar he lunched at sometimes in Ouray. If he and Dusty made it that far without freezing to death, he'd ask Brian to take care of the animals, and sweeten the request with several hundred in general currency.

Closing the door, he left, half-convinced he would never see his cabin again.

Chapter 8

OVER THE NEXT WEEK, WHENEVER I CAME INTO RAFE'S PRESENCE, HE STOPPED whatever he was doing to concentrate on me. He asked what I liked to eat and *voilà*, those dishes appeared. Even more meaningfully, he remembered what I had loved in the past, and watched with satisfaction as I devoured Dale's made-from-scratch carrot cake, for instance, heavy on the icing.

An unexplained absence equated into a diamond bracelet and a cobalt blue scarf with a subtle underpainting of gold. A couple of days before Mother's Day, he sent me a masseuse, of all things. Stepping out of the shower in the guest bath and hearing someone knocking, I answered the door wrapped in a towel, surprised to see McKenna and a strange man holding a folded, padded table.

"Daddy thought you might enjoy a massage," she said. "This is Anthony. He's very good. He'll massage you, remove all your...you know...hair...and make you feel like a new woman."

"No. No way." The ugly revived image of me being forcibly shaved in the Quonset hut while those men looked on had me breaking into a sweat and taking an alarmed step backward.

McKenna's smile turned into an astonished frown. "Daddy said you used to get massages all the time."

Anthony bowed. "I am doing this for all great families for fifteen years. Never have I had complain."

I bit my lip. I didn't want to hurt his feelings, but there was no way that man was putting his hands on me.

"Oh, I get it." McKenna grinned. "He's a eunuch. He doesn't care what you look like."

I was hotly embarrassed that she would say such a thing right in front of him. "I just got out of the shower and that thing is like getting a massage, with all those rotating jets and sprays and the waterfall. No. Thank you, but no."

She shrugged. "Well, Anthony, you can give me one since you're here."

He bowed again, this time snippily. I felt so guilty at how I'd handled the situation that I almost called him back, but didn't. There was no way. He'd have to think whatever he liked.

Later that afternoon, Rafe set me up with a holo cell, a painless, seed-like implant in the wrist. I could now make and receive calls, and apparently much more. There was all of *Ticolo*, as he called it, to explore. It was the one and only authorized online browser where I could shop—he thoughtfully linked it to a currency account—have things delivered, listen to and watch a universe of music being performed, make notes, take 3D photos, watch projected 3D movies, enjoy holographic books read by their authors or actors representing the authors, track my health, get advice, find health programs, and too many other things, he said, laughing, to remember. He then called me from his own holo cell to get me started.

He didn't bring up the slap. Typical of Rafe, to want me to simply forget it had ever happened. Unfortunately, that only served to remind me of the stereotype of abusive men, who hurt, showered the victim with apologies, gifts, affection, and promises, then hurt again. Wash, rinse, repeat.

Every time he brought me a gift, he also had one for McKenna and Brianne. Brianne waltzed about with a perpetual smile, saying, "It feels like Christmas or my birthday!"

"I've never seen him act this way," McKenna said. "It's like aliens have taken over his body."

"He's happy, Mommy." Brianne unwrapped a chocolate from the pirate's bag of gold doubloons Rafe had brought her. "Meemah makes Granddaddy happy." She popped the chocolate in her mouth with absolute assurance.

I flushed as my daughter stared at me. McKenna's brows descended. She left the room.

I sat with Brianne for a while, but McKenna didn't come back. "I'm going to check on your mom, okay?" I said finally.

"Okay." Brianne opened the holographic book on her lap and a delicate, white-haired fairy lifted above the page, wings fluttering.

I grabbed the bouquet of gladiolas, daffodils, and lilacs the gardener had brought in but hadn't yet put into a vase. He'd told us he couldn't remember a more prolific blooming season or an earlier one, then Rafe told me it was because I had returned life to Ramandu's Dawn.

His comments often verged on the annoyingly manipulative, but I smiled and kept that to myself. I was keeping a lot to myself these days.

"McKenna?" I knocked on the bedroom door and took the muffled sound I heard for *come in*. My daughter lay face down on the bed.

"Did I do something?" I dropped onto a corner of the cloud-like mattress and laid the flowers beside me.

For a long moment she remained silent. Finally, she sat up, wiping at tears. "Why couldn't I make him happy? I tried, but all he wanted was you. It's not fair. You let him think you were dead. Now you come back without any explanation, and it's like magic to him. It shouldn't be that easy. You don't deserve that."

"I know." I reached out and tentatively rested my fingertips on the back of her hand, half-expecting her to wrench away, maybe even hit me, but, surprisingly, she didn't. "The last thing on earth I want to do is hurt either of you more than I already have. I love you. I know it's hard to believe, but I do."

Her face showed no suspicion or bitterness, only distrustful hope. With the makeup washed away she seemed about the same age as her daughter, her eyes as big and dark as the disks of chocolate Brianne was consuming apace downstairs.

Half-fearful my heart might shatter, I whispered, "I'm here."

"You're not going to leave again?"

Ludicrous ideas ran through my mind in a split second. Running. Taking her with me, and Brianne. All three of us. But how?

She looked into my eyes. I could not, would not, give the wrong answer.

"I won't leave you again, McKenna."

She burst into a storm of fresh weeping and leaned in, resting her head on my shoulder. "You *promise?*"

I saw what it meant. "I will never leave you again, McKenna, unless you want me to." It didn't matter how I felt about Rafe or how much I missed Will. I would make it work, somehow, for McKenna.

"You love me? Really?"

"More than anything. Really."

And so, my future was decided.

WE MADE COCOA AT HER SNACK BAR AND CRAWLED THROUGH THE HOBBIT DOOR into the secret garden room. I pulled back the same yellow dotted swiss curtains I'd installed not long before I left, tucking them behind their hooks. Light flooded through the round window.

Breathing in that delightful old book smell and falling into happy memories, I ran my fingers over the spines of books in their little shelves.

The artist had included scenes from some of the books. On the forest wall, I had her place a few silvery-white unicorns and translucent-winged fairies amongst the trees, barely-there hints to tempt McKenna to search for them. Memories returned of brainstorming sessions with the artist, a woman by the name of Eugenie Bellerose, whose mind ran along similar paths as mine, who understood what I wanted to create. She disappeared not long after finishing the room. Lunacy, no doubt.

Had she survived? Was she now confined somewhere, her wild colorful personality stifled behind a mask, her talented hands restrained by a tether?

Drawing my knees to my chest, I browsed more of the hardcover classics I'd chosen for McKenna's four-year-old self and beyond. *Journey, Sweet Moon Baby, The Twelve Dancing Princesses, A Fairy Went A-Marketing. The Sky Jumps into Your Shoes at Night. Goodnight Moon. Grimm's Fairy Tales. Nancy Drew. The Black Cauldron. A Wrinkle in Time. The Narnia Chronicles.*

McKenna sipped her cocoa and watched. When I came to a gap, she told me it was an interactive version of *The Faerie Handbook* that was missing. It was Brianne's favorite, and what she was currently reading downstairs.

I pulled out *Prince Caspian* and flipped the pages, remembering fondly the illustrations from when I was young. It had been quite the challenge to find these books. Old fashioned hardcover books that you had to hold in your hands and read, word by word, had become priceless relics by 2045, when she was born. Everything had moved to streaming and later, to holograms.

The other wall held the books my mother had read to me when I was young. *The Wizard of Earthsea. The Mists of Avalon. The Golden Compass.* She'd loved fantasy, and instilled the same love in me. It had been our special bond, and she continued to read aloud to me until I was thirteen.

"Daddy said you picked all the books in here. I've read them over and over. They were what I had of you."

I grieved for my lonely little girl. In another state, high in the San Juan Mountains, her mother had treasured a green crayon. Over the years it darkened considerably from being handled over-much, but in the beginning, it was chartreuse. I'd taken it from McKenna's little box with a hundred different colors. She couldn't say the soft ch. It always came out *Char* like charcoal, with a *roose* at the end. The t got lost somewhere. It was the one thing I had the night Will found me wandering in the forest.

The flowers I'd carried in filled the room with heavenly scent. The blooms were exquisite. There was not a single wilted petal or brown spot.

"Tell me how you and Daddy met."

"Let's see. I was…nine. Wow. It seems like yesterday."

"Nine?" Surprise flickered across her face. Apparently, I'd found something Rafe had kept to himself.

"My best friend Maya and I were dancing on the playground at school." I laughed. "The Nutcracker. I was the Sugar Plum Fairy and Maya was the Cavalier. We'd been taking ballet, and thought we were prima ballerinas. It was freezing, but I said the show must go on. We had an audience of four captivated girls. Maya and I were dancing the *pax de deux* in our winter coats."

"Where was Daddy?"

"Staring at us from outside the fence. Even then, at twelve, he was so handsome! I remember seeing this cloud of color around him. Fire colors, red and orange. It felt like the Universe was saying, *Pay attention! This is important!*"

She said nothing, but her gaze was rapt.

I peered at the ceiling, working to bring it all back. "I was freaked out to have the undivided attention of an older boy. He watched until the bell rang and we had to go inside. Every single day after that he was there, waiting at the fence when we came out for recess."

"Was it love at first sight? Why did he watch you? Was it just you, or did he watch Maya, too? I remember her a little. He never talks about her."

"We stopped seeing each other after you were born. Something I'm very sorry about. Maya started things off. She approached him and asked him where he went to school. He pointed down the block, to Scarlet Mesa. That was the name of the neighborhood he lived in. Very exclusive. It took me awhile, but I finally got up enough nerve to say hi. The next day he brought me a dozen roses and told me he was going to marry me. He had to pass them one by one through the chain links." I reclined onto my elbows and crossed my ankles. "They were lavender. I'd never seen roses that color." I laughed. "He hadn't even asked me my name! It was almost like he *knew*, even then, that we were meant to be together."

"I bet he did."

Her voice jarred me from my memories and I realized I'd inadvertently spoken my thought aloud. "We never dated other people. The two of us fought and loved our way clear through puberty."

"And you married when you were—"

"Seventeen." My cheeks heated. This conversation could go too deep in a minute.

"Because you were pregnant?" McKenna's eyelids flickered downward, then she met my gaze directly.

"I don't really know." It was the truth, I didn't. It seemed like I never had a choice about Rafe, but I didn't want to say that to his daughter. Actually, I'd begun to feel suffocated. There was a cute basketball jock putting heavy moves on me. *You're only young once*, Maya said, urging me to go for it. Before I could make up my mind—it seemed like a stupendous decision—Rafe bought a bottle of champagne, got me deliciously tipsy, and blindfolded me. We made love four times.

So it was, at seventeen, I learned how young women could get pregnant without intending to.

An innovative birth control implant was developed in the early thirties. Placed in the upper arm, it was effective, had no hormones and few side effects, was painless and inexpensive, and didn't upset a woman's monthly cycles. Women bought it in droves. So did teenage girls. The implant was blamed for riling up the evangelicals, getting them onto the streets and into Washington to demand action. Eventually, they won the day. Abortion was federally banned in 2034. The ban on birth control came two years later. For a while there were various black market birth control methods, but as the years passed it grew harder and harder, and very expensive, to find anything, even outmoded things like diaphragms.

On the night Matthias was conceived, Rafe and I had only the "pull-out" method to use as a contraceptive. Champagne dulled my inhibitions and somewhere along the way I forgot about being careful. I guess the same thing happened to Rafe.

He was ecstatic when I gave him the news.

All those years with Rafe, and I'd never met Will. I'd heard of him, but he was never at home. He didn't even come back for the wedding. While we dated, Rafe kept me from his family with the excuse that they were constantly hounding him to dump me. *She's not from a good enough family*, he'd say in mocking imitation of his mother, and I was "mixed blood." He laughed at that, and made a face of mock horror. "Little Hitler," he called Cordelia.

Brianne knocked on the hobbit door and we welcomed her. She told me how McKenna transferred ownership of the room to her when she was six, and how she had read most of the books on the shelves too.

"Wait here," McKenna said, and left. She came back a few minutes later with a bundle, which she placed in front of me.

It was an old homemade quilt. *What colors shall I use?* my mother had asked. *Blue, white, gold, purple!* I'd said without hesitation.

I held it to my cheek, keeping my eyes closed. "Is Mother alive?"

There was a pause. "No. She got pancreatic cancer before they figured out a treatment."

"Dad?"

I heard her sigh. "He died later, at a rally of some kind. He was protesting. Daddy's never told me the details."

Both my parents gone, both no doubt thinking me dead too, but they never could be certain, as there was no body to cremate.

This room wouldn't exist without my mother and the love of fantastical worlds she'd planted in my imagination. I was such an introverted child. I'd had only the one friend, Maya. I would often leave my house on weekends and spend the entire day by myself in a nearby wilderness, one of the few places that hadn't been turned into a parking lot, or apartments, offices, a shopping center, or a housing addition. There was a creek and a forest maze that nobody, as far as I could tell, owned. My favorite pastime was pretending that one day, if I timed it just right and if the sunlight slanted a certain direction, I would find the door to a magical land. Not Narnia, though I'd read those books multiple times. For me, the magical country was hidden in the ocean and contained a palace made of pearls and rubies and amethysts. It was populated by a race of very tall, very beautiful men and women with eyes that were many layers of blue upon blue. Once I made it there, I would have countless adventures and never come back unless I wanted to.

Will had encouraged me to become familiar with the primeval land around Dallas Creek. As I explored, that old daydream regenerated. Dallas Creek, Blue Lakes, and the Sneffels wilderness was similar to the forest I'd explored as a girl, on a much grander scale. Will gave my precious, nearly-forgotten child-hood fantasies back to me.

"Are you sorry you married Daddy?" McKenna asked, returning me to the present.

"No, McKenna." I bit my lip, trying to keep my voice steady. "Without him, there would be no you. He will always be a major part of me, as you are."

"Rafe." I gave his bedroom door a halting rap. "Can we talk?"

He opened the door and stepped back, smiling. "I was going to deal with some boring correspondence. Thanks for a much better option."

I stepped inside, hiding a twinge of unease. He must have just come out of the shower. He had on a sleeveless white undershirt and a pair of low-waisted drawstring sweatpants. His hair was damp and the ribbed tee stuck to him in several places. Damn. Fifty-two years old, and no hint of a belly. This man would be sexy in a garbage bag.

"Aren't you cold?" I asked.

"No." He led me to the chairs in front of the fire. "A bit hot, actually."

That might explain the eddying color, curls of red sparking into brighter crimson as I entered, outlined in fiery orange. The phenomenon was brief, gone by the time we sat down.

I looked around, remembering the last time we'd been in here alone, and the many times before…before I ran away.

"Want a drink?" he asked.

"No. Could you turn off the charm and listen? This is important."

"All right."

"Do you love our daughter?"

His brows shot up and his smile faded. "Of course I love her. I love her, Brie, and you, more than anything else in the world. I'm surprised you have to ask."

"McKenna's been eating her heart out, believing you don't care about her."

He glanced into the crackling fire before answering. "I've already told you I was terrible with her. If I could go back in time, I'd try to do things differently. I was a selfish son of a bitch. Pretty much all I cared about was my own pain. She paid the price."

"Have you ever told her you were wrong? Maybe apologize?"

He rubbed his palm over the side of his face then across his mouth. "She makes something like that very hard, Erin. She's as prickly as a porcupine. Secretive, reckless, sarcastic. Has she told you we don't know who got her pregnant?"

"Yes. She wouldn't tell me either."

"It's like she'll do anything to piss us off. Sometimes I think she's got a death-wish."

"Don't say that!"

He shrugged. "It had to be one of the sentinels. Those are the only men she's ever exposed to, but I put them on hi-tech lie detectors, and they passed."

"She did say the father was gone. Did any of your men leave around that time?"

"I'm not sure. There have always been men who don't last. Maybe they think working for me will be easy, but it's not. Life is never the same for them if they lose my trust. A breach of faith follows them wherever they go. They can't hide it or lie about it."

"Why didn't you put her in therapy or something?"

"I did get her a therapist."

"What about telling her you love her? Making her feel like she's important to you?"

I knew I'd gone too far when Rafe blasted out of his chair. He paced like a tiger to the wet bar. I heard water running, and he returned with a glass.

"It's easy for you to come in here full of accusations and judgment." His voice sounded like a wood saw working its way through oak, and he kept his face turned away. "I did the best I could at the time. Nobody knows better than me that it wasn't good enough. I think the thing I'm most ashamed of is how I let the public embarrassment affect the way I treated her. I was called a hypocrite among other things, and for what seemed like forever, I had to run the gauntlet of difficult questions. The leader of Aquilo's daughter, unmarried and pregnant. Mother and Father suffered, too." He released a deep sigh. "Things were unpleasant for a long time."

He approached my chair and stared down at me. "You can't fix the last twenty years in a week, Erin."

I leaped to my feet, placing my hand on his arm. "You're right," I said, and meant it. "Honestly, I blame myself for your pain, McKenna's unhappiness. It happened because I left and never came back. It happened because of the way I left. A child doesn't get over that. This isn't your fault. I know you did the best you could."

He pulled me in and kissed the top of my head. I needed comfort and part of me wanted to comfort him, too, but I couldn't forget what he'd done. I stood passively, neither encouraging or discouraging.

Surprisingly, he backed away. "Now that you're here, I'm trying harder. Who knows?" The stunning smile made an appearance, along with a dimple in his right cheek. "Maybe this will be a Mother's Day full of miracles for everybody."

Chapter 9

EVEN BEFORE THE ARRIVAL OF THE SECOND MOON AND THE LUNACY IT CAUSED, I'D been famous, thanks to Rafe. I couldn't go anywhere without being bombarded for selfies and autographs. It was hard, but I tried to emulate Rafe, who was so comfortable in the company of crowds and strangers.

We were referred to as America's prince and princess. My clothing was copied. If I styled my hair differently, it was a big deal.

Rafe's thoughts, theories, and solutions about everything from climate degeneration to Grigory Novikov's endless wars were discussed and analyzed by leaders and pundits across the globe. His speeches changed national and international policy, and his face appeared in as many commercials, fashion outlets, and online venues as mine. Journalists talked about us far more than Rafe's boss, Henry Montague, president of the United States. Good thing he wasn't the jealous type.

We were a striking couple to be sure, me at 165 centimeters tall with black hair, eyes, and a Mediterranean complexion, next to Rafe, Nordic pale and green eyed, with hair like ripened wheat, standing at a full 196 centimeters.

In those bucolic days, I would search out images of us, print them, and keep them in a special box. I thought it would be fun to relive our fifteen minutes of fame when we were old.

Was the box here, somewhere? I'd have to ask. McKenna might like to see those; she was in some of them. Maybe I could lose myself in the past and forget about my hiatus with Will.

Even as I thought it, I knew it would never happen.

After the lunacy began its toxic, creeping advance across the globe, I grew to appreciate my fans. It warmed my heart to hear that they would never trust the government if it weren't for my assurances and endorsement. The hour-long documentary Doctor Provost and I made, detailing one of the quarantine residences—a renovated sanatorium in New Haven, Connecticut—was a huge step forward. We conducted tours of the exam rooms, the restaurants, the tennis courts, and the grounds, all free for patients. I interviewed on-site doctors, nurses, and invalids, those who weren't too ill to interact, and sampled the food on air, standing next to smiling chefs. The documentary was televised across the world. America was praised as a leader in the fight against our latest malignant epidemic, and I was honored for contributing so much to the healing effort.

Where had it all gone wrong?

Numbed by grief and loneliness, I lay in bed, losing myself in vignettes of my life with Will, the life I was renouncing for McKenna and Brianne and false intimacy with a man I no longer loved. It was a worthy exchange, I knew that, but it hurt.

I took out the memories, one by one. Daisy and Dusty nickering as they came out of the barn…Duke whoofing at some imagined threat…the rumble of an early thunderstorm…the distant, continual roar of Dallas Creek…Will pulling me closer in his sleep.

They would remain my secret treasures, dusted off in private and wept over until they grew nebulous and fell apart with age.

From the moment he'd picked me up off the floor in that Quonset hut, Rafe had seen me as recovered property, and he wasn't about to lose me again. Would he feel that way if he knew about Will? Especially if he knew how I was lying here wishing I was with him?

An insidious thought came out of nowhere, swooping in and lodging at the edge of my mind like a vulture.

Could Will have had something to do with me leaving Rafe? Could he have kidnapped me, drugged me, lied to me, or planted the idea that Rafe had done something so awful I would never want to return to him? Could he have brainwashed me into believing I had come to him of my own free will?

It didn't feel right. A man couldn't hide his true nature for over twenty years. Could he? Maybe a very disciplined man, like Will, could.

If only that night would come into focus. That one damnable night.

If I'd never left Rafe we'd be celebrating thirty-one years of marriage. I pictured him passing one perfect lavender rose, then another, through the fence at my elementary school, curling his fingers through the links as I performed my most graceful arabesque, which had no doubt been laughably awful.

We were innocent at first. At least, I was. We hiked in the mountains, swung on park swings, and attended church side by side. As the years passed, those chaste interactions gradually gave way to the inevitable awakening awareness of our bodies. We spent hours kissing, but after a while that wasn't enough.

If I hadn't left Rafe, that slap in the face might never have happened. I had seen the split second of satisfaction. He was doing his level best to hide it, but he *was* angry. He might not even realize how much anger was simmering inside, anger that would triple or quadruple when I got around to revealing who I'd been living with.

A knock on the door put an end to my tortuous pondering. "Come in," I said, sitting up.

Rafe entered, bearing a tray with mugs of coffee and a squat vase bursting with hyacinths and sweet alyssum. Alyssum, a flower that shouldn't be blooming for another month.

"Happy Mother's Day, McKenna's mother." He placed the tray on the bed.

"What's going on with the flowers? Do your gardeners perform magic spells?"

"The magic is you. I told you. It's because you've come home. The very air and soil are affected."

"Oh, stop. Jeez."

"You think I'm flattering you? My horticulturist showed photos to the members of his association, and none of them are having this kind of spring. Not even in other Utah gardens."

"I'm pretty sure there's another explanation."

A week had passed since he'd slapped me. I wondered, as he stood there, waiting for me to invite him to sit, if he'd expelled his buried anger with that slap. Perhaps he was truly sorry, and would never lose control like that again.

But in this spine-chilling new world, girls and women were subject to the kind of control I'd never imagined in my most nightmarish feminist thoughts. There was really no reason for Rafe to feel sorry for striking me.

Hoping I looked and sounded neutrally friendly and was giving off no suggestion of my inner turmoil, I invited him to sit. If I was really going to stay here, it would do no good to let him see my true feelings.

"Thanks," I said, as he handed me a mug.

"I didn't wake you, did I?"

At that moment, the sun lifted above the mountains. Its light captured a diaphanous cloud of snowflakes, transforming them from white to gold. The sight was a comforting sign of normalcy.

"No, I've been awake. I've been thinking about us. Remember how we met?"

"You were thinking about that?"

"Yes."

He grinned. "So was I. See how meshed we are?"

"Why did you hang around, watching me when I was so young?"

He laughed. "You know why."

"Pedophile."

"No," he said, sobering. "Don't even think that. I never touched you until you were old enough to know what you were doing."

Was I? Or was he simply tired of waiting?

"You know why I watched you," he said. "Why I talked to you, gave you presents, walked you home from school. I swore you would be mine forever the day you danced for me."

"I wasn't dancing for you, and fifteen is not old enough to make adult decisions about sex and pregnancy."

"*You* were old enough, Erin. You weren't some silly airhead. You were a smart girl."

"You're right about one thing. I was a girl, and while I may have been book smart, I wasn't street smart. You saw to that."

"You're lying to yourself, or maybe you've forgotten how it was with us. From the second you saw me watching, you danced for me. You knew, even then. Like I did." He took the cup from me and placed it on the tray, then brought my hand to his mouth and kissed my fingers. "For as long as the pyramids stand in Egypt." Leaning forward, he kissed the tip of my nose. "That's how long you and I will be together. Nobody, nothing, can separate us. Fight it. Ignore it. Curse it. It's never going to change."

There was some lingering vestigial thing inside me, left over from romantic girlhood, that wanted to buy into the fairy tale he was trying to construct. That little organ envisioned a future where we magically overcame pain and anger and recreated the perfect little bubble we'd lived in, once upon a time. I tried to hide this fact, but his twitch of a smile told me he saw something in my expression. Something he wanted to see. I retrieved my coffee and sipped, taking in courage with caffeine.

"The surgeon called," he said. "He's gone over the scans we sent him yesterday and says you're healing well. He wants to remove the scars on the nineteenth."

"Okay."

"I've reserved Le Melon d'eau for the night before. The whole restaurant will be ours, and we'll spend the night at the bungalow. Have you missed it?"

My mouth watered at the thought of the French cuisine, and the bungalow on the grounds had been one of my favorite places to get away and relax. I was happy to hear that this convoluted world had left it standing. "I suppose I have."

Then I realized he would expect me to sleep with him. If I refused, there would be a fight. All this beguilement was a means to an end. He was pushing me into a corner where it would be difficult to maintain my free will. It was no mistake, him making reservations there. He wanted to take me to a place of happy memories. He definitely meant for this celibacy to end.

The crescent scars over my pulses burned in unison. I put the mug on the tray so I could rub one wrist, then the other. The scars were raised and red. As I rubbed them, the burning subsided into itching and Will's face formed in my mind, bringing with it another round of longing. If only I could see him, touch him. If only I could say goodbye.

Here I sat, drinking coffee with Rafe in a luxurious mansion, while Will didn't know whether I was dead or alive.

There was another knock and Brianne peeked in. "Are you awake yet, Meemah?" She stopped, blinking. "Granddaddy," she said. A smile lit her face.

"You ready for Mother's Day, punkin?" he asked.

"Yes!" She ran to the bed and he ruffled her hair.

"Good morning, child of my child." I got up, bundling into the dark green cashmere robe I'd left hanging on the bedpost. It was too big, way too long, and sometimes I caught a transitory whiff of Rafe's aftershave. I had to roll up the sleeves and Brianne laughed at how I had a "train." It had been hanging in the closet when I came. I suspected he'd put it there on purpose.

She and I shuffled downstairs as Rafe returned to his room. "Mommy didn't want to get up yet," she said. "She told me to make hot chocolate. Meemah, do you love Granddaddy again?"

What had she seen in that bedroom? A couple enjoying coffee in warm camaraderie. Why wouldn't she draw such a conclusion?

I had a subliminal conviction that I loved him—was *in* love with him—the night I left, or was taken. Every time I thought of him during the years, my heart twisted in my chest, and that wouldn't have happened without strong, persistent emotion.

Was I destined to live the rest of my life donning a façade of contentment while inside, I slowly turned to stone?

It will be what you make it, I chastised myself.

"Do we ever stop loving someone we've loved?" I said carefully. "I don't think so. Some part lingers on." She was a child. I wasn't going to dump my crap on her.

"Sometimes it changes, though."

"You're very smart, Brianne."

"I know."

We entered the kitchen. Brianne fetched the cocoa while I poured milk into a saucepan.

"Great-grandmamma says it's a sin when I see things," Brianne said. "I'm supposed to close my eyes and pray to make it stop."

The milk steamed. I stirred in the cocoa. "What do you mean, see things?"

"In dreams and stuff." Brianne gave me a shy glance. "I knew you were coming back. I knew you were going to stay."

"You did?"

"There was a lady. She said you would come and promised she would come with you, but you didn't bring anybody with you, Meemah."

"Dreams can seem so important, but in the end, they don't usually mean much."

"I also saw the sky and grass and flowers getting better when you came back, and they did."

"They weren't like this before?"

She shook her head. "None of Granddaddy's gardeners could make things grow like he wants, till now."

"You'll have to show me."

McKenna scuffed into the kitchen in her robe and slippers. "She telling you about her Sight?"

"A little bit."

"When she was four years old, Brie said there was going to be an earthquake. 'The earth will shake and buildings will fall.' Those were her exact words. She threw up. Then it happened. We have earthquakes all the time, but this was the first one in a hundred and sixty years that caused a lot of damage."

"That is weird."

Rafe entered, freshly shaven, dressed in jeans and a crew-necked sweater the same shade as the robe I wore. Dark forest green was definitely his color.

"Time for presents!" Brianne cried.

"Meemah already got hers," Rafe said. "She's with her daughter again. What could be better than that on Mother's Day?"

"That's true," I said, even as inside, I resented his blatant manipulation of every scenario.

Brianne laughed. "And Meemah loves Granddaddy."

Rafe put his arm around me, casual yet possessive.

McKenna squinted and an awkward few seconds passed. I had to force myself to remain compliant under Rafe's arm like I wanted to be there.

Something passed through her face. A flash of ardent hope, there then gone in one fleeting instant.

She doesn't dare trust you.

"You really are staying?" she asked, keeping her voice unconvincingly noncommittal.

"I meant what I said, McKenna."

"Come on!" Brianne cried. "Don't you want to open your present?"

We adjourned to the terrace beside the infinity pool, where three brightly wrapped presents were perched on the table between the chaise lounges, couch, and chairs.

"Should we wait for your parents?" I asked Rafe.

"They aren't coming. I thought it would be nice to spend the day without them. We'll see them later, for dinner."

I was grateful to have missed that scene. Cordelia, denied access to her son's home, and on Mother's Day? Not a pretty picture.

"My three beautiful ladies." Rafe handed us each a gift wrapped in red paper covered in hearts.

"Me too, Granddaddy?" Brianne asked.

"Of course. They wouldn't be mothers without you."

McKenna got hers open first, then Brianne. Identical velvet boxes.

"Open yours, Meemah," Brianne said.

I tore the ribbon and paper, my fingers caressed by the velvet of another jewel-box. Rafe sat on the couch, his arms stretched along the back, smiling. "Open them together."

Reluctantly, I flipped up the lid. McKenna and Brianne did the same.

Three golden necklaces. A heart cut into thirds, each with its own faceted ruby.

"Take good care of them," Rafe said. "You three possess my heart."

"It's like a puzzle ring!" Brianne cried. "Give me yours, Mommy." When McKenna handed it over, she fitted it and hers on either side of mine—the centerpiece. "They make a whole heart! How pretty!" She ran to Rafe and gave him a smacking kiss. "I'll always wear mine, Granddaddy."

"So will I." McKenna sent her father a shy smile.

"Samson, play *The Nutcracker*," he said, sending me a secret smile.

The opening notes flowed through hidden speakers. He rose, holding out his hand to McKenna. She blinked and held back but Rafe leaned down, pulled her up, and waltzed her between the couch and the outdoor fireplace like a polished gallant. When the Grossvater Dance ended, he stopped, twirling her, and kissed her on the cheek.

"Look, Meemah," Brianne said quietly.

I caught my breath, seeing it too. My daughter's face was glowing.

Throughout the rest of the day, Rafe showered us with indulgent attention. Even church, Cordelia, tethers, and masks hardly dampened the celebratory mood. I started to feel better. Perhaps I was being melodramatic with all my inner misgivings.

When the day ended, Rafe kissed his daughter and granddaughter tenderly, as did I, and sent them off to bed. He invited me to join him in the study and Dale brought us mugs of mulled cider.

"Remember the first time we made love?" he asked, so soon after we were alone that I knew it was part of some hidden agenda. Still euphoric from McKenna's earlier happiness, I played along.

"I was awkward, but you weren't, even though you'd never had sex either."

"You were afraid you'd get pregnant. I hoped you would."

"You're kidding."

"I wanted you to have my child. If we lived in a different kind of world, I'd have begged you for five or six children."

The doctors zapped my tubes after McKenna was born. Rafe said it was our duty as responsible citizens. We had to set an example within the limits of the law. I agreed, yet…I would have liked more babies, too. I remembered wondering what was the use of having such a powerful husband if we had to follow more restrictive rules than everybody else, who went on producing as many children as they wished? Far too many people seemed to think overpopulation was somebody else's problem, or that it would never affect them, only future generations. It didn't seem fair that we had to give up our dream because of others who were so selfish.

Shaking my head, I murmured, "I'll never figure you out, Rafi."

"Remember how I botched up the seduction?"

"Yeah. Your parents were gone on that church thing. We were going to do it at your house, with candles and the hot tub and sheets covered in rose petals."

"But we didn't quite get there."

We'd parked in the driveway at his house and he'd leaned over to give me a kiss. Though it sounded cliché, passion overwhelmed us.

We never made it into the house. Instead, young love was consummated on the impossible front seats of the black Jag he'd received for his eighteenth birthday.

"Rafe."

"What?" He leaned in, running his fingers over my hair. His presence affected me, but it didn't feel like love or excitement. It felt like danger, like I was again treading a narrow precipice with dizzying drops on each side.

"Do you know where Maya is?"

He drew back. "No idea. Because of the note you left, she was questioned, but she claimed she didn't know anything and she had an alibi. She was with some man. Frankly I don't care. She was a major part of every problem you and I ever had. Good riddance."

Again, with this mysterious note. I'd give anything to talk to her. Logical Maya looked at everything with common sense. She always had. Where could she be? Was she alive? Had she found a way to survive in this horrible dystopia? I needed to verify the things Rafe had told me with someone I actually trusted. That would be Maya.

"I don't suppose you have this note, do you? I'd like to see it."

"I'm not sure," he said indifferently, annoyed. I'd ruined the scene of seduction he'd hoped to create. "I'll look for it."

He escorted me to my bedroom and left me at the door with a soft *goodnight, Erin,* and a kiss on the temple.

Chapter 10

THE SKY WAS CLEAR, GIVING THE ILLUSION THAT THERE WAS HARDLY ANY DISTANCE between the skylights over my head and the nearest star.

I punched the pillow, but Rafe had expensive ergonomic pillows. Punching them made no difference. As I watched, it returned to its original shape.

I kept thinking about this note I supposedly left. It said I was flying to Rhode Island, where Maya lived at the time while she was attending Brown University, but I'd actually flown to Denver and rented a car. Why had I lied? Why didn't the safety systems on the car protect me? How had I ended up with Will? That small, specific part of my life—writing a note, flying to Denver and renting a car—was completely blank. My memories started up again after I'd been with Will a week, so I thought, anyway. Everything in me was certain I hadn't known him before I left Rafe, but what if I was wrong? What if I had been given some fancy drug that made me forget?

What if Will hired those men who kidnapped me? What if he arranged for me to end up in that kennel?

Speaking of insidious thoughts, why not go all out? What if Rafe and Will cooked the whole thing up between them?

That's what happens with memory loss. It leaves one floundering, drowning in conjecture.

My thoughts wouldn't slow down. Maybe a glass of whiskey would help me sleep.

DISGUISED IN A GHILLIE SUIT THAT PERFECTLY MATCHED THE SPRING GRASS UPON which he stood, Will watched the Deer Valley house for three days. Using high-powered binoculars that could switch from daylight to night vision with a spoken command, he memorized the overly-predictable patterns of the guards and the precise moment each of the seven drones swept the area he'd pinpointed as the easiest place to break in.

The dogs would be more of a problem.

But late in the night on May eighth, Mother's Day, two guards went off to one of the adjoining buildings talking about coffee, and took two of the dogs with them. That hadn't happened before. He decided not to squander the chance.

He jogged across the lawn, keeping a close eye on his watch in order to merge into motionless grass whenever a drone hummed overhead. He came to his chosen spot at the rear of the chateau, beneath the terrace. Jumping over a low drystone wall, he padded to a rectangular window and used a heavy cloth and hammer to break the glass. He hadn't seen a light shining out of this particular window, not once. He waited, listening. No alarm sounded, but it could be silent. Time would tell.

Nobody came running. No snarling dogs. Rafe had grown lazy, trusting his security to imperfect men rather than infallible, tireless electronics.

He slid in, feet first, and dropped to the floor. Everything down here was dark and silent. Shrugging out of the ghillie suit, he made his way through the room and into the hall. Lighting came on at floor level, but no alarm sounded. He passed more rooms and open, spacious areas until he came to a staircase.

At the top of the stairs, he breathed a silent laugh. For there, beyond an arched opening in a room across a hallway, was Erin, alive, half buried in a deep armchair, one leg slung over the armrest, gazing at liquid in a crystal glass. There was something odd about her face, but the light was dim. He couldn't tell what it was.

Joy made him careless. He almost called to her before remembering where he was. He waited, but she spoke to no one. There was no indication of another person in the room with her.

Five more agonizing minutes he waited, while she sipped. "Pssst," he tried.

She didn't hear.

"Pssst. Erin."

She looked around the room, frowning.

"Pssst. Erin."

Her head turned his way. He ascended to the top step, making sure to keep out of sight of the enormous windows beside the front door in the nearby foyer.

Her mouth fell open. Without looking away—without blinking—she set the glass on the table and ran across the hall. "Will. Will. Oh, Will."

She sobbed against his neck and he held her, refamiliarizing himself with her flesh, her hair, her bones, her curves, her scent.

"You're alive," he whispered, hardly able to give this moment credence. "Come on." Keeping hold of her hand, he led her down the stairs and back to the room where he'd climbed in. Rays of light filtered through the window from the spotlight in the back yard.

"You broke the window?" she asked.

"Yes. Be really quiet so the dogs and drones don't hear us. Your face, Erin. What happened?"

"It was a chain. A man did it. Rafe killed him. How did you know I was here, Will? How?"

"I'm the one who told Rafe you were missing."

"What?"

"When I got back to the cabin, you were gone. I tracked you. I found a tree limb, blood, signs of a fight. What happened?"

"I was hiking by the creek. I heard men coming and hid. I thought they'd gone. I came out and waded into the water after something I saw out there. When I got back to shore, they attacked. One of them wanted to kidnap and keep me. The other wasn't so sure, but he was the one who knocked me out with that branch. I...I don't know if they did anything to me. When I woke up, they were nowhere around and I was in a kennel. I'd say it was a dog kennel, but it was bigger, and I was wearing a gunny sack. It was the most horrible place. Women locked in these plastic kennels, maybe hundreds of women, all of us at the mercy of the male guards. It was one of them who had fun with my face." She gestured at the raised, puckered gash curving around her left eye, much like his own scar, but worse.

He felt defeated and sick. If only he hadn't gone for supplies. If only the border police hadn't detained him. Another thought struck. "I wonder..."

"What?"

"I've heard rumors, but I couldn't believe we would—*they* would do that. That they could get away with it."

"With what?"

"Cage farms. I've heard that's where they keep women. I mean, they have to be somewhere. Nobody really knows where. There are hardly any women, Erin, anywhere. You and I, we escaped all that. Either the women in this country were murdered, or they're being held somewhere. I've heard stories about how salt mines and other underground places were turned into women prisons."

She was quiet for a moment. "I wasn't underground, but there was camouflage over us. Rafe said that after the lunacy resolved itself, women were released, but that it didn't work out. Will, you told Rafe about me?"

"I was desperate. I know you know Rafe is my brother. You've known almost from the beginning. Don't deny it."

"It's true. About a week in, my memory loss cleared up and I remembered Rafe and my life here. A few days after that, I saw the deed to your property in one of the bedroom drawers, and your name. I knew then you were the brother I'd heard of but had never seen."

Will nodded. "I figured as much."

"Did I ever tell you why I left Rafe? I've tried so hard to remember, but there's nothing. It's like a black hole."

"No, you never told me and I didn't ask. I'm ashamed to say I didn't really want to know."

"It's all right, but you and I, we didn't know each other before, did we? We didn't plan what happened?"

"No," he said, obviously surprised. "I swear, Erin. I had no idea who you were the night I found you. No idea."

She was quiet again, rubbing his cheeks and just looking at him.

"I knew if anyone could find you, it was him," he said. "He has the resources. It worked. I can't be sorry. You're alive, Erin. That's all that matters."

"That liar. He never mentioned you. He took all the credit, except for the little he gave his private detective. He said he's never stopped searching for me."

"That could be true. When Rafe thinks someone or something has stolen from him or cheated him, he can be like a Doberman. He had conditions, though. He made me swear not to contact you. He threatened to throw me in prison and abandon you if I did. I had no choice but to agree."

"Oh my *god*. I can't believe it. He *knows* you and I have been together all these years?"

"He knows. But I had a condition too. I made him promise he would post a photo of you when he found you, so I would know you were okay. He never did. That's why I'm here. I had to see for myself if he'd found you or not."

He kissed her fiercely, drowning in her whiskey mouth and hair, kissing her until she fell limply against him and he had to support her. She started crying again.

"Come with me," he said. "We can go right now. We'll run."

She kept her cheek cocooned against his shoulder, weeping, for a good minute before she lifted her head and looked into his eyes. "No, Will. It won't work. Like you said, he can be a Doberman. And now he knows I'm alive. He would see this window and he would never stop. We couldn't ever go back to the cabin. He would kill you, Will, and maybe me, too, for leaving. There's something very different about him. He never raised a hand against me, ever, but the day after I got here, he did. He hit me in the face. He is not the Rafe I used to know."

Will had to grind his teeth to keep from shouting. "Are you all right, baby?"

She nodded. "It was just a slap. It doesn't hurt anymore."

"He's one of the most powerful men in the world, Erin. There are rumors about him, too. Bad ones. His nickname is the Cannibal. I don't know why, but that says something, doesn't it? You can't stay here. I can't leave you here."

She placed her hands on his cheeks and kissed him. "If I stay, I'll be all right. I'm learning how to deal with him, how to play his game, and I'll play it better than he does, that I promise. That's what I was doing when you saw me just now. Making plans. I've got to make plans. Good ones."

"You're overconfident. You don't know him as well as you think you do. Don't ask me to go away and leave you. I love you, Erin. I'm half dead without you."

She caressed his face then his hair, drawing it through her fingers. She stared at him in the half-light, tears streaking her cheeks. "You're strong, Will," she said gently. "My daughter isn't. I've come back into her life and I can't abandon her again, no matter what it costs. No matter what price I have to pay. She needs me. She doesn't trust me, and I have to fix that. I have to try to make things right with her. I can't let her down. Not again." She drew in a deep, shaking breath. "I will stay here until my last breath rather than do that again to my child. I love you too, but she is my child."

This was an argument for which he had no rebuttal. He saw her resolve. He knew he couldn't break it. He wasn't even sure he wanted to. He knew, though Erin had never talked about it, that the guilt, remorse, and ache for her child had never relinquished its hold in all the years they lived together.

"Now I have a grandchild, too. Brianne. She looks at me like I'm an answer to her dreams. I can't imagine what it would do to her if I left."

He felt as though he was splintering like the window he'd broken. "This is it? We never see each other again?"

"I don't know. Maybe the world will reject this madness. Maybe Rafe will decide he doesn't want me after all and kick me out."

They held each other and didn't speak. They both knew Rafe would never let her go.

Without looking into her face, he released her. Seizing the ghillie suit, he vaulted through the window and was gone, leaving behind his broken heart.

ALL CRIED OUT, I CLUTCHED MY PILLOW AND WATCHED THE DAWN BLOOM BRIGHTER and brighter as it turned from ice-blue to crimson to yellow and the sun uncoupled from the peaks outside my window.

Mornings in the mountains around Mount Sneffels were crisp and cool, redolent with forest smells. As sunlight heated the wood, the rails on the veranda popped and crackled and filled the air with the smell of pine sap.

The horses would neigh their good mornings as Will went in the barn to feed them. Then he'd come back and offer me eggs, or whatever we had on hand. He'd put his rough, perpetually chapped hand on my cheek. Every morning. Never fail.

The anguish I'd seen in his eyes, felt in his embrace, made me want to cry again, but I was too tired. How could I have ever thought, even for an instant, that Will would have me kidnapped and put in that kennel, or any of the other preposterous things I had considered? It took a massive amount of love to humble himself and ask for Rafe's help.

I remembered. I remembered.

He'd gone to town on an unexplained errand. When he returned, he told me he was going to make supper. "Go take a walk," he said. "I don't need help."

I liked to hike in the evenings before the deer bedded down. Will, in his amazingly cognizant way, never asked to come along. He seemed to sense my need for solitude, perhaps because he felt the same way.

I idled away an hour, exploring. I saw two deer and moments later smelled something very pungent. A well-hidden bear, I guessed. Or a moose. Pretending I was a pioneer woman making my way through the West in search of a new home, I clambered over an enormous scatter of boulders and arrived at noisy Dallas Creek, flanked by well-traveled foot paths. Already, after only a month and a half at Will's cabin, I felt as shy as a lynx and merged into the shadows when I heard a strident conversation between a group of hiking men.

Night had fallen when I returned to the cabin. Will had drawn the curtains. Muted ivory light flickered through the fabric, pooling into neat squares on the ground.

The interior stopped me flat. Arranged throughout the room that comprised our living, dining, and cooking areas, were more candles than I'd ever seen, some fat and short, some tall and narrow. A vase of wildflowers decorated the center of the smooth white pine table. The scent of simmering pork and rosemary drifted from the stove and a wine bottle jutted from a wooden ice-bucket. Sauvignon Blanc, my favorite.

I stammered. "W-what is this?"

Will stepped from the bedroom where I'd been sleeping since I'd come to live with him. He spent his nights on the couch in the living room.

Speechless, I stared at this no-nonsense trapper/hunter/mountain man, dressed just now in a denim button-down shirt and a vintage Jerry Garcia tie. His beard was trimmed to shadow-stubble and his dark hair fell like a waterfall. At first, before I knew who he was, I'd assumed he had an American Indian heritage, but he'd told me that was just a coincidence, that his ancestry was Greek and Norwegian.

I was younger in those days, but not slow. "Tired of the couch, huh?" I asked.

He grinned and blushed.

Afterward, nestled half beneath his body, Dallas Creek murmuring through the open window and the smell of hot candle-wax heavy in the air, I said, "Just so you know. Wine alone would've done the job."

His laugh, rare and honest, entranced me then and had never failed to delight me since.

Would I ever hear it again?

A MAN IS A MAN IS A MAN, BUT A CHILD IS FOREVER.

I hadn't said it out loud. Saying something like that to the man who risked his life to see me would be cruel.

The phrase was from *Cobalt on Shadow and Glass*, by Françoise Babineaux. It had replayed for years, every morning when I woke, every day as I went about my chores, every night as I fell asleep next to Will. It finally faded, but now it was back, compounded threefold by sweet little Brianne with her fathomless brown eyes. I had looked into those eyes and was lost. They held wisdom and a kindness one seldom saw, except in very old women.

Françoise Babineaux was tortured and murdered in France by Christian zealots, angry at the heresy in her book and because she was an outspoken atheist.

I could never make up for the pain I had caused so many, including Will. If I hadn't taken off into a Colorado thunderstorm, I would never have met Will, and wouldn't have destroyed him just a few short hours ago.

Why the hell did I leave? I suspected those few hours were the missing key that would provide every answer I longed for, if I could only remember them.

When you fuck up, Erin, you really fuck up.

AFTER SAMSON ANNOUNCED THE TIME, THE VARIOUS PARTICULARS OF MY SLEEP quality (not good), the weather report, and the readiness of coffee in the kitchen, he went on to inform me that there were police and detectives in the house. Did I intend to go downstairs, or would I prefer to have coffee brought to the bedroom?

Police and detectives. Shit. "Why are the police here?"

"Mr. Konstantinou said he would explain when he sees you."

"I'll go down." Might as well get it over with. Likely as not, they knew what had happened and who broke in. For the first time I considered security cameras and what they could have recorded. I might very well be handcuffed and hauled off to some kind of prison. In this world, I'd probably earned myself the death penalty.

"Your heartbeat has increased to one hundred and thirty-six beats per minute, Erin. Is there anything I can do?"

"No, Samson. Nothing." Couldn't hide a damn thing from this AI.

Wait. That was true. So why hadn't Samson sounded the alarm last night?

"Mr. Konstantinou asked me to remind you that you will need to wear a visitor mantle."

"What might that be?"

"There are several approved mantles hanging in your closet, Erin."

The overhead light came on in the closet and Samson told me which of the robes were appropriate. Loose and long-sleeved, the shapeless thing included a hood and an attached scarf that stretched across the lower half of my face. When everything was donned and fastened, only my forehead, eyes, and hands were visible. I glanced in the mirror before leaving. The getup accentuated the fact that I'd slept badly and had been crying. I'd already splashed several liters of cold water over my eyes without much improvement. There was nothing more I could do.

I went downstairs and was confronted by no less than seven detectives and policemen. Earlier, the dogs had caught Will's scent. His footprints were visible in the dew. Shortly after, the broken window was discovered and then the hammer and cloth, in a mess of slivered glass.

I tried to make my forehead and eyes appear bewildered and concerned and went off for coffee as the investigators, along with Rafe and Oliver, the youth who served as his home secretary and personal assistant, inspected every room with a myriad of detection gadgets.

I wasn't surprised that nothing was missing, but I frowned as though I thought that very odd. I rubbed the charcoal-colored fabric covering my arms and spoke the right words during a moment when Rafe and I were alone.

"Do you have any idea who did this? How did it happen? Don't you have security cameras and alarm systems?"

Anger emanated from him like heat off a furnace. "I haven't used them since Brie was born," he said. "I relied on them, never contemplating how they could be shut off by a disloyal sentinel intent on screwing my daughter, or a daughter intent on being screwed. I *thought* that drones and specialized guards with dogs would do a better job and the men would police each other."

"What about inside?" I asked. "No cameras inside either?"

"I have Samson," he said. "Better than any camera, or so I *thought*." He glanced at me and his gaze sharpened. I held up my coffee cup, lifting the scarf to drink and using the action to cast my gaze downward. The captain came in, murmuring crossly at a small gauzy figure hovering above his wrist, and Rafe turned away.

It was puzzling. Why would someone risk being ripped apart by attack dogs to break in to a rich man's house stuffed with priceless artwork, expensive gadgets, and countless other valuables, and take nothing? They tested the cloth and the hammer, but whoever used them hadn't left a single fingerprint. No DNA.

Perhaps something scared him off, the captain offered.

Will and I were damn lucky. Through sheer happenstance, there were no security cameras. If there were, I would be trying to explain why there was footage of me crying in another man's arms.

I breathed a little easier.

Detectives spent the whole day at the chateau. I avoided them as best I could, but I was called to the first-floor study once to answer questions.

As I sat down, I saw my abandoned glass, half full of whiskey, on the table by the chair. *Holy crap*, I thought, but as Oliver spotted it and picked it up, I knew what to do.

"That's mine," I said. "I had a glass before I went to bed last night."

Rafe again, with the penetrating look. His frown hammered at me.

For once I was grateful for the disguising face scarf, though it wasn't completely opaque.

"How late was that, Mrs. Konstantinou?" the captain asked. "You didn't hear anything? See anything?"

I was already shaking my head. "No, I would have told you. It was fairly early. Eleven, maybe? I'm sure it was before midnight. I never heard a thing."

The man turned his gaze to Rafe, one brow lifted, but Rafe said nothing, did nothing, and wouldn't meet his gaze. After a moment the man shrugged and stood. "We'll keep working on it, Mr. Konstantinou. I have men spreading out over the property, looking for clues, and asking around in Park City. Something will turn up." He glanced at me. "It is strange, though."

As soon as the door closed behind the investigators, Rafe collected the bottle of cognac from the study and went in search of Erin. He found her lying on the bed in the guest bedroom, hands behind her head, watching fat cumulus clouds sail across a pink evening sky. She'd changed into his cashmere robe; the visitor mantle lay crumpled on the floor.

His face must have held some kind of question, because she said, "Felt like I was in a straitjacket." She added, "I'm not hungry. Go ahead and eat without me if you want."

"I'm not particularly hungry either." He purposely kept his tone mild as he poured them both a brandy, noting how the flowers from yesterday were still releasing heady scent. "I was in the study last night at eleven. I had already told the captain."

She sat up to take the glass. "Thanks for covering for me. It was later when I was in there. I couldn't sleep. I was afraid of being accused of something. Not being in bed or whatever." She gave a brittle smile. "Seems like women are blamed for all kinds of things these days. It's enough to make a person paranoid."

He read nothing on her face. Not anger, hate, fear, or love. Nothing. It was too neutral. "Do you know something you're not telling us?"

"How could I? And why would I?"

"There was a break in, but nothing was stolen, and you're different somehow than you were yesterday." He didn't even blink, not wanting to miss the slightest subtle hint her face might reveal. "Maybe whoever broke in did get what he came for. Could that have happened?"

"I'm 'different,' somehow? Looks like I wasn't being paranoid after all."

"I'm not accusing you of anything. Just asking."

"Good cognac." She set the glass on the bedside table and leaned towards him. "You seem to have forgotten how to trust." She looked at him dead on, her eyes open and guileless.

He put his thumb and index finger on her chin. Her mouth was so close. He couldn't resist. She returned his kiss, at first indecisively, then with growing passion. Just like before, after that disastrous supper with his parents. Her tongue touched his. Her hand slipped around his neck.

That first night roared through his mind as he tasted the velvet cognac on her lips. She'd almost succumbed, no doubt due to the compound he'd had Dale mix into her cheesecake. It was similar to the drug he'd given her long ago, but newly tweaked and in a tasteless powder form. As soon as the doctors assured him of her recovery, he began fantasizing about using it on her. One of his tech friends at UCLA had slipped him several packets. "Let me know if you need more," he'd said, laughing.

This modified formula, dubbed *Sappho*, supposedly made sexual desire almost impossible to resist. That's what members of the Brotherhood claimed, anyway. President Warwick liked to say that it was a good thing the females dosed with it were kept under lock and key. Otherwise, he drawled, they'd be screeching like feral cats for anything with a dick.

It had almost worked. He didn't understand how she managed to fight it off. He'd grilled Dale, who'd been offended. The chef insisted he'd used the prescribed amount, and showed Rafe the empty premeasured packet.

Officially, *Sappho* was only offered to men in the Reformation Brotherhood. It enhanced docility and prevented pregnancy like the Cage formulas, but the intensified sexual desire made it very popular with owners.

No doubt with the Cage guards too. In this world, like any other, the black market thrived.

"You're more than enchanting," he said against her mouth. "You're an enchantment. A heroine of the untold Arabian Nights."

She said nothing, but her eyes opened. He put his hand over her breast. There it was, the hard, rapid beat he wanted to feel.

"I'm completely under your spell." His lips trailed across her cheek to her ear. His tongue circled her lobe; he reveled at the soft sigh it elicited. He moved his hand down to the belt, which he easily unwound, and ran the tips of his fingers across her stomach and lower, to the magic. He brought his fingers to his nose, inhaling, and spoke into her ear. "Yours is the most addictive drug in the universe. When I had the scent of you on my fingers, Erin, I thought I might die of fulfillment."

She shivered. Her mouth opened. Her pupils expanded, swallowing her irises.

Even as suspicion muttered on at the back of his mind, he dropped his brandy glass and kissed her more deeply. He pushed her backward across the bed and followed, stripping off his trousers, pressing himself against her, feeling like a teenage boy having his very first sexual experience.

She'd stated with unequivocal certainty that any chance at reconciliation was lost when he struck her. Now here she was, spreading her legs, kissing him as if they'd never split up. Women were weak, slaves to their desires. The early Christian prophets knew that. When he'd drugged her, hoping for this, she'd resisted, but here she was, drug-free and acquiescing.

So much for Will, he thought triumphantly.

When he'd struck her in the limo pod, pleasure flooded, reminding him of the initial rush of his own favored euphoria drug, *Mozart*. Then rage took over. He'd had to physically contain the scream pounding against the back of his throat. *You were with my brother for twenty-three years!* He'd wanted to hit her again and again.

When she'd come downstairs this morning her eyes were swollen and bloodshot as hell. He'd noticed her lips seemed redder than usual when she lifted the scarf to sip her coffee. Maybe she'd been biting them. They looked like he remembered from the old days, after she'd been thoroughly, competently kissed.

Was she that unhappy here, that she spent her time sobbing in secret?

His mind stopped obsessing when her hands drifted to his hips.

For as long as the pyramids stand in Egypt. He didn't know where he'd picked up that line, but it expressed his sentiment perfectly. In his worst moments after she left, he believed he would never say it again, but here they were. Together.

"Elfin Erin. My Erin."

"Rafi."

He buried his face between her legs and drank her in. When she cried out and her fingers spasmed, digging into his upper back, he released his suspicion.

It wasn't an act. She was back. Erin had come back to him. The nightmare was truly over.

Chapter 12

THANKS TO MOONLIGHT, I COULD OBSERVE MY HUSBAND AS HE SLEPT. HIS ARM WAS flung across his forehead. His lips moved without making a sound. He sighed once, seemed to relax, then resumed tossing and turning, letting me know the old nightmares were still around, plaguing him. He used to call me by a different name when I shook him awake. I couldn't remember what it was.

I didn't wake him this time. Let him dream of her. She didn't bring him any pleasure, twenty years ago or now.

He was enduringly beautiful, his smile breathtaking, torrents of hair that remained more tawny-blond than gray, eyes that could be as cold and fierce as a dragon's or soft and seductive, depending on his mood.

But there was something new to me. A tattoo. At first, since he lay on his back, all I could see were thick black curves wrapping beneath his arm and coming to a point adjacent to his navel. Running my fingertip lightly along one of them caused him to roll onto his side, facing away from me, and I saw what had been hidden.

A lion. The profile of an open mouth, bared fangs, and corrugated snout lay between his shoulder blades. That part was realistic. The mane grew looser and more conceptual the farther it flowed from the head. Under his arm and on his stomach, it resembled licking flames.

As tattoos went, it was more dramatic than attractive. Bold and black, menacing. A lion on the attack, wielding fangs and fire.

He'd kept his shirt on during the encounter in the guest room, so I hadn't seen it. Afterward, as we lay propped on pillows, sipping what hadn't spilled of the cognac, his mouth slid into the suggestive smile that always meant trouble.

"Come on, Erin." He ran his index finger beneath my ear. "Throw me a bone. Can we finally move you out of the goddamn guest room?"

I agreed, pretending shyness. I would agree to anything to throw him off the track he'd been racing down when he came in, hoping to trick me. I had to stop him following his suspicions before they led him to Will.

I would play his game, and I would do it better.

Of all the destinations that existed in the world, why had I chosen that corner of Colorado when I abandoned Rafe? What if I'd gone to LA, Chicago, or Tibet?

Hindsight wouldn't help me now, not in this wrong-side-up world, where my husband publicly demonstrated his authority through physical violence.

I can't take this. I slipped out of bed, donned the robe, and left the room. Should I go downstairs and find oblivion in alcohol?

No. Not again. Nothing got solved that way, and it would only remind me of Will.

Instead, I journeyed to the chateau's fourth story for the first time since I'd returned. I took the elevator and approached Rafe's private loft, half expecting alarms to go off or a lock to stop me. Neither happened. Samson remained silent and the latch turned easily. Odd. I remembered Rafe keeping his office strictly off limits to everyone, but I wasn't about to complain. I had a vague notion that spending time in his work space might help me understand him, or reveal something important.

There was the familiar air of masculinity that hit me as soon as I entered, the smell of leather, polished wood, and a hint of bergamot. The silence. The dark hardwood floors and rich, purple-taupe walls. The bookshelves I remembered.

There were changes, though. The rectangular mahogany desk that used to dominate the center was gone, replaced by a crescent shaped, narrower surface of gleaming black glass and a sleek black leather chair. Three transparent screens curved around the outer rim of this crescent, facing the chair. Computer screens, surely, but there was no keyboard on the desk, nothing but the glass, as unmarred as a pool of deep water. It was not like anything I had ever seen, but then again, Will's cabin only had electricity because of an old rusty generator.

A tall case behind an arrangement of chairs and couches displayed a corroded sword and a helmet with a slot on top for a feather plume. They'd been fished from the ocean, judging by the pits, dents, and patina. Rafe must have continued to indulge his passion for archeology while I was gone. Before I'd disappeared into the wilds of Colorado, he'd attended several digs, and had taught me some of what he knew. I could, therefore, date the helmet and sword to the Greek Classical Age, and the style told me the articles were Spartan.

Ambient light came on as I approached another, lower case, running the length of the west wall. Inside lay a collection of exquisite Bronze Age seal-rings and hammered gold pendants. Seven miniature golden axes, a curved blade on either side of the haft, lay on a raised shelf covered in black drapery, next to a small vase of alabaster and three spear tips. The axes at least were from Crete, famous for the number of double-axes found in caves and ruins. Several pottery items were reassembled from fragments, with faded images of octopi, squid, and seaweed.

I returned to the desk and ran my hand over the back of the leather chair. The computer he'd used decades ago was gone, long gone, probably. The desktop had at first glance seemed unsullied by even a fingerprint but now I noticed the outline of a rectangle embedded in the surface. I had no idea what it could be, and briefly regretted that so much had passed me by while I lived the life of a primitive. Hesitantly, I touched it. Nothing happened.

I dropped into the chair and opened two narrow drawers, looking for some kind of technology I could put a name to, but they were nearly empty. I ran my fingertips along the edge of the desk. Almost immediately I discovered a small depression that cupped around the tip of my little finger. I pressed it without even thinking.

An invisible panel on the far wall of the adjoining room slid open. I jumped to my feet, wondering if an insane wife or three-headed dog would appear.

Hundreds of chiming beads, silver, turquoise, and cobalt, swung from lintel to floor.

I had to see what was behind those beads. I walked to them and pushed through. More lighting switched on, illuminating a square, windowless room. Recessed lamps in the ceiling focused on a raised pedestal in the center of the south wall, setting off a large sculpture.

The figure of a bare-breasted girl, carved in white marble, was poised upside-down above the head of a black marble bull. The bull, front legs splayed, head lifted, was forever caught beneath his toreador. If the scene were to come alive, the female would continue her flip and land feet-first on the bull's broad back.

Unlit candles framed the bull-leaper and her fearsome partner. Two incense burners hung suspended from chains on each side.

No way could this room have been here before I vanished. He couldn't have had it built without me knowing.

Opposite the statue was another opening, inviting me into a large, circular library. I walked in, bringing up the lighting, amazed to see two stories; a spiral staircase to the left led up to the second story, the same size and shape as the first, with a circular witch's cap ceiling of stained glass. It must be gorgeous in sunlight.

Rafe had built a turret library. It was like something from a fairy tale. The maple walls, decorated with rune-like carvings, were lined with bookshelves and doors. Loveseats and oversized leather chairs were grouped near the fireplace. Behind them was a spacious worktable.

I perused the nearest shelves as I passed. Real hardcover books, like those in McKenna's hobbit room. Old tomes on archaeology, ancient myth, ritual, and religion. Mostly from Greece and the Aegean islands, but some on Egypt, Mesopotamia, and ancient Africa.

Behind the worktable there was a well-preserved Victorian wardrobe, an oval mirror inset in the front. I opened the doors; it was empty but for a stone statue positioned on its side, carved from dense rock, perhaps slate. I struggled to pick it up and bring it out for examination. Touching the stone caused my scars to tingle as though electrified.

I could tell this was a valuable artifact. The female figure's face, and the nursing child in her lap, were worn by age. It ought to be in a museum, not stuffed in a private individual's closet.

"I'm sorry," I said, caught in a flood of miserable emotion I couldn't understand.

The female returned my gaze from blank, enigmatic eyes.

A sudden thump sent me pivoting with a gasp, sure I'd been caught. A book had fallen from the shelf opposite me and now lay on the floor, open. I crossed to it, wondering what had happened. I hadn't been anywhere near it and hadn't felt any tremors.

I sat cross-legged on the floor and picked it up. *Secrets of Bronze Age Goddess Cults*. Its augmented hologram technology activated automatically; I was greeted by the representation of a female in Victorian dress, sitting at a table with nothing on it but an oil lamp. She held the book in translucent hands and began reading aloud, looking up at me every now and then. Her voice had a Celtic-flavored accent.

Intrigued, I flipped back to the beginning. The first copyright date was 1886, the authors listed as M. A. Ramsay, E. Graeme, and D. Sinclair. A forward, dated 1903, by someone named Curran Ramsay, identified himself as the deceased M. A. Ramsay's husband. In a few succinct lines, he stated the book was the effort of three women—Morrigan Ramsay, Eleanor Graeme, and Diorbhail Sinclair, all residents of a place called Glenelg, in Scotland. He added that the chapters were transcribed from dreams and visions each experienced.

A second forward by the publisher and dated 2016 for the third edition, explained that historians who investigated the authors' lives discovered that all three were users of hallucinatory mushrooms and were probably addicted, much like opium junkies of the time.

I switched off the tech and thumbed through the book the old-fashioned way, studying the photographs and drawings. I read how invading hordes conquered Greek farmers and fishermen, how they maimed the religion and stole the native peoples' deities for their own, warping them in the process to support their own ambitions. Before the onslaught, Hera was not the jealous, petty shrew of a wife I remembered from my ancient world religions class. Rather, she was a symbol of fertility, connected to the stages of the moon. Hera had presided over the original Olympic races, run by women from the most archaic of times, long before men took over and banned females from competing. She became the wife of mighty Zeus only much later, so she would fall in line with the new beliefs.

The writers had a different take on Athene, too. I'd been taught that she was a martial goddess born directly out of Zeus's forehead, fully-grown and armored, but this book declared that she actually lived before the Classical, Golden, and Hellenistic Ages in Greece, long before Zeus was even a thing. Supposedly, she was worshipped on the isle of Crete and before that, possibly Africa. She taught writing, weaving, and pottery-making, passed on the method of extracting dye to color cloth, and gave the early Cretans the secrets of olive grafting. She reigned as a goddess of peace and promoted harmony with nature. I remembered learning that Athene was an eternal virgin, and always took the side of men, yet this book claimed she was the mother of more than one child, and the meaning of her name was, "I have come from myself." In Ramsay's version of history, Athene's son became her lover; she gave him in holy sacrifice each year to fructify the crops for her cherished mortals then resurrected him to renewed vitality every spring along with the planet. I couldn't help but compare that theory to the Christ story.

Was the impassive female statue a goddess, or merely a representation of motherhood? Why did Rafe have her tossed in a closet? Did she not fly in the face of his evangelical convictions? Did his Christian friends know of this room and what it held?

I realized suddenly that there were no Christian symbols in this room. No crosses, no artwork of Jesus, no Bible verses. Nothing. Then I realized for the first time that I'd seen none of these things anywhere in the entire chateau.

Exhaustion flowed over me. I rubbed my eyes and yawned. No doubt I could sleep now.

Maybe the answers I sought would come in a dream. They did for little Brianne, after all. I returned to the statue and touched the stone woman's forehead. Again, my scars tingled, as though the stone was generating conductive energy.

Hurry.

I studied every corner and shadow in the room, finally deciding I'd imagined the voice. I touched her cheek.

He lies.

This time I scrambled away. I ran into the outer office, but the lights had dimmed. The room was empty.

I returned to the statue. "Do you have the answers?"

Silence.

Silly. Stupid. Yet so much in this room called to me, inviting me into a world of basilisks and minotaurs and omnipotent deities. I wanted to go through every shelf, every drawer. I wanted to open each of these doors and see what worlds were hidden behind them.

I picked up the statue and returned it to the closet. This time when I touched it, I heard nothing.

"I'll come back," I promised. In the main office, I pressed the button and the panel door closed.

"I'll come back," I repeated, not knowing why it seemed so important, but unable to resist the impulse.

Chapter 13

I COULDN'T OPEN THE DOOR LEADING FROM THE MUSIC ROOM INTO THE SUNROOM at the back of the house. I pulled on the scrolled latch. I pushed. I threw my weight against the wood. It wouldn't budge.

"Samson," I said. "Why won't this door open?"

"Only authorized people are allowed in that room, Erin."

"Why?"

"I'm not sure, Erin." There was a pause.

"Samson?"

"I'm asking Mr. Konstantinou now."

"Oh, forget it." I would get a cup of coffee and find a room I *could* go into. Hard to believe I'd overseen the remodel on the chateau. Now locks restrained my movements like I was an interloper.

As I crossed the room, running my fingers irritably over the keys on the grand piano, Rafe bounded in. "What happened? Samson says you're having trouble."

"I wanted to go into the sunroom, is all. Why is it locked?"

"I'm sorry, sweetheart. I completely forgot about this. Samson?"

"Yes, Mr. Konstantinou?"

"Give Erin the same access to everything in the house that I have, please."

"Immediately, sir."

Rafe beamed as though he'd presented me with the password to Fort Knox and told me to help myself.

"Why is it locked?" I asked.

"Because the sunroom has exterior doors that lead onto the estate."

"I suppose those doors will remain locked to me."

"Well, Erin. I told you about going outside."

"A sentinel. Yes. A mask. And a…leash, is it?"

"You don't understand—"

"Oh, I think I do. Even with my poor little female brain."

He scowled.

"Are you going to hit me?"

"You're in a hell of a mood."

"I wasn't. Would you like being a prisoner in your own home?"

"You're not a prisoner. These things are for your protection. Just tell me if you want to go outside. I'll arrange it. You don't even have to tell me. Samson can arrange it, too."

He could have told me I gave up the right to call this house mine when I left it, and him. Nevertheless, my anger simmered on. "I wonder how many women have been reassured by such patronizing statements through the centuries? How is a *leash* for my protection?"

"It's mostly subliminal." He sounded eager, as though he was sure he could get through to me this time and make me an ardent supporter of my own subjugation. "It was studied extensively. It sends a message to those who might want to harm you. It's like saying, 'Watch your step. This woman is protected. Threaten her at your peril.'"

McKenna came in holding two cups of coffee, and glanced between us. "I was going to take you coffee and heard you talking."

Now, when I tried to open the sunroom door, it gave way without issue. I pointedly turned my gaze to McKenna. "I wanted to see how my plants have fared while I was gone," I said. "Join me?"

McKenna nodded. "Sure."

Rafe sighed and left, throwing back a growled, "I have work to do, thanks."

I noted with satisfaction how everything I chose so long ago had flourished. The room was a tropical paradise. I climbed the curved steps in the southeast corner and made myself comfortable in the hammock next to the reflection pool; McKenna dropped into a canvas chair and we were instantly plunged into privacy and shade, provided by a multitude of enormous Colocasia plants. Kingfishers and broadbills flitted among the branches of the taller foliage, eying us suspiciously, and in the adjacent corner, the waterfall bubbled.

"Were you and Daddy fighting?" Before she lowered her gaze, I caught the wariness she tried to hide, and I understood, maybe better than she did. Things were precarious. She feared another abandonment.

I wanted to weep, but that would be a mistake. "Not really." I sipped coffee. "Thanks for this. It's so good. McKenna? What is it like for you, living here? Do you have friends? Things have changed so much. I feel lost. Angry, if you want to know the truth. Is that just me and my age? Everyone else seems okay with the way things are, but I hate it. It might be dangerous for women out there, but this alternative doesn't seem like the answer to me. You've given up almost every freedom. In this world, maybe I would never have met your father, because—I don't know, do girls go to school? Are they allowed to play outside during recess?"

"No." She stirred her coffee with a small silver spoon, watching the flavored cream swirl before it blended in. "The only education girls get is if they're attached to wealthy men, like Daddy. If that man decides it's worthwhile to educate his women, then a home tutor comes. It's up to the man. We're told in church that an educated woman leads to violence, rape, and anarchy."

"I can't believe we're going through this crap again. Now we're back to Victorian times. Women have to be imprisoned because the alternative is rape?"

McKenna looked up from her coffee. "You really don't know, do you? Before, when you were asking me about Brie's father, you weren't just fishing for Daddy's sake."

"Of course not." I was surprised. McKenna thought I was acting as Rafe's spy? "No way."

"You really don't remember anything from before Daddy found you?"

It was my turn to pause and inspect my coffee. This was it. I could either continue to lie or I could take a leap of faith.

A man is a man is a man, but a child is forever.

I returned her direct gaze. "I remember everything. Well, that's not quite true. What I can't remember is what happened the night I left you and your father. Why I left, where I went, the car wreck. All that is gone, but where I've been? Yes, I remember."

"I knew it." McKenna drew in a deep breath and blew it out. She probably expected a magical adventure story, like *Treasure Island* or *One Thousand and One Nights*. "Where were you?" She gestured with one hand to indicate our surroundings. "Someplace where this isn't the way, obviously. I've heard of countries where women are as free as men. Daddy says that's a myth, but I think he's lying. Is that where you were?"

"No. Much closer, in Colorado. I was…with a man."

McKenna's hand crept to the heart necklace her father had given her. "You left us to be with another man?" She sighed sharply; the spark in her eyes receded.

"Your Uncle Will."

McKenna stared. "You left us for my uncle?"

Pain bolted through my sutures. I felt hot all over. "It wasn't like that. I didn't know him. He can't have been the reason I left. I didn't have an affair. At least, not before. It was—it was—I don't know what it was, McKenna. I don't know how I ran into him, of all the men in the world, but it happened. Your father has told me that when I left here, I flew to Denver and rented a car. Somehow, I managed to wreck it within hearing distance of your uncle. I had never met him. I didn't know who he was. He and I never exchanged a single word in all the time I was with your father. I'd never even seen a photo of him."

"I've never met him either," McKenna said.

"Will was out hunting and he heard the crash. He found me, covered in glass and blood. I guess I was lucky to be alive. He cared for me until I recovered."

I paused. McKenna went on staring, her coffee forgotten.

"At first, I really did have amnesia. I didn't even know my own name. Things started coming back after a few days. I remembered you, and your father, and my life here, but not anything about why I left. Sometime later, I ran across the deed to Will's cabin and land. There was his name, William Camael Konstantinou. At first, I thought it had to be a coincidence. They don't look alike. Your uncle must take after Dillon, while Rafe is definitely from the Norwegian side. Then I saw Dillon's name. He was listed as Will's beneficiary."

"So after you knew who he was, and who you were, you chose to stay with him. You chose him over me."

How to tell her? How to explain? *Truth, Erin. Truth.*

"Why?" McKenna asked bluntly.

This was even harder to answer. Not long after Will found me, he'd come home from a trip to town and he seemed different. He offered to take me to Ouray and help me find my family. He said people must be worried, that they must be searching. I could tell he was reluctant, but that didn't stop him. He offered, and offered again the next day, and a third time.

Every time, his offer sent me into floods of primal dread. I didn't know why. Had Rafe hurt me? Kicked me out, threatened my life, attacked me, or done something illegal? I didn't know. The last thing I remembered was standing at our front door, greeting the presidents of the United States, Ukrus, and North Korea, then escaping to the terrace. That's where my memories halted.

I put Will off with vague excuses. *I need more time. Maybe later. I'm not up to it yet.* Eventually, he stopped asking.

How to explain? She had just started feeling closer to Rafe. I didn't want to harm that newfound affection.

"It's hidden in my subconscious, McKenna. I don't know why I didn't want to come home, but I have no doubt it was something between your father and me. It had nothing to do with you. You were only four years old. Later, I told myself it was kinder to let you believe I was dead, and Will agreed. He believed you were better off with Rafe."

"He would, wouldn't he? Another man's child. A constant reminder."

I couldn't let her dismiss Will as a selfish creep. "We lived off the grid. Way, way off the grid, on a mountain, in a drafty cabin. I had no friends, no job. No phone, TV, or computer. I never, ever went off the mountain. He did, once a month. He drove to Montrose for supplies. He knew more than I did about the world, but he never discussed it with me. I think he sensed I didn't want to know. I'm sure he was aware how famous and important Rafe was. He never said it, but I suspect he believed you wouldn't want to give up what you have here—" It was my turn to indicate the magnificence of the chateau with a wave of my hand—"for a two-room cabin and an outhouse."

McKenna blinked. She frowned and was quiet for a while. "I don't know," she admitted. "So, you didn't leave me, just Daddy. What did he *do?*" Before I could reply, she added, "It really destroyed him, you know. He was like a wounded animal."

"Believe me, since I've come back, I've questioned what I did that night. It was so long ago, and I was suffering from severe anxiety, so bad I was having hallucinations. I suppose it's possible that I was kidnapped like everybody thought, and my memories were wiped, but from what your father has told me, about the flight and the car, that seems unlikely. I should have stayed, no matter what. I should have stayed and had it out with him, whatever 'it' was, instead of running away. I can't express how sorry I am. I made an impulsive, disastrous choice."

McKenna looked down at her coffee cup. She lifted it, sipped, and made a face. "It's cold."

"Mine too."

"He tried to be a good father. I blamed him because he was the only one left to blame."

"I'm sure he made mistakes, but none of them were malicious."

She nodded. "Yeah."

"I only had one thing from this life after the car wreck," I said. "Your crayon. Your chartreuse crayon. I kept it until there was nothing left."

Her jaw clenched and her lips whitened a little.

I dried my eyes with my sleeve and we sat in silence, watching the iridescent birds, listening to the waterfall and below that, the masculine voices and laughter of the guards as they patrolled outside.

"You wanted to know where Brie's father is."

"Do you want to tell me?"

Tapping her index finger on the edge of her cup, she said, "He was one of Daddy's sentinels. I was starting to show, and I caught Grandmother staring at my stomach. I knew the gig was up. She would tell Daddy and he would fly into a rage, and Brie's father…well, if they figured out who he was, he would disappear in some horrible way. I had to do something. The next time I saw him alone, I told him I was moving on to another man, and I didn't want him around anymore. I told him if he didn't leave, I was going to tell Daddy that we'd had sex. It was actually pretty hard to make him go, even saying all that." She looked at me, her eyes brimming with tears. "He really did love me. I don't know why."

I can think of a few reasons.

"I finally had to hook up with another sentinel. The Sunday after, he wasn't there. He'd gone. Grandmother told Daddy and I was taken to the doctor. I overheard Daddy ordering his captain to bring in everyone for questioning and lie detection. I heard him say when he found out who knocked me up, he was going to tear that man's flesh off with his bare hands. I was right to chase him off."

"Sometimes people say things in anger they don't really mean, McKenna."

There was that puzzled look again. "You really don't know, do you? Daddy has a thousand faces, and he's hiding most of them from you. It's funny. You'd think, of all the people in the world, you would be the one who knows him best. It makes me afraid for you."

I had noticed how his men seemed to fear him but had assumed that was because he wasn't easy to please and it would be difficult to find another job if he fired them.

"It must have been a challenge, having a romance around here," I said.

"We found a way." Her voice took on a note of pride that didn't surprise me. She would have liked giving the proverbial finger to those who tried to muzzle her.

"One day, he and I were left alone for a couple of minutes. It was my sixteenth birthday and Daddy was taking me to Le Melon d'eau. He'd forgotten my present and went back inside. Brie's father and I were standing next to the limo. He told me he'd been falling in love with me from a distance for a long time. He tried to fight it. It's a death sentence for a sentinel to have unauthorized intimacies with women in his pledged family. I'd never realized. I didn't pay much attention to the sentinels. I hated them for their control over me, for what they symbolized. I hated everything about them. He was different. I did notice him after that, and eventually, I fell in love too. Brie has his hair."

I could see how much she missed him. I wondered where he was. Her first and only romance.

"I told Daddy if he tried to marry me off, I would kill myself. I guess he believed me."

That explained why she remained here at the advanced age of twenty-seven.

"Tell me about my uncle," McKenna said.

Stories rose to the surface, one after another. "When I was a child," I said, "there was a popular idea about special humans who could communicate with animals. They were called 'Whisperers.' Dog-whisperers. Horse-whisperers. Will is one of those. He can charm almost any animal. Deer aren't afraid of him. Once he gentled a black bear just by speaking quietly, and once, when we came across a fox in a bear trap, he managed to get it to stop snapping at him so he could open the trap and free its leg. I'll never forget how it lay there, wagging its tail and whining."

"You said he doesn't look like Daddy."

"He's tall and dark, but for his eyes. They're blue. Will resembles an American Indian at first glance, probably because his hair is long, and he has that kind of compelling nose and cheekbones, but his beard is dense if he doesn't shave. He's very strong. He could toss bales of hay that I couldn't even budge." I remembered then who I was talking to and tempered my enthusiasm. "He's not like Cordelia, Rafe, or Dillon. Will doesn't believe in the Christian God, or any god. He's quiet, soft-spoken, and he listens. Really listens. That's probably the most unique thing about him."

Blinking desperately, I lowered my gaze to my coffee cup, not wanting to weep over another man when speaking to Rafe's daughter, but I feared it was too late. I'd probably betrayed my true feelings.

She gave me a moment and I used it to shut the door on my grief. Then she leaned closer and lowered her voice. "Brie's father asked me to run away with him. If I tell you this, you can't ever tell Daddy. Do you promise?"

"I'll never repeat anything you don't want me to."

McKenna looked at me long and hard. I waited. Hope sprang, not because McKenna might tell me this secret but because I could see how she wanted to trust me.

"He was part of a group that hides women. Mostly women, and some men." She added, shrugging, "They aren't really free, but at least they aren't rich men's toys, displayed, handed around, or killed. No tattoos to pinpoint their every movement, whether they're white or black, their age, whether they've ever had a baby, and who knows what else?"

"That's what those tattoos do?"

"Yeah. I guess you got out before that started. Otherwise, Daddy could have found you in less than a day."

"There are groups that hide women? How do they do it?"

"I don't know. He said I would see."

"Oh, McKenna. This is so much worse than I imagined."

"I know Daddy downplayed it that day after church. I bet he never used the word ownership, but that's what it is. You're Daddy's property. He can do whatever he wants with you. Sell you. Kill you. Rape you. Starve you. Make you disappear. Give you to his friends. Whatever he wants. You're literally no different than a prize pig. Owned women are status symbols. Only a few men who can afford it, like Daddy, have women living openly in their houses."

"There are no families?"

"Ordinary men don't have wives and daughters. That's just a fading memory from before." Her hands clenched. "I don't know very much because Daddy sure as hell has never told me the truth. Brie's father told me some. Mostly, I've had to figure things out on my own." Drawing in a deep breath, she said, "It's different with you, though. You're not a status symbol to him. He loves you. If he didn't, you would have disappeared. He probably would have done away with you as soon as he found you."

I pressed my lower lip between my teeth, working to tamp down the sickening horror coursing through my blood. "How did this happen? McKenna, your father supports this?"

"I'm guessing he's one of the founders. I used to ask questions. He'd just say not to worry, that I would always be taken care of, and so would Brie."

"Why didn't you run? You had a way out."

"If I ran away with Brie's father, I'd be risking his life and the lives of every person in that group and everyone they might save in the future. Daddy would never give up searching, or let me go. I couldn't do it."

Some of the same reasons why I hadn't gone with Will.

"Oh, McKenna. I wish I'd been here."

She set her cup on the floor beside her chair and smiled. "I forgive you. I'm actually a little envious. You got something almost no other woman in this country got. Twenty-three years of freedom with a man you loved. No leashes, no masks, no humiliation. No house arrest. I can understand the feeling that you have to escape, just run and figure it out later."

"Thank you," I said, and this time I didn't try to stifle my tears.

"This may sound bizarre, but I *felt* you in my mind. I never felt like you abandoned me. I only said that because I was angry."

"Same here. I felt like I was seeing you, then I told myself I was imagining things. It was so vivid, though. Sometimes I had thoughts, and I swear they were your thoughts, not mine."

"Mother," she said, and I thrilled to hear her use that title, "don't ever take those pills Daddy wants to give you."

"I haven't. I refused and he hasn't brought it up since. I don't need them anymore. Why?"

"Those pills aren't what he says they are."

"They aren't?"

"No, Mother. No."

"I used them before, you know. You and I both did. Yours treated your ear infections and mine were for anxiety and panic. You only had a couple of ear infections after you started taking them, and my anxiety improved a little. Not enough, to be honest."

"I don't remember."

"You were only two."

"After you left, you didn't take the pills anymore, right?"

"That's right."

"What happened?"

"I never had another panic attack. The anxiety vanished too. I felt better than I had in a long time. I could concentrate again for one thing. Something I really hated about those pills was how they made it hard to think."

"Daddy took me for an exam not long after I hooked up with Brie's father. The doctor said I had ovarian cysts, and that's why I had painful periods. He prescribed a once-a-day pill. He said it would break them up."

I waited quietly, but inside, I was putting two and two together.

"Right away I felt sluggish. I lost any desire to stand up for myself, no matter what Daddy said or did. I turned into an obedient little robot. You may not get this because you weren't here, but that isn't me."

I smiled. "I've kind of figured that out, McKenna."

She nodded, shrugged, and smiled too. "I had just enough cognitive ability left to wonder what was happening, plus, my guy saw the change in me. He said I was acting like I'd had a lobotomy. He knew about the pills being given to women. He told me about them and showed me how to convincingly pretend to take them. In those days, Daddy insisted I eat breakfast with him. Dale would put one by my plate every morning. I'd act like I was popping it in my mouth and comment on the flavor, but I'd keep it behind my thumb. When nobody was paying attention, I'd get rid of it in a pocket or a tissue."

"So what happened?"

"My mind cleared up. And I got pregnant."

"You're saying your father or that doctor wanted you drugged. Why, McKenna? Why would anyone want that?"

"I was embarrassing Daddy, that's why. I was disrespectful and rude in front of the guards and sentinels, like a typical teenager. Well, maybe a little worse than typical. I was ten when I first started sneaking around. I wanted to have some control over my life, and it was fun evading the guards, fooling everyone. I shut Samson down when I left and switched him on when I came back, but once, after I started meeting with Brie's father, I guess he reactivated on his own and reported me when I came back in. Two days later Daddy had me on those pills. I know Grandmother put him up to it. If not for her, I could have convinced him I hadn't done anything wrong."

"Sometimes I feel weird after I eat. It's hard to think. And..." I stopped, realizing I was about to reveal too much, like that first night. I'd gone to Rafe's bedroom wanting to talk. It had been difficult, very, very difficult, to resist giving in to him.

"That's what those pills do, Mother. Make us good little girls."

"But I haven't taken any."

She scoffed. "He probably has Dale putting some form of them in your food. They would do that to me for sure, except I've learned how to con them. I pretend to be well-behaved so they don't suspect. You'd be better off agreeing to take them. At least then they won't put them in your food, and you can palm them like I do. Those pills will destroy your soul, Mother."

There must be different formulations of the damn things. One that increased sex drive, and others that didn't, or even did the opposite. Rafe wouldn't give his daughter a pill that would make her horny, certainly not after the embarrassment she'd already caused him.

Suddenly I remembered something one of the guards at the kennels said. *That powder should have tamed her.*

I wanted to ask more questions, but a voice interrupted.

"Meemah? Mommy?" Brianne stood in the doorway, holding the stuffed elephant I hardly ever saw her without. The poor thing had lost most of its plush fur, but she wouldn't hear of replacing it or having it redone. She'd had it since she was a baby.

I couldn't figure Brianne out. Sometimes she seemed younger than her age, which made sense, as she'd been cooped up in this prison without friends or social exposure. Other times, she seemed far, far older, mostly due to those unflinching brown eyes.

"Brianne. Come sit with us." I wiped away the last traces of tears.

"You're what's been missing this morning." McKenna held out her arms.

Brianne grinned and ran forward, snuggling into McKenna's embrace. "I couldn't find you. I looked everywhere. Granddaddy told me where you were."

I studied the edges and corners of the glass ceiling. I saw nothing, but that hardly mattered. Had he been watching us from some hidden camera? Maybe even using Samson to listen to our conversation?

I looked at my daughter, and my daughter's daughter.

Oh, McKenna. Be careful.

Chapter 14

I HEAR VOICES IN THE SEA.

The man leaned in. There was something about him that called to me, yet at the same time I was frightened.

I can swim without being cold and I don't need to breathe.

Shadows made a sinister mask of his face. *Once she has you, she never releases you. She will take all of you without remorse. The sea claims final possession.*

And leaves nothing behind, I said, my tongue knowing the phrase without help from my memories.

I rolled over, kicking off the blanket, aware of everything in the Deer Valley bedroom even as a fishy-smelling ocean lapped at the shore. The man gave me a kiss that would send me tumbling off course into a precarious future. He had Rafe's eyes, but his hair was dark, ill-cut, his cheeks covered with dirty stubble. His fingers were callused and grimy, his old-fashioned clothing threadbare.

The words we spoke were innocuous, yet fragrant with allusion. I could see he was drawn to me as I was to him. He wasn't very happy about it. Nor was I.

Now I was walking in the way of dreams, where it was hard to make headway, like toiling through mud. A small room, a wooden table, fire flickering in a hearth, and another man.

My brothers tell me that women have no souls, that they are barely above swine. If that is true, why am I angry? Pigs are not angry. Sheep are not angry!

This man resembled Will, but his eyes gave off a radiance that seemed unnatural.

Eamhair, he said.

Eamhair…Eamhair…Eamhair.

I sat up. The echo circled, faint and low, before dispersing.

Rafe continued to sleep beside me. He'd thrown off his covers too, and lay on his stomach. Blue-white moonlight pricked at the snarling lion etched between his shoulder blades.

I lay down, pulled the sheet up, and drifted into new dreams.

You are the woman my father said I'd find. The one who would bind me, make me a willing slave. When you leapt the bull, I had no more doubt.

Rafe had changed again. He was younger, bearded, scarred. His tawny hair flowed wildly.

For longer than can be dreamed, I am yours. Even death will never break our bond. Even in death, Aridela, I am yours.

For as long as the pyramids stand in Egypt.

I TRIED TO WAKE ONCE MORE WHEN SOMETHING ICY COLD PRESSED AGAINST MY arm. My left hand reached for my right arm, but something bore me down, deeper into insensibility.

When I did finally wake, someone had closed the blinds over the skylights and windows. Rafe sat in a chair beside the bed, gazing at me.

"What-what time is it?" My tongue felt thick and clumsy. I felt like I had drunk too much, but I hadn't had anything other than a glass of wine with dinner.

"About one."

"In the afternoon? Wh-what—"

"Easy, Erin." He rose, bent over me, and placed more pillows behind my head. "The doctor said you should rest today. Would you like some tea?"

"Why do I need to rest? What happened?"

"We just had to get your tattoo inserted. You slept through the whole thing."

"Tat—" I slapped my left hand over my right arm. "Ow, damn it." I craned my head. There it was, the intricate black marks, patterns, and dots, covered with some kind of greasy salve, five centimeters above the red, healing wound where I'd been attacked in the Quonset hut. "You didn't even ask—"

"You have to have it, Erin. It's the law."

"Bullshit! You want to track me like a cow!"

I knocked his hand away when he tried to touch my cheek. "Don't even," I said through my teeth.

Was this because he'd been eavesdropping on McKenna and me yesterday? I couldn't tell by looking at him. He was too good at hiding his thoughts.

He sighed. "Do I need to explain again?"

"Please don't. Our protection. Our safety. Do you think I'm an idiot?"

He rose, his jaw clenching. "It's interesting to me how you're such an expert on the world, though you've been holed up somewhere for twenty-three years and can't remember where you were, what you did, or who you did it with."

You know where I've been! I wanted to scream, but that would give Will's break-in away, and who knew what kind of sick revenge Rafe would take on him?

Or who you did it with. If that wasn't an accusation, my hair was purple.

"You drugged me, Rafe. You let some faceless asshole cut me open while I was unconscious. I never consented to this."

"It had to be done. I knew you wouldn't agree so I chose this way. The appointment to have your scars removed is next Thursday and I can't legally put you on the jet to see the surgeon without a tattoo."

I knew, and Rafe knew I knew, that he could do anything he wanted. I had flown home from the hospital without a tattoo.

I shook my head and said nothing more. At all. Soon he said he had to work and left.

No doubt about it, this new relationship with Rafe was going downhill fast.

I NEEDED TO VENT, AND DIDN'T HAVE ANYONE I COULD VENT TO. McKENNA MIGHT understand, but this was her father; as angry as I was, I didn't want to put her loyalty to that kind of test.

Rafe was calmly inscrutable, which further infuriated me. Why shouldn't he be? He believed he had me. No way to ever escape his reach again, no matter what I did. Totally worth a few days of anger on my part.

Tapping the window sill impatiently, I watched the front of the chateau until he came out. He pressed two fingers behind his ear, which McKenna had told me kept callers and holo images private. I could see his mouth move, but I heard nothing. When he reached the limo pod he spoke to the guard and got in. The guard closed the door; others took up their places inside and on the fenders, and the limo pulled away.

Alone at last. Except for Samson. Like God, Samson was everywhere, watching and listening.

This time, Rafe's office door was locked. "Samson?"

"Yes, Erin?"

"Would you unlock this door, please?"

"Certainly."

There was a soft click and I triumphantly entered, wondering if maybe Rafe had made a critical error when he ordered Samson to give me access to every-thing. Samson, with the unerring logic of an artificial intelligence, took those words literally.

I opened the sliding panel. The lights came on, illuminating the frozen dance between the bull and his human partner. Sunlight through the stained glass in the library sent showers of color into the room. I stepped from a pool of violet into a circle of buttery yellow and from that into a waterfall of scarlet. I turned my face up and closed my eyes, feeling color seep into my skin, and simply stood for a while before getting to the task at hand.

Retrieving the statue from the Victorian closet, I set her on the Turkish rug. "Here I am."

I felt silly, yet also comforted to speak to this figure who showed such love in the embrace of her child. "You'll never believe what Rafe did." I held up my right arm.

No otherworldly voice replied. There was no sound at all in here. Just thick silence and the intoxicating scent of old books.

Then I remembered. I had touched the statue when I heard it speak before. Hesitantly, I pressed my index finger to its forehead.

He lies.

Seconds ticked while I questioned my sanity. "I think you're right about that," I said.

I waited, but when I heard nothing more, I rose and crossed to a set of drawers next to the only area of the walls that had no artwork. When I opened the top drawer, I let loose a frightened squeak as the wall slid away and I found myself staring into yet another room.

How far did these rooms go? Did they wind through the chateau and into the mountain's core? I entered; recessed lighting came on. It was set up like a museum, with inky-dark hardwood floors and benches down the center. Art was everywhere, glass cases of artifacts and wall displays, each with its own focused light. I mentally identified two of the paintings as Caravaggios. They appeared to be originals, though I was no expert, and hung on opposite walls. *Medusa* on the south wall, *Bacchus* on the north.

Reconstructed frescoes hung on the east and west walls. There was a fortune in this room.

What about the cases? I scrutinized the largest, lit from within. Clay tablets were propped on artist's easels, each covered in some type of unfamiliar syllabary. They were dry and fragile, the edges crumbling. Several were damaged, two cracked clear through.

I started to speak, croaked, and had to clear my throat. "Samson?"

"Yes, Erin."

"Where are these tablets from?"

"Mr. Konstantinou discovered them on Crete, in a cave in their White Mountains. The Cretans call those mountains—"

"Lefka Ori," I said. Wait, how did I know that?

"Yes, Erin. He and his assistant smuggled them out to prevent the local government from confiscating them."

Hmm. I put aside the morality aspect of stealing artifacts from their mother country for the moment. "I don't suppose they've been deciphered?"

"Mr. Konstantinou hired expert linguists. Would you like to see the files?"

I switched my incredulous laugh to a cough. "Yes, I would. Is that possible?"

"Certainly. If you will return to the outer office, I have pulled them up for you."

"Thanks." *I bet Rafe never thought I would discover this. Oh, no, he wouldn't have granted full access if he'd had any idea how snoopy I can be.*

The rectangle on Rafe's desk had changed. It was now translucent. Above it, revolving slowly, was a holographic image of one of the tablets. Beside it floated an image of parchment, stylistically rolled at the top and bottom.

The title at the top of the virtual parchment was "Tablet One." Below that, the script read, *Death cannot stop the thinara king **** will **** me until *****

The note below the translation talked about the words the translator could not determine, and gave possible interpretations. His last asterisk detailed that Mr. Konstantinou provided the word "thinara," and added the translator's doubts about it being correct, as he had never seen that word in connection with ancient Greeks or Cretans.

I studied the holo-parchment, trying to match the English words with the symbols, but I finally gave up. Whoever Rafe hired to decipher these had his work cut out for him. The markings looked more like chicken-scratches than any kind of writing.

If the tablets came from Crete, that would mean the writing was Linear A or B. I guessed A, because of the translator's difficulty in cracking so many of the symbols. When I'd left Rafe, Linear A had only been partially decoded.

"Show me the next one, please."

The hologram dissolved and was replaced by another. Alongside it the parchment appeared, but this time it showed more pages stacked behind the first. I read all nine pages explaining how the translator came to his conclusions, along with reasons why some words couldn't be deciphered. The tenth page held the actual words he successfully translated from the tablet.

*One more completes **** a child will ***** (the translator noted this word was worn away but guessed it would have been something meaning "be born") *from the **** Velchanos god of **** her **** brother **** without her all will ***** (again the translator had to guess, as that part of the tablet was damaged. Logically, he wrote, it would have been either "fail" or "succeed.")

The third tablet spoke of the female child again.

*Should this child **** she **** blind and deaf to **** things **** to others will **** to her she will see **** what Potnia **** this holy child will **** moon*

The translation for the fourth tablet introduced a new topic.

*Our **** king gives **** does not Velchanos **** sacrifice **** death, no **** god **** wise men **** and **** punishment*

Velchanos, god of…something. I'd never heard that name or title, though Maya and I had been fascinated by ancient world myths. We'd even taken two online courses on the subject. It had been one of the things Rafe and I had in common, an activity that bonded us during those awkward teenage years.

"Who or what is Velchanos, Samson?"

"He appears to be a local Cretan deity who was later absorbed into the persona of Zeus. Very little is known."

I ordered the holograms to go on turning until I arrived at the last tablet and several words caught my attention.

***** so shall **** and **** will **** me from **** and **** into **** in an **** line will **** my **** will **** Eamhair of the sea who **** Shashi **** names are Caparina Lilith **** Morrigan seven times far into **** too will **** me **** will **** for as long as **** for **** are the earth **** yet **** will be **** will **** until these *****

The notes explained how the translator came up with the names by transcribing each symbol he'd already deciphered and extrapolating from them. He underlined his declaration that he couldn't be sure they were correct, but that Mr. Konstantinou wanted the work kept on file.

I rubbed my arms, suddenly cold. "Would you print out copies of these for me, Samson?"

"Certainly, Erin."

There was a brief hum and a sheaf of paper protruded from a slot in the desk.

Eamhair. Shashi. Caparina. Lilith. Morrigan.

The names were exquisitely familiar, as if I'd heard them moments ago, but I could put no faces with them.

My stomach growled. I'd been in here a long time. Brianne or McKenna might be looking for me. Rafe could return any minute. I would come again next time he left. I knew I'd hardly scratched the surface of what there was to discover in these rooms.

Perhaps I should just approach him and ask. He might surprise me and be willing to talk about the treasures he'd collected while I was gone. We used to share such things eagerly.

But those days were over. Will had gone to Rafe and told him about us. Rafe had never once admitted he knew that. Rafe might well know why I left him so long ago. If he did, he was keeping it to himself. There was not one iota of trust between us anymore.

He might order Samson to keep me out of here. I couldn't bear the thought.

The nursing mother sat where I'd left her, patiently waiting. Dropping down and crossing my legs, I placed the translations beside me and contemplated her face. What was left of it looked stern, but not cruel.

Once more I touched her forehead.

Go now.

Was the statue telling me to run away again? "I can't." I half-turned so my upper right arm was clearly visible. "He put a GPS in me. Do you know what that is? He's made sure I can't get away, and I won't leave McKenna or Brianne. McKenna is tattooed too."

The fingers of my left hand remained on the statue's forehead. I waited. Listened.

Go.

The voice was fainter, but no less firm. It was imperative. I was to go.

Maybe the statue simply wanted me to leave this room.

No. I was certain the message meant *leave this house.* Leave Rafe. Run. I would do it, if only there were a way to take McKenna and Brianne. If there were a way to do it and succeed. If there were a way to do it and survive.

The memory of stinking dog kennels and sadistic men flooded my senses. I wasn't about to put my daughter and granddaughter at risk for that.

I removed my fingers from the statue and pressed my palm to the slightly swollen place on my arm, hissing at the zing of pain.

"Tell me how," I said. "How can three females leave this house without getting caught?"

He lies.

The back of my neck prickled. *I don't have to be touching her to hear her voice.* The words, though not corporeal, were clear.

I waited, but there was nothing more. "Tell me *how.*"

Nothing.

Sighing, I rose and picked up the papers.

Take them. Almost inaudible now.

"I intend to." The statue was bossy if nothing else. I made sure everything was as it had been before, the drawers and panels closed, the statue in the closet, before I returned to the outer office.

My gaze was drawn to a narrow, targeted shaft of light rising from the case along the wall.

I edged closer. The light came from a sickle-shaped artifact, covered in intricate carvings. A weapon maybe, made entirely of old, off-white material. It looked like an elephant tusk; I was certain it was bone. There was no formal haft, but one end of the knife was smoothed and rounded, so I guessed that served as one.

Use it.

I spun, staring at the wall where the sliding door was hidden.

"He'll notice if it's gone," I said. "I can't see how to open this case, anyway."

No response.

I heard a door slam. I knew I couldn't let Rafe catch me in here, but the mystery of the weapon wouldn't release me. I pushed on the corners of the cabinet, then pulled. I tried to slide the glass.

As I had done at his desk, I inspected the molding, running my fingers over every bit until I came to the slightest depression, no bigger than the tip of my little finger. I pressed it and the glass slid open.

Hurry. Not the statue talking this time but my own mind, warning me. I lifted the knife. It felt warm; I nearly dropped it as a series of shocks ran through my arm.

I pushed the spot on the molding and the case closed. Hopefully, he wouldn't notice anything missing, at least for a while.

The pinpointed light vanished.

I almost ran out, barely remembering to tell Samson to lock the door after me. It wasn't failsafe. Samson could very well tell Rafe about me being in his office. Hopefully he wouldn't consider it important, since Rafe had given me permission to go anywhere I wished.

I zipped into the elevator and back to the main areas, pondering where to hide these items until I could figure out why I was supposed to take them in the first place.

Chapter 15

BRIGHT SUNLIGHT WOKE ME AND I RUBBED MY EYES, FEELING THE RAISED SCAR, BUT in an oddly deadened way because of nerve damage. Tomorrow I would say goodbye to the scars. The doctor had described the miniature lasers he used to accomplish this miracle with many before and after photos.

Yawning, I sat up, startled to discover Brianne standing beside the bed, staring vacantly.

"Brianne?"

No reply. Alarmed, I tried again. "Brie?"

"Return me."

I leaped out of bed and gripped her ice-cold arms. "Honey, wake up."

Brianne blinked and sagged. I caught her, placed her on the bed and covered her with blankets.

"Meemah?"

"I'm right here. You must have been sleepwalking."

"Mommy. Mommy."

"Shall I get her?"

"He's hurting her."

Someone was hurting McKenna? I immediately thought of Rafe, or one of the guards.

Brianne held out her arms and I hugged her. "Mommy," the child wailed.

"I'll check on her, okay? I'll bring her here."

Brianne nodded.

I ran to McKenna's room and flung the door open without knocking. The room was empty. The bed hadn't been slept in.

Though I methodically searched the house, I didn't find McKenna. Dale and Oliver both said they hadn't seen her. They asked their assistants, but everyone denied seeing McKenna.

I returned to her room and looked for clues. Finally, I crawled into the secret garden alcove and there I found a note stuck to the forest painting.

I've always been defiant and called it courage. Now I know what courage is. I'm going with Brianne's father. I'm hoping that somewhere there is a country where everyone is free. I want what you and Uncle Will had. I want freedom. I want that for Brianne.

I know you're only staying because of me. You'll never be free again as long as I'm here.

Go back to him, Mother. Take Brie. Her father and I will find you.

I crumpled the note in my fist. "I wasn't free, McKenna," I said. "I hid every day, from everyone except Will. That isn't freedom. I was not even happy, because I didn't have you."

No more children. No more love. The voice of the nursing mother in Rafe's office was tinged with sadness. *Not until they all lie dead. Then we will begin again.*

I FOUGHT TO CONTROL MY FRUSTRATION AND WEARINESS.

The house was once more swarming with detectives, along with some dangerous-looking men who didn't seem to have titles or rank or anything to show where they came from or who they worked for. The way they looked at me, even covered up, with that mix of lust and hatred I'd seen all too often since my kidnapping, made my flesh crawl, but when Rafe was near, their faces were carefully expressionless.

There was something about that hatred. It nicked at my brain, but I was too terrified to give it attention.

Detective Ronald Dempsey tapped his wrist then pressed two fingers behind his ear. He listened, nodded, then said, "As soon as you contacted us, we put a lid on the case, but this sort of thing has a way of leaking. It looks like the underground press has gotten wind of your daughter's disappearance."

Rafe paced, giving the detective a glance that sent concern for the man's safety scattering through my already shredded nerves. "If they know what's good for them, they'll back off." His voice was hoarse from shouting.

One of the non-titled, mysterious men stepped in. "There's nothing when we scan for her tattoo, sir. You're sure she had one and it was functioning?"

High five, girl.

Maybe, just maybe, McKenna knew how to make this work.

The note was in my pocket. I hadn't shown it to Rafe or anyone. I could only hope I was doing the right thing.

Exhausted, afraid, I closed my eyes and rubbed my lids.

"Would you like coffee, Mrs. Konstantinou?" Dale held out a cup.

"Thanks," I said.

I caught movement out of the corner of my eye and glanced into the hall. Brianne was there, one hand on the staircase bannister, staring at me.

Setting the cup on the table, I rose casually, saying, "I'll be right back."

Nobody responded or seemed to notice. I went into the hall. "Are you okay?"

Her nose was red, her eyes enormous. "He's hurting her! He's hurting her right now!"

"Do you know who your mother is with, Brie? Can you see him?"

She shook her head. "No, but I see his hands…"

"You've seen something?" Rafe had come up soundlessly behind me. I jumped.

"Come with me." He herded us to the music room and closed the door. "Tell me everything."

She crossed her arms and kept her mouth shut.

"Brie!" He grabbed her little shoulders. "You've got to tell me, do you understand? Don't you want to help your mother?"

"Rafe!" I hissed.

She stood defiantly, scowling, and refused to speak.

He paid no attention to me. "Brianne!"

I pried his hands off her. "You're making it worse."

"She sees things, Erin. She's never wrong. If she sees someone hurting McKenna, then someone's hurting McKenna."

The note felt like it was burning a hole in my pocket, but McKenna's words had seemed confident, like she knew what she was doing.

I thought I knew what I was doing that day by Dallas Creek.

I was torn. Brie wasn't lying. She was certain someone was hurting her mother, but showing Rafe the note could put McKenna, and maybe others, those who might be helping her, at risk.

What should I do?

Brie's eyes gleamed with tears. We stared at each other. She seemed to be asking the same question. *What should I do?*

There was no reason to trust Rafe. None. He'd proven that.

Nevertheless, I brought out the note. He'd said time and again that he loved me. I knew he loved McKenna. The repercussions could be bad, especially for me, but if McKenna was in trouble and needed help, so be it.

"You can't show this to those men," I said as he scanned the handwriting. "If you do, I swear I will hate you until the day I die. This is your last chance, Rafe."

He let out a shaky breath. "We have to tell them. They know everything there is to know about the insurgents. There is no way she could have done this on her own. You should have given this to me immediately. Do you realize he's probably the one hurting her? He must have gained her trust and now he's got her."

He walked to the door. "You don't have a clue. There are people out there who would do *anything* to harm me, including harming her, or you, or Brie."

"Rafe!"

He opened the door and left, striding purposefully.

I stared after him. "What have I done, Brie?"

She said nothing, but took my hand.

Five days passed. No news. No results. No change.

"Mrs. Konstantinou?"

I lifted my blank gaze from the smoldering logs in the fireplace. I'd come to one of the lesser used studies, wanting to be alone.

Dale stood in the doorway, working a dishcloth in his hands. "One of the groundskeepers is asking to see you about the lilacs on the south lawn."

"What? Oh, all right." It was the first time any of Rafe's employees had asked to speak to me; it made me slightly nervous. Then I scoffed. How quickly I was becoming inured to this world, where females were held in such contempt they couldn't even speak to a gardener. Not to mention I couldn't leave the house to see the damn lilacs. Not without a mask, a chain, and a sentinel.

A tall man, dressed in grubby overalls but with immaculately combed salt and pepper hair slithered past the cook as I fastened the requisite scarf across my face. He held out his hand. "My name's Geoffrey, Mrs. Konstantinou. Barrander. Geoff Barrander."

I didn't shake his hand. "How can I help you?"

Dale took this as his permission to leave, which he did, quickly.

The man dropped his hand to his side and the obsequious air vanished. "I work for the Sharpe Eye. Your story is fascinating. Missing for twenty-three years. I remember, you know. I was seven when it happened. It was all over the news. Your husband cried on TV. He begged you to come home."

"I don't understand. What is the Sharpe Eye? What does this have to do with the flower garden?"

"I'm sorry for that subterfuge. It was the only way I could get in to talk to you." Barrander reached in his pocket and pulled out a device that looked like a marble. He twisted it and a flat edge appeared. He placed it on the table between us, and as he did, I noticed a tattoo on the back of his hand. The letter J inside a black square outline that curled over on one corner. "I wish I'd known about your return before Mother's Day. It would have made the greatest inspirational piece."

Nervousness fell away beneath real fear. "You're a journalist? You've got to leave." Who knew what could happen? I might be blamed. "How did you get on the property? How did you get past the guards?"

Barrander's eyebrows puckered. "Don't you understand? The entire state cried along with your husband when you disappeared. Now he's a world-famous personality. He's the one who brokered the coalition with Ukrus, you know. Frankly, I'm amazed you haven't been inundated by reporters."

"It's a private situation. How did you get past our sentries?"

One thing after another with these supposedly highly-trained guards. At this point, I had no faith in them whatsoever.

"Forgive me, but your husband gave up his right to privacy, first when he went on television to advertise your disappearance, then again when he became the Lion of Aquilo and the president's principal advisor. Raphael Konstantinou has changed the world more than any war this country has ever taken part in." He frowned. "You do realize that, don't you?"

I didn't say anything, but his words made me very uneasy.

The reporter's eyes changed and his lip curled. Was that my imagination? It was gone almost instantly. Rafe's warning about subversives clamored through my mind.

Would someone hear me if I shouted? Was Dale in on this? Then I realized help was always close at hand. "Samson," I said.

"Yes, Erin?"

Barrander stepped closer and all I could see was the point of a knife a few centimeters from my nose.

"Never mind, Samson," I said.

"Erin, your heart rate has accelerated to one hundred sixty beats per minute. I see that there is an unauthorized male in your presence. I am calling the guards."

"I will slice your throat," Barrander said quietly.

"No, Samson," I said. "He's not unauthorized. Everything is all right. Don't call the guards."

There was silence, which was strange. Samson usually replied immediately.

"Yes, Erin," he finally said.

"All I wanted was a feel-good story. Men need to believe life is worth living."

"Please go," I said. "If I talk to you, I'll be killed. I told Samson not to call the guards, but he's very intuitive. You might be able to kill me, but you'll never get away."

I saw hatred in his eyes. I had seen this so much. What had females done to cause so much hate?

He gave a derisive bow, snatched up his device, and left. The front door slammed.

Would he make it? Ought I to follow and yell for the guards? I placed my hand on my throat, grateful to be breathing. Then I fell into a chair, trembling, and gave it over to fate.

Samson displayed drone images of reporters huddled at the main gate over a kilometer away. Rafe ordered him to lower the steel window and door screens. Even then, it wasn't enough to block out the buzzing of the extra drones. An answering service intercepted every incoming message, sifting through each one in case McKenna called.

I walked into the dining room the day after Barrander's intrusion to see Rafe standing at the table, his clenched fists pressed to the wood as he scrutinized a real, live newspaper. I hadn't seen one of those since I was a little girl, and even then, they were rare. I joined him, shock and anger coalescing as I absorbed the big black headline and story.

WIFE OF PRESIDENTIAL ADVISOR RETURNS ALIVE.

GROWN DAUGHTER DUPLICATES MOTHER'S DISAPPEARANCE.

A second valuable female attached to the preeminent Konstantinou family has disappeared. How do these well-guarded females keep escaping? Perhaps our cabalistic leaders are not as untouchable as we have been led to believe.

Scattered throughout the lengthy piece were four photos. The first was of me, before I'd vanished, at the height of my youth and fame. The second was of Rafe, half-hidden behind a forest of microphones as he begged for information about his missing wife. The third was a blurry photo of McKenna, taken as she climbed a staircase into Rafe's private jet, and lastly, the most famous photo of Rafe, smiling as he shook hands with the youthful leader of Russia—or Ukrus, as it was renamed after the subjugation of Ukraine and assimilation of many countries.

"I didn't tell that man anything." Fury and panic made my voice shrill. "How did he find out? He didn't even ask me about McKenna."

"I want to know how the hell he wandered all over the property and got in the house."

"I've told you I don't know. Shouldn't you be asking your guards those questions?"

"Oh, they're being asked."

His expression sent my anxiety soaring. I supposed I ought to consider myself lucky I wasn't being questioned the way they were. Rafe had been frighteningly enraged when Dale and I told him what happened, but he seemed to believe we hadn't revealed any family secrets.

"I haven't seen a newspaper in years. I thought they'd gone out of business."

"There are still a few underground papers. The Sharpe Eye is the worst. It's put out by subversives. Full of stupid conspiracy theories. They leave them everywhere because no one will buy them, and their lies keep people worked up. Did he tell you he was a reporter?"

"Yes, after Dale left and we were alone. He told Dale he was a groundskeeper. He was dressed the part. He looked at me with such hatred, Rafe. Do you know why?"

"Everyone who works for the Sharpe Eye is an insurgent. They hide in the shadows like rats, moving their presses from place to place. Sometimes we catch them, but they always seem to come back. They want to overthrow our country and cause anarchy. He probably hates you because he believes you're one of us. Which you should be. They sow chaos and destruction."

He snapped the paper, smoothed it, and pointed. "It looks like he managed to get his hands on McKenna's confidential therapy reports. No one knew she was addicted to yage but me and her therapist."

A moment later, he hissed, "Fuck," and left, shouting for Oliver.

I picked up the sheet. The paper was thin and grimy, like it had been recycled many times. Right after the part about McKenna being a hallucin user, the article stated, *One by one, the women closest to Salt Lake's charismatic religious leader disappear and he publicly proclaims his devastation. First his wife, now his daughter. One wonders if any fate, even risking capture by sex traffickers, is preferable to living with Mr. Konstantinou, as luxurious as that life must be.*

A source close to the family reports that Mrs. Konstantinou—Ms. Aragon, as she was known before her marriage—spent most of the last quarter century with her husband's brother, William Konstantinou, of Monticello.

Conspiracy theorists? One thing was for sure. They did their research.

OSCAR TORRES, A FIERCE-EYED HULKING MAN WITH AN UNRULY MOUSTACHE, HAD been promoted to the rank of captain after Will broke into the chateau. He came and went without asking permission or announcing himself, and had several times surprised and creeped me out with his shadowy presence, staring at me as if he would like to slit my throat or maybe other things.

Rafe had laid into him for not preventing the Sharpe Eye reporter from getting onto the property and lying his way into the house. Subsequent interrogations revealed that Barrander had deceived a guard, who he tricked into opening the gate with fake credentials. Then he pretended to work in the gardens like he belonged there, fooling others until a chance moment when no guards were close by. He used that moment to sneak up to the front door and lie his way past Dale.

The guard who had allowed him through the gate was sent away for "reconditioning" and Samson emotionlessly informed me that if he made another mistake, he could be dismissed, thrown into prison, or, if his next error was as egregious as this one, put to death.

I was certain Torres blamed me for his own negligence. Rafe warned him that one more mistake would mean his end, and embellished the threat with a few raging lines about how every man he hired was incompetent and useless.

Torres appeared in the entry to the study, inclining his head and removing his castro cap as I, then Rafe, noticed his presence.

"I need to speak to you, sir," he said, sending me a cold squint.

Suppressing a sigh of annoyance, I left the room and sought out Brianne, who was lying in the hammock in the sunroom, listlessly rocking it with one foot.

"How are you holding up?" I asked.

Her eyes were red. "I miss her."

"I know." I joined her on the hammock. "Me too."

I wanted to ask if she still thought McKenna was being hurt, but didn't. This was too raw for a ten-year-old to endure. "I think your mommy had a plan when she left. I bet she knows what she's doing. I'm going to try to have faith."

Brianne didn't perk up, but she said, "Okay."

"How about you read to me from *The Faerie Handbook?*"

"Okay." She left to get her book.

Rafe came in.

"Torres has been investigating the guards and sentinels. One of the guards left a week before McKenna disappeared. He had permission, but now we can't find him. It's suspicious, but he passed the Hawk course, in fact scored in the top ten of his class."

I shrugged impatiently. "What the hell is that?"

"A regimen we used for many years, until we formed a better replacement. All the older guards and sentinels have passed Hawk. It conditions a man, makes him loyal, in fact willing to die before betraying the family he serves."

"Maybe you should tattoo men, so you can keep better track of them."

Rafe scowled. "I really don't have the patience for your snide comments today. Did McKenna say anything to you about any of the sentinels?"

I thought about the man who had escorted her to the restroom at church. Then I thought about Brianne's father. *You can't ever tell Daddy,* McKenna had said, and I promised. I wasn't about to make that mistake again. "No, not a word." If only I knew McKenna's plan. But she had kept me in the dark.

Had that one sentinel been in church last Sunday? I'd been too upset to notice.

"Was McKenna friends with them? The guards?" I asked.

"They aren't here to make friends. Interacting with the females of the house is prohibited."

I had a feeling McKenna would take that prohibition as a challenge.

He turned away, tapping his wrist. A hologram appeared, blurry to me as I was sitting in the hammock.

"Who is this?" Rafe said.

"That really doesn't matter," a voice replied, disguised so thoroughly I couldn't tell if it was male or female. "The question that matters is, do you want to see your daughter again?"

I jumped off the hammock, staring at the holo. The image was scrambled too.

"Go public with your crimes," the voice continued. "Get the US out of Ukrus and rejoin the Western Alliance."

"When I find you, I'm going to skin you alive."

I seized his forearm. "He has McKenna."

"We don't know that."

"You might not want to threaten me," the voice said. "Release the women. Shut down Carnevale. Tell the world you're sorry for what you've done, and turn yourself over to us."

"You'll be dead in twenty-four hours," Rafe shouted.

"Then so will she." The holo blinked out.

Rafe shook off my hand and strode from the room, shouting for Torres.

I hurried after him, trying to tamp down my terror. "Rafe!"

He caught up to Torres and said something. I couldn't hear anything but one word.

Kill.

Chapter 16

I DROPPED INTO A PLACE OF DARKNESS, A COLD TWISTING PIT WHERE I COULD NOT feel or see. I could only hear distant screaming.

For the first time in nearly twenty-eight years, there was no McKenna in my psyche.

I carried her beneath my heart. My blood nurtured her. I talked to her and played music I thought would inspire her. I believed we could communicate in a way that was not understood by doctors or scientists. After I gave birth, I often wondered if that entangled union is what humans unconsciously seek for the rest of their lives, especially when they make love, until they grow older and realize sex is the least part of true intimacy.

The severing of that rapport was partly why Matthias's death was so hard to overcome. Rafe didn't understand, and I caught glimpses of impatience at my grieving. I could tell he thought it went on too long.

Transformative communion. That's what I dubbed this gift, given to women and the children that grow in their wombs.

Now I was cocooned in a chrysalis nothing could penetrate, not after the image I saw in my sleep. My daughter, nailed like Jesus upon a concrete bridge over a busy subpod route.

I even saw the heart segment, its chain dangling over her breast.

The chrysalis could only protect me for so long. It ebbed, leaving behind a pulsing crimson throb that increased with each breath into a searing white-hot brand.

I felt Rafe, but I didn't want his comfort. I struck him and tumbled to the floor.

Blood of my blood. Heart of my heart. Mind of my mind. We remained connected in some fashion even when I was with Will. Every now and then, there were flashes of her face, laughing, weeping, angry, bored. Even more rarely, a random thought I believed was hers. I had always known she was alive. I knew now she was not.

She'd said the same thing. She felt me. She knew I was alive. She knew I thought of her.

I only just found you again.

Blood of my blood. Heart of my heart. Flesh of my flesh.

She was gone.

THE CALL CAME A FEW HOURS AFTER RAFE TRIED TO CALM ME WITH WATER, WITH brandy, and with patient, logical declarations that dreams were meaningless.

The detective in charge of the investigation, Ronald Dempsey, was at the gate.

We were dressed and waiting when he reached the front door. His face wore uneasy sympathy, betraying the truth before he spoke a word.

"There's no good way to tell you." He glanced at the fireplace. "Your daughter has been found. A man was discovered nearby, also dead, stabbed multiple times. We've identified him, and our records show he worked for you, sir, long ago. He's been missing a little more than ten years."

I fell bonelessly into an armchair. The room whirled. I'd known, but until the words were spoken, I could tell myself I was wrong.

The detective cleared his throat and shifted from one foot to the other. "We're sure it's her, Mr. Konstantinou, but as next of kin, we need you to make a positive identification."

The statue warned me. I was supposed to take McKenna and Brianne and go. It's my fault she's dead. My fault. But how? How could we get out? The house is guarded by men, by dogs, by drones. Our tattoos would reveal our location. Rafe would send his sentinels after us.

The reporter got in. Will got in.

I should have tried.

My fault.

My fault.

"Erin? Erin."

"What?"

Rafe had on a jacket and was leaning over me.

"I'm going with Dempsey. I'll be back soon. Will you be all right?"

Is that snow?

It *was* snow, blowing off the eaves even though the sun was shining. Tiny flakes dancing like party glitter.

Rafe's hands clenched. I sensed the urge to kill and the desire to rescue, battling within him.

Dempsey pulled a clear bag from his pocket. "Was this hers?"

Before Rafe stepped between me and what Dempsey held, I saw it, lying forlornly at the bottom of the bag. McKenna's segment of the heart necklace Rafe had given her on Mother's Day, stained with blood.

"I have a car," Dempsey said.

"We'll take mine." Rafe swung around. "It will be faster."

"I'm coming."

"No, Erin. You stay here."

"I'm coming with you. Don't try to stop me."

Rafe sighed and nodded.

RAFE REFUSED TO IDENTIFY MCKENNA FROM THE HOLO SCREEN. "I WANT TO SEE her." Everything about him was predatory—the sneer, the clenched jaw, the turbulent fire in his eyes, the way he was stalking rather than walking.

We waited in the stale-smelling morgue for an attendant to locate the wall chest. Dempsey touched my forearm. "Let your husband handle this. It isn't the way you want to remember her."

Adrenaline surged, subsided, then surged again. *It will be the last time I can ever see her,* my mind shouted. Yet I nodded.

Rafe entered the inner sanctum with the medical examiner.

"Could I get you some coffee?" Dempsey asked.

I shook my head, hardly hearing.

When Rafe returned, he staggered to a chair and dropped into it as though his bones had melted.

"I'm sorry, Mr. Konstantinou," Dempsey said. "Were you able to identify her?"

I stared from one to the other. Dempsey's face exuded sympathy as he handed Rafe a cup of water. Rafe's hands shook. Water spilled over his chin and spotted his white shirt.

"Erin? Erin?" The voice was far away and raspy at first but gradually the ringing in my ears faded and I opened my eyes. Dempsey had caught me before I hit the floor. Rafe frowned into my face, fanning me with his hand.

"There's a storage room," Dempsey said. "She can lie down. I'll get her something. Maybe I can find some brandy."

They assisted me into a dim room, cluttered with shadowed furniture, a dusty old desk, dented filing cabinets, and a couple of grimy bioplastic chairs. Rafe helped me lie down on a backless bench. Dempsey left on a search for alcohol.

Rafe dropped into one of the chairs.

"Was it McKenna?"

He stood abruptly. "Her cheeks were mangled. Her skull fractured. There was a gun; whoever did this wanted to let me know that guns can still cause a lot of damage even if they don't shoot." He sounded incredulous.

I couldn't breathe. I tore the mask from my face, crushed it in my fist, and threw it on the floor.

Shuddering, I leaped off the bench and ran to him, needing one of his all-encompassing hugs, needing the warmth and life in his body. He was the only other person on earth who could possibly understand. He must feel even worse than I did, for he hadn't abandoned his daughter. He'd been there, at least at the periphery, every day of her life.

As I pressed against him, I felt him recoil. His hands lifted; he shoved me so hard I stumbled and fell, bashing my elbow on a corner of the desk.

"Don't touch me," he said through lips drained of color. He paced, stepping over me like I was nothing more than a pile of debris. He struck the wall so hard he punched a hole in the plaster and blood sprang from his knuckles. "Goddamn it! I'll kill that son of a bitch. I'll kill him!"

Dempsey rushed in, yelling for help as I pulled myself off the floor. Two uniformed policemen joined the fray. My husband was forcibly conducted to another room.

I dropped onto the bench.

"Mrs. Konstantinou?" It was Dempsey, back to check on me. "Are you okay?"

"Who was the man you found?" There was no use asking if he was Brianne's father. Nobody would know unless they ran the DNA, which I didn't think Rafe would allow.

"Your husband said he looked familiar, but he wasn't sure."

"Did he have red hair?"

"Why, yes. How did you know?"

I shook my head.

"Don't worry. The doctor will give your husband a euphoria shot. He'll be fine. Terrible shock for both of you." He patted my forearm, at first kindly. Then his hand began to rub. I jerked away and glanced into his face. I saw what was there before he had time to hide it.

"Get away from me." My voice sounded like it was coming through a tunnel.

His cheeks reddened. He fetched a cup of ice water and handed it to me. "We'll be right across the hall." He bent and retrieved the mask. "Here," he said emotionlessly. "You had better put this on."

I took it from him and he hurried out, leaving the door ajar.

I dropped the mask on the bench and closed my eyes. The chain around my wrist jingled. I heard Rafe cursing.

"Did you see that girl they brought in?"

I opened my eyes. Two young men in lab coats had entered the hallway and were strolling towards me. One loosened his tie.

"No, but about two hundred men did, from what I hear. She was nailed up over the Parley's Canyon sub rails."

"I was there when they brought her," the first said. "Somebody had a real hard-on for that one."

"I heard about that. Raped with imagination." The second man didn't sound particularly horrified. In fact, if anything, his tone carried respect.

They came abreast of the storage room. "Her earlobes were slit," the first one said. "Dempsey said it was for the earrings, said she came from a rich family. That's a given. Her face looked like an animal got ahold of her, but the coroner said the saliva was human."

"He must have thought her some tasty dish, huh?" They passed on and turned a corner.

"He couldn't stop at one bite."

"Guess she gave him some cheek."

"Oh, you're bad, man. You're so bad." The voice shook with laughter.

"What do they expect? Assholes."

A door slammed and all was quiet.

I simply stared, I don't know for how long, or at what, until my stomach let me know it could take no more. I retched and threw up. Denial drifted into hopeless, unbearable belief.

Rafe had seen the truth in my eyes when I reached so desperately for him. I might have been able to go on hiding things, but McKenna's note made the truth all too clear. She wanted me to leave Rafe and go back to Will.

That must have been so painful to read. It must have felt like such a betrayal.

He could no longer deny it was Will I needed. Now he believed it of McKenna, too.

Chapter 17

THE MORNING OF MCKENNA'S FUNERAL WAS COOL AND MISTY. I STOOD ON Brianne's right, holding her hand. Cordelia stood on her left.

After Rafe was given some calming drug at the morgue, he'd apologized. "Don't be sorry," I said. "That's the first honest emotion I've seen from you since the day I woke up in the hospital."

Since then, we'd avoided each other. Even now, he stood on the opposite side of the grave, stiff and morose in somber black, eyes hidden behind opaque sunglasses. Dillon stood on his left. Church members, business associates, and many of Rafe's Aquilo partners pressed in around him.

But that was nothing. The president stood at Rafe's right hand, next to his vice president, the secretary of state, and several senators. A crowd of armed military circled. Security drones buzzed overhead beneath the invisibility shield provided by the thermal infrared tower. Hopefully, there would be no news leaks for insurgents and underground journalists to exploit.

Cordelia, Brianne, and I were the only females. We wore encompassing black masks and long, loose black dresses. Chains of white gold and diamonds, any of which would have made the fortune of a man brave enough to steal one, ran from our wrists to the hands of the two sentinels behind us.

I didn't care. I couldn't muster any outrage. Even if I could, I would not mar McKenna's funeral with a scene.

For the first time I saw the Aquilo symbol Rafe adopted when he took over the organization. Several of the men had it embroidered on the breast pocket of their coats. He'd discarded the lightning bolt with the arrowhead, but his replacement was similar—a trident, like the Greek god Poseidon's. All three prongs had deadly-sharp, arrow-like points. The new logo still resembled a penis as a weapon, but now there were three instead of one. Behind the trident was the cyclone he'd mentioned my first night back.

The minister was reading from his Bible. Something about bodies being killed and souls living on. He held a clump of dirt over the casket as the attendants lowered it into the ground. I tuned him out, hearing only the words *confess, before men, son of man,* and *paternal God.*

McKenna would have despised this service. There was nothing in it to speak to her as a woman.

A federal law, passed thirty years ago at the height of the population explosion, required cremation. There was no more room for cemeteries, and in fact many bodies were exhumed and burned to create more living space. But, as with everything, the rich and powerful had different laws. This cemetery was a beautiful swath of green rolling hills set apart for those of importance.

Halfway through the sermon I looked over the heads of the men on the other side of the grave, and nearly cried out as my gaze landed on Will, standing on a knoll beneath the branches of a tree, beyond the ring of security and obscured by mist. It didn't matter. I knew him.

I locked my gaze on him rather than the casket or the minister or these men I didn't know.

Go home, Will. Forget about me.

The only thing keeping me from falling into despair was Brianne. I knew McKenna was counting on me to protect her, maybe even save her.

I'd always pictured God as a grizzled white-bearded colossus in flowing robes. His blazing eyes matched the flaming sword of vengeance in his fist. I imagined Jesus the same way, only younger. Then came the disciples, the Holy Ghost, and the major angels. Lucifer, Michael, Gabriel, Raphael, and Camael. Only two women stood out from the New Testament. Mary the mother of Jesus and Mary Magdalene, each at her own end of the extreme spectrum. The pure, unsullied eternal virgin and the dirty prostitute. Nothing in between.

But long, long ago, according to *Secrets of Bronze Age Goddess Cults*, religion was dominated by women. Women, not men.

Don't do it, McKenna, I thought. *Don't kneel before their male god and ask forgiveness for sins you never committed.*

The group was focused collectively on the casket, the handfuls of earth that fell with hollow thuds. Oliver wiped his nose with a handkerchief.

Only Brianne wasn't watching the burial of her mother. Her eyes were centered gravely on me.

 legs stretched out, wrists hanging limply over the arms of the wing chair. Dillon hovered behind her, his gaze darting from Rafe, who leaned against the corner of the fireplace, to me, on the couch.

"My granddaughter murdered," Cordelia muttered. "And Brianne hasn't said a word since McKenna was found." She dabbed the corners of her eyes with a handkerchief. "This—wasn't—supposed to happen any longer, Raphael!" She glared at him as though he'd had full knowledge and allowed the atrocity. "You swore those days were over!"

Her glare settled upon me. She sniffed and jerked the hem of her skirt closer around her knees.

I knew what she was thinking. Their lives had been just fine until I reappeared from the dead. I had polluted Rafe and caused McKenna's death.

Remembering McKenna's note, I could not say she was wrong.

It must be so hard for Brianne to wake up in this house. Even I heard McKenna's voice through the suffocating silence. How much worse was it for her clairvoyant daughter?

"Is the FBI doing everything it can?" Dillon asked. "They've got to turn this state inside out. The whole country if necessary. It isn't only a crime against us, her family. It's an attack on the framework of our society."

"They say they are." Rafe paced to the plate-glass window that looked out over the front garden in the circular drive. The blooms that had been flourishing were now wilted. Maybe the last few nights had been too cold for them.

"Any new information on the guards and sentinels?" Dillon asked.

"I made a clean sweep. Sent them all for restructuring. I've brought in a whole new cadre. These have been through Black Scorpion Therapy."

"Ah." Dillon nodded. "Good work, son. There's no way any of them will disappoint you."

"I never thought I needed that level of security. I have been far too complacent."

Before I could ask what Black Scorpion Therapy was, Cordelia changed the subject. "We couldn't even have an open casket." She pressed the handkerchief to her eyes.

I had been trying to block the memory of what had been done to McKenna. Now it rushed in, an agony of raw emotion.

A strong drink would be helpful right now.

She continued her tedious complaints and my mind wandered. The night I'd given birth to McKenna, cramps had plagued me for hours. Rafe made love to me slowly and gently. Afterward, I drifted to sleep against his chest, wondering how he understood a pregnant woman's needs so well.

My water breaking and contractions woke me just after midnight. I timed them as Rafe's driver brought the car. Two minutes apart.

McKenna slipped into the world twenty minutes after we reached the hospital. I hardly worked up a sweat. Rafe said he felt cheated because he didn't get to coach me, nor did he have the opportunity to experience the stereotypical resentment women showered upon their husbands during labor. He'd smiled, leaned down, and kissed my forehead.

Somehow his kiss that night, after I delivered our daughter, held a different message than any before. It communicated love in a way words never could. In the recovery room, he rested his cheek on my shoulder as I encouraged McKenna to nurse for the first time. He ran one finger over the dark fuzz on his child's head and sighed his contentment.

"Erin?"

Jolted into the present, I blinked and realized I was weeping. "I'm fine," I said, wiping my cheeks and repeating by rote what I'd said for days.

Rafe knelt by the couch and clasped my hand. "Erin."

No, not tenderness. I couldn't take that. I'd cry myself into a puddle. "I'm okay. Were you saying something about Brianne?"

Cordelia rubbed her eyes. They were red and watery. She looked her age today. "I said it will be a miracle if we can ever find a man willing to marry her. There isn't a male in this country, or even the world, who won't hear of her shame."

"Her shame?"

"Are you being deliberately obtuse? This taint will follow her the rest of her life."

I shot off the couch. "*What* did you say?"

"You may not like the truth. I don't care for it either, but that's what people talk about, and their sons listen." Her lips turned down at the outer corners and the lines around her mouth deepened.

Rafe sighed and rose.

"How *dare* you! Get out. Get out of this house!" I faced Dillon. "Get her out of here before I tear her in half!"

"Erin." Rafe imprisoned me in his arms. "Hush. Hush, now." He pressed my head to his chest.

"No. Stop it. I won't listen to this. I won't have it."

"You can't change human nature," an unrepentant Cordelia said.

"Can't anybody shut her up?"

Was she right? Would Brianne be marked by the crime committed against her mother? Would people make fun of her, gossip behind her back, write derogatory articles about her in their underground papers?

Cordelia sat in our living room like a queen on her throne. Dillon remained behind her, the ever-present jester.

"Fuck this," I said.

Her cheeks suffused. "I thought I told you—"

"Fuck this, and fuck you." I ran out of the room before it could get any uglier.

I DIDN'T EXPECT RAFE TO COME AFTER ME, AND HE DIDN'T. HE WOULD DO THAT later, after Cordelia left on her own terms. She would probably stay longer now, just to prove she commanded more loyalty from her son than I did. No doubt it was true. I didn't care.

Brianne was asleep, her elephant tucked under her chin. I eased her door closed and made my way to Rafe's office. I needed to put my hands on the stone statue and ask forgiveness. She had warned me, ordered me to leave, but I allowed fear and inertia to hold me in place.

The office door was unlocked. Intending to open the secret panel, I crossed to the desk, but something was different. The screens above the desk were not blank. They were translucent, the light within them pulsing. I touched one. Nothing happened, nor when I waved a hand in front of them. I pressed my palm to the black rectangle on the surface of the desk. Nothing.

"Samson, are these on? How do I get them to work?"

"They're locked, Erin. I cannot control Mr. Konstantinou's private files. I can access the archaeological records if you wish, but not his personal documents."

"Something is running."

"He may have left the screens on. Mr. Konstantinou prohibits me from seeing inside his office when he's working. He values his privacy."

I ran my hand over the rectangle again, feeling like it was the brains of the computer. *Do something, you stupid piece of crap.*

A click preceded a blossoming of color from the screens. The whole room was speckled in violet-blue-green incandescence. I drew back, surprised. Had it responded to my thought? Would Samson shut everything down now, or alert Rafe?

The bookshelves on the wall to my right swung out then swiveled backwards. The wall became a screen.

Two words appeared in fancy cursive and floated horizontally.

The women.

"S-scroll?" I tried.

With a soft susurration that convincingly imitated the crackle of old-fashioned paper, the screen turned a page, at first slowly then speeding up until I said, "Stop."

She is my Goddess, my queen, my wife. Our daughter will be queen after her.

What was this? Had Rafe written it? Who did it refer to? What the hell?

"Scroll," I said again. The pages rustled, one after another.

"Stop. Go back."

Eamhair. Shashi. Caparina. Lilith. Morrigan.

Aridela. Oh yes, Aridela.

I have known them. I see them laughing, crying, making love to me, giving birth to my children. Somehow, they all become Erin.

Those names were on the translations of the tablets I'd read nearly a month ago, but I had already known them. I dreamed of women with those names. Perhaps Rafe dreamed of them, too. Especially Aridela. Seeing it brought back how I used to wake him out of nightmares where he called out that name in his sleep, then got angry when I asked who she was.

The crescent scars over my pulses throbbed, just once but quite painfully, and a new dream played out before my eyes. A waking dream. I sensed a presence behind me. Invisible but palpable. A female presence. I wanted to turn but I couldn't. I was frozen.

Right before me, Rafe took shape. I had to look twice but it was Rafe, though his hair was longer, his skin darker, marked by wicked scars, and his aspect more intimidating. Instead of his customary crisp shirts, trousers, and ties, he was dressed in a knee-length tunic and leather sandals. The vision or hologram melted, much like the old hallucination I used to have of the youth who dissipated into copper dust. Another man took the place of the first, wearing the habit of an ascetic monk. Again, the basic form and face was Rafe. Before I could take in any but the most superficial details, he became a priest from a later era, one with a singularly arrogant cast. Another shift, and I gaped at a pale, bearded blond wearing a Turkish kaftan and turban.

As that Rafe vanished, I saw the figure I'd dreamed of the night Rafe had me tattooed. The impoverished man who spoke of the sea as a living female.

Each had unique characteristics separate from the previous presence, yet each was also Rafe. The eyes were the same in every form, green and long-lashed.

Then there he was, my Rafe in his twenties, the seductive, charming up-and-coming headliner, vivid and real then fading away, imbuing me with sad memories of happier times.

I returned to my senses. I was in Rafe's office. I heard the distant voices of the guards outside, and I stared at the translucent wall, still displaying the last lines I'd read.

Eamhair. Shashi. Caparina. Lilith. Morrigan.

Aridela. Oh yes, Aridela.

I closed my eyes and dropped to the floor, exhausted, bewildered, sure of nothing.

Wake, Mother.

I looked up. "McKenna?"

Color burst on the wall screen. A different page of writing appeared without any input from me.

Something beyond reality was happening. Rafe's computer was being manipulated. It was not me, and Samson said he couldn't. I didn't think Samson could lie.

They all live in Erin. I see her in them at night when I dream. I see them in her when I'm awake.

They tell me we have come full circle.

I don't know what it means. Am I losing my mind?

I stared until the words blurred. When I first saw those names, my mind instantly assumed he was writing of other women he'd been with. Now I realized that wasn't it at all. In his mind, *I* was Eamhair and Shashi. I was Lilith and Morrigan.

Morrigan. That distinctive name stood out from the others. I searched for the reason and soon remembered. Morrigan Ramsay was the author of the book, *Secrets of Bronze Age Goddess Cults*.

Kaleidoscopes erupted. The scars burned intensely. I jumped away from the desk. The crescents were swelling, turning bright red.

As though ghosts were in the room, I heard sighs that became names. *Chrysaleon, Menoetius, Selene, Themiste, Iphiboë, Helice.* Each name had a face, and I knew them. I knew every one of them.

Cailean, Taranis, Ula, Meraud, Rhalanse.

Nuren, Shashi, Halldór.

A young woman appeared before me, leaping over the curved horns of a huge black bull, touching his back, propelling off, and landing in the arms of her half-brother.

The statue in the hidden room, come to life.

Aridela.

She slipped inside me. My eyes looked out from her eyes. Together we examined the crowd. Two men stared, one angry, the other awe-struck, lifting his dagger in salute. Two men, who would go on to love the princess of Crete. One would die for her, the other would kill.

Aridela gave them those names. Chrysaleon. Menoetius. I knew them as Rafe and Will.

The panel door into the secret room slid open and McKenna stepped out, wearing a sleeveless white gown bound across the breasts with silk ribbons.

They did love her, Mother, but Chrysaleon betrayed her. He murdered his brother. He murdered Aridela. He destroyed Crete and decimated the lady's worship. Who knows of her now? Who is she? A fanciful story from the ancient past, nothing more. A myth. The word itself declares it fiction.

"Why did you have to die, McKenna? Why do I have to lose you right after finding you again?"

You never would have done a thing if I'd stayed. Guilt would have forced you to surrender the rest of your life to me. Now, you can do what you're meant to do. My death sets you on your path. You will see.

She came closer, the hem of her gown fluttering. I saw that her feet weren't touching the floor.

"What is Rafe hiding?"

For thousands of years, he has been forced to follow and suffer, strive to possess, and fail. His curse has been to remember, to be punished for what he has done. This time, Athene keeps his memories hidden. He sees the lives he has lived only in dreams. He is drawn and repelled by them; they feel real, but he does not believe they are real.

"Why?"

If he knew who Maya truly is, he would kill her. He cannot know who Brianne really is, or Will. And you, Mother. You most of all. He cannot know who you truly are. She keeps his memories hidden to protect you and your followers, but the past lives are so strong within him, they try to break through when he sleeps.

"He says I'm these women. I've also dreamed of an Aridela, and an Eamhair, and the others. Am I having the same dreams as Rafe?"

Your dreams are your own memories. He dreams his. Take Brianne and go, Mother. Hurry. If you and Brianne are here when his memories return, he will kill you, or arrange for you to be killed.

Fear came over me in waves. *I've been tattooed. Brianne is ten years old. The house is guarded. Any woman caught outside without permission is arrested. I woke in a dog kennel. Those men. I can't, I can't, there is no way. What if Brianne wakes in a dog kennel? What if the guards take a liking to her?*

"I can't," I said. "I *cannot* risk Brianne by taking her from this house. This is the only place she's safe. Rafe has told me how criminals will hurt anyone he cares about. They did it to you, and I have seen their hate. I can't. Don't ask it of me, McKenna."

There was something else. I didn't believe Rafe would kill me. Deep down inside, he might hate me. He would manipulate and imprison me without blinking an eye, but kill? Nor would he harm Brianne. He couldn't.

McKenna rose higher. I saw her anger. *Now is the time for courage. Throw off the lies you have told yourself. He is not what he seems. He never has been. Be stronger than your fear.*

Flaming heat came off her. Her mouth opened, wider and wider until it resembled a scene from a horror movie. The room became a vortex.

I was in the center of a tornado, clinging to the floor. My flesh tore off and vanished into the cyclone. My skeleton hands came up to my skull. I heard the click of bone on bone.

Then I heard and saw no more.

"Erin? Wake up."

Don't let him—

I felt myself being lifted and shaken.

Fool you again.

The last thing I wanted was to be shaken. Through the throbbing in my head, I cried, "Stop," or thought I did, but the word came out more like a groan.

"Erin, open your eyes."

I did, squinting, though the light was muted. "Where am I?"

Rafe was bending over me. "My office. What happened? Are you sick? I couldn't find you. Samson told me where you were."

He helped me sit. Everything looked normal, though I was certain something extraordinary had happened. Propping me against the bookcase, he said,

"Stay there. I'll get water." He disappeared, coming back a moment later with a glass. "Here. Take this. It's aspirin."

I opened my mouth and he placed a pill on my tongue, then immediately held the glass to my mouth. Too late, I felt the shape. And it wasn't water he gave me, it was brandy. He tipped the glass and I swallowed to avoid choking.

I protested through a coughing fit. "That wasn't aspirin."

"Don't be angry. You're having a panic attack. You need that pill."

He set the glass on the desk. "Better?"

The rapid effects washed gently around the edges of my ability to focus, bringing a fuzzy sensation that would get worse by the moment. Before McKenna warned me, I'd blamed the dullness on too much alcohol, but no. He'd been drugging me. I could remember at least three times I'd felt this way since coming home from the hospital.

The instant of clarity was subsumed in a murky cloud. I nodded. "Yes."

He hauled me to my feet.

I stared at the desktop. The black glass was spotless and empty. The panels were dark. The wall was again ordinary bookshelves.

"Where are the pages?"

"What pages?"

"On the wall." Awareness briefly rode back in on a spurt of anger. "Have you hidden them? It's too late. I know what they said."

"You must have had a nightmare." Rafe guided me to the leather chair and pushed me down. "Things seem so logical and clear when we're dreaming, then we wake up and find there's no way to make sense of them. Surely you understand that, Erin."

"Don't patronize me! I *saw*." I waved my hand. I slammed my fist against the rectangle. Nothing happened. The panels remained blank. The bookshelves didn't budge.

Rafe crossed his arms, his face betraying hints of resigned indulgence. I hated that.

"What are you trying to do? Maybe I can help."

"The pages…I read them on your wall. Turn your computer back on."

"I haven't worked in here since before you came home. My computer's been shut off. Erin, I heard you scream as I was coming up the stairs. I found you out cold on the floor." He took a step back, studying me intently. "I'm calling the doctor."

I tried to piece together the last few hours. After Cordelia's stupid announcement that Brianne would be rejected by every male on earth, I cursed her and left the room. I came here seeking comfort from the statue.

Then what? I'd had a dream. McKenna.

Why did the sight of Rafe fill me with fear?

He will kill you.

"What about your secret room?" I searched for the depression that would open the hidden door, half-afraid it would be gone, another figment of my imagination, but there it was. I pushed, and the panel slid open.

I faced him, watching for his reaction.

"Yeah?" Shrugging, he crossed to the opening and stepped through the hanging beads. The lights came on around him. "So?"

I followed. Everything was as I remembered, the bull and its leaper, the incense burners, the candles, and the bookshelves, fireplace, tables, and chairs in the attached library.

It was becoming increasingly difficult to concentrate. The urge to give in to him was taking over.

"I keep artifacts in here, partly because when McKenna was little, she got into everything, and partly to protect them from thieves. Over the years I've picked up several extremely rare antiquities. How did you find it?"

"I couldn't sleep one night and came up here."

"If you'd told me, I would have given you a tour. You're not a thief, are you?" His eyes twinkled. They were awfully pretty, those eyes. I wanted to be closer to them.

Wait. No way I could have dreamed those phrases or faces. What faces? My mind could bring forth little but color and mystery, a sense of questions, but I couldn't remember what they were.

"It wasn't real?" I stared around the room as my righteous outrage deflated.

He spoke softly. "Honey, I don't know what you saw or thought you saw."

"What about this?" I opened the Victorian closet and heaved out the mother and child. I was trying to hurry and lost my balance. I dropped her. She landed on her side with a distinct thud.

"Careful." Rafe squatted. He tilted her, eyeing her critically before setting her upright. "We dug her up on Cyprus a few years ago. She's early Bronze Age, about 1700."

"Why is she stuck in the closet?"

His brows drew together. "She's in a dark, dry place, on her side in case of earthquake. Better than a table she could fall off of."

Biting my lip, I swung away and pulled *Secrets of Bronze Age Goddess Cults* from the bookshelf. "Is this yours?"

"All these books are mine. What's the point of these questions? You've always known my interest in archaeology."

I wanted to punch him in his high-handed, arrogant face, but it was a dull, faraway sensation. "I came to your office. Those displays on your desk were turned on. The bookshelves on the wall changed to a...computer screen. I saw stuff. Like a dream journal, or a stream of consciousness, or...names. Of women, I think. Have you become a novelist, or are they women you've been involved with?"

Rafe stared at me from his position in front of the statue. His frown communicated puzzlement but as the seconds ticked by, amusement took over. He rose.

"Let me get this straight. I'm in trouble because of a dream you had. Is that right?" He leaned against the closet, shoving his hands into the pockets of the black dress trousers he'd worn to the funeral. "Typical female logic."

"It wasn't a dream, unless it was yours. You called me Aridela. There was another one. Lilith. Yeah, Lilith. There were more. I can't...I can't remember."

He rubbed his cheeks, pushed away from the closet, and left the room, shaking his head.

"Where are you going?" I followed him. "Why do you have all this stuff about ancient religions? I don't think your mother would like that. Why are there no pictures of Jesus in this house, or crosses, or Bibles for that matter, other than Brianne's? What about the thousands of men who hang on every word you say about Christianity?"

"Hundreds of thousands," he corrected mildly.

"Damn it, do you believe what you preach, or is it bullshit?"

"I don't know how to reach your doctor, or if he even practices anymore. Mine doesn't know your history, but it can be retrieved easily enough." Rafe touched his wrist and a moment later, a bored-looking receptionist flashed to life in a holo.

"I don't need a doctor." I shook Rafe's arm. "I need you to be honest with me."

Even as the next words formed on my lips, McKenna, or the statue, called from the other room.

He's lying.

"You're lying! You're going to try and make me believe I imagined everything."

The male in the holo interrupted. "Doctor Quinlan's answering service." He peered at me with new interest.

"Have him call me right away. My wife is ill."

"Is this an emergency?"

Rafe paused, glancing at me.

"We don't need a doctor." Reaching out, I added, "Sorry to bother you," and pressed my fingers to Rafe's wrist. The holo scrambled then vanished.

"Why did you do that? You're obviously caught in some kind of psychosis."

I drew in a deep breath, desperately grasping at shreds of clarity. "Just talk to me, Sigmund Freud. I don't claim to understand, but you've got to take a chance and tell me what's going on."

Rafe gazed steadily into my eyes, then he brought my hands to his chest and drew me in.

"Let me go!" I struggled.

He spoke against my ear. "How did you activate it, Erin? It's set to only respond to me."

I sensed he was close to giving in. "The computer? I didn't. The screens were already on when I came in."

He frowned. "That's impossible."

"They were."

He stared at me. "They're dreams, Erin, nightmarish dreams. I have them all the time. I can't stop them. I've tried everything. Doctors. Meditation. Drugs. Alcohol. Nothing works. I'm so damn tired. I found very old clay tablets in the Middle East and those names were on them. The same names. Those women lived, somewhere in history. I feel like I know them. Sometimes I think I'm trapped in a never-ending hallucination."

I tried to decipher what he was saying, comparing it to his body language, searching for the lie I knew must be in there, somewhere.

"I started writing down what I could remember, hoping I could explain or exorcise them. I don't want to turn the computer on. I want you to see me as a strong, steady man. A provider. A protector. A man you can respect. Not some weakling who can't control his own dreams."

Everything caught up with me at that point, that or the pill took over. I shuddered. My teeth chattered. Hot tears flooded from my eyes.

McKenna hadn't been here. I, too, had been the victim of a dream. I knew how he felt.

Rafe caught the back of my legs in one arm and scooped me up like a child. "Give it to me. Give your grief to me. Give me your hate. I can take it all."

I sobbed, shutting away the past hour as he carried me from the office to his bed. At that moment, there was no other place I wanted to be.

Chapter 18

BOTH MOONS FLOATED ABOVE ME, FILLING ME WITH THEIR FROTHY LIGHT. I WASN'T sure if I was sleeping or awake. The moons seemed more like a pair of lopsided eyes than lifeless rocks.

"It is time to finish."

I lifted my head from the arm of the chair. My neck felt stiff as old wood. Fighting through mental fog, I realized I was in the observatory, where the walls and ceiling were glass.

I vaguely remembered wandering up here after Rafe made love to me and fell asleep, although "made love" was not exactly accurate. It had been more like combat, with biting and fingernails, pinching, and driving lunges. I was sore.

I rubbed my eyes. "Brianne?"

Her gaze turned from contemplation of the moons to rest on my face. "I wither. Only you can restore me."

"You're talking." I was overjoyed until I saw her vacant expression. She was once again walking in her sleep.

Sitting up, I took her small, cold hand and drew her onto my lap. This time, instead of jarring her awake, I would let the fantasy play out.

I felt suddenly clear and sharp. The pill had worn off. *Damn* Rafe for drugging me. Those pills were nothing more than strong aphrodisiacs and mind controllers.

But revenge could wait. "Who are you?" I asked, keeping my voice soft.

"Mother of the white tiger and the field mouse, the wildebeest and the gnat."

"Who am I?"

"Maiden, mother, and crone. My Erinys."

I brushed downy hair from her forehead. She seemed no longer a ten-year-old. Moonlight leant her blue-white agelessness.

"Did you kill McKenna?"

"What she endured is multiplied one hundred thousand times throughout your world every day."

"You did kill her," I whispered, trembling.

"Not I," Brianne replied. "It was the man."

"You allowed him to kill her."

"Men choose their paths. This is what they, and you, must face. Your fight will not find reckoning through blame. You do not fight for land or power or wealth, those things for which men are willing to die. Your war is waged for hearts and minds. For the future. For life. Force them to face their choices."

She spoke with authority and wisdom. This was not Brianne. It couldn't be. This was Someone Else.

"Raise your sickle. Return the sacred, before it is too late. Before I fall into the abyss."

"How?"

"Free the child."

My mind was by now adept at constructing the worn protests. *We can't leave the house. The sentinels will stop us. We'll be forced back and watched even more closely, or something worse.*

I breathed in and closed my eyes. I held Brianne's hand and stopped thinking.

A moment or two passed, and a thought I'd had before made a tantalizing return. *Will crossed the property. He broke in and left again.* Of course, Will had military knowledge and experience that I lacked.

The journalist had done it too, using trickery and audacity.

The main problem was this: Will and the journalist were *men*. That made a huge difference.

A little hand pressed over mine and I opened my eyes.

"Trust."

With that word, the true memory of Rafe's office returned. I saw the words I'd read on the screen, and McKenna's toes peeking out from beneath the flutter of her gown. She might be dead in this world, but she was not gone.

Now is the time for courage.

Throw off the lies you have told yourself.

He is not what he seems.

Be stronger than your fear.

Brianne woke. At first, she was afraid. I hugged her and tucked my robe around her.

"Are you going to leave me, Meemah?"

"No, Brie. I will never leave you." I kissed her forehead.

She snuggled against me. I carried her to her room and her elephant, and she fell asleep quickly. I sat beside her on the bed. Her face was pure, untouched by these horrible events.

I was warned to leave before McKenna died. Now, it seemed, I was being given another chance.

I would trust. I would take a leap of faith.

And I would get us out of here.

Archive Four

June, 2072

ROBBER'S ROOST

A Triad Forms

Chapter 1

Sunday. At last.

I felt like I'd been locked in a tower webbed with entrapment spells. Ramandu's Dawn was a luxurious prison, but any prison, luxurious or nightmarish, is still a prison, and to top things off, every room reminded me of McKenna.

Even putting on one of the moronic masks and accepting a tether around my wrist could not fully spoil the simple pleasure of going outside in June.

The air was warm and there was a honeyed scent of alyssum. A few patches of snow remained on the mountain summits but on the estate, tulips and daffodils were bravely reemerging after their recent decline. As I approached the limo with the blacked-out windows, I glimpsed a few gardeners, and was jealous of their freedom to wander freely among the flower beds.

Why did Rafe bother with gardens if no one but him and the hired help got to enjoy them? He might as well let it go wild.

Remembering McKenna's advice, I waited until the limo was well under way and broached the subject.

"I've changed my mind about those pills, Rafe."

He turned to face me. "Yes?"

"I've been having some anxiety since the funeral. It feels like it's getting worse. I think they might help."

Saying he would find them as soon as we got home, he reached over the seat and ran a finger down my cheek reassuringly.

He and Dillon exchanged one of those glances that told me they were communicating silently. Cordelia went on reading her Bible, paying no attention to any of us.

Had they ever drugged her? What about Brianne? I would probably never know.

He was so pleased at the idea of his dutiful, uncomplicated wife coming back to him that he oh-so-generously granted me permission to use the first-floor terrace whenever I wished, no sentinel needed, saying he remembered how I used to love spending time out there. I smiled and thanked him, knowing I would never take advantage of his offer. It wouldn't be the same, not just because of all the patrolling guards, but I knew he'd have Samson watching. Besides, I resented the fact that I needed his dispensation.

Unfortunately, I'd had an extra cup of coffee before we left. As the sermon droned on, I wondered if I could make it to the end. We were not allowed to leave for any reason while Jasper Simonson lectured us.

By the time it was over, I thought my bladder might burst. I told Cordelia, who tsked and gestured to a sentinel. He was the same one who had taken McKenna to the toilet before she was killed.

I wanted to grill him about her but I couldn't, as there were more sentinels in the hall and we females weren't allowed to speak. Defying that rule would get him reprimanded and I might be punished in any number of ways, with the old but effective paddle on the palms of my hands to wearing the witch's mask, which made my punishment visible to everyone.

Had they been close? Was he mourning my daughter?

Another sentinel stood before the restroom door, which meant a woman was already in there. Though the restroom had four stalls, only one was operational; the others had been shut off. My theory was that nobody wanted women to congregate or have an opportunity to whisper among themselves.

She came out and I was allowed to enter. My sentinel remained in front of the door, his enhanced assault rifle held across his chest.

I walked in, thinking only of peeing, and, with a heavy heart, of McKenna. I glanced at the sink, trying to picture my daughter standing there, washing her hands and touching up her hair, but movement out of the corner of my eye elicited a gasp, which in turn brought my sentinel barreling in to see what was going on.

A man in coveralls stood at the far wall, using a stiff brush and a bucket of soapy water to scrub at a smear of white paint.

The paint was running, but I could make out the design. It was a Chinese character, drawn in large strokes. I knew it because Maya and I had used it to communicate with each other in school when we couldn't talk openly. The symbol's meaning was "eternity."

In typical dramatic teenage girl fashion, we would text it to let the other one know something had happened or we needed to talk. Sometimes we would draw it on the bathroom mirror with lipstick, giggling at the conjectures it sparked among the other girls who had no idea what it was. For us, the symbol was a signal. It meant there was a message hidden behind the second toilet.

Our secret symbol. Here. *Here,* in this horrible church in Park City, Utah.

"I—sorry," I babbled at the suspicious sentinel, and turned my gaze to the floor. "The man surprised me."

"Hurry up," the sentinel barked. I wasn't sure if he was speaking to me or the janitor, but I couldn't lose this opportunity. I fled into the open stall and closed the door. Immediately I felt behind the toilet and there it was.

A piece of paper.

My heart thundered. I sat down to pee and unfolded it, shaking with hope.

The vintage Lykan doesn't use face/wrist ID. The fob is in an unlocked cabinet.

That was it. I couldn't be sure if the note was from Maya, or if it was meant for me. I had no idea what a "vintage Lykan" was. Something that used a fob, so maybe a vehicle. Older cars had been controlled with fobs, though by the time I was driving, most had graduated to more secure means. I turned the paper over. The Chinese symbol was scribbled there. Nothing else.

It had to be from Maya. There were too many similarities for it to be coincidence.

The sentinel would be getting suspicious. I stood up and the toilet flushed. I threw in the paper and waited to make sure it was gone.

I washed my hands and left, not daring to glance at the janitor. There was a line of women waiting to get in and my sentinel prodded me away.

In the limo, I kept my face turned down meekly. I didn't want to see other women being led around like pets on leashes. Cordelia was quiet as well, her attention on the holo figures displayed above her Bible. The one glance she sent me indicated she was satisfied with my docile silence.

If I kept up this act, they would become complacent, and I would make my move.

I glanced at Brianne. She smiled, which made me wince inside. It was almost like this child was trying to heal me, when it should be the other way around.

I smiled back.

Soon, sweetheart. Soon.

Night after night, I lay beside Rafe, making one plan then another, discarding each as impossible.

At breakfast, a week after I found the note at church, Rafe watched as I pretended to pop the icosahedron pill into my mouth.

"Doctor Cohn messaged me," he said. "Now that the funeral is over, he wants to get you in for the surgery. If we wait too long, he won't be able to erase the scars as thoroughly as you might like."

Beneath the table's surface, I slipped the half-dissolved pill into the pocket of my robe and rubbed my palm on the cashmere to wipe away the residue. I would erase the evidence of what I'd done later, in the bathroom.

I picked up my coffee cup and sipped, mentally exploring why his suggestion pissed me off while presenting a perfectly serene façade.

I didn't understand the anger. Every time I saw my reflection, the scar was there, reminding me of how it was created. I ought to want it gone, but for some reason, I didn't.

"I know it's hard to think about things like that right now," Rafe said.

Was it because I felt like he wanted it gone so I would look younger? Prettier? To him the scar was ugly, but the damn thing was now a part of me, a part of my history. Honestly, I didn't want it gone for that very reason—because he did.

"I don't think I'm up for it yet, Rafe," I said. "Maybe next month."

His frown let me know I'd disappointed him. "I'm afraid next month might be too late, and Cohn told me he's going to be out of the country. Let's get you in, Erin. You'll thank me later."

"All right." I gave him my best *Stepford Wives* smile. "Just give me a few more days to feel stronger."

That pleased him.

Another week passed. I managed to put off the question of the scar with one excuse after another.

The next Sunday after church, Brianne and I spent the afternoon in the secret garden room. We talked about McKenna. We read from a few books and drew with crayons.

Without much hope, I asked her about Rafe's cars. He was a collector, and had many. I'd never been particularly interested.

She knew more than I ever had. Like most children, before they become teenagers and decide adults are stupid, she was interested in the same things as her parental figures.

She described some of his old-style vehicles and told me their names. *Venom, Bugatti, McLaren, Tesla.* Soon, there it was.

Lykan.

"Lykan," I said. "What a strange name."

"Granddaddy took me for a ride in it once. He had to drive it himself, and it runs on gasoline." She wrinkled her nose. "That stuff smells. He said it reminds him of the good old days."

A vintage Lykan.

I wasn't going to make the same mistake I'd made with McKenna. I would take my leap of faith tonight, before I could talk myself out of it.

RAFE WAS FAST ASLEEP. FOR ONCE HIS BREATHING WAS CALM AND REGULAR. I KNEW I would get the credit for this miracle were I to ask, for I'd made love to him, acquiescing to everything he wanted and more, hoping for this result.

I'd already decided what to take. I wouldn't pack any extra clothing, because I feared it would alert Samson, but I had collected protein bars, apples, crackers, and jerky, and a few biodegradable bottles of water. A couple of days ago I lucked out when I happened to notice the safe in the wall of the bedroom closet and decided to test Samson's literal understanding of Rafe's directions once more.

"Samson, can you open this for me?"

"Of course, Erin," he replied and a blue light went off on the front.

Inside, I found several credit card sized devices I couldn't figure out. "What are these?"

His answer was candid and honest, as always. "General currency. Mr. Konstantinou keeps them on hand for emergencies, and for keeping his identity private. The blue one purchases commercial airline travel. The red one is for lodging. The purple one is for dining out, and the green one pays for sundries. Groceries, alcohol, clothing, and other miscellaneous items."

Each one was conveniently labeled. "When you say 'general currency,' do you mean it's like having loose cash?"

"Mr. Konstantinou never uses cash, although he keeps some handy for overseas travel. There are several countries that have returned to a cash system over virtual currency, so he likes to have some on hand."

I tried again. "These aren't like cash, then? They're linked to an account?"

"The cards are stocked with untraceable currency. When they are emptied, they can be discarded or reloaded. Mr. Konstantinou has problems with people recognizing his name and harassing him, so he sends Oliver to purchase the cards whenever he needs more. Oliver acquires them from a black-market dealer."

I peered into the recesses of the safe. Sure enough, there were old-fashioned bills. A lot, from what I could see, and moreover, neat stacks of Krugerrands.

"Okay, thanks, Samson," I said.

"Would you like me to add you as an authorized user of the safe, Erin?"

"Um, yes. Please."

"From now on, look into the iris detector and the door will open."

"Thanks."

"You are welcome, Erin."

I decided to be discreet and wait to steal the currency until the last minute, which turned out to be a wise decision, for earlier when I'd come into the bedroom after taking a shower, Rafe was shutting the safe door.

I got out of bed and tiptoed soundlessly into the closet. The iris detector worked as expected. I cleaned out the cash, Krugerrands, and the currency cards.

The food was stashed in a cloth bag beneath the bed in the guest bedroom, along with the blade made of bone, the translations of the tablets, and that book, *Secrets of Bronze Age Goddess Cults*. I wanted to take it, though I wasn't sure why.

Carrying my shoes, I left Rafe's bedroom. The hallway floor lights came on as I padded to the guest room, but Samson gave no challenge. No doubt he was too well-trained or too familiar with the inexplicable nighttime skulking of his human beings to interfere.

I wondered again where the hell he'd been the night Will broke in. My lover had shattered a window and entered the house. He'd walked around, got my attention, and spent thirty minutes talking to me and kissing me in the shadows. Samson had done nothing. I hadn't heard a word from the detectives about this drastic failing on the AI's part, nor had Rafe brought it up, at least in my hearing.

Did Samson turn off at night? That didn't seem plausible. Maybe there was a defect in his programming. It was puzzling, but I could only hope something similar would happen tonight.

I retrieved the bag then went to Brianne's room.

"Are we leaving, Meemah?" she asked after I gently woke her.

This child was astounding. It was like she'd known all along.

I nodded. "Yep. We're getting out of here."

Brianne threw back her covers. "Good." She dressed quickly. The only thing she wanted to take was her stuffed elephant.

We descended to the kitchen, where a door opened into a corridor which led to the underground garage. I motioned to Brianne to be quiet, as Dale slept nearby.

I had no real plan. I was taking this one step at a time and hoping for luck. Right now, the goal was simply to open the door.

I depressed the latch and pushed. Nothing happened. I tried to turn the deadbolt. It wouldn't budge.

"I'm sorry, Erin." Samson's voice broke the silence and made me jump. "You aren't allowed in the garage. That isn't part of the house. Isn't it past Brie's bedtime?"

Crushing disappointment engulfed me, but I wasn't ready to give up. "Not that it's any of your business, Samson, but Rafe left something in one of the cars and asked me to get it earlier. I couldn't sleep and just now remembered."

"Mr. Konstantinou only gave you access to everything *in the house*, Erin. I cannot understand why he would request such a thing of you, when there are many others who can retrieve items for him. Perhaps he forgot to let me know. I will ask."

"No, Samson. He's sleeping. Don't wake him. He's had a hard day."

Through this, Brianne pulled on my sleeve. I looked down. She placed a finger over her mouth then tiptoed to the wall. She pushed something and a section of the wall slid away. A translucent panel appeared, and an interface.

She motioned, indicating I should join her. Reaching up—it was almost too high for her—she placed her thumb and middle finger against two separate circles outlined in flashing red. She used her head to point at a third she couldn't reach, outlined in green, and mouthed, *Push.* I put my finger on it and at her nod, we pressed all three at the same time. A few seconds passed then the interface turned dark.

Brianne smiled. "He's gone, Meemah."

"Gone? Who's gone?"

"S-A-M-S-O-N. Don't say his name, or he'll wake up."

Glancing at the dark, unresponsive interface, I said, "He won't start singing 'Daisy,' now, will he?"

"What is that?"

"Never mind. It's not important."

I gave her a silent high five and mouthed, *Let's go!*

Now I was able to turn the deadbolt and open the door.

We raced down the corridor to the garage. No guards were there, for which I thanked providence. "Do you know which one is the Lykan?"

"That one." She pointed at the third car in, a wicked piece of gleaming black machinery, like a leopard on wheels.

I wasn't sure I could control such a powerful beast, but I wouldn't allow myself to fall into the trap of thinking too far ahead. We crossed to the wall and opened a cabinet. There was a fob. I removed it and pressed the button.

The Lykan's headlights blinked and I heard the locks click. The windows were as black as the body, thank goodness. That would be in our favor.

"Brie," I said. "When this car starts, I have a feeling it's going to be loud. The guards will hear. They'll see the garage door open, too."

"They'll just think it's Granddaddy. Go fast, Meemah. That's what he does."

I tossed the bag onto the passenger side floor and we got in. The bloody thing still had that new car smell.

"Ready?"

She nodded.

I took a moment to check the mirrors and the transmission. A six-speed manual. There was first, and there was reverse.

I can do this.

Now or never.

I pushed the ignition. The engine roared and the garage door opened.

I floored it.

I NEARLY RAN OVER A MAN AND A GERMAN SHEPHERD. HE FELL BACKWARDS. I SAW him in the rearview mirror, gaping.

It's okay. He'll assume it's Rafe. Who else could it be?

I chuckled when the guard at the edge of the property hastily bent, using his iris to open the gate as I blasted closer. Then I was through, hopefully before the man glimpsed me through the windshield.

I raced down the winding road, the headlights illuminating much of the wilderness on either side. At the bottom I faced a choice. Left or right. One narrow mountain road would take us to Park City. The other led to Heber. The car didn't seem to really want to stop. I had to push hard on the brakes; they squealed in protest.

The holographic display in the windshield showed me all kinds of constantly-changing technical things. I didn't know what some of them were, but it was nice to see the road and my position on it, as well as the blinking red outline of a deer off to the right.

"They'll expect us to go through Park City," I said, "so we'll go the back way, through Heber."

"Okay," Brianne said.

I turned left, remembering I had to get off the mountain then go east to the highway.

"You knew Samson could be turned off?" I remembered McKenna saying something similar from when she sneaked out.

"I know lots of things. Sometimes I see things in dreams."

"I'm impressed."

"Turn on the stealth mode, Meemah."

"How do I do that?"

"That button."

I pushed it and a female voice said, "Stealth mode activated."

"What does it do?" I asked.

"It sends out a signal that this car isn't to be stopped or searched. Only really important people have it."

"Hmm," I said. My mind latched onto another question. "Why am I always 'Erin' to Samson? He calls Rafe 'Mr. Konstantinou,' and he used to call me Mrs. Konstantinou, but now it's Erin."

"Because you're the same as Samson, Meemah."

I was confused. "I'm an artificial intelligence?"

"No." She giggled. "You belong to Granddaddy, like Samson does. So do I."

"Is that so?" I muttered, but let it be. Elation was taking hold. "We'll go through Midway and around the back of Timp."

"What's that?"

"What's Timp? Timpanogos? You don't know?"

She shook her head.

"It's a mountain, child. A gorgeous one. I've climbed it."

"I wish it was daytime so we could see."

I was saddened and angered. This rotten society had stolen the childhood she deserved. No hikes, no whitewater rafting, no camping, no friends, no slumber parties, and no school but for male tutors who brainwashed her about her subservient role in this world.

As we came to the bottom of the twisty mountain road and I slowed to check for oncoming traffic, my pulse-scars tingled.

"Meemah!" Brianne cried.

A detonation left our ears ringing. The two front tires rapidly deflated. Glass exploded; both side windows shattered. I reached for Brianne, who was crying, and pulled her across the center console, tucking her against my body and covering her head with my arms.

The doors were flung open. I couldn't see who our attackers were; their bodies and faces were completely covered.

Cloth was shoved over my head. I tried to fight, but arms far stronger than mine held me down.

A tube pressed against the side of my neck. My ears started buzzing. "No," I cried, but I couldn't stop my eyes from closing.

It was a trick.

Chapter 2

Water dripping.

Distant voices.

Menoetius will bring a rabbit. We'll roast it in the embers.

My mind veered into grief and hopelessness, the only two emotions I'd had in a long time.

Yes, Menoetius would bring a rabbit. He would place it in the fire pit and try to tempt me to eat. I wished he would stop. I didn't want to eat, or breathe, or think.

Chrysaleon is dead.

The sound of running water separated into individual echoing drops. I felt a sensation of movement near my head.

I opened my eyes and there was Maya.

Chiseled, strong, almost manly, a face I didn't want to stop looking at. Eyes as fierce as an eagle's, irises with the clarity and color of a turquoise sea. Like most people these days, she was the product of various bloodlines. Maya was proud of her heritage, which was an intriguing mixture similar to my own but with a few key differences. We shared an ancestry of African and Japanese, but where I veered into Portuguese and Hispanic grandparents and parents, she had Ute, plus a squiggle of Scots, from which she got her last name. She was only a month younger than me, but she didn't look much different than she had when I'd last seen her.

Her hair had always been blue-black, a crown of naturally springy coils.

She'd never had the patience for styles, even as a teenager. Now it was long, smooth, and creamy white. Nevertheless, I knew her instantly.

She was the most beautiful thing I could imagine waking to.

"Maya!" I cried. Then we were hugging, weeping, and laughing.

She dabbed at her eyes with her sleeve. "I didn't think I'd ever see you again. I thought you were lost forever."

"Merely misplaced." My words were casual, but my voice trembled. I'd thought the same thing about her.

"I'm as sorry as I can be about McKenna. I wish I could have seen what was going to happen. I would have done anything, Erin, to prevent it. I swear that to you."

I was nearly undone. "I know." I glanced around this shadowy…room? No. It was a cave, like the dream I'd just had. "Where is my granddaughter?"

"Currently being spoiled. She woke up about an hour ago. Come, I'll show you."

Brianne was playing holographic Chinese Checkers with a girl who looked about her age, in a cozy, well-lit rock chamber. An orange sherbet moustache was drying on her upper lip, the elephant was tucked beneath her arm, and two adult females danced attendance in the background. She ran over to hug me and chattered about the game, and Dharma, the girl she was playing with.

"She sure lights up the place," Maya said.

I bit the inside of my cheek, using pain to help me hold onto self-control.

Maya, with one penetrating glance, fetched coffee and led me back to the room I'd awakened in—her bedroom, I discovered.

"Where are we?" was my first question.

"In a canyon," she said, waving her hand.

"It's a damn cave."

"Lots of caves. At the bottom of one of the most remote slot canyons we could find, hidden behind a mess of flood debris and boulders. I won't say which one. The less you know, the better. That's the rule for everybody who doesn't need to know. We call it the Catacombs."

"Are we in Utah? Can you tell me that much?"

"Yeah. We were inspired by the Anasazi. We're under more than 180 meters of rock and earth, beyond the reach of drones or curious military."

I'd only seen two chambers and a corridor, but Maya told me the Catacombs wound into the earth for nearly two kilometers. An underground spring had performed most of the original work. The people who lived here did the rest, digging, jackhammering, and blasting. They gradually carved out fifteen rooms and created a sprawling commune.

"They co-opted the underground for their Cages. Salt mines, mostly. We took their idea and used it to our benefit."

Questions raced through my mind so fast I couldn't keep up. "Cages" made a mark, bringing back Will saying something about "cage farms," but I was already caught by another. "You put that drawing on the wall?"

"I hoped you hadn't forgotten."

"I found your note, but I had no idea what a Lykan was. Brie had to explain. Was it you who blew out our tires and drugged us?"

"It was my people, yeah. I'm sorry. I know it was frightening. We had to put you under. Almost no one knows how to find this place. Besides, they had to cut the tracking tattoo out of your arm and take out your wrist phone. You didn't want to be awake for that."

"Oh. That's what hurts." I pulled the collar of my shirt down over my upper arm and saw a clean bandage. It throbbed dimly, like wounds do after surgery, and was sensitive to the touch. "Good riddance." The extraction on my wrist was just a tiny nick. "Why did you have to take the phone out? It was pretty handy."

"No way could we leave that. None of us have those, except for the occasional burner phone. They're as bad for pinpointing your location as the tracker." She inspected the bandage on my upper arm. "You'll have to take antibiotics for three days to ward off any bacteria that might have slipped past during the removal."

"There was bacteria in there?"

"Oh yeah. Deadly stuff. They know how desperate women are to escape, and what they'll do to get that tracker out. They want women who try to remove it to die, painfully, from sepsis."

"Bastards."

"That they are, my darling. Do you need pain meds?"

"I'm okay for now. I thought Rafe had played a trick on us, or the guards called for backup."

"I'm going to try my damndest to keep Rafe from coming anywhere near either of you ever again, boo."

Nostalgic tears filled my eyes at her use of the old endearment.

"What happened to your face and your arm, below the tracker? Did Rafe do that?"

"No, no. He saved me from getting worse."

She scowled as though she didn't believe me.

"He did. We were going to fly to LA to have the scars removed, but McKenna went missing, and I guess I didn't care enough to reschedule. It's a long story."

"We do have a lot to catch up on, don't we? Damn, it's been twenty… twenty-two—no, twenty-four years."

"Are you sure it's not twenty-five? We didn't see much of each other after Rafe and I married. We shouldn't have let that happen."

"I concur. Do you mind if I have gin? It's my drink, and noon somewhere."

"Go right ahead."

When we were settled, a tray of snacks on the table beside us, Maya's gin and tonic fizzing and giving off the tart aroma of lime, she said, "Now."

"I don't know where to begin."

"I do. I thought you were dead, Erin."

"That's what everyone says." Suddenly, I knew where to begin. "I've been longing to ask you about the night I left Rafe and McKenna. I can't remember. He's told me things, but I don't know if I believe him. He claims I left a note saying I was flying to Brown to see you, but apparently, I really flew to Denver and wrecked a rented car. The investigators figured I'd been kidnapped and the note was a decoy. Please tell me you know something about this. Anything."

"You called me, half out of your mind, screaming about Rafe. A monster, you called him. And a devil. I think you mentioned Nazi, and I distinctly remember asshole. You said he and the president were plotting to sever our coalition with the Western Alliance in order to join Ukrus, China, and North Korea—the three worst governments in the history of the world for a democracy to be aligned with. You said the borders would be sealed and they were laughing about using the second moon to enslave every living female. They were going to use women like cattle, for profit. You told me Grigory Andreiovich Novikov had weaponized his satellites to force compliance. On the phone that night, I couldn't fathom what you were talking about. It made perfect sense not long after, when that's exactly what they did, but that night I wondered if somebody had slipped a hallucin in your drink. I'm the one who calmed you down, a little. I told you to get out of there. I knew Rafe wouldn't give you a minute to think. He'd brainwash you into believing there was no truth in the world but his truth. I'm the one who advised throwing him off with a note, because I knew they would trace your call to me and would look at me first. Remember my summerhouse? The place my dad left me near Telluride? I thought it would be safe to hide out there for a while. I was going to meet you as soon as I could, but you never got there, and neither did I. Rafe sent the black suits after me the minute they found out you hadn't flown either to Providence or Boston. I was interrogated for days."

"I'm so sorry I did that to you."

She laughed as she offered me a plate of croissants, cheese crepes, and apple slices, which I refused. My stomach was flip-flopping.

"No worries. I like to think I'm at least three steps ahead of your personal Nazi. Right after I talked to you, I picked up one of the adjuncts and spent every minute of that weekend with him. Made sure we were seen in a lot of public places. An airtight alibi. They didn't like it, but there was nothing they could do. I told them you'd called, but it was just a chat, and you hadn't said anything about coming to visit. Thankfully, I had scramblers on my phone because of the work I was doing, so they couldn't disprove my story."

I gazed at her, half in love. Had she been Rafe's wife, put into my situation after twenty-three years, I had no doubt she would have found a way to escape or kill him within a week.

"So, I wasn't kidnapped. I wrote the note of my own free will." It sank in. "I abandoned Rafe and McKenna of my own free will. I left McKenna with a man I'd called a monster and a Nazi."

"That was on my advice too, so blame me if you want. For one thing, it would have been so much harder for you to get away with a four-year-old. You were taking off with nothing but the clothes you were wearing, and I didn't want you to feel pressured into going back to him because of McKenna. You were leaping off a cliff, so to speak, into the dark. And if you had taken McKenna, Rafe would have gone bat-shit crazy. He would've turned over every clump of dirt in the country to find you. If I hadn't believed that McKenna would be completely, one hundred percent safe with him, I wouldn't have encouraged you to leave her there. I can't stand that man, but even I will admit he doted on her." The melting ice in Maya's glass clinked as she sipped her gin. "You had to be able to make decisions without consideration for a child, but if I had known you were going to vanish for over twenty years, Erin, I might have advised you differently. I remember telling you to take a few days, maybe a week, to think things over. I thought you would go home and divorce him. That's what I hoped, anyway."

Another jolt of sentimentality brought a shaky smile to my lips. Oh, how those two hated each other. Their hatred was larger than life, and all because of me. If not for me, they would never have even met, and certainly would have no reason to interact.

"Well, let's hear it. What happened?" She leaned forward. "Where did you end up? I hope I can bear to hear this story." Her gaze moved to the scar around my eye. It had been painstakingly stitched and after two months had healed, but there was a pronounced red scar, and now that I'd abandoned Rafe again, I'd best get used to having it for the rest of my life.

"You're not going to believe me—"

"Erin, somehow you managed to keep yourself alive and out of Rafe's clutches for a hell of a long time. I'm impressed." She held out her hands questioningly. "And why would you lie to me?"

I conceded the point. "As I said, I wrecked the car. I must have turned everything off and unbanded, damned if I know why. The detectives who found the car told Rafe my head hit the windshield."

"That's what happened to your eye?"

"No. I have no visible scars from that night. A man found me."

Surprise and concern sharpened her gaze.

This was in some ways harder than telling McKenna. I wasn't at all sure how Maya would take it, so I barreled on to get it over with. "I've been with that man all this time."

She regarded me, missing nothing, not the sweat I felt trickling down my temple, or the wobble in my voice.

"A good guy, I hope."

I realized what she was thinking. "Oh, yes. Fantastic. The thing is, Maya, he was—is—Rafe's brother. William. Will Konstantinou."

Seconds ticked by. She stared as though frozen. Then she started laughing. At first it was a mere snort, but it grew and grew, expanding until tears streamed from her eyes and she sloshed a third of her gin on the floor.

I managed another smile, though it felt rusty. Two smiles in a matter of minutes. *You have to admit it is kind of funny, if you're not Rafe.*

She wiped her eyes. "I didn't know Rafe had a brother. Talk about revenge served cold!"

I spent the next half hour describing my life with Will, our mountain cabin, how I learned to ride a horse and never, ever went into town, or anywhere. How Will knew things about blending in and being invisible, how to move between states without getting caught, and, best of all, how he lived, so deep in the wilderness that we'd escaped notice for twenty-three years, and probably would have gone on doing so if not for that disastrous morning when I let my guard drop. Then I had to explain how I was taken that last day.

"A True Phantom." Maya's expression was one of wonder. "I've heard of them, but I didn't believe they actually existed. Not after all this time."

"What's that?"

"They're legends. True Phantoms have never been caged. They escaped the Protective Quarantine and round ups. They figured out what was coming and hid so well that nothing and nobody could find them. Not drones, not public records, not family members, not even satellites."

"Aren't you that?"

"Nope. None of us down here are. We've all been caught and imprisoned. One by one, we managed to escape and eventually find each other. We're ingenious, but you're different. You were never caught. Well, you were, but damn, what a long run you had! The guy who removed your tracker said it was new. He couldn't get over it. A grown woman with a new, barely-healed tracker." She blew out a low whistle. "Did you tell Rafe what you've told me?"

"No. It never seemed to be a good time, but he knew, Maya. He knew all along. Will went to him after I was taken. He confessed and asked Rafe to find me. Rafe made him agree to never see me again. That was his price. Of course, that's not what I was told."

"Always the price to pay with Rafe, that and the lies. How did you find this out?"

I told her about Will breaking into Ramandu's Dawn.

"He sounds like a valuable asset, and just about the polar opposite of his brother. How did he get past the AI?"

"I don't know. I haven't figured that out. Samson was right there, Johnny on the spot, the instant I tried to leave through the kitchen door."

"Hmm. Interesting. With you vouching for him, I'd support bringing him into our group. If Rafe knows about the cabin, though, I'll bet you ten thousand rubles he's having Will watched. We'll have to be careful."

"That would be wonderful, but I'm not sure Will would want to give up his home and go into hiding underground, with...how many people are down here, anyway?"

"Twenty-one, as of last month. A baby girl, born to one of our couples. Tarryn."

"That might be too many for him. He's a true loner."

"We won't worry about it now. I want to know how you got those scars, which was, I believe, how we started this convo."

She refilled my cup for the third time. I was beginning to experience the jittery sensation that comes from stress, no food, and too much caffeine. I set the cup down and had a croissant to balance things out. "This is delicious. It's like eating a butter-cloud."

"Don't change the subject."

"I haven't told anyone about this. Rafe doesn't even know, I don't think, anyway." I inhaled and braced myself. "I told you I was taken by two men. One of them knocked me out. When I woke up, I was in a dog kennel. You know, one of those plastic travel kennels, but bigger. Big enough to accommodate a human. A human kennel, I guess."

She gazed at me, motionless, then nodded and placed her hand on my forearm.

I did my best to maintain detachment and tell it objectively, but when I got to the part where the men took me to the Quonset hut and all that happened there, I couldn't stem the shuddering.

Maya listened, squeezing my forearm every now and then.

"Rafe told me he killed them both. I think that's true. I remember hearing the shots."

Her eyes blazed. "Good."

A woman came in. Her gaze was somber as it met mine and she didn't return my smile. She spoke into Maya's ear. I waited for Maya to introduce us, but she didn't. The woman took away the coffee and food.

"That's interesting," Maya said when we were alone.

"What?"

"She told me every one of the vegetable plants shot up six centimeters overnight and the tomatoes went from green to fully ripe."

"You have vegetable plants?"

"Sure. We have a whole gardening chamber. It's difficult to get clean potting soil, so we make our own, with mulch."

She leaned forward, resting her elbows on her thighs. Her regard was somber. "You were in a cage farm, Erin."

There it was again, that ominous-sounding term. "What is that? Will mentioned it the night I saw him at the chateau, but we didn't have time to get into it."

She rubbed her temple, closed her eyes, and sighed. "I swear there's an icepick stabbing me right here." She opened her eyes, adjusted her seat, and finished off her gin. "I wish I didn't have to do this. It's one thing, to call your husband an ass. It's another to reveal what a monster he truly is."

I didn't like the sound of that.

"From what you've said, I can see that you know almost nothing about what's happened in this country. I think I'm going to have to start at the beginning."

"I'm ready. Tell me everything."

"I will, but Erin, are you hungry? One croissant isn't much to go on. Brie must be hungry by now, too."

"I guess so." I didn't want to stop. I wanted to know the truth, horrible or not, and I had a feeling it would be. But I didn't want Brie eating alone, or with strangers. Plus, I had to pee. "Do you guys have bathrooms?"

"What do you think?"

"I don't want to assume."

"Of course we do. They're very nice, for underground self-contained composting toilets. We have all the comforts of home here. I'll show you how to use them."

"I need instructions?"

She laughed. "It's simple. What did you have, anyway? Three liters of coffee? No wonder you're fidgeting."

"I'll be peeing on the floor if we don't get a move on."

"You're too thin," Maya said as we left the chamber.

"Really?" I glanced down. The shirt I'd thrown on when we escaped hung loosely and my wrists were bony, hardly bigger than Brie's. Hadn't I been stuffing my face since the day Rafe carried me out of the Quonset hut? It seemed like it, and thinking of those heavenly meals at the chateau made my mouth water. Maybe I was hungry after all.

Maya gave me a speed course on compostable toilets and a brief version of how some of the men stayed above, blending in and working various low-level jobs. Once a month, they brought supplies like water, perishable foodstuffs, compost material, and manure for the vegetables.

"They're the bravest of us," she said. "They have to pretend to be supporters of the Brotherhood and sneak here very carefully. Avoiding drones, highway patrol, and border guards is a delicate balancing act. They're stopped frequently, so they've honed their lying skills. Those guys could talk their way out of quicksand. We couldn't make it without them."

This reminded me painfully of Will's monthly excursions for supplies, and how he played a similar game.

As it turned out, Brianne was too busy with Dharma and another girl to stop for food. We had to coax her into it with promises that she could come right back after she fortified herself. My heart ached to think of the lonely life she'd lived. How could Rafe do that to his own daughter and granddaughter?

In this primitive underground hiding place, she was laughing and giggling, dressing and undressing a pile of dolls with her new friends and making up adventures for them.

Seeing her happy like this in the midst of sorrow and uncertainty, gave me hope that she might recover, someday, from all that had happened. I'd often heard that children are resilient. I didn't think that statement was as true as people wanted it to be, but maybe it did have some merit.

Maya brought us each a plate of steaming turkey and pasta goulash, with a side of artisan rolls. We went into a nearby chamber furnished with several dining tables made from reclaimed wood. While Brie and I tucked in, Maya went off again and brought back milk and a glass of wine.

"Have you ever had a friend before, Brie?" I asked.

She shook her head to say no, then forgot her manners about talking with food in her mouth and explained. "Granddaddy brought girls to the chateau sometimes. I didn't know them and grownups were always watching us. Some of them were snotty. Some of them were too afraid to do anything. They wouldn't even talk."

"I hope you can make friends here," I said softly, and was rewarded with a grin. I could see she believed she already had.

Turning to Maya, I asked, "How do you cook? How do you keep the food from spoiling? For that matter," I added, looking up at the ceiling, "what about the lights?"

She scraped the tines of a fork over the surface of the tabletop. "Ten generators. They run the refrigerators, heaters, ovens, and lights."

"I don't hear them."

"They're solar powered and insulated. They have to be silent. Can't have any inquisitive canyoneers hearing and investigating. I'll show you sometime."

"Hey," I said as it occurred to me. "You knew about Rafe's cars. You knew which one could be started with a fob."

Maya didn't smile at my sudden comprehension. Soberly, she said, "Many have died to collect knowledge from those in power, Erin."

Which sobered me right up, as well.

"How do you think we knew you'd chosen last night to take the car and escape?"

I drew in a breath. "An infiltrator."

"Can I go play, Meemah?" Brie asked.

"Sure." It said something, that she was more interested in playing than hearing about the group's abilities. Or, knowing Brianne, she might have discerned where my thoughts were headed, and knew I needed time alone with Maya. "Where are we sleeping?" I asked.

"I've put you two in the same room. Unless you want to share a room with some of the other girls, Brie. They have a dormitory kind of thing going. Do you?"

"I'll stay with Meemah," she said, in a way that made it sound like she was protecting me.

I blinked away a tear and kissed her. "Have fun, babe."

She ran out and I regarded Maya across the table. "Who is the infiltrator?"

"I can't tell you that."

"Okay." I felt like I'd dropped into a political espionage movie, but she had a point. If I were recaptured, it wouldn't do for me to have too much knowledge. "After McKenna's funeral, Rafe sent the guards and sentinels away for something he called restructuring."

"That's double-speak for torture and lie detectors."

I took that in, unsurprised. He'd been so enraged. "The new guards and sentinels he brought in were supposedly better. They passed something he called Black Scorpion Therapy. Their tattoos were different. The ones he sent away had crossed sabers on the backs of their hands. The replacements had scorpions." I shuddered. "With gaping pincers and oversized stingers."

"Yeah. Those tattoos are given to graduates of an elite training college the Reformation Brotherhood set up. They're enrolled at age four and train every day of their lives to swear a loyalty oath to one man. By the time they're seventeen or so, they're ready to die for that man, and they've been trained to kill without hesitation."

"They did seem young."

"That tattoo marks them as ready for imprint. They're safe to be around their man and his family, if he has one. It's also a sign that they're enthusiastic supporters of the dynasties running this shit show. The boys enrolled in Black Scorpion Therapy are chosen for their build, their aggression, their willingness to kill, and their fighting abilities. Sort of like the old Navy Seals."

"The sentinels Rafe had when I first arrived wore shirts with a red lion and crossed sabers over the suggestion of a female. The design on the shirts worn by the new sentinels was simpler. An apple with an eye in the middle."

"Not very imaginative, is it? Sentinels are specifically trained to secure, control, and protect the females belonging to the man they've imprinted on."

"What's the Reformation Brotherhood?"

"That's the regime you're living in. Rafe is one of the founders. It's called 'Brotherhood' for a reason. There are rumors they have tattoos too, but none of my people have ever seen one."

"What are they supposed to look like?"

"A lion. A big one."

Everything slowed, the coursing of my blood, my ability to reason. Here it was, verifying what I had subconsciously suspected. My husband, who worked overtime trying to make me believe he was a good guy, was one of the creators of cage farms and sentinels. Of leashes and masks. Of sermons harping on our sins and never-ending debt of submission to men. He was a founding member of something called the Reformation Brotherhood, a title with an ominous undertone.

"Early on, the Brotherhood designed something they call Carnevale, to reward the sentinels. I don't know very much, because none of our guys was ever considered loyal enough, or elite enough, to be invited. All I know is, once a year there's a big party to reward the proven loyalists, especially the sentinels."

"Maya. Do you know who McKenna ran away with?"

"I know everything about that, Erin."

"I told her the truth," I said, not sure why, maybe to delay hearing what Maya was about to tell me. I had a feeling it would be unbearable. "She forgave me. Not sure I deserved it, but at least I have that."

She looked away from me and released a stifled sob.

"What, Maya? Tell me."

"She sent a message to Brianne's father through our infiltrator, asking him to come for her." Maya's voice got that waver that comes from trying not to cry. "His name was Noah. He lived here, with us. We offered to help. I was the only one against it, because we knew you were back. I didn't think it was the right time. I wanted all three of you, which was a much more delicate operation."

I nodded. "She told me about Brie's father. He sounded like a good guy."

"He was. He refused to let any of us go. He said it was too dangerous and put us at risk. The only person he took was Levi, his brother, also a member of our group."

I waited impatiently.

She swiped away a tear with her thumb. "Levi wasn't a good guy, Erin. After they left here, Levi killed Noah. He waited for McKenna at the arranged place, which the infiltrator helped her get to. I'm guessing Levi told her he would take her to Noah, but instead he—he did what you know."

The dead man they found not far from McKenna. The redhead. Here was proof of what I'd suspected. He was Brianne's father, McKenna's lover, and he had a name. Noah.

Brianne was an orphan.

Pain and anguish flowed over me as though I had just been told of McKenna's death. "Why? Why would he do that?"

"I'm not sure. We think he went mad. Lots of men have. They're called the Confounded. Stupid name. If it were up to me, I might call them the Confounding, because that's what they do. They fool everyone with lies, surface congeniality, and gaslighting. Behind the façade, their minds and souls are rotted with hatred and the need for violence. Revenge. They're insane, with that kind of horror movie insanity one wishes couldn't exist in the real world."

"I don't get any of this! What the hell are you saying?"

"I'm sorry, Erin. This is hard. What Levi did was meant to hurt Rafe and send a message. Noah and McKenna were just convenient mechanisms. He wanted to hurt Rafe because of what he's done. What he stands for. I guess he wanted to hurt Noah and McKenna too, because of what they wanted. A happy ending. That's the simple truth."

"It's not simple! He tortured her, Maya! She didn't do anything to him!"

I covered my face with my hands and sobbed.

I felt her. She had come around the table. She held me, gradually slowing my tumble into bitter agony and imbuing calm with her soothing embrace. It reminded me of how Will gentled the horses when they got spooked.

Maya was not a toucher. She was the type who had a "boundary," and didn't want it invaded. That she would voluntarily hold me like this spoke volumes.

Eventually I regained control. She produced a box of tissues and I wiped my eyes.

Tucking my hair behind my ears, she murmured, "There are no words for a loss like this. I would take it from you if I could."

"Every time I think about her no longer living or breathing, it feels like someone is tearing my heart from my chest. Brianne and I just have to make it, one hour, then one more, and another, until the pain becomes bearable. She and I will help each other survive."

I blew my nose and glanced around, hoping no one had witnessed my collapse. I was relieved to see we were alone. "Can you explain to me about this 'confounded' thing? You're right about me knowing almost nothing. Like I said, I never left the mountain, and Will never talked about what was going on. Rafe told me a few things, but I bet he was lying most of the time. McKenna told me some too." I huffed a short, sarcastic laugh. "The first time I saw the masks women have to wear, I nearly threw up. That was just last month."

"Some men couldn't take it. This regime. It's funny. They were either all in, one hundred and fifty percent, or they went nuts. There are so few who are just ordinary men anymore, good men, I mean. Men who were able to hold on and hope for better times. We think Levi lost his mind because his wife was taken and he never saw her again. Who knows if she's alive or dead? Levi lost himself over a long period of constant rage, of never having closure, of unending grief. We'll never know what kind of man he would have been if she hadn't been stolen. At first men were in favor of female quarantine and all for the Reformation Brotherhood. They were brainwashed by the things they were promised, but after ten years or so, these episodes of insanity started. I wasn't a firsthand witness, but some here in the Catacombs were."

I stared at the cheap framed prints on the walls, depicting nature scenes of forests, mountains, and waterfalls.

"Erin."

I turned to her, blinking.

"You need rest. Those drugs we gave you linger in the system. Let me show you where you're sleeping, and we'll take this up again tomorrow."

"There's no way I can sleep."

"I have some Fenyl. Come on, Erin. Listen to your doctor."

I didn't have the will to argue. After collecting Brianne, Maya took us to one of the newer chambers. It was necessarily small, filled with two twin beds, one nightstand, and a white pine trunk against the wall. A circulator embedded in the ceiling freshened the air and added a hum I knew would lull me to sleep. Upon entering, I saw the bag I'd packed at the chateau sitting on one of the beds. I opened it to make sure everything was there.

"Someone spotted it on the floor of the Lykan and brought it along," Maya said.

"I'm so grateful. I'd really like to thank those guys. They risked their lives for us."

"Sure, later. Are you going to be okay?"

"Yes." I looked at Brianne and received a nod. "We'll be fine." I told her I didn't need her drugs, and kissed her.

"The lights switch off at ten. If you want to read, there are candles in the drawer, or that oil lamp is filled and ready. Tomorrow we'll go up above and hike, if the weather cooperates."

This excited Brianne and me too, but it also scared me. "What about drones, and Rafe's henchmen? Won't they be searching for us?"

"We have clothing that makes us blend into the landscape. Also, drones out here are rare. We're quite a distance from Deer Valley." She laughed. "Talk about being off the grid. It's never occurred to them that we could do what we've done, or that anyone would choose to live down here. Now, you two. Goodnight. Sleep well." She untied the rope by the doorway as she left; a Navajo blanket, woven in gorgeous geometric patterns of red, brown, orange, and turquoise, fell across, giving us privacy.

Brianne looked as tired as I felt. She was almost asleep as I tucked her in.

It was harder for me to drift off, even though I felt flattened by an asphalt roller. Rafe knew by now I was gone, and that I'd taken his granddaughter. What must he be thinking? Feeling? A horrible déjà vu?

Knowing as I did his famous rages, I capitulated to a shiver of trepidation.

Chapter 3

These damnable rooms. They weren't just big. They were pompous. What a delusion, thinking he and Erin could be happy here. It was nothing like a real home. Ramandu's Dawn was designed for rich socialites and celebrities jetting in for gilt-edged weekends, a luxurious retreat for those who wanted to be seen and photographed with high-priced skis and prostitutes.

The chateau was built in the days when the population was skyrocketing and life everywhere was becoming a stinking, congested bottleneck. Every highway, street, and commuter line—even the sky—was intolerably crowded, and there was precious little beauty to be found anywhere. Then came the financial crash of 2028, which sparked the beginning of the end.

Rafe leaned on the railing at the edge of the second-floor deck. He could just make out the old asphalt pavement below, chipped and decaying under an inexorable growth of weeds and scrub. Once upon a time, that road or a helicopter was the only way to get to the chateau, but after the destruction of roads and bridges, he installed one of the new polymer surfaces with built-in sensors to guide autonomous and hover cars.

At first, there had been a glut of appreciation, especially as it became clear how many good jobs were suddenly available. Just rebuilding the roads and bridges took years. Nowadays, men drove their solar powered cars on near-empty highways and shopped at well-stocked stores or on *Ticolo*, the American-specific, community search engine. They could chase after jobs they wanted, even if they weren't qualified, with no competition from better-educated women, no having to share the benefits or, for that matter, wages, and none of the financial hardship that children inevitably cause. Depending on personal preference, they hiked or biked on carefully maintained trails in wilderness areas, visited national parks, or gambled in Las Vegas to the sound of rolling dice and rock music. They were able to purchase houses they never could have aspired to in the old days, indulge in hobbies, and save for old age. There were no jealous women at home making demands, and they had Carnevale to strive for every year, a week of enjoyment and commendation, if they were good enough. But after the passage of a generation these conveniences were taken for granted. No one gave a thought anymore to how it had been so painstakingly devised and executed.

Would they ever realize the only reason they could enjoy life in such a manner was because he and Henry Montague had the courage to do what was necessary?

He might be condemned to hell, but he'd saved the goddamned planet. He, Novikov, Soung Jae-jin and Henry. The four of them had made it possible for future generations to live on instead of yielding to annihilation. Sooner or later, without the choking infestation of human beings, the earth would recover and become fertile again. A paradise. It had to. It just had to.

No matter what the grumblers claimed, they'd paid a very small price.

You're whining. Old, sad, pathetic Rafe.

Staring blankly, he wandered through his enormous, empty hotel.

Every now and then he thought he heard Erin's voice, or McKenna's, or Brianne's. He would stop, turn, and search.

He came to the guest room where Erin had slept until he finally seduced her.

Had he seduced her? Or had she merely let him think so while she plotted her escape?

A mirror hanging on the far side of the bed showed a haggard face. Who was that? Dull, drooping eyes, lank hair, shirt half-unbuttoned and wrinkled.

Was that *him?* Raphael Alexandros Konstantinou, presidential advisor, architect of the new world order?

She saw through you the instant she woke up in the hospital.

As if of its own accord, the brandy glass he always seemed to have in his hand flew through the air. It was well-aimed, shattering the mirror and breaking the frame. One side swung before falling to the floor.

"Mr. Konstantinou?" Mild as always, Samson's voice intruded, followed by the cloudy, emotionless face. "Are you well? Do you need anything?"

"Leave me alone," Rafe muttered, but, as Samson started to dissipate, he amended. "Wait. Contact Darko. I need—want—two—no, four grams of *Mozart.* Tell him to bring it to the gate and there's an extra thousand in untraceable if he gets it here in half an hour."

"Yes, Mr. Konstantinou." Samson vanished.

The light in the closet came on as Rafe stepped inside. He'd chosen the dresses and gowns, the sweaters, even the underwear, while Erin recovered in the hospital. Oliver was the grunt who took care of the boring details. He'd kept the young man hopping as he rejected first one thing then another, until he was satisfied.

He pulled the dress Erin had worn to church last Sunday off its hanger. There was no scent, nothing to ignite any memory of her. She hadn't used any of the perfumes he'd bought for her, not even once. It was like she'd never been here.

The FBI had found no trace. It was McKenna all over again. Erin had vanished and somehow subverted the subdermal tracker beneath the tattoo.

Had she cut it out? He'd heard of women who tried that. It was placed deep to discourage such measures, but desperation sometimes overrode pain. Not that it did them any good. They usually died after unknowingly breaking the bacteria capsule placed oh-so-meticulously at the center of the tracker, but if they didn't, there were other fail-safes. Hunger alone would drive women out of hiding eventually. The reward for turning in a lone woman was enough to set a man up for life. Long-term escape was impossible.

Not even Erin managed to evade her destiny forever.

Samson claimed he prevented Erin and Brie from leaving, but his memory chip stopped recording at about the same time he said they tried to get into the garage.

"Damn it," Rafe shouted at the closet wall. "Did you have help? Where are you?"

The first thing he'd done after being informed of the theft of his Lykan, and after discovering who had taken it, was to send Flannery to Will's cabin. In a matter of hours, his private investigator reported that Will was at that moment chopping wood, alone. He continued to watch but Will never left the area and no one else ever appeared. He promised he would make certain, but it looked like Erin was not there and that Will had no involvement with her disappearance.

At this news, Rafe swung back and forth between relief and apprehension.

He would not entertain the idea that she and Brianne had been taken against their will. This time, he would see things with reason and logic. No one could break into this house, steal people, and get away. They never had. Erin had left him. Once again, she'd deliberately and maliciously stomped on the love he longed to give her.

Redmond Warwick would be calling soon to inform him his advice was no longer required. His value to the vice-president-turned-president had never been as strong as it had with Henry Montague. Aquilo would follow suit. They wouldn't want a leader who allowed his wife to turn him into a public laughingstock. Twice.

"Oscar Torres is at the front door, Mr. Konstantinou," Samson announced.

He threw the dress on the floor and hurried downstairs. Oliver had just closed the door on Torres. He turned upon hearing Rafe and held out a box.

"Don't let anyone disturb me," Rafe said, grabbing the box. "I don't care what happens."

"Yes, sir. What should I do about your parents?"

He'd completely forgotten they were coming over for a late supper. "Call them and cancel." He couldn't take his mother's endless interrogations and criticism. Screw them.

He heard a rumble of thunder and the driving thrum of rain striking the outside walls as he left the entryway and entered the study, slamming and locking the door behind him.

Opening the bag inside the box, he cut two fat lines of pure *Mozart* right on the coffee table. The glittering orange granules vanished up his nose, followed by half a glass of GlenDronach, which he downed in three wasteful gulps.

He would obliterate Erin's face, and McKenna's, and Brie's, laughing the day he gave them the heart necklaces symbolizing his everlasting love.

RINGING. ALMOST INAUDIBLE, AT THE FARTHEST EDGE OF AWARENESS, DEMANDING attention by its persistence.

Charon's bell reverberating over the river Styx.

A deadly, incessant tone, accompanied by black and crimson explosions.

Erin's come back. Erin's at the door.

Why was no one letting her in?

"Answer the door," he muttered, shifting onto his back and throwing out one arm. It connected with the edge of the table. A thud was followed by the odor of whisky and wet carpet.

He tried to speak. "Oliver. Let her in."

The bell rang on, undaunted, growing louder then softer.

"Why the fuck is no one getting the door!"

He rolled over, landing in the spilled whisky, and pushed onto an elbow, cursing. How had he ended up on the floor? His lower back throbbed.

At least he hadn't dreamed. There were only vague memories of spectral streams of light, intensely blue.

Ringing.

Ringing.

A monstrous roar of thunder shook the table and knickknacks. Something fell nearby.

Ringing.

He staggered to his feet. That hammering sound wasn't coming from his head after all. It was rain. Hail, maybe. Here on the first floor, with so many stories stacked above him, the outer walls and ceiling far removed, one never heard such things, no matter how hard it poured. This must be an epic storm.

Another peal of thunder and immediately a flash lit up the wall in the hallway. The storm was overhead.

Who had opened the study door? He'd locked it when he came in so he could drink and snort drugs in privacy. Hadn't he?

Step by slow step, he lurched out of the room.

Who could it be? His new guards never let anyone through the gates without permission. Was it one of them?

He reached the door, struggling with the handle before remembering it was always locked.

"Samson, unlock the door." His voice sounded hoarse and unfamiliar.

The door flew open since he was already tugging on the latch.

Thunder exploded, so deafening that for an instant, it severed the connection between his mind and body; he imagined he was no longer on firm ground but a kilometer up inside storm clouds. A wicked bolt of lightning momentarily blinded him. Rain slashed sideways, sluicing in beneath the porte-cochère, stinging his face like needles.

Ricocheting shadows coalesced into one single black outline, a motionless figure in silhouette.

He squinted, blinked, and blinked again.

"Erin?"

The only light came from small overhead lamps set in the porte-cochère, the lampposts spaced at intervals along the drive, and reflections from pools of water. All he could discern was the impressive height of the figure before him, a long black coat, a raised collar…

And dazzling blue eyes.

A human shadow with fire-demon eyes.

For a split second, he thought he heard the rattling screech of an angry pterosaur. Then he saw them, three monstrous females, ebbing and flowing, their shrieks ripping through his brain. He covered his ears with his hands, turning to run and striking the edge of the door. He slumped, surrendering to apathy.

The figure spoke. The sound was like thunder coming down from the heavens and taking human form.

"Hello, Father."

With the voice came the memories.

Chapter 4

ONCE, DURING A HOLIDAY FROM PREP SCHOOL BEFORE CORDELIA PERMANENTLY severed their fragile connection, Dillon took nine-year-old Will on a three-day backcountry hunt. Will used the opportunity to ask about their last name.

He was being teased and wanted to know why their name was so different from everyone else's. There were many Christiansens, Allreds, and Bensons, but no other names like his.

William was so common as to be invisible. It was Camael and his surname, Konstantinou, causing the problems. Perhaps the teachers had been gossiping, and some child had overheard. Sniping began. He was a "dirty Greek," a "goatbanger," and a "popeblower." At nine, he didn't know what the last two meant, but the older boys hurled the insults like bullets.

Dillon tried to change the subject, but Will would not be sidetracked.

"Your mother and I…um…argued," he said reluctantly. "She wanted to give you and your brother religious names. I wanted traditional Greek names. Neither of us were of any mind to surrender, but finally, we compromised. Your mother chose Raphael's first name and I chose his middle name. Alexandros. I chose your first name and she chose your middle name."

"Why am I William, then?" He didn't think William was Greek.

He relented and explained more fully. "It was my gift to her. A secret message. You see, I convinced her to marry me by getting down on my knees and reciting *Aedh Wishes for the Cloths of Heaven*, by William Yeats. You know, the poem on the dining room wall? I relinquished my name choice so that she would always be reminded of that poem, whenever she said or heard your name. I thought—I hoped…well, never mind."

Will could only remember the last three lines of that poem. Whenever he read them, he pictured himself as a poor supplicant, and his mother stomping around on his passions.

"There was something else," Dillon said. "Don't tell your mother, but your Christian name came to me in a dream. I saw a woman. I think she was actually a goddess. Athene, in fact, the Goddess of Wisdom. She ordered me to name you William and I didn't dare defy her."

Dillon often mentioned the ancient deities of his homeland when Will was young.

He'd asked what his father's Greek choice would have been.

"My favorite uncle's name was Sisyphus," Dillon said gravely.

Will's mouth fell open as he imagined what the boys would have done with that, until Dillon laughed and said he was teasing. He would have named Will after his grandfather, who raised him. Demetri.

Dillon had been happier then. Kinder. He'd had a sense of humor before Cordelia's fanaticism corrupted their marriage and everything became hard, cold, and oppressive.

Will heard his father's voice echo as he left the dream. *I didn't dare defy her.* He blinked, trying to clear away the fog.

He was lying on something hard. His head was pounding. He opened his eyes and sat up. He was in the living room, on the floor.

A stranger sat on his couch, gazing impassively at him.

Every fiber of his being kicked into alarm. Only habitual discipline kept him from jumping up and, perhaps, making things worse. Instead, he looked around, maintaining an air of calm. He was not tied up, but then, he didn't need to be.

The man held a sleek black Glock on his lap. One operational bullet from that pistol would shred his chest with nothing more than a muffled thump. The man held it casually, but his finger was on the trigger.

It had been a long time since Will had seen a viable firearm. He knew they existed, but not for common men. About thirty-five years ago, shells and cartridges stopped working as expected. Some disintegrated like sugar in the chamber when the trigger was squeezed, and some backfired, killing the shooter. Only old stockpiles fired as expected.

Will was certain by this man's relaxed confidence that his cartridges would be operational.

The last thing he remembered was buckling the girth on Dusty's saddle. The horse hadn't been ridden in a few days and was antsy. He'd planned to ride him and lead Daisy on a long wilderness excursion. He'd already loaded the saddlebags with water, a blanket, rations, and a tent.

He'd heard a faint scuff. As he pivoted, something hit the back of his head.

Slowly, so he wouldn't earn himself a quick death, he raised a hand and felt the exquisitely painful lump.

"Sorry about that," the man said.

"I don't suppose there's any use asking who the hell you are."

The man smiled. "Why are you keeping Mrs. Konstantinou's things, Will? Her underwear, her gloves, her shampoo. It's a little perverted."

Ah, they'd figured out it was him who broke into the chateau last month. "Fuck off," he said mildly, even as his heartbeat sped up. Sure as shit, on Rafe's orders, this man was going to slaughter him. There was no use answering his questions.

Smile fading, the man got to the point. "Has she contacted you? Have you seen her? Think very carefully before you answer."

Will hadn't expected this but he continued to wince and rub his scalp without any change in expression.

"Good poker face," the man said. "Impressive. The thing is, it sort of makes me feel like you have had contact with her."

Will didn't know what to say or do. This wasn't about the break-in. This was something else.

Erin's run away again.

And Rafe believed she would run right back to him.

His heart thudded with silly joy. Erin had left Rafe. He should have known this would happen. After McKenna died, there would be nothing to keep her there, other than McKenna's child. Maybe she'd taken Brianne with her. He hoped so.

On the heels of joy came overwhelming sorrow. This man was going to kill him. He would never have a chance to see her or tell her how she'd made his life complete.

Lifting his gaze, he stared coldly, refusing to say a word. Let Rafe wonder for the rest of his miserable life.

The mercenary's head slanted and his eyes narrowed. "I was wrong. You haven't seen her."

He got up off the couch and Will stood too, careful to make no sudden moves.

"Friendly warning," the man said. "If she does show up, I'd advise you to let your brother know immediately. He told me I could kill you if I wanted, but I think you'll make the right choice. The only choice."

Will said nothing, just let one quirked brow answer for him. He knew what the man was really saying. He was going to be used as bait. There would be eyes on him from now on.

He hoped Erin would not make the mistake of coming here.

His visitor waved the pistol and nonchalantly left.

WILL HIKED TO DALLAS CREEK. HE DIPPED A SPONGE IN THE ICY WATER AND pressed it against the lump on his skull until the ache eased and there was no more bleeding. Then he sat, watching white-green water spray and bubble over boulders.

He fished the necklace from his pocket, glad the man hadn't searched him and taken it while he was unconscious. The silver rim caught at sunlight like a beacon; the milky veins in the blue jewel winked slyly.

"Are you all right, Erin?" he asked it. "Is there any way to find you?"

Light flared off the water and he felt himself falling like he'd tumbled head-first into a well. Stars formed, thousands, millions, converging, filling his eyesight.

His last conscious thought, as he dropped into a trance edged in white-veined lapis lazuli, was that he must have a concussion.

He dropped into a scene of bustling activity where everyone was dressed in tunics and sandals, the kind worn by people in antiquity. He wore similar garb, with the addition of bronze-plated leather armor. Looking above the crowded marketplaces and beyond the cypresses, he saw the walls of the famed temple. Labyrinthos.

Crete's queen and the moon are sisters.

Then he was standing in the courtyard of that temple. A line of richly-attired women approached, eying his brother with curiosity.

Keeping his helmet on, he studied the high walls, the balconies, the russet pillars with their vivid blue capitals, the fountains, potted trees, and bystanders.

His brother—*Chrysaleon*—removed his helmet, shook out his hair, and bowed to the queen. Women and children leaned over the balustrades, staring and pointing like they'd never seen foreigners before.

His gaze soon returned to the young woman at the center of the approaching group. Garbed in an open-faced blue blouse and long, layered skirts flashing with disks, she moved gracefully and proudly, her gaze unequivocal, in patent opposition to the females at Mycenae, who might receive a bruising cuff for such overt postures.

She held the hand of the woman next to her, who leaned in close and said something. When his brother turned away from the queen to observe them, Will caught her sudden pause.

He knew her. She was the vision in the pool on Mount Ida, hair slicked off her face as she laughed and splashed with her dog. She was the girl in the cave, illuminated by flickering lamplight, ready to join with a man in honor of Crete's rite of fertility.

She was the enticement he and his brother had come to blows over. His cheekbone still throbbed from Chrysaleon's punch.

She was Aridela, all grown up.

For longer than you can imagine, I will be with you, in you, of you. Together we bring forth a new world, and nothing can ever part us.

Will lifted onto his elbows. Night had fallen and the air was sonorous with cricket song. The water in Dallas Creek rushed on, quiet now, carrying the last of the snowmelt from the highest peaks; both moons floated in the heavens, one close and bright, the other bluish. Ghostly. Mysterious. *L'ombre Moon.*

He watched them slip from one side of the sky to the other and knew what he would do.

A hot, dusty place. A place of magic, where the world began.

He stood up, stretching and giving the bump from the attack a cursory exam. "Crete." He tasted the word on his tongue. "Nothing can ever part us."

Getting out of this country wasn't easy, but he could do it. In fact, he looked forward to the challenge.

When Cordelia and Dillon disowned him, they assuaged their guilt by providing him with a trust fund. He'd used some of it to buy his land and build his cabin.

High time he dug into it again.

Chapter 5

"Let's go above," Maya suggested after Brianne and I had a hearty breakfast of bacon, toast, and oatmeal. She was already dressed in dun-colored zip-offs, boots, a loose, long-sleeved, dun-colored shirt, and a big brimmed dun-colored hat. A coil of rope and other gadgets hung from carabiners on her belt and she carried a beige backpack.

"Doctor Livingstone, I presume?" I saluted. "Or Edmund Hillary?"

She laughed. "We won't be reconnoitering Africa or ascending Everest today, and you're going to look just like me after you change."

Brianne asked who Livingstone and Hillary were. We explained, then I asked, "What say you, child? Wanna go hiking?"

"Yes!" Her excitement was infectious. This was exactly what she needed. New distractions. If McKenna could see her now, she'd be overjoyed.

Maybe she can see. Maybe.

"Okay then." Maya accompanied us to our bed cave, where two sets of clothing like hers were laid out. "Let's see how good I am at guessing sizes. What about the pain, Erin? Need some meds yet?"

"I could use something mild to dull the soreness."

"Okay. I'll get an analgesic cream."

"When are we going to meet everyone?" We'd passed four people on the way here, and I'd smiled, but they all looked away.

My senses tuned in to Maya's hesitation.

"Later." She eyed the bag I'd packed at the chateau. "Right now, I think getting fresh air and the last of that drug out of your system is more important. What's in here?"

"Stuff I stole from Rafe." I opened it and placed everything, one by one, on the bed.

She noticed the currency cards first and fanned them out, touching them as though afraid they might bite.

"It's all right," I said. "They're untraceable."

"Are you sure? If Rafe could track these…"

"I'm sure. I asked Samson, and he never lies."

She fingered the bills. "It's been years and years since I've seen money like this. Not sure they can be used anywhere."

"Rafe wouldn't have them if they weren't any good. Samson said he uses cash overseas."

She stared at the Krugerrands. "This is a hellacious amount of scratch."

"He can spare it."

She picked up the book and examined the cover as I explained.

"I was snooping in his office and found this little button that opened a hidden door into a secret room. Three rooms. Maybe more, who knows? I found three. There's a bunch of ancient stuff, things he's collected from archaeology trips, and a big library, and a museum with priceless art and treasure." I pointed at the stack of papers. "These are translations of some hieroglyphic tablets he has. Samson printed them for me. I skimmed through that book you're holding. There's so much more I think I can learn from it, although the forward says the writer was a drug addict. Maybe that's part of the attraction."

Maya put the book aside and sifted through the translation sheets, one by one, her brows lowering. I saw her precise scientific persona coming to the fore.

"This was in one of his display cases," I said, picking up the bone knife. "I guess I should have told you first about the statue in the hidden library. It spoke to me. It ordered me to take Brianne and get out and it told me to bring this knife and the translations."

Brianne frowned. I realized how I sounded and hoped she didn't think I was bonkers. I couldn't read her expression.

"Can I hold it?" She gestured to the knife.

"If you're careful," I said. "It's sharp. Here." I placed it on her palm.

"A statue spoke to you, eh?" Maya's age-old skepticism. I'd missed it.

"I know, I know, but it did. I swear."

"Did its lips move? Had you tried some of your author's drugs, maybe?"

I laughed. "No, Maya. I was stone cold sober. And it was more of a telepathy thing."

Brianne held the knife across her palm, looking down so I couldn't see her face. She hadn't moved since she'd taken it from me.

"Brie?"

No response. I lifted the knife from her hand. Her gaze followed, and I recognized that blankness from before, when she saw and heard things nobody else could see or hear.

She spoke quietly. "The Lady sends swans to carry his soul to Hesperia."

"Brie?"

Maya held a finger to her lips and shook her head.

"What seems the end is only the beginning." She sounded like an adult. She turned her gaze from the knife to my face. "We will make ourselves barren."

I frowned. That line…

Then I remembered. "No more children," I said. "No more love."

"Not until they all lie dead," my granddaughter responded. "Then we will begin again."

Maya and I exchanged a glance.

"She's done this before," I whispered.

"Meemah?" She blinked and rubbed her eyes. "Aren't we going hiking?"

I pasted on a smile. "Yep. Right after we put on these delightful outfits."

We changed. Maya sprayed our hands with UV block as she told us what to expect.

"I hope we find some wildflowers. The area can be so pretty when desert flowers are blooming. Where there are flowers, there are sure to be butterflies, so let's keep our fingers crossed."

"It's really safe?" I asked.

"We'll be careful. That's why we're dressed like this. You'd be amazed how thoroughly we'll blend in, and I've got a drone alarm. It will warn us if one happens to come along, but they don't very often. That's the beauty of the Canyonlands."

She hadn't been kidding about the inaccessibility. We had to suck in our stomachs to slink around several boulders before emerging on a shelf no wider than my foot. Dropping to the canyon floor, we clambered over a noxious pile of debris that poked and prodded and scratched and tried to pluck out my eyes. Once we got through that we hiked, single-file, along a narrow boulder-strewn wash, then rappelled into a lower canyon—Brianne laughing all the way—and inched through a claustrophobic seam before we finally came to the exit, made of nine scary-shallow "moki steps" and rock ridges. Eventually we hoisted ourselves over the edge and onto the surface of the earth, where we rested and drank from the water bottles Maya had brought.

"Why aren't we wearing shorts?" I was drenched in sweat and splashed water on my face. "Two months at Rafe's and I'm completely out of shape."

"Now, Erin, surely you had to be careful of the sun in Colorado. You really need to watch it here. I don't know the state of the ozone anymore, so I'm erring on the side of caution. The clothing we're wearing blocks UV rays."

"I've never had a sunburn in my life, and I doubt you have either. We do need to be careful of Brie, though."

"True. Pale-face." Maya tugged the brim of Brianne's hat, making her giggle. "Is this your first ever hike, child?"

Brianne nodded, though she seemed to be barely listening. She stared in every direction, at distant, hazy blue mountain ranges, buttes, and the red rock dotted with sagebrush. How must this seem to a child essentially imprisoned inside a building her entire life? I sensed her desire to run, to explore.

I felt it too, the limitless space opening up around me. Freedom, transcending everything I ever thought I knew of freedom. It had been stolen from me as well for the last two months.

We headed for a series of formations and chose one with steep sides, topped with fantastic hoodoos. A ring of boulders lay around the base. What must they have sounded like when they tumbled from the summit? One resembled the petrified head of a Tyrannosaurus Rex, or, no, maybe more accurately an alien turned to stone. A sly smile stretched across its face.

Maya brought out a book on wildflowers and we examined every blossom we found.

"These flowers seem healthier than they did last time I was up here," Maya said. "There's more, too. Look. They're everywhere! This is weird, because it hasn't rained. They must be getting water somehow."

"Let's not pick any," I said to Brianne. "If we do, they'll die. The bees won't have nectar to drink and the spiders won't be able to catch the little bugs nesting in the blooms. The problems go on and on. Enjoy them on their stems, child."

"That's good advice for every living thing," Maya said, "except that the bees have left this area by now and I doubt there are any spiders either, because there are no little bugs. There's no water out here except in early spring, and everything needs water. There's a mass exodus when summer hits this red rock land. We probably won't see anything but ants. I don't know what the hell they drink."

At that moment a bumblebee buzzed past her head. She stared, nonplussed. Finally, she shrugged. "It's almost July. This is weird, believe me."

"I believe you," I said. "But there is a bee, nonetheless."

We watched it meander.

"Listen," Maya said. "Do you hear it?"

"What?" Brianne's eyes were big and round.

"Nothing." Maya's lips twitched.

I turned in a circle. No jets. No drones. No birds. No animals. Not even a breath of wind. Only our voices and the sound of our boots on earth and rock. When we stopped walking and talking, we were engulfed in silence.

Before I left Rafe the first time, I'd lived with constant noise. The ringing of phones, the chatter of TV, endless music pumping from players into ears stuffed with headphones, people talking, crying, screaming, fighting, advertisements blaring, the bellow, hum, or roar of machinery like lawnmowers and air conditioners, trucks, cars, and trains, and the rumble of jet engines. It was quieter at the chateau, but not silent. There was the never-ending backdrop of the waterfall in the sunroom, the clatter of dishes in the kitchen, music from hidden speakers, guards talking and laughing, mulching machines, tillers, snow blowers, and snow shovels grating against the walks, planes humming on their way to the Salt Lake airport. And the wind. It was never calm on that mountaintop. Even at Will's cabin, the rushing water in Dallas Creek never stopped, wildlife squeaked, sang, cried, or growled, and there were almost daily thunderstorms. The many sounds of a living forest. I had grown so accustomed to underlying racket that I quit paying attention. It was just part of life.

To be outside, to see no other humans, to hear nothing, not even wind, was eerie, like something gigantic and invisible was watching us and everything familiar had shrunk away. It reminded me of the time I'd been in Texas during a tornado warning. Everything fell silent just before it struck, and I joined in the silence. Uneasy. Waiting. My ears straining. Knowing something dreadful was coming.

This eeriness was not dreadful. It was wonderful. Invigorating. Life pulsed through me in a new and vibrant way. Will's cabin in the San Juans had offered something similar, but it was closed in. We were surrounded by forests and mountains. This was the opposite. Endless heavens. Endless earth, and we alone walked upon it.

Brianne climbed the formation joyously, her laughter echoing. "Look at me, Meemah!" she cried from the top, waving.

I returned the wave and drank in the empty, sage-scented land stretching into infinity. "No masks," I said. "No leashes. No sentinels. No church."

Maya laughed. "You know why?"

"Why?"

"No men. At least, none who are followers of the current administration. They don't think this land has any value. They don't think humans can live out here."

"I was cooped up in that stupid chateau for two months, and Brie has been her whole life. McKenna too. It's a wonder they didn't both go insane. If I hadn't escaped, I would have gone stark, raving mad. How could Brie ever heal there? That place is a tomb, pure and simple. A tomb for living women." I started crying helplessly. "Once upon a time, I loved it so much. I wanted it to be a happy home."

"It must have been ten times worse for you, because you were free before."

"I miss him, Maya."

"Rafe?"

"Will."

"Contacting him would put his life and ours at risk. Someday, maybe..."

"Do you know that men's group, Aquilo?"

"Sure. Aquilo is a major brainwashing venue. They gotta keep these men motivated, right?"

"Apparently Rafe is its figurehead now. I about fainted when he told me. It used to be geared toward subduing women. But now that women are beyond subdued, I can't see what the purpose is. What do you think? Has it changed from what I remember?"

"What do I think? You probably don't want to hear what I think. That it's a racist bunch of women-hating bigots that helped mold America into what it is today."

She looked into my eyes. "Tell me the truth. Did Rafe hurt you?"

"Of course not," came out of my mouth automatically. Then a creeping itch ran through my cheekbone as I remembered that slap. Not to mention being repeatedly drugged, or a nameless, faceless doctor implanting a tracker in my arm while I was unconscious. He'd hurt me in other ways, too. Psychologically. Emotionally. "You've never liked him," I said, buying time while I inwardly faced what had to be faced.

"For good reason. He never let you think for yourself. He took over when you were still a kid and turned you into his little house frau. He stalked you, Erin, like any run-of-the-mill pedophile. You couldn't see it because you were too young, and he was so damn charming."

She swung away from me.

My face burned. One of my biggest regrets was the flippant way I'd rejected higher education in favor of marriage and motherhood. I'd believed I was choosing independence. It was years before I realized I'd gone for the opposite.

Up until this moment, I hadn't realized just how much Maya hated my husband. I wasn't angry. Blunt she was, always had been, but until now, she'd obviously tempered her words. "I wonder what he's thinking? I hope he can understand my motives. He's so different. Do you know what happened to him?"

"I can guess. He was given unlimited power. I have things I need to tell you, Erin, but first, let's have lunch."

"You have food?"

"Sure." She searched out Brie at the top of the rock formation. "You hungry?" she called, shading her eyes from the intense sunlight.

"Yeah."

"Come on then. Your Auntie Maya brought snacks."

We feasted on sandwiches, apples, cheese, and brownies, and washed it all down with cold water in insulated bottles.

"Look at the clouds, Brie." I stretched out my legs and supported myself on my elbows. "I see a dragon. That long tail and the fire coming out of its mouth, see right there?"

She peered into the sky in a way that told me she had never once laid on the ground and invented images in the clouds.

"I'll bet you see things up there, don't you?" I asked softly.

She guided my hand, maneuvering my index finger so that it was pointing at a big, fluffy cloud floating apart from the others.

"You see something in that one? Is it pretty?"

"A face. She's looking at us, Meemah. She's smiling."

I watched her. She went on staring at the cloud, then she smiled back.

AFTER WE'D EATEN AND CLEANED UP OUR MESS, WE HEADED FOR A BUTTE MUCH higher, longer, and wider than the others, squatting grandly on its own like a giant's anvil. That's what I would have named it, but Maya said it was commonly known as Citadel Butte, since its original name was lost to history. Brianne, with the inexhaustible energy of childhood, ran on ahead.

She stopped abruptly, almost falling over. "What's wrong?" I shouted.

"There's a white butterfly. I bet at night it turns into a fairy. Do you think it's drinking nectar, Meemah? I wish I'd brought *The Faerie Handbook*."

She was the sweetest child. "Maybe it's having a late lunch. Nectar is fairy wine, I seem to remember."

"Fairies love nectar, and honey, and milk, but there's no milk or honey here." She frowned. "I wish we had some."

We walked on, enjoying the sunlight, the earthy smell of sage, and a sense of peace that made reality seem like a bad dream. Somewhere out of sight, a bird released one disconsolate note. Brianne ran from one formation to another, her natural curiosity emboldened, perhaps for the first time. She brought back a rock with multicolored stripes like a rainbow.

"Uncorrupted," Maya said, turning it in her hands and brushing off the dirt.

"What does that mean?" Brie asked.

"It means this rock, this whole place, is untouched. Not ruined by humans," I said. Without warning, I started crying again.

"What the hell?" Maya said. "I've never seen you cry so much."

"Don't you remember?"

Maya stared at me then grinned. She turned to Brie. "I used to talk," she said. "Just talk, normally, but Erin didn't like some of my words. She thought they were pretentious. It was just talking to me. I never could figure out how I was supposed to know which word she would take as pretentious."

"Showy, too," I said.

"Isn't that what I said?"

"Big words."

"Pretentious is a big word?"

"It is if you don't spend twenty-four-hours a day with scientists. That and 'reconnoiter.' Jeez!"

We giggled, embraced, and brought in Brie for a hug. She ran off in ever larger circles.

"Tell me how you and Rafe got tangled up with Henry Montague," Maya said. "I didn't see much of you during those years. How the hell did that happen?"

"It wasn't my plan, that's for sure. It totally messed with everything. Me remodeling Ramandu's Dawn, having society parties, and being a house frau..."

She had the grace to blink.

"We were living in New Hampshire while Rafe attended Dartmouth, then we went to Oxford for his year of study abroad, then back to Dartmouth. We'd agreed to make our home in Utah when he graduated. The plan was for him to go on to law school with the goal of joining his father's firm in Salt Lake City, but what is it you and I always said?"

She grinned. "Never. Make. A. Plan."

"Exactly. Something will always come along to screw it up. In our case, it was Henry's cousin, who happened to attend two speeches at Dartmouth defending the nearly one-hundred-year-old conservative club. He asked the name of the speechwriter. Consequently, Rafe was invited, just days after graduation, to Washington, with a promise of meeting the president. Henry was impressed and invited Rafe to stay on as an intern policy advisor. Within a year, he was promoted to Senior Policy Advisor and Henry's aide-de-camp. I had to fly back and forth overseeing renovations to the chateau by myself while Rafe attended Georgetown Law and grew ever closer to the president of the United States."

"Was this before or after Henry revitalized the defunct Republican Party?"

"After, and after he gave it its new, radicalized mission. I watched Rafe turn into an ardent supporter. He'd always been conservative, but that word took on a whole new meaning when he started working for Henry. I had to swallow my opinions so often I should have had chronic acid reflux. Rafe and I never discussed politics for the sake of our marriage."

She laughed. "Chronic acid reflux. Yeah, that about describes being around Rafe."

"Maya, you've hated Rafe since we were kids, but it seems like lots more people hate him now. He's got armed guards everywhere and drones buzzing all over the place. It's like a high-security prison. The Rafe I remember was admired. Respected. Envied. Everybody wanted to be him, or at least have sex with him." I paused, but Maya didn't return my smile. "After McKenna went missing, he said there are people who would do anything to harm him, including harming her. You said Levi killed her to hurt Rafe. What happened? What changed? Do you know?"

She took a deep breath and I saw that she was struggling to keep her voice neutral. "It's because of what he did to the women. He stole us and turned us into profit machines. He makes men pay to be with women, and women have no choice in the matter. He's kind of a glorified pimp. One way or another, men pay, either directly if they have the funds, or in service, like the military. If they make their superiors happy, they get rewarded with sex. If they're disobedient, they get cut off. Sometimes for years. I'll tell you something. Men seem to have it all in this sick world, but they're prisoners too. Men are controlled through the control of women. Every one of us is a prisoner, trying to survive the dictatorial whims of the Reformation Brotherhood."

"'He stole us.' What the hell does that mean?"

"Exactly what you think. He had help, of course. I'm not implying he did it alone. This had to be a carefully coordinated effort, probably between several countries. I'm willing to bet the rudiments were hammered out the night you ran away, between those four men, the leaders of the most powerful countries on earth. Women were never released from quarantine, Erin. They were transferred into cages. Kennels, as you call them. That's where women are, where they live, those who aren't owned or under the protection of rich old bastards, escaped, like me, or in mass graves. They're in cage farms. At least, that's what we've been able to cobble together by hearing each other's stories. It's not like they published a 'how to take over the world' manual."

She saw my shock and nodded. "It's true. You would still be there, if Will hadn't gone to Rafe. Rafe and the others in the Brotherhood are the only ones with the means to undertake finding a lone female in all the cage farms. We think there are farms throughout the United States and across the world, in every country aligned with Ukrus."

She looked out over the desert, where Brianne laughed as she climbed another formation, shouting, "A lizard!"

We waved.

"You were actually one of their major helpers." Maya reached out and took my hand as though she wanted to soften her words. "Although I don't believe for a minute you knew that. When the second moon came and women went berserk, the government set up the Protective Quarantine. Remember?"

I nodded. My lips felt too numb, my mouth too dry, to form words, though my mind shouted. *Of course. How could I forget that?*

"Women were asked to turn themselves in for testing and treatment. They were told it was the best way to keep themselves and others safe and limit the spread of infection."

Nausea began the process of curdling lunch. My knees trembled. I could barely manage another nod.

"That was the start. Massive numbers of women cooperated to protect their loved ones from their own uncontrollable violence, and to take part in finding a cure. We were so trusting. The government used you as the face of their social media campaign. You convinced women it was legit. Safe. Millions of women voluntarily turned themselves in, partly because you told them to."

"I was there. I traveled across the country and saw the places. They weren't those kennels. They were nice. I toured them. Some were renovated hospitals and auditoriums. Some had been built specially. I interviewed the women. The doctors. The scientists. Everyone was hopeful. Not happy about being separated from their families but resigned. They knew it had to be done. I saw the laboratories." Rising desperation crept into my voice. "They let me see the studies they were running. They explained how they were searching for changes in DNA and chromosomes. They showed me the instruments they'd set up at various places to test for contaminants in the air and water. They wouldn't have done all that just to fool me into lying to American women."

"Would they not? It was very effective."

I didn't know what to say. The idea that I played a part—any part at all—in the imprisonment of millions of women was too much to bear.

Maya threw me a bone. "I suspect it was real in the beginning, when you were being used. In the US, anyway. Later, things changed. After you ran away, they started rounding up the rest of us. Damn, we made it easy, since most of us had already put ourselves into their hands. All they had to do was send out the military, town by town. Montague had never rescinded martial law, and most likely, he gave them carte blanche. They bombed bridges and roads behind them so that it became next to impossible for people to travel. I doubt there were many women left in the wild, so to speak. Just those few who were hiding, or who hadn't caught the lunacy and refused to go into quarantine, and scientists, like me, working on a cure."

"You were one of the scientists?"

"Yeah. A molecular geneticist I was friends with wooed me out of my psychiatric residency in order to help. We worked twenty-four hours a day, catching naps on cots, trying to figure out how to reverse the lunacy or develop a vaccine. Something. Anything."

"A molecular geneticist," I heard myself repeat. I sounded like a parrot. "You didn't get the lunacy?"

"Actually, I did. I tried really hard to hide it, knowing they'd remove me from the work and send me into quarantine. Because of my background, I had access to all kinds of drugs, and I found one that helped me control the symptoms. It was experimental and unapproved, a dopamine blocker called Monopsyphrenohexamin. It didn't have a brand name, so I started calling it *Moshe*. I knew it wouldn't last forever though. Every day, I felt that rage trying to break through. I kept having to up my dosage, which caused terrible stomach pain and weird hallucinations. I suspect I didn't do my liver any good. My urine turned fluorescent and burned. It was actually that drug that got me thinking about the brain differently."

I was never infected with the lunacy for some reason, but Rafe would have sent me into quarantine anyway. We'd discussed how important it was that I join the other women, to show solidarity, our trust in the process, and to set an example. He would have sent me there if I hadn't run away.

Would he have let me come out?

I could no longer answer that.

"Men just accepted this?" My voice was oddly hoarse. "There were no standoffs? Not one single man in this entire country tried to fight? They let the government take their wives, their daughters and girlfriends, their coworkers?" I remembered an armed confrontation that happened some years before I was born. A cattle rancher held off the government over grazing rights. I'd learned about it in American History class in high school. If they would do it for cattle, surely…

"It's hard to believe, isn't it? That in America, land of the free, the entire female gender could be caged like nuisance animals. Many claimed it wasn't happening, despite the actual evidence of no women anywhere. They declared their political opponents were making it up in a power grab. We figured out over the years that the Cages were built in remote areas, usually underground. Heavily guarded, fenced, the works."

Maya's tired shrug let me know my question had been asked innumerable times. "Lots of things conspired to make it successful. First off, men were terrified of women's rage. The lunacy was mysterious, caused by the second moon. It only affected females, making it mythical and evil in a subliminal way, a way that made them see women differently, like they weren't really human. I'm sure you remember. Some were afraid for themselves. 'They'll arrest me too. I'll disappear too.' Apathy played a part, as it always does when the opposite is needed. Some of the guys in the Catacombs have told me they were tired of the never-ending conflict between the sexes. Once the women were gone and men had access to new jobs and opportunities, they decided they would give this brave new world a chance. Time passed, the roads were rebuilt, and everyone seemed to accept the changes. And, lest we forget, there were the very loud, enthusiastic supporters. More than you want to know. They were promised rewards for their support. They would be paid well, they would have power, and they would get women. New, fresh women, without commitment. Those men blamed women for the loss of their age-old privilege. They wanted revenge. With the government putting the blame for everything on us, including the illness we had no control over, the world got the lowered birth rate it needed and at the same time satisfied the evangelical groups, who wanted women biblically punished for stepping out of line. I remember seeing Rafe during one of his rallies on TV. He said men made a terrible mistake when they allowed the liberation of women. He said that out loud, for millions to hear. It was exactly the message the religious groups wanted. It came to be accepted fact that if anyone was to blame for the state of things, it was women. Overpopulation? Women's fault. Mental health problems? Women caused it. Violence and crime? Look no farther than women. They were even blamed for the appearance of the second moon and lunacy. Because they defied their place in God's structure."

How the hell had I been married to Rafe for so long without ever seeing the contempt he bore towards other women? I had no answer but that I saw what I wanted to see, true or false.

"Men were methodically conditioned to think of us as things, not people. Some men resisted the brainwashing, but in the beginning, when this was being set up, we were all isolated from each other. There was no way to congregate and form a plan for fighting back. No way to find out if there were others who felt the same way. Oh, I almost forgot. At first the government reported that the lunacy victims died. What man is going to fight if he believes there's no one to fight for? Lists of the supposed dead were distributed and men were told their loved ones had been cremated to limit the spread of disease. It was complete fiction, of course. The first questions arose when a few women were seen. Then it was grudgingly conceded that yes, there were survivors, but they were so few and rare that they were too valuable to be released. They were moved to special places for their own protection and the continuation of the human race. Here's the truth. Not many women died of lunacy, if any, but lots of women did die. Those who were considered useless to the Reformation Brotherhood were murdered. Sick women, handicapped women, old women. The young ones, the pretty ones, the viable ones, those were kept. Some were given to members of the Brotherhood and other high-ranking toadies. If they were lucky, females with powerful family members were taken home to live out their lives in isolation. The rest, the vast majority, were dumped in the Cages for future use and pretty much forgotten."

"Rafe told me the women were released and sent home."

"That never happened, Erin."

I stared at her, weighted down with guilt and hopelessness, hating what I had done to bring about this world. Once it was accomplished, I ran away. I lived with a man who loved me, in a forest in the mountains, while almost all the other women were packed into plastic kennels.

Maya gripped my hand tightly. She knew. I didn't need to say a word.

"You missed it," she said. "All but the very beginning. The rest of us were fools. We didn't believe an entire planet of males would sit back and watch the wholesale imprisonment of women and never lift a finger in protest."

"Really?" I was at one of the lowest points of my life, and I heard it in my voice. "I know you haven't forgotten Germany, and the second world war. This sounds like much the same thing, on a larger scale."

"Yeah, I take your point," she said. "There is good news. Even as the government strengthened their hold over the years, we've grown stronger as well, and trickier. We figured out how to communicate with others in hiding. The Catacombs is not the only place protecting subversives. There are many. We're working together to locate the cage farms. We know where some of them are. One day, at the right time, we'll attack. Sometimes I fear it will take an intervention from some omnipotent deity. A miracle. Other times I think we'll manage on our own. We always have."

"Tell me more about the beginning. What you saw and experienced."

"There aren't many specifics, because almost every means of communication went dead. My colleague, Pascal, said it was digital darkness, and we wouldn't know how to handle such a massive regression. He, like many scientists, had been expecting it sooner or later. It was like every satellite shut off at once and the fiber optics were cut. Online, there was nothing but shopping sites. That's how we knew it was deliberate, because you could connect to a few of those, but at others, especially where there was any kind of news or social interaction, there was nothing, and no way to communicate via comments on any of the sites that did work. They were turned off. Calls and texts never went through. The TV channels at every provider disappeared except for one with a recorded message that ran constantly. A man sitting behind a desk relating a problem with sunspots. Not to worry, he said, everything would soon be up and running."

She took a moment to breathe. "It reminded me of a movie I saw when I was little. The only way people had to communicate an emergency between large distances was by lighting bonfires on mountaintops. I wondered if we were on our way back to those days. How spoiled we were, with our instantaneous gratification. News, services, porn, entertainment. For the first time I realized how much I was relying on the web to do my research. We took it for granted until it was shut off. It was freaky, Erin. Scary. We'd huddle at work. Everyone had an opinion, or had heard something somewhere, but nobody knew anything for sure. Conspiracies ran rampant. I tried not to listen. That way lies madness."

"Yeah."

She shrugged free of her backpack, plopping it on the ground. Taking out her water bottle, she drank, offered it to me, and squinted as she watched Brianne. "A scientist I was working with came in one morning saying he'd heard Pyongyang was bombed from space, killing Soung Jae-jin. It was one of those viral rumors, impossible to verify. He heard that Novikov did what you told me that night on the phone. He weaponized his satellites. He could bomb any city on earth with the push of a button, and he had them cloaked so nobody could shoot them down. The scientist said the reason communication was disrupted was because Novikov had blown up everyone else's satellites. His were the only ones left, so he controlled everything. That rumor wasn't true. Novikov didn't blow up everyone else's satellites, because they did start working again. They were only down for a couple of weeks. But that's what happens when rumors get started. Some are right, some are wrong, and nobody but those at the very top know the truth."

She tucked the water bottle into her pack and shouldered it again, shrugging so it sat evenly. "You're right about the standoffs. This is America, after all. It's a matter of pride to distrust the government and go for your guns if confronted. There are a few older men back at the Catacombs who were able to fill in some important blanks. Like I said, the military was sent out town by town, rounding up women, but their secondary agenda was to take the weapons. Wherever they were confronted, wherever they met resistance, they killed everyone. Men, women, children, animals. People were given one chance to turn over women and guns. Anyone who refused or shot at them was slaughtered. Two of our guys witnessed it in real time in Baltimore. They watched with binoculars from a high-rise. The resisters were bombed by some kind of guided missile from a drone. There was a lot of collateral damage, bystanders disappearing into the dust cloud. Nobody seemed to care. Another one of ours, Zachary, saw something even worse in Colorado. A military drone dumped a white cloud over an armed, fortified camp that was resisting. Zachary heard a lot of screaming, but nobody came out. We think it was a nerve agent. Another guy told us about working at a nursing home in Louisiana. Military stormed in and went room to room, shooting the patients. We figure it happened all over the country. Old, sick people contribute nothing and eat up assets. So, away they went."

Brianne came up to us excitedly, a butterfly perched on her index finger. It seemed content to allow this human to ferry it around.

"It's so pretty," I said. Orange and black, with a rim of light blue around the edges of its wings.

Maya brought out her book and they looked it up. "A Western Pygmy-Blue," Brie said, before gently urging it to fly away.

She nodded to Maya's offer of water and had a drink before she ran off again.

Maya went on with her explanation. "We think it was a country-wide effort, aided by the inability for regular people to communicate. They couldn't prepare and set up effective blockades or bunkers or anything. Even if some of the more paranoid did hunker down, what good was that when the military was using gravity bombs and nerve gas? They'd passed those laws, too, the national gun registry, the ban on military weapons. And the price hikes. Remember when they did all that? Somewhere in the twenties, wasn't it?"

"2029."

"You always had a head for dates, boo. Anyway, the government had twenty years to collect information on the biggest troublemakers and make a real dent in gun ownership. We think they had a good idea who owned most of the guns and where the worst resistance would come from. Our best guess is that those people were targeted first."

"This is whacko," I said, but I knew it wasn't. All those women locked up in just the one cage farm I'd been taken to. Hundreds. Women being led around at church like docile pets, forced to listen to sermons drilling in their servility to men. The masks and tattoo tracking, and Rafe so complacently informing me I wouldn't be leaving him again.

They'd pulled all that off. They would have thought about guns, and found a way.

I did leave you though, didn't I? You're not as omnipotent as you like to believe.

"Of course, there are guns," Maya said. "Plenty of them, I'm sure. Why else do people like us need to be in hiding? They're accessible to powerful men, their guards, the military, and sentinels."

"How did this happen?" I asked, but I wasn't really asking. I was simply trying to wrap my mind around all she'd told me.

"Everything you said that night on the phone came true, Erin. The very last thing any of us saw on TV before it went dead was Henry Montague. He unloaded a crapload of bullshit on us. He said the US was leaving the Western

Alliance and joining Ukrus. He said the US and Ukrus were embarking on a partnership of collaboration, equality, and environmental regulation that would clean up the air and water. He attacked the Western Alliance. Said it had done nothing to address world problems, and existed merely to threaten Ukrus, who was the only one, besides ourselves, actively trying to find a cure. He said he preferred the US to be at the forefront of technology, at the head of deciphering the risks of the second moon, rather than the whiny tail end. He confirmed that he was sending our scientists to work side by side with the Russians in Moscow, and that for the first time in a long while, he felt confident there would be a swift, effective outcome."

I waited.

Maya glanced up into the deeply blue sky. At this moment, her changeable eyes matched the heavens perfectly.

"Turns out lunacy was only part of the problem. At any rate, it stopped as suddenly as it began. From what we can tell, no more women were infected after early summer in 2049."

"Right after I left?"

"Yep. No one who has come to us in the Catacombs has heard of anyone having lunacy in years and years. The younger ones have never seen it in real time. Of course, Ukrus claimed the win. Novikov announced that his scientists had devised a vaccine and released it into the air."

"Rafe told me no one knew how or why it ended."

"Yeah? That surprises me. I would have thought he'd be the first to give Novikov credit. Anyway, great news, right? Quarantined women could gather their belongings and go home."

I nodded hesitantly.

"Instead, it was the Cages for us, the ones who didn't get a death sentence."

"Maya, Rafe acted like he didn't know what that place was. He shot and killed those two guards, and he told me he sent in the police. I figured it was some kind of illegal thing, like a sex trafficking ring, and he didn't correct me."

I thought back to that conversation, trying to remember the nuances, and my heart sank. He'd lied. Rafe had done nothing but lie since the moment he picked me up off that plastic floor in the Quonset hut. It was a hard thing to stomach, how little respect he had for me. "Gemma, the woman in the cage next to mine, was so kind. I can't bear the thought that she's still there."

"I'm afraid that's true for thousands of women. Maybe millions. We think they started the roundups on the east coast. We're not sure why. Because that's where almost all the genetic testing was going on, at the universities? Or because that's where many highly educated women seemed to gravitate? I have a reason for saying that."

"What?"

"It was something someone said. See, I was taken in late June, just a month after you ran away."

All my senses sharpened in bitter understanding. She nodded. "I was in the Cages too, Erin."

"Oh, Maya. You know, then. You know."

She nodded again. "I do."

"Tell me everything you've gone through since I last saw you. Everything."

"We have time, boo. Time to get to know each other again."

Her smile vanished as a rapid vibrating hum rose from her belt.

"Drones!" she cried.

Chapter 6

"Pas, look at this."

"Whatcha got?"

Sliding his glasses up into his hair, Pascal leaned over the desk. Maya scooted her chair away to give him room at the AFM.

"Am I seeing what I think I'm seeing, or am I just tired?"

He frowned at the computer screen, made an adjustment to the parameters, and restarted the scan, watching as the images clarified.

"That is weird." He rubbed his eyes and loosened his tie. "Let's try it on the 3D imager."

"Do you see it?"

"I see something."

"Open the full specimen in the volumetric display," Maya ordered. A model of what Pascal had been looking at on the AFM screen appeared before them, rotating slowly, expanding on the sample taken from a woman with lunacy to a likeness of the entire brain the cell came from, incredibly detailed and clear, aligned in separated slices that could be manipulated however the viewer wanted.

Pascal used hand gestures to stop its movement, back up, or enlarge a specific area. He concentrated on the hippocampus, looking at it from every angle, finally zooming in on the right amygdala.

This was what Maya had been impatiently waiting for. "Do you see it?"

"Hand me those dissecting forceps."

She did. He returned to the atomic microscope and lifted the lid. The volumetric display followed him so that he could observe what he was doing in close-up, three-dimensional view.

"It's too small," he said, sighing irritably. The object seemed to actively move away from the microscopic tip of the forceps, though Maya thought that could simply be tissue reacting to the invasion of a foreign instrument.

"Looks like e-coli," Pascal said.

"I know, but something is off. The way it's moving, like it's intelligently avoiding you. It's way too small for e-coli, Pas, not to mention it's in the *brain*. It looks…" she stopped, not knowing how to finish that sentence.

"Artificial? I think we agree, but let's try the electron microscope. It might show things a little differently. I want a neuroscientist to verify, too."

"Who? With every means of communication down, who the hell can we show this to? Must we send up smoke signals?" Maya struggled to control the anger rising like a lava surge. Clenching and unclenching her hands, she took several deep breaths trying to slow down her heartbeat, but it hardly made a dent. She should have taken another dose of Monopsyphrenohexamin forty-five minutes ago, but she'd been too engrossed in what she'd found. A break-through, she hoped. Something not identifiable in the preserved brain of a woman who had died twelve hours ago, while infected with active lunacy. A quick-thinking resident had imaged the brain before she'd been dead five minutes. The object did resemble a common e-coli bacterium, yet it didn't. The revolving flagellum, for instance. She had seen that, hadn't she?

Pascal thought a moment. "Doctor Singh. He's a neurologist at Massachusetts General. I'll get in my car and drive there. I'll show him. I don't suppose we have any old memory cones laying around, do we?"

"I think so." She triumphantly produced one from a cabinet. "What about the roadblocks, though? Wasn't the bridge over Seekonk blown up? Not to mention the bridges in Boston." *Stop babbling. He can't know you're affected.*

"I'll walk if I have to." Pascal placed the cone on the AFM and ordered a backup of the system. "You discovered this. You should go with me."

"It might be safer if we split up, Pas."

They regarded each other somberly, turning as one at the sound of boots stomping up the stairs. The handle skidded across the floor as the door was forced open.

"Pas!" Maya cried as a sea of rifles pointed at them.

"Don't worry, my love." He placed his hand on her shoulder then stepped in front of her. "What do you want? You're interrupting our work. We're researchers, authorized by the president to be here."

"Not any longer," one of the men said. He motioned with the barrel of his gun, but Pascal remained where he was.

"Go," Maya said. "Move away, Pas."

"She is not infected," Pascal said forcefully, "and she has just made the most important discovery of this entire endeavor."

"Move aside," the soldier, or more likely a mercenary, ordered.

"I will not. I demand you follow the chain of—"

The soldier shot him. Even before Pascal finished falling, six others swarmed forward and seized Maya's arms.

WITH HER WRISTS BOUND BEHIND HER, MAYA COULDN'T DISLODGE THE COVERING thrown over her head and tied around her throat, though she could see, in blurry fashion, through the coarse weave. The men propelled her down the stairs, into the elevator, and out of the building.

She smelled rain through the fabric. It was a scent she always associated with childhood and puddles and joyfully turning her face up to catch drops on her lashes.

Will I ever smell rain again? she wondered as the men shoved her into a van. Tears streamed down her cheeks. She relived the horrible instant when Pascal clutched his chest and slumped to the floor. Maybe the bullet had missed his heart. *Someone, find him. Please find him. Please save him.*

There were others in the van. She heard breathing and felt the heat of crowded bodies. She inadvertently stepped on a hand and someone cursed. The side door slammed and all was darkness, pierced with soft weeping. As the van peeled out, Maya tumbled onto women, by the sound of their protests. "Sorry. I'm sorry."

They couldn't talk. There was an armed male somewhere near the back and whenever anyone tried, he threatened to shoot. Maya listened to sobbing and sniffling as the van raced along, taking corners recklessly.

Where were they going?

To quarantine, she told herself, filling her mind with images of her old friend Erin, smiling enthusiastically for the TV cameras as she toured luxurious facilities with an adoring entourage of doctors, nurses, and a few happy, obviously non-lunatic patients, who were enjoying massages and gourmet meals.

Now something else was happening. Her ears picked up a disturbance. It was too dark to tell what the male was doing, but she heard cries of fear, shock, and protest then interludes of silence, before it started up again. *Stop! No!* Silence. *Don't! No! What are you—*

The man was either killing the women one by one or anesthetizing them.

When her head was yanked backward, she kicked with all her might. If she was going to die, she would go out fighting. Her shoe connected with something, maybe a shin. She hoped so. That would really hurt. It definitely hurt her foot.

The man wrenched again, so hard she saw stars.

Something was smashed against her nose and mouth, on the surface of the sack. At the same time, she felt the press of a round injection tube against her upper arm.

There must be more than one man.

She tried not to breathe but failed almost immediately, due to the adrenaline rushing through her body. A sickly-sweet scent filled her nose.

Sevoflurane, maybe, though that was antiquated.

A metallic taste imbued her tongue then she experienced a rush of euphoria, followed by the uncaring awareness that she was about to lose consciousness.

A barbiturate with a side of propofol. These Neanderthals don't know what they're doing. I'm going to die, even if that's not the plan.

What the hell. There were worse ways…

Chapter 7

MAYA WOKE TO DIM LIGHT, A STALE SMELL, AIR SO DRY IT HURT THE INSIDE OF HER nose, and goosebumps.

She lay without moving as she fought off disorientation and fear.

Impenetrable darkness lay on every side but one, which provided a faraway, cold blue light.

She seemed to be alone, but she heard an occasional cough, suggesting others were nearby. She sat up, groaning when the top of her head struck something hard.

I'm alive, she thought. As she started putting together her memories, she patted her cheeks, her chest, and her stomach. The men in the van had managed to anesthetize rather than kill her.

How long had she been unconscious? Where was she?

When the mercenaries broke into the lab, she'd had on black pleated trousers, a white shirt with a crisp wing-tip collar and French cuffs, black suede Louis Milan boots and a lab coat.

All gone. In their place was a shapeless, sleeveless, knee-length shift of some scratchy material like burlap. Her legs, feet, and arms were bare.

Someone had stripped her naked and put this shift on her. She felt over her body a second time and after a moment of hesitation, probed between her legs, breathing a quiet sigh when she discerned no soreness, stickiness, or smell.

Vertical bars separated her from the pale light. She pushed and pulled, but they didn't budge. Beyond them she saw a line of small enclosures that gave her an idea of what she was trapped in. They looked like large animal trans-portation kennels.

The light came from three feeble lamps in the ceiling, which was a streaky, dirty gray, same as the floor. Reaching through the bars, she scraped with her nails, revealing a whiter substratum. She smelled what she scraped up, then touched her tongue to the particles.

Salt.

A distant motor started. When it stopped, there was an echoing clang and a smoky stench followed by a number of male voices. She heard disconnected phrases. "Latest shipment," "Look them over," "Bound for the trench."

A group of men wearing hardhats came closer. "Hey!" she shouted. "Hey you! Where am I? What the hell is going on?"

The men stopped. One laughed. Another came over and squatted. His companions followed.

"What's wrong, Ma'am?" he asked, concern furrowing his brow.

"Why am I locked up in here? Where are my clothes?"

"You're in a special place, darlin'. Because *you're* special. A doctor, right?"

"That's right. Whoever kidnapped me took me from important work. Work that could make a difference to the entire world."

The men laughed like they would at a child acting silly. Rage made her foolhardy. She could no longer separate reasonable rage from blood-tinged lunacy. "Let me out of here!" she screamed, trying to shake the bars loose through sheer will then reaching through, her fingers curled into claws, but she couldn't reach the asshole's face.

They let her shake and shout. When she stopped, the man squatting in front of her grinned. "You've got it bad, don't you? Poor little thing. Fetching, though. A real spitfire under all that insanity. Like a wild Mustang. God, your eyes are pretty. You could have had men fighting over you, but no. You had to go and get smart. That's why you're in this room, with the other smart ones."

"Smile, why don't you?" another man said. "Maybe then you'd be pretty enough to keep."

"Fuck you," Maya snapped, and added for good measure, "I like women."

"Why am I not surprised?" the squatting man said. "Too smart and a dyke to boot. We're going to change all that. We've learned our lesson, sweetheart. As our Lion says, the biggest mistake men ever made was allowing women to think they have choices."

His gaze lowered; she realized the burlap was gaping at the top. She scrambled back from the bars.

"A real shame." He rose and rejoined the other men. "Too dangerous to keep alive."

She wanted to shout but something stopped her. She'd been so angry she'd hardly heard what he was saying.

He might be trying to frighten her, or he might be serious.

The men walked on. One of them said, "Do we get to have any fun with these bitches before they go to the trench?"

Laughter drowned the reply.

Chapter 8

THE TIC BENEATH HIS LEFT EYE TWITCHED ABOMINABLY, PULLING RAFE OUT OF drugged sleep. He slammed two knuckles against his cheekbone. "Stop, goddammit."

The answering whine twisted down through his sleep fog like a screw.

He jerked upright.

His bedroom shimmered in blue-white light from the second moon. The original moon had traveled beyond the skylights and was hidden.

L'ombre Moon. Trickster Moon. Shadow Moon. Sly Moon.

A shape like a dog sat on its haunches not far from the bed. Its eyes picked up the moonlight and flashed emerald green, like an imp's. The whine repeated.

"What the hell?" He blinked, sure he must be dreaming, but the dog remained.

His gaze drilled into the gloom beyond the dog. A human figure sat in one of the wing chairs that was usually by the fireplace. One ankle was crossed lazily over a knee, which was about all Rafe could discern, other than his eyes, which also reflected moonlight.

Rafe knew those eyes. He shuddered as the chateau at Deer Valley fell away.

"Cailean," he croaked. "Vita."

He no longer knew which life he was in. Hadn't Cailean and Vita died at Uisge Bealach, the sea inlet at the northern tip of Scotland? Hadn't he watched them die, along with Eamhair?

Memories ricocheted like bullets, not from this life but six others, spread out through history. His heartbeat fell into wild disarray.

"Jesus Christ," he said out loud. "Erin."

Erin was Aridela, his lover and queen from the Bronze Age. His wife! Legally, romantically, emotionally. McKenna's mother, Brie's grandmother, was the woman he'd loved for nearly four thousand years. Until this moment, he'd had no idea, though he'd always known there was something different about her.

He was all of twelve when he found her, without the benefit of past life memories, but they must have been there, subliminally guiding him to the black-haired child who danced in the schoolyard. Somehow, he'd known she must be drawn in, held close.

What about the rest?

Disconnected scenes of him snorting *Mozart* and gulping whisky. Incessant ringing. Stumbling to the front door. A pair of blue eyes like knife blades.

Swift vignettes clarified then faded, his many mistakes, bad choices, and crimes running through his mind in full unbridled replay.

For as long as he could remember, nightmares had haunted his sleep. Erin often woke him, afraid of his thrashing and shouting.

Nightmares? They were memories, fighting to break through.

What did this man, sitting there so calmly, have to do with it all? It would seem he had awakened the memories without using any incantation or drug, at least that Rafe could recall.

He called me Father. That was an outright lie. In the Bronze Age, after Chrysaleon left Mycenae and became Aridela's consort on Crete, the wrath of her Goddess never again allowed him to sire any male offspring, never in that life, and never in any life since.

Bit by bit, his thoughts cleared. The man in the wing chair was not Cailean reincarnated. Cailean was gone forevermore, as was Taranis, and Eamhair.

Menoetius though, his Mycenaean half-brother, whose spirit lived inside Cailean's body, was another thing altogether.

Could this ghostly figure be Menoetius?

An intense burst of understanding set another puzzle piece in place. Menoetius was alive. He'd been alive for forty-seven years, inside Will. If it was Will in that chair, waiting for him to wake up, death was close. Revenge would be the only reason he would risk breaking in.

Rafe's temples throbbed. The animosity he felt for his little brother had always seemed irrational, but he must have unknowingly perceived a whiff of the Bronze Age bastard, the thorn in his side. He had hated his brother from the moment Dillon brought him home from the hospital. *No wonder.*

He stared blearily at the form in the chair. He should be afraid. Will or whoever it was had bypassed his guards and Samson. Now he sat not three meters away, and was probably armed.

Everything was murky. Rafe couldn't remember getting into bed. It had been storming, but now the heavens were crystal clear.

I'm too old for this. I need peace.

Why had it taken fifty-two years for his past life memories to return, and what the hell good were they now? They hadn't come back in time to stop Erin from running away. The only purpose they served was to confront him with his own mistakes. His own…evil.

"You just want to make me relive everything I've ever done wrong. Kill me and get it over with, you bloody damned whore."

Nothing happened. The creature didn't move. The man, or apparition, remained silent.

This psychic cacophony was too much. "Samson! Lights."

Recessed lighting switched on discreetly.

It was Vita. Of that he had no doubt. He would never forget that wolf, or its eyes as it closed its jaws on his forearm and snapped the bone on a beach thousands of kilometers away and over a thousand years in the past.

The man, though, was a true enigma. Youthful. Hair of copper, like Eamhair's, but darker, and the shadows in it seemed to move like fluid. His expression was a motionless pool of water, his eyes as deep and unreadable as the pit of hell. "Samson! Identify this man and…wolf."

"I am sorry, Mr. Konstantinou. Man, and wolf?"

"How did they get into my bedroom? Why was the alarm not sounded?"

"There has been no intrusion, Mr. Konstantinou. There are no unaccounted-for individuals inside, and certainly no wolves."

"They're right in front of me! I'm looking at them!" This was the same shit excuse Samson gave after the May break-in. He had asserted that no trespass had occurred, despite the broken window, the dogs going nuts, and footprints in the dew. There was obviously some error in the AI's code.

Samson materialized. "I detect 420 micrograms of *Mozart* in your bloodstream, Mr. Konstantinou. That is more than enough to cause hallucinations."

Rafe threw back the covers and jumped out of bed. He was naked but for black briefs and had no memory of undressing.

Suddenly he understood Erin's anger when she woke up to find a tattoo on her arm.

He stared through Samson at the wolf, and beyond, to the man in the chair. "Bloody hell," he snarled, and drew back his fist. Samson's gray-blue image swiftly dematerialized.

The wolf bared its teeth. Its pelt bristled.

Rafe's fist loosened. "I'm not hallucinating."

"No, Father." The young man uncrossed his legs and stood. He had Cailean's impressive height. Rafe was 196 centimeters. This man was taller. "You are not."

"Who are you?" The man's accent was not pronounced but had a Scottish flavor. "Why do you call me that?"

"Do you not remember the young woman you raped on the beach near the fortress of Dunaedan?"

At those words, Rafe's head felt as though it had disengaged from his neck and was slowly spinning around the room. Or was the room itself spinning?

He couldn't tell up from down. Why had he snorted that *Mozart?* This was the worst trip of his entire life. If he could get through it, he would never abuse drugs again. *So help me, God.*

In a daze, he saw clouds of white swirl around the stranger, white with hints of pale green and intermittent sparks of copper so bright they nearly blinded him.

The aura.

He staggered, flinging out a hand to catch the bedpost. "I—I did not…"

The stranger stepped forward. "Do you deny raping my mother?" His eyes turned as hard and cold as obsidian, so much like Vita's he nearly gagged. He could believe that inside this human, if he was human, there lived a wolf.

"Yes! No! I—we loved each other. How do you know these things? How *could* you?"

"I know because I am the product of that rape. I am your son."

"She didn't…this is insane. What the hell is your name?"

Under the young man's gaze, Rafe felt stripped and pinned by a thousand knife points.

"Adamantinus."

It was stated simply, softly, yet the word echoed, and Rafe thought he glimpsed those three harpies, staring, mouths foaming.

"Ada…"

The wolf growled.

Rafe snapped his mouth shut. He had to get ahold of himself. "You cannot be Eamhair's son. It was over a thousand years ago." But he knew that was a lie. Cursed Harpalycus had devised a way to continue living, a way that was different than the repeated incarnations Athene forced upon him, Menoetius, and Aridela. Perhaps this young man used the same mysterious method or had discovered another way.

"One thousand five hundred and seventy years."

"Why are you here?"

"Can a son not want to know his father? I am here to meet you. To know you. To be your son."

"And that?" He gestured, and again the wolf growled. "Why is *that* here?"

"She is my companion."

Rafe's forearm throbbed in spiritual remembrance of the night it was mangled. He breathed in through his nose, willing a return to mental and emotional control.

The wolf appeared quite ready to mangle him again. Rafe's gaze moved on to the young man, who waited as if he had all the time in the world.

In the year of our Lord, five hundred and two, I, Taranis, a woodcutter, left my mother and traveled to the edge of Scotland, searching for something I could not name, until I saw it. Not it. Her.

It hadn't taken him long to recognize the tall, copper-haired lady at Cape

Wrath's fortress as the rebirthed Aridela, queen of Crete. Some inexplicable homing instinct had brought him to her.

In that life, she was called Eamhair, and Eamhair's brothers had thrown her off the cliffs for refusing to marry the man of their choice. Taranis had believed her dead, crushed by rocks or the sea. He never found her body, though he searched for many days.

A month later she reappeared in the company of Cailean and his wolf. To make amends for what he had done to her, he'd revealed the secret of the hidden routes through the fortress, which made it possible for them to sneak in, find Eamhair's mother, and escape.

But his stupid bloody jealousy got the better of him and he betrayed them, only to get trapped in the middle of their confrontation with Bericus, his sons, and Fathna, the king of Innse Orc.

Fathna. *Harpalycus!*

Eamhair, Cailean, and Vita died that morning. He distinctly remembered the village boys, and Eamhair falling beneath the onslaught of stones. A moment later Vita succumbed to the same injuries. She placed her head on Cailean's thigh and drew her last breath.

It was harder to recall Cailean's death. Everything was blurry, probably because of his own wounds.

Yes, Eamhair might have been pregnant, but she died long before a babe could be born. This man was lying.

He wanted Adamantinus to be Eamhair's son, *his* son, but it could not be true.

He searched the intruder's face. What he saw was Eamhair, in the bone structure, the shape of the eyes, and the flowing, darkly copper hair. Eamhair and something else. Something…not entirely human.

Rafe could not read those eyes. Not even the tiniest bit. The man standing before him made his blood run cold. At the same time, they fired strands of hope.

"I have returned to you, Father," Adamantinus said, placing his hand on the wolf's head. "Like Mordred returned to Arthur."

Chapter 9

"Brianne!"

She turned and I motioned for her to get down. Without question, she dropped. I could barely see her as she tucked her hands under her body and kept her face pointed to the ground.

"Wait a minute." Maya whipped out a pair of binoculars and slapped them onto the lenses of her sunglasses, swiping at the edge to focus the view. "Unless they've developed something to make them invisible, I don't see anything. They can make them tiny, but these Ocs are supposed to be able to detect the slightest artificial movement. There's a bumblebee, but it's a real bee, not a machine."

We sank to the ground anyway, making ourselves as small as possible to lessen any chance of discovery as she went on with her inspection. After a few minutes, she peeled the binoculars off her glasses. "There's no drone. Something must be wrong with my alerter." She removed it from her belt; holding it upside down, she gave it a tap and a shake. "Dust maybe. Sand."

I motioned to Brianne and she ran to us.

"Maya thought there was a drone," I said. "You were amazing. You knew exactly what to do." I high fived her and she grinned.

Maya replaced the alerter on her belt. "I don't know why it did that, but we need to get back. I don't want you two navigating the canyon in the dark."

Subdued and not quite reassured, we made our way to the shelf steps and climbed down. Once at the bottom, we felt safer.

Maya brought out headlamps. Brianne strapped hers on and zipped in front of us, calling herself Doctor Livingstone.

"Erin."

I glanced at Maya as we scrambled around a mess of branches. "Yeah?"

246

"I've been trying to figure out the best way to tell you this. There are people who weren't happy to know you were coming to the Catacombs. They blame you. Some blame you as much as Rafe, and some blame you more. Some think Noah would be alive if not for you. Some would like to turn you in, knowing you'd probably be killed. For your own safety, I don't think you're going to be able to stay very long."

I stopped walking. Now I understood the looks I'd been getting.

"I know," she said quickly. "You were lied to. Duped like everyone else. But you were the smiling face of it all, Erin. It's going to take time and I don't know what else to change minds."

I had already thought these things. In my mind I saw faces of women who left their families and submitted themselves to the quarantine on my word of honor.

There was nothing I could ever say or do to make amends for the lies I told the American people and the horrible consequences those lies inflicted.

Maya wasn't finished. "Then you ran away. You could have blown the whistle, Erin." She hastily added, "Nobody knows that but me."

I hung my head. I'd taken off. I chose to hide from my husband and child. From the entire world. The masks, the leashes, the Cages. It was all on me.

"Now Erin," she said, gently giving my arm a shake. "I know what you're thinking. It's typical for victims to blame themselves. I want you to tell yourself this a hundred times a day till you get it. The fault belongs with Henry Montague and Raphael Konstantinou. It's on Grigory Novikov and Soung Jaejin. The Reformation Brotherhood. That's who to blame for the world we live in."

I wasn't ready to think so clearly yet. "Can Brianne stay? I'll go. I'll go tonight. Please, please don't make her suffer for what I did."

"I don't want you to suffer either, Erin! I *know* you. Something happened. Maybe something psychological. You would never abandon your child. I *know* that, as sure as I know myself."

A little hand slipped into mine. "I know it too, Meemah," Brie said.

I knelt and hugged her. "Thank you."

"Wherever you go, I'm going with you." Her mouth tightened into a stubborn line.

I felt like living again. Seven words. That's all it took from the right person. I was able to stand without feeling like I might topple.

Maya urged us to walk on. It was getting very dark. "I'm certainly not blameless. Based on what you told me on the phone that night, I should have tried warning everyone myself. The thing is, I don't think it would have done any good. I had no proof. They would have denied everything. I decided to put my energy towards curing the lunacy. Knowing what I know now, if I had come out and accused Rafe and the president, I probably would have mysteriously disappeared, never to be seen again. Same goes for you, Erin."

"At least you did something."

We hiked in silence.

"It's interesting to me as a doctor that you can't remember that night," she said suddenly. "Dissociative amnesia. It's quite rare, but that's what you've got. Whatever you saw or heard or were subject to was so traumatic, your brain locked it up and threw away the key. It's curious, too, that for some reason you shut off the safety mechanisms in your car. You must have even disengaged your seat bands, to be thrown into the windshield. I would like to be able to explain that but I can't, other than to posit the obvious. That you were trying to kill yourself, in a very gruesome way."

"Oh, wow, I'd completely forgotten, but that's what the psychiatrist at UCLA said I had. He assured me such things were transient and that it would heal within a matter of days. I didn't tell him I'd been trying to remember why I'd left Rafe for twenty-three years. It drives me nuts, Maya. Every night when I go to sleep, I try to bring it back. There are voices. Faces. Terror, revulsion, and pain, but nothing gels."

"He was right. Most cases of dissociative amnesia are short-lived. I've never heard of a case lasting as long as yours."

"I wonder..."

"What?"

"Could Rafe have done something? Dosed me with something, or done something that erased that night?"

"Something that would last twenty-three years?" Maya shook her head. "It's possible. The Reformation Brotherhood could have developed a new drug that I don't know anything about. What do you think of trying hypnosis?"

"You know how to hypnotize people?"

"It's been years, but yes, and I had good outcomes back in the day."

It was nice to experience a ray of hope after the dark moments of self-recrimination. Casually, I said, "Depends how much you charge. I've recently lost my job."

Her smile was relieved. I realized how hard it had been for her to say those things. "For you, gratis. Let's do it tomorrow."

I slept badly. Any noise in the corridor beyond the Navajo blanket had me tensing, fearing someone was coming to slit my throat. Maybe I deserved such a fate, but Brianne didn't deserve to see it happen.

When the old-fashioned wind-up clock on the table by the bed told me morning had come, I rose wearily and dressed, but was hesitant to leave the chamber. Thankfully, Maya soon arrived and requested permission to come in.

"Do you have a wolf?" she asked.

"A wolf? There's a question I never expected to hear."

Brianne, slipping on her sneakers, paused and looked up.

"Three people told me there was a wolf outside your doorway all night, stretched across so no one could pass unless they stepped over it. I was kidding by the way. Thomas—the guy who removed your tattoo and holo cell—would have mentioned a wolf in the car with you. But I swear, three unconnected people say there was one outside your doorway last night."

Why were three people snooping around this room?

Keeping my uneasy fears to myself, I said, "I've never seen a wolf in my life. Why would they make up something like that?"

She laughed. "Bored troublemakers. I've had problems with them before, although never of the supernatural kind. Come on, ladies, it's breakfast time. Then, Brie, would you like to play with Dharma? She's already asked if you can."

"Yes!"

I'd noticed nothing was blasé to this child. She approached every day here with new excitement. I started to mentally curse Rafe for keeping her in isolation her entire life, then switched the condemnation to myself. After all, I had run off in true cowardly fashion instead of staying and fighting for my daughter and granddaughter.

Silence fell when we entered the dining cave with our dishes, which we'd filled in the kitchen. My face heated as about ten people stared at me, but Brianne cracked the tension when she saw her friend and ran forward, shouting, "Hi, Dharma!"

Maya and I sat near the girls and everyone went back to their conversations, though one or two of the men continued to scowl. I felt guilty for eating the food these people worked so hard to acquire. I knew without them saying so that they didn't like sharing with a traitor.

Maya ignored them. "Ready?" she asked as I finished.

I realized I hadn't even tasted my sourdough toast. I was itching to get out of this room. "Yes."

"Let's do it in your sleeping cave, where we'll have quiet and privacy."

I told Brianne where I would be then followed my doctor.

Maya delved into a leather bag she'd brought along and withdrew several candles. We stood on the beds and taped fabric over the lights in the ceiling to dim the room then she lit the candles, making things more intimate. "Okay, lie down on the bed, on your back. Comfortable?"

"Sure. I warn you, I've never been to a shrink. I don't think my mind will allow itself to be manipulated."

"Don't worry, I won't force you to bark like a dog." Maya pulled up a chair, sat, and brought a pen and notebook from her bag. "We do things the old-fashioned way here. I no longer trust electronics, not even my drone detector, after yesterday. Hey, that reminds me. What was going on with Brie? She was in a trance."

"She has the ability to see things, according to her mother and Rafe. Clairvoyance, I guess it's called. She walks in her sleep, too. She predicted an earthquake once, before it happened, and Brie knew someone was hurting McKenna before anyone else even knew McKenna was gone. I've seen her in that state a couple of times. The first time, I woke her up and disrupted the vision. The second time, I let it play out. What you heard was pretty strange. It seemed to me like that knife caused it to happen."

"Interesting. Makes me wonder what we might learn if I hypnotize her. With your permission, of course."

"Let's see how today goes."

"Sounds reasonable. First, we need to get you relaxed, okay? Then we'll continue."

For nearly half an hour, we worked on releasing tension and breathing properly. Maya helped me visualize myself inhaling white light and loosening each muscle, beginning with the toes and working up through the legs, torso, and finally, my face, which was far more tense than I'd realized.

She rose and stood beside the bed, placing her hands, palms down, above my body. My eyelids were half-closed, but I watched her sweep her hands from my feet up to my head and, once there, make a sharp flicking motion. At first, I wanted to laugh. Then I realized things were changing. Every time she cast away whatever invisible substance she'd gathered beneath her palms, I felt lighter and lighter until I was almost intangible, like a soul freed of physical boundaries.

"Little by little, you're going deeper," Maya said. "Your muscles are warm and heavy. You don't want to move. Can you hear me?"

"Yes." I forced my lips to reply. As if from a distance, I observed how relaxed I felt.

Apparently, I could be hypnotized.

I HEAR A VOICE. IT'S SOOTHING AND REFRESHING, LIKE A BREEZE.

"Erin, I'm going to count backward from ten to one. By the time I reach one, you will be deep inside your mind. It will feel like a warm, supportive cloud. You'll be weightless, buoyant as a rubber ball and cushioned in mist. While you're in this mist, you're completely safe. The mist separates you from worry or harm."

Each number diminishes the pain and fear of the last two months. My breathing evens out.

"Can you describe this room?"

"It's cozy. The fan makes the perfect white noise for sleeping."

"Do you like the Catacombs?"

"I could stay forever, as long as we could go hiking once in a while. See the sun and moons."

"Okay, Erin. I want you to go back in time. You're twenty-six. You've given birth to McKenna. Will you describe it for me?"

"The nurse brings her. She's got lots of black hair, like mine. I'm tired, but I can't sleep. I want to hold her. I want lots of babies, three or four brothers and sisters for her, but it's impossible. I had a tubal ligation."

A tear slips out of my eye. I'm tenuously aware as it trickles over my temple.

"Is Rafe with you?"

"Yes. He must have bought out the flower shop. He says nobody has ever loved like we do, and that we'll be together for as long as the pyramids stand in Egypt. He's been saying that since we were kids."

"You're doing well, Erin. Now go forward, to the night you left him. Tell me what's happening."

I pause. It all evaporates, my joy over McKenna's birth, my pride in the delivery of a healthy child, my happiness with Rafe.

"I'm on the terrace. I've come out to relax and have a glass of wine."

"Can you describe the terrace?"

"There's a big stone fireplace in the corner, but no fire right now. There's chairs and loveseats and tables. The only light comes from a solar powered flame-light on the other side of the infinity pool, but it's faint. I lie down on one of the chaise lounges and cover myself with a blanket. It's chilly, but not too cold. The Milky Way is right above me. So many stars, blazing in perfect silence. So many silent stars, watching our little blue planet. What do they think of us?" I pause. "They're disappointed."

"Why do you think that?"

"There's always a war somewhere. People hurting each other, lying to each other. Humans want to wipe each other out. I'm surprised we've made it this long. Rafe is right about the overcrowding. He says humans can't live this way. We'll eventually destroy the whole planet out of sheer rage."

"How do you feel now?"

"My son. My son."

"Matthias? What about him?"

"Adam. He is here, with me."

No more questions come out of the mist. I am left to explore on my own. "Meraud named him Adamantinus. She calls him her eidolon."

"Your voice sounds different. Where are you?"

"Inis Tearmann. Sanctuary Island."

"Where is Inis Tearmann?"

"I don't know."

I drift awhile, holding my baby, happy but for one thing. I'm afraid for my mother.

"Is your son still with you?"

"Yes, he's grown up. He's handsome, but sad and angry and lonely. It breaks my heart. Did I do the right thing, bringing him into this world?"

The voice in the fog redirects me. "Erin, let Adam go. Tell me more about the terrace. Is anything changing?"

My son extends his hand and I reach back. Our fingers touch, the barest kiss of sensation. I stare longingly as he fades. The last thing to vanish are his eyes. I realize he is the hallucination I have seen so many times since the second moon came.

"Yeah." Tears clog my voice. "There's cigar smoke. I hate that smell. I hear men talking. I'm waking up. My scars hurt. The moons have moved. I must have fallen asleep. I start to call out, let them know I'm here, but something Henry says stops me. I don't want them to know I'm listening."

"What does he say?"

I feel the softness of the fleece blanket and biting night air on my cheeks. I smell the acrid cigar smoke and a more subtle scent of Scotch whisky. I am in two places at once—on the terrace and in this warm cloud, separated and safe from all that is real and frightening.

A voice comes out of this cloud. A male voice, far away then growing clearer. It's Henry Montague. I can't see him. My back is to him and the chaise lounge is tilted, but I know his voice.

"I needed this fresh air," he says. "It was getting smoky in there and I've had too much good whisky."

"It is bracing," someone I can't identify answers.

Henry speaks again. "Are we really going to do this, gentlemen? Keep females in cages? Own them, fuck them, share them, sell them, kill them? Excuse my language, Doctor Petrov."

I hear a female giggle. "Please do not apologize. I am on your side, remember? You will soon see how much." Her English is almost flawless, only a hint of her native tongue coming through.

"It is not so hard to imagine, is it?" The low, coarse pitch and Russian accent tells me the speaker is Novikov, the president of Ukrus. "For most of history, females have been our property, to do with as we wish. It is only recently they have risen to independence, and I think we can agree that their taste of freedom has gone on too long. Look at the chaos it has caused. What we are doing is returning order. They will thank us in the end. Females never know what to do with autonomy. You will see. They will quickly adapt. That is the one thing females have always been better at than us. Accepting their role in servitude."

"But why?" Henry asks. "I'm not against it, don't get me wrong, but I'm not sure I see the long-term benefits. In fact, I'm imagining some mind-boggling repercussions."

Careful to make no sound, I shift so I can peer around the edge of the chaise lounge. The members of the secret meeting are clustered by the infinity pool, their faces marginally illuminated by the solar flame-light and violet lamps in the water.

Rafe, Henry, Soung Jae-jin, Novikov, and the unidentified man and woman.

They are all there, holding glasses of scotch. Novikov, Henry, and Rafe are smoking cigars.

The man I earlier assumed to be a scientist says, "I worry about that too." His accent is also Russian. "Will they not fight? How do you get them to accept what you are doing? Especially here, in your America. I have heard that for every man, there are something like fourteen assault rifles."

"Not anymore," Rafe says. "Congress helped solve that problem during Henry's first term. Americans wouldn't give up their guns. They slobbered on about revolutions and civil war, and there were so many shootings. Drastic measures had to be taken."

"What was the solution?" Novikov's tone is only mildly interested. Guns in his country have always been strictly regulated, so he's never had a gun problem.

"Assault weapons were banned and restrictions placed on gun ownership. Serious fines and prison time were levied against those who hid banned weapons. Simple things like that can make a big difference. What helped most was the gun registry, licensing, and forcing up taxes on guns and ammunition. There are fewer guns out there than you might think, plus we have a good idea who has them. Plus...we have bigger, better guns. And bombs."

"Rafe," Henry says. I hear a reprimand in his tone.

Rafe gives a slight nod.

"A well-planned initiative," Novikov says.

"Men across the country are taking their wives, their sisters and daughters, even their neighbors, to the nearest quarantine," Rafe says. "They drop them off and wave as they speed away. No doubt many of them have an inkling of what's really going on. There will be those who fight us, no doubt, but we're ready."

I think about how right now, at this moment, men, women, and children are sleeping in every town and city across America, without the slightest idea that these four men are plotting an upheaval that will change the world for all of us, forever.

"It's the perfect solution," Rafe says. "By controlling births, everything from overcrowding to climate change will improve, plus we'll control *who* can have children. You want white babies? Done. Heirs for our class, to carry on the power and bloodlines. Common stock for labor. How long have we torn out our hair trying to come up with a fix that wouldn't drive away our supporters? Here it is. The ban on abortion and birth control will remain, but the birth rate will instantly nosedive. Incorporating well-calculated gaps in births means recovery can get a solid foothold. I'm working on those details, but I think once a year, in select cities, with a select group of participants, we can keep things maintained so we don't go too far the other way and end up exterminating ourselves. I've put our best mathematicians to work on the numbers."

Rafe, my husband, speaks these words, and I grow cold. It is a unique, penetrating cold, the sickening emotional cold that occurs when the hidden, cataclysmic truth of someone long loved and trusted is exposed.

"Controlling births is necessary and of great importance to Mr. Konstantinou," Novikov says. "There is more to consider, however. When females are turned into rare and valuable commodities—virgins and fertile women even more so—it will be men like us who reap the rewards. They will be the red diamonds of our species, and we will be the dealers."

A clear note of admiration comes through in the hushed voice of the man who came with Novikov. "Men can have sex, if they can afford to. Some will give their life savings for ten minutes with a woman."

"Hell," Henry says, "I'd do that right now. Ten minutes. That's all I ask, with anyone other than my bitch of a wife."

Which sends them all into a round of callous laughter.

I believed Henry loved his wife, and I have never heard him curse. I have never seen him even slightly tipsy, but he is obviously drunk now. I stare at this stranger from my hiding place then I stare at Rafe, desperately hoping this will prove to be a terrible dream. Perhaps the wine was corked. I didn't taste anything off, but I'd heard old wives' tales about corked wine causing hallucinations, like moldy psilocybin.

The laughter dies out. Henry spews a cloud of cigar smoke and follows it with a sip of scotch. "It will be done before they can even begin to realize what a mistake they made, and by then it will be too late. People are sheep, and we've been herding them into this pasture for years, never knowing how or when we would get there, but herding nonetheless."

"Yes." Soung Jae-jin nods vigorously. "Well put, Mr. President."

"Women were designed for this," Novikov says, quite calmly. "That is the only reason they exist, to serve us and bear children. Patience is needed for grand, transformational changes, as President Montague suggests. I can attest to that, having much experience with your American concept of 'playing the long game.' At first, there will be problems, yes, but we have the means and might to quell them. Mark my words. One short generation and the females who have grown up in cages will think that is the way of the world. They will have no other expectations. The idea of equality and freedom won't even be a memory."

As icing on the cake, Novikov adds, "The younger men will come to see this as the natural order even more quickly. We will show them all the new opportunities they can expect and enjoy, now that women are under control. Their quality of life will improve. Their choices will multiply. Given time, men will see females simply as useful resources, like cows. Not human beings."

Silence blankets the terrace for a moment. I imagine they are picturing this future, as am I.

"Now that the papers are signed and you are the official owners of our women, our future, our country, and our souls," Henry says, "I think I deserve to hear those details you've been teasing us about. Like, how you got this idea in the first place, and how you linked it to the moon."

Novikov inclines his head. "I am happy to share some of our proprietary developments. We began the project long ago, my friend, eleven years before the second moon arrived, long before anyone knew it existed. It was happenstance, maybe, or luck, when the moon was first discovered by the Thirty Meter Telescope on Maunakea, very far away, yes, but we could extrapolate from its course that it would come to Earth unless something caused it to stray. My philosopher-scientists understood what we could accomplish by linking our research, which was still in the realm of the hypothetical, to the moon. They ramped up production so we would be ready, all the while inventing other scenarios we could use if the moon didn't come."

"His laboratories were quite a sight," my husband says. "Very impressive."

I remember the trip Rafe took to Moscow. He must have seen Novikov's setup then. That might explain the change in his personality after he came home.

"All right." Henry waves his cigar. "I saw the damn thing under that fancy microscope, but you haven't explained how the hell it actually works."

The female receives a nod from Novikov, possibly giving her permission to speak.

"Our nanobots are propelled by an artificial flagellum—a revolving tail— and each one has its own computer chip. A brain, if you will, just enough to process orders and carry them out. We made them to resemble a common bacterium, in case one is accidentally seen."

A soft gasp nearly breaks my connection to the terrace, but after a few floundering seconds, I'm able to return to the chaise lounge and the conversation.

"These are what we can thank for the lunacy?"

"Yes, sir. They have a tiny homing device that is attracted to human pheromones. They are lighter than mosquitoes, made to float in the air until inhaled. You might think many eventually fall to the ground and are wasted, but that is not so. The slightest breeze lifts them again, even if they are wet, and sends them back out to complete their mission. Once inside the body, the first thing they do is determine if the host is male or female. If male, they go inert and the body eliminates them. If female, ah, that is where the magic begins, Mr. President! They travel through the blood to the host's brain, and implant in the right amygdala."

"Where they turn women into lunatics."

"They follow whatever commands they receive. After the nano sets up, data begins streaming between it and our computers in Moscow. Moment by moment, the nano can use specific electrical stimulation to affect different areas of the brain. Attacking the parietal lobes causes the host to become confused, unable to understand and navigate. Concentrating on the occipital lobes would cause her to hallucinate. Just as easily, our nanos can attack the temporal lobes to make her aggressive and violent. We can provoke many emotions. Depression, fear, anxiety, paranoia. Even pleasure. Whatever we want."

Soung Jae-jin's English is almost incomprehensible. "Can you turn them off? I am not in favor of having to control lunatic females forever."

"We can activate and deactivate the nanobots at will. Not each one separately. Having a control code for each individual nanobot would require a planet-sized computer. We assigned codes to batches of 50,000."

I watch Henry squint, first at Novikov, then his scientists, for a good fifteen seconds before he says, "I should have you tossed in Guantanamo for cyberattacks on our citizens."

After a startled moment of silence, everyone joins in forced laughter.

"Yes, you should," Novikov says. "No doubt."

"I suppose you have already given the order to arm your satellites if anything happens to you, am I correct, Grigory Andreiovich?"

Novikov says, "I have taken the necessary steps to preserve peace between our countries. Of course."

"If I were a man of honor, I would eject you and dare you to blow up Miami."

Novikov's voice becomes smooth as melted caramel. "Would it be Miami, though, Mr. President?"

Silence.

Another burst of laughter, but with a strained undertone.

"Now that you have joined me," Novikov says reassuringly, "I will give the order for your satellites to function again. Life will return to normal. You will have your GPS, your communication, your shopping, your TV soap operas."

Soung Jae-jin tilts his head back and captures the dregs of his scotch. "It is not only the good doctor here who has made this miracle possible. I have watched your wife on television, Mr. Konstantinou. Because of her, the majority of women are already locked up. Please extend our gratitude for her invaluable help."

"Ooh." Henry wags his index finger. "Can't do that. She has no idea. He even lies about the pills."

"What do you tell her?" Novikov asks.

"Henry's exaggerating. I tell her the truth. They're formulated to control the anxiety she's had for years. I just leave out their primary function. The pills we give our daughter treat her ear infections. That is also true." Rafe sets his half-smoked cigar in a nearby ashtray and thrusts a hand through his hair.

He always does that when he's uncomfortable or angry. If I could see his face more clearly, I would detect the twitching beneath his eye. It happens when he lies or is stressed. I take hope from the gesture. Outwardly, he shows nothing but confidence, but he isn't as complacent as he sounds.

What the hell is the "primary function" of the pills? What don't I know about those little icosahedron shapes he places on my tongue every day?

Novikov turns his attention to Henry. "I am told you did not give the pills to your wife."

"Are you kidding? As soon as this thing started, I was dreamin' of her being put away. I wanted a good excuse to be rid of her without being accused of anything. I told Rafe to flush her pills down the toilet. She got it, gentlemen. She got it bad."

More laughter. Drunk Henry is proving to be the life of this party.

Balancing the cigar between his index and second fingers, Henry places his hand on Rafe's shoulder. "Your wife is one gullible lady. She believes whatever you tell her, unlike mine. It's a nice personality trait. She's a treasure, my friend. Funny. I don't remember her being that way."

Novikov's male scientist explains. "I think we forgot to mention the ingredient in the pill that generates manageability, Mr. President."

"Manageability? Nobody told me about that."

"Docility, if you will. Agreeability. A sweetness of nature that we have come to miss in our women."

"I'd rather not discuss my wife like a lab rat, if you don't mind," Rafe says tightly.

Henry breaks the awkward silence by changing the subject. "This moon has been a godsend, and you, Grigory Andreiovich, a prophet. Connecting the lunacy to the moon? Damn, I have to admit that was brilliant. Everyone blames the moon, everyone. Even liberals have put their blessing on a quarantine."

He pulls heavily on the cigar and turns his attention to Rafe. "I remember the very first time I saw you, when my cousin brought you to Washington. You were wet behind the ears, but I knew then I wanted you on my side. I was right, as usual."

"I have more ideas for the transition," Rafe says. "I've been working on this for two years. There's a lot more to tell, but I'm sure we've all had enough for one night."

"Yes. I'm tired, gentlemen. I'm older than the lot of you put together, and this fine whisky has scrambled my brain. Let's take it up again in the morning."

Rafe and Henry head for the doors, followed by their guests. Rafe holds the door for Henry. I hear him say, "It's important that men feel like they're an active part of the new order. I'm playing around with an annual gala. The females will go for it too. It'll be a status thing for them, plus they'll get medical care and better food. Win-win, for everyone involved. I'll tell you more at breakfast."

"Your aide-de-camp is a valuable asset, Mr. President," Novikov says. "His ideas are bold. He reminds me of my philosopher-scientists. I may steal him from you."

The last thing I hear Henry say is, "If you go that far, you'll have your war." He doesn't sound like he's joking.

My heart is broken. Gullible is the nicest thing that can be said about me. Not only do I not know Henry Montague, far worse, I don't know my husband.

Before I can succumb to useless, enraged tears, my attention is caught again. Novikov's female scientist has taken his sleeve to keep him from following the others inside.

"Did it work, *Gospodin* President?" the woman asks. "Are they convinced?"

"Have you had too much to drink?" Novikov replies. "They were always ours. Always. Tonight was just a little artifice to let them save face and pretend they had a choice."

"It was worth the trip, then." The scientist nods and steps inside.

Novikov is right behind her, but he stops. He swivels and stares right at me. I don't even breathe. I hope it's dark enough to hide my presence.

But it seems the gig is up. His gaze doesn't waver. He smiles.

Every crescent scar on my body bursts into flaming pain. His face melts away and I see another. It is one of the most terrifying things that has ever happened to me. His eyes drill into mine and as I gasp for breath, I experience something. I cannot tell if it is real or a dream. I see this man threatening to give me to his soldiers. He calls me a slave. He rapes me, laughing. He does not look like the man in the doorway, yet they are one and the same.

Time slows. Scenes play out. A tiny black-shelled snail slides over my wrist. A man carries me into an icy night.

By forcing yourself to suffer, by blaming yourself for what he has done, you help Harpalycus achieve his aim.

Cave crystals glisten in firelight.

I will have victory.

The soothing voice intrudes, grounding me. "Erin, leave the terrace. Go forward to Colorado. You're with Will. Describe the night you met him."

Evergreens sweep past, glimpses in the headlight beams before merging into formless black night.

"Help me, Mother. Help me."

You're coming straight to me. My hand holds you safe.

I accept the inner voice. It is no stranger than anything else that's happened. If I can believe that my government, with my husband's assistance, is going to imprison females, infect our brains with machines…

Leave that behind for now. *Ahead lies salvation.*

"Salvation," I repeat, appreciating the word's kick-start of joy.

Right turn off the highway onto a dirt road that winds steeply. I'm bouncing and scraping over rocks and through potholes. The road grows ever narrower, ever rockier. Soon, I will be wrapped in the contentment of a radiant ember fire. A man's boast echoes through the mist. *Look what I found.* Kneeling, his hair brushing against his chest, he holds a limp rabbit for me to admire.

I have touched the curved moon-scar on his cheek, but his name won't form. I speed up, knowing the answer lies ahead, hidden in darkness.

The windshield wipers scrub at freezing rain. I pay scant attention, for now something is returning my soundless call. *Where have you been? Hurry please hurry, I need you.*

It's not real. Nevertheless, my heartbeat thrums and I floor the accelerator. "This automobile has exceeded prudent speed limits for current conditions," the computer tells me. "The rate will automatically slow for safety."

I'm coming. I send the message into the night. *I'll be there. I'm coming. Find me.* I switch off the blaring safety system and unfasten the bands across my chest and abdomen.

When the tires lose their grip, it takes precious seconds to realize what's happening. The car spins, squeals, and careens.

I slam on the brakes but that does no good because I am now flying.

There is a horrible jolt. Glass explodes. Cold darkness. Metallic shifting, grinding. Losing consciousness, waking up.

We will make ourselves barren. No more children. No more love. Not until they all lie dead. Then we will begin again.

"Rafe?" We've been fighting. Cordelia has taken McKenna for the night, the hag. She always tries to insert herself between me and my child.

The family will be angry. Cordelia loves to see me mess up, and isn't this a mess? A wrecked car, and I have no idea where I am.

I'm stumbling through a forest. I wipe blood from my eyes. My breath is visible. All is silent but for dripping rain. I am easy prey, and a hunter is watching. If I don't freeze, I will be a bear's midnight snack.

How the hell have I landed in this predicament? I have to get home. I can't give Cordelia time to poison McKenna with dirty cow's milk and beef stuffed with antibiotics. If she does, I will throttle her, mother-in-law or not.

"Hey!"

Bright light bounces across my face. A gruff, half-annoyed voice. "Damn, lady, what happened? You're hurt."

Salvation. The word reverberates. As it fades, it takes the memories of everything…my years with Rafe, the terrace, the vicious plot. Happiness and horror slip into oblivion.

The light is aimed away from my eyes. After a moment I see a face that holds wisdom as old as Earth herself.

I will have victory.

"My Menoetius," I whisper, and fall into a twenty-three-year dream.

Someone is sobbing. Brie. I must get to her.

"Erin? You're not there any longer. You're safe."

"Brianne."

"She's playing in the other room. Don't cry, Erin. You're right here with me.

Everything is all right, boo. I'm going to count to five, and when I get to five, you will open your eyes and you will feel safe. You'll remember everything you've seen, but it won't bother you."

I hear the voice slowly recite. The closer it gets to five, the smaller the face in the forest grows, until it pops like a bubble and is gone.

Maya smiles as she wipes away my tears.

Chapter 10

After a courteous invitation to "call me Adam. My mother did," Rafe and his son settled into a wary sort of amicable existence.

Whenever Adam referred to his mother, it sent a shock through Rafe's system. He heard in memory the roar of a cold ocean, the howl of stormy sea wind. He saw Taranis stroking Eamhair's hand, making her laugh and firing the spark that accompanied them through every life.

And that last morning. Sand in his eyes, the awful stench of blood, the screams of the dying, the thud of stones and excited whoops of boys...until they brought Eamhair down and fell silent, understanding too late the horror they'd wrought.

Taranis was a simple woodcutter from a village far south of Eamhair's wild fort. He lived with Breda, a prostitute. Everyone thought of her as his mother, but she was not. She had found him in the wrack left by a terrible storm.

It was staggering to be told Taranis had planted a child inside Eamhair the evening he hauled her out of the ocean so many centuries ago. A son! Here was that son, born again or never died, he didn't know which.

Rafe's logical present-day intellect argued that it was impossible. Yet he believed. He needed no DNA test, and doubted a DNA test could reveal anything, anyway.

I love you, Adam. Rafe held back the words, not trusting this swell of emotion. He couldn't love Adam. He didn't know him. He loved the idea of Adam. They were very different things.

Adam called what Taranis had done a cold-blooded rape, but that wasn't true. Adam didn't know the subtleties of that night. Taranis saved Eamhair from suicide. She kissed him. Hadn't she kissed him? He remembered her lips moving beneath his. The tenderness of her voice.

Then she asked him to save Cailean.

He couldn't bluster away what Taranis did next, or that it had been done for any reason other than blind rage. That short, repulsive act lived on, almost more vividly than any other in his seven lives. Never again had he taken her by force, not in any life. That didn't help, though.

At least Adam didn't know that Taranis betrayed Cailean and Eamhair and caused the attack at the edge of Uisge Bealach.

The relief he felt brought awareness that some part of him feared this young man. Something about the youth who called himself Rafe's son kindled a primal reaction. His voice was unfailingly soft and subtle—Rafe couldn't imagine him shouting or losing control—but he sensed that Adam was a being one would not want to get on the wrong side of. It was there in the diamond gaze when he spoke of Eamhair's rape. It showed in the way he walked, like a hunting predator. It declared itself by its very invisibility. Not to mention those women. Furies. Had he seen them, or had it been a hallucination caused by his *Mozart* induced trip? He could not be sure.

If Adam had been alive since the Dark Ages, what had he seen? What had he done? The tingling, electric spark was so strong that Rafe could feel it even when his son was across the room. It radiated and pulsed in time with his heartbeat.

On day two, Rafe noticed his guest wearing the same clothing he'd appeared in, and he called for Oliver. His assistant happily and with furtive infatuation questioned Adam about his preferences, then purchased new clothing on *Prism*, the private, highly-secure search engine that connected the highest echelon and members of the Reformation Brotherhood to a massive, world-wide web. He spent hours examining attire on holographic models using Adam's exact measurements. "I never get to do this," he gushed when the parcels were delivered. "Mr. Konstantinou has a personal shopper who takes care of his clothing. In the old days, I would have been a fashion designer."

"Why can you not be that now?" Adam asked.

Oliver glanced at Rafe and stuttered. His cheeks reddened. "I have no relations who rank highly enough."

Adam nodded and said nothing more. Silence throbbed.

Deep in the night, Rafe ascended to his office. He entered calmly enough, but after standing near the door, looking into a gloom broken only by the muted light in the display cases, a haze of fury erupted. He strode to his desk and punched the button that opened the hidden door.

He only realized what he'd done after, as he was confronted with the destruction.

Books ripped from shelves and thrown against walls. Priceless ancient pottery, smashed. Mementos of his archaeological adventures ground beneath his feet.

His fist was closed around something. A ring.

He clutched the doorjamb as his legs grew weak. It was the Cretan king's seal ring. Chrysaleon's ring. He ran his fingernail along the notch that ruined the perfection, remembering the day his royal hunting eagle's claw had caught, nearly ripping off his finger and leaving this flaw.

Longing for that life, for Aridela, took him to his knees. It was like cancer eating away his soul. He would give anything, *anything*, to go back, to breathe in that hot, fragrant air and hear the cheering in the bullring. To touch her again.

The engraving was holy. Goddess Athene giving the bull-king three golden apples, the token that carried every Cretan king to Hesperia after his death.

A few years ago, while on a sponsored excavation at Knossos, he went off one rainy day to explore Heraklion. He came upon the ring in a lean-to designed to attract tourists and almost bypassed it, assuming it to be a well-crafted fake, but something brought him back. He ended up paying eight thousand in Alliance silver, no doubt because the savvy shopkeeper marked the passion in his eyes. As the man retrieved a box, he confided he'd found the ring using a metal detector. It was buried in the ground right outside the palace.

Rafe berated himself for succumbing to the lure, but was vindicated when he brought the ring home and had it dated to the Early Minoan period.

The ring was yet another case of following deeply submerged instincts, like courting the inappropriate child, Erin Aragon, without understanding they were bound through time, or telling her he would love her as long as the pyramids stood in Egypt, which wasn't his phrase at all, but Chrysaleon's. Or choosing "Aquilo" for the new name of Jasper Simonson's organization. Or how he'd paid a fortune to have a sculptor create the bull and its female leaper, without any conscious memory of the day he'd watched Aridela dance with a wild bull.

The shopkeeper had told the truth about finding it. Rafe could recall the very day Chrysaleon's slave, Alexiare, had attempted to defend Aridela in the face of Chrysaleon's murderous jealousy and impotent fury. Jerking the ring off his finger, Chrysaleon had thrown it over the palace balcony, watching as it soared out of sight.

You are eager to believe Queen Aridela betrayed you, Alexiare had rasped. Taking her side. As he always did in those days.

Here was that ring, the symbol of his kingship, returned through the gauzy labyrinth of time. The shopkeeper was, in the end, a fool. The ring was worth twenty times what he was paid. It should be in a museum, beyond the reach of any ignorant tourist. Rafe lifted it to his lips and kissed it before slipping it onto his middle finger.

Books and broken glass lay everywhere. He'd even exhumed the stone goddess. It lay on its side, blank eyes staring. The only thing he'd left untouched was the statue of the bull and its leaper.

He couldn't deal with this. Scuffing through glass and debris, he left, locking the door behind him.

AFTER A SHORT, RESTLESS NIGHT, RAFE ESCAPED TO THE TERRACE, TAKING PLENTY of coffee.

Images of Erin monopolized his thoughts. He saw her in the hospital, looking at him with badly disguised fear, and that first night at the chateau, when her gaze changed to gratitude, hope, and desire. Despite his best efforts, it all went to shit. She rejected his love, his forgiveness, even his rescue. Selfish bitch! She scorned the good life and love he wanted to give her, preferring to be a runaway female. A wanted criminal. And she had put his granddaughter in danger. He wasn't sure he would ever forgive that.

Beneath surface anger, the welling ocean of his past lives brought everything into glorious synchronicity.

From the moment he'd glimpsed her through that chain link fence at her elementary school, nothing could stop him from pursuing her. Not her age and ethnicity, nor Dillon and Cordelia's violent objections. Somehow, he'd known that he had to bind her to him. No matter the cost. Now, after forty years, he finally understood why.

If he could have one more chance, he would do everything differently. She would never again hate him, fear him, or want to run away. Her face swam through his mind as it had been during the first years of their marriage. Young and vibrant. A loving mother, a trusting wife. His helpmate.

She looked quite similar to Aridela, with her black hair and obsidian eyes. There was even a replica of that birthmark on her wrist, and he was Chrysaleon again, right down to the tic beneath his eye, and the honorific title of "Lion." Did it mean something, that they had adopted forms so similar to those from the Bronze Age? Was it a suggestion that this life might offer a new ending?

Will, too, was dark like Menoetius. He even had a similar facial scar, though it wasn't as horrifying as what the lioness had doled out thousands of years ago.

One day, when Rafe was seven, he came home from school and Will wasn't there. Neither was Dillon. Cordelia was, but she was in one of her moods, trembling, distinct spots of color high on her cheeks, and a shaky voice. Rafe at seven was quite familiar with this mood and absconded to his bedroom. Later, he was awakened by his mother's screaming, the shattering of glass, and Dillon's voice, unusually threatening, but he caught only the word "betrayed."

Two-year-old Will didn't show up for three days. When he did, the left side of his face, near the temple, was covered in bandages. Eventually the wound healed and the bandages came off, but the scar remained. Rafe never did learn what happened.

His reminiscing ceased as Adam emerged from the chateau. It was still early; he suppressed a flash of annoyance. He needed time to think about what had happened before the house came to life and there were people everywhere and neither love nor money could grant a moment's privacy. He'd wanted to lose his worries in the sun peeking over the mountaintops, its light turning from red to yellow and sending shadows running in fear.

When he purchased this mountain, he'd thought there would be plenty of solitude and private time. He could not have been more wrong.

Adam wore a dark gray rollneck and over that, a cobalt blue jacket, faded jeans, and black suede boots with a subtle Victorian flair. It might be July, but mornings at this elevation were always chilly.

He couldn't have asked for better choices in the clothing his assistant purchased. They fit well and enhanced Adam's elegance. He ought to promote Oliver, though such things were never done, especially for a twink. If it got out, there would be an uproar. Rafe had an image to uphold as the Lion of Aquilo, a men's group virulently opposed to homosexuality, and as advisor to Redmond Warwick, who had signed into law the death penalty for any man caught in homosexual relations. But he could at least give Oliver a generous bonus.

Every step Adam took as he crossed the flagstones flowed as smoothly as water. Vita prowled one step behind. The effect was spellbinding.

Something suspiciously like pride flared through his chest and stuck in his throat. Adam had the air of a mythical, otherworldly priest, ardent and pure, volatile and holy. Not just a priest, not in the way one generally pictured those pale, black-robed, double-tongued milksops. Adam's bearing was that of a warrior, and Rafe would be lying if he denied a subtle likeness to Cailean— especially in the eyes.

Many characters in books and movie dramas were dubbed warrior priests. Adam was one in the flesh. This rotten earth, filled with lazy, self-absorbed human beings, had not seen a man like Adam in centuries.

"May I join you?"

Rafe beat back his emotions. It would not do to reveal how moved he was. Not yet, anyway. He nodded. "Be my guest."

Why hadn't he offered a car and driver so Adam could go to Park City or Salt Lake and make his own clothing purchases?

As wary, fearful, and suspicious as he was, he didn't want to take the chance. Rafe was afraid if Adam left, he would never return.

"YOU HAVE QUESTIONS." ADAM REACHED INTO THE INNER POCKET OF HIS JACKET AND brought out a slim silver cigarette case. He opened it, took out a cigarette and lit it before settling into the chair across from Rafe and resting his right ankle upon his left knee. The breeze brushed his hair into his face and he pushed it back without seeming to notice. Like Rafe's, it fell in luxurious layers, and out here the sunlight picked up reflections of copper and gold, inset with deep shadows. For the first time Rafe noticed the miniature stud in Adam's right earlobe. It looked like lapis lazuli. Perhaps its likeness to Aridela's necklace was a coincidence. Perhaps not.

When the breeze again ruffled Adam's hair and he tucked it away, Rafe noticed that his ear had a subtle point. His skin was slightly translucent, something that hadn't been visible inside. It was more than the aura, which Rafe could see even now. This was a sense of glittering, like sun striking virgin snow.

The more he saw, the more mysterious his unexpected guest became.

"You smoke?" Rafe didn't know why it surprised him. Cigarettes and their electronic cousins were banned at the federal level in 2027, to be replaced with a facsimile that was supposed to be safer, but the outcry was so intense and long-lasting that the government relented and allowed the old-fashioned variety to be manufactured again on a limited basis.

"Sometimes." Adam sipped the coffee Rafe poured for him. "I have questions too."

A ring on Adam's left pinkie finger flashed. Rafe grabbed his hand without thinking. "Menoetius's seal ring! It's silver, but the image is the same."

The detail was raised rather than the original intaglio, but Rafe remembered as though he had seen the ring on his bastard half-brother's finger yesterday. A warrior, dagger in hand, holding off a charging lion.

He glanced at his own ring, the one he'd discovered mere hours ago. Premonition trembled, shortening his breath.

Adam didn't ask who Menoetius was. "A gift from my grandmother, in memory of my father."

"Your father? You said I am your father. This has never been my ring."

With a nearly imperceptible smile, Adam replied, "I seem to have multiples."

"Is Cailean your father, or am I?"

"Cailean was my father on Inis Tearmann. You were the one who planted the seed during your rape of my mother."

Adam's face grew hard as stone and warned Rafe against protesting his use of the word rape. There were so many questions he was afraid to ask. So many riddles he was unwilling to solve. So many particulars he didn't have the courage to challenge.

Something else sent his mind cartwheeling. When he'd pulled on Adam's hand, the sleeve of the jacket had shifted. There, on Adam's left inner wrist, was Aridela's birthmark. The bull horns.

Erin had it too. Her soul was Aridela's, which was also Eamhair's. Did that make Erin in some fashion this man's mother? He wished he could observe them together.

Barely able to move his lips, he said, "You mentioned your mother called you Adam. So you knew her." *How could he have? She died, damn it, on that beach!*

"No." Adam gave a brief shake of the head, causing his hair to ripple like wind upon the sea. "I was a year old when she died. My grandmother told me." He paused, his eyes narrowing, before adding, "She told me many things. Like how you tricked Cailean and Eamhair into trusting you, then sent the warriors of Dunaedan to slaughter them. I suppose your punishment was to watch her die slowly by stoning."

Rafe froze. Adam knew every sordid detail. He had to clear his throat before he could speak. "It is one of my greatest regrets."

Adam gently withdrew his hand from Rafe's numb fingers. "Shall we get started?"

Rubbing his palm over the stubble on his cheek, Rafe said, "You grew up on an island?"

"Inis Tearmann. With my grandmother."

"Where is it?"

"Hidden in the ocean where ships never travel."

Rafe's frustration intensified. "I dragged your mother out of the sea the night she was forcibly married to Fathna, king of the Orkneys. Her brothers later threw her off 300 meters of sheer rock cliffs. I believed her dead, but she miraculously returned, very much alive, a month later. I was with her when she did die. Yet here you are. Did she lay you like a chicken egg and leave your grandmother to hatch you?"

"I am not sure I can explain. Time does not progress in linear fashion in all places at all times. It has not for me, and it did not for my mother."

Rafe scowled. He was fighting an overwhelming urge to reveal every secret he'd ever kept even as Adam gave nonsensical, meandering answers and non-explanations. He glanced at his coffee, wondering if it could have been doctored with some kind of truth narcotic, like the top-secret *Pink Fizz* under development in government labs. No, it couldn't be that. The scientists hadn't figured out how to rid the substance of the severe side effects and telltale odor, which was why Rafe had never used it on Erin.

"You don't take very good care of yourself, Father. Why is that?"

"What do you mean? I'm perfectly healthy."

"You drink and you use drugs. That is the sign of an unhappy man."

"My life is stressful. Sometimes I need a break."

Adam's head tilted. Ah, damn! The affectation brought Cailean sharply to mind. How clear it was, that long-ago life at the northern tip of Scotland.

"You have many responsibilities."

"More than anyone can comprehend."

"This world you helped create. Would you tell me how it was conceived? It seems strikingly violent and coercive."

Adam would never understand. For the moment, he would allow the arrogance of youth, but he wasn't sure how long he could maintain such long-suffering patience. "What do you want to know?"

"This is a house of men. There are no women. No girls."

"No." Rafe couldn't meet that dispassionate gaze and locked his gaze on the snow at the summit of the mountain behind Adam's head. "No women. No girls." *I was supposed to be one of the elites. The privileged. The cabal of victors. Yet here I am in the same boat as any other common grunt.*

A complete lie, of course. One barked order would bring any number of women to the chateau. Common grunts couldn't do that.

"Why?"

He didn't answer as another memory clarified. Cabal was the word used both at Mycenae and on Crete for "brother." Nowadays, its meaning had transformed so completely it was the opposite of brother. When had that happened? He didn't know.

"What?" he asked.

"Why are there no females?"

"Because my daughter was murdered and my wife couldn't stand the sight of me. She left and took our granddaughter. No. She stole my granddaughter. That's why there are no women or girls."

Adam's gaze remained composed through Rafe's angry outburst. Had he already known? It was impossible to tell. "I had the impression that women cannot leave their men. Are there not many safeguards to prevent this from happening?"

"There are." Rafe brushed a wasp away from his coffee cup. "She circumvented them. Twice." The words Adam used seemed deliberately chosen to suggest that women might not need safeguards and punishments if they were happy.

Adam's brows lifted and Rafe described how Erin vanished the first time, but that was before America shut down every avenue of escape and imprisoned the rest of the free women. That time, all she had to do was get to the airport and engage a flight. It was easy to understand. This time it wasn't. How had they hoodwinked Samson? How had they passed every guard unchallenged? How did they know to take the Lykan? Why was her tracker not responding?

"Tell me about the safeguards." Adam tilted his head again.

Rafe wished he would quit doing that. "No woman is allowed in public without a mask, a leash, and her husband, owner, or sentinel. Any woman spotted in public without those things would be immediately arrested. All women have tracking devices, anyway. They're implanted deep, to prevent removal."

"In your country then, women are property?"

"Yes. Valuable property." He didn't have the strength to banter with euphemisms.

Adam dropped his right hand onto Vita's head and scratched behind her ear, earning a pleased whine. "Even with these measures, your wife and granddaughter have not been found. What could have happened to them?"

The young man sitting before him had also evaded the guards. He had pressed the doorbell and gained entrance. He'd made himself and Vita invisible to Samson.

"I wish I knew. Brianne's too young for a tracking device or a holo cell. Erin had both, but nobody's been able to detect a signal."

Adam glanced at Vita. She looked back at him, grinning, thumping her tail. "I can see this situation causes you pain. Tell me more about this land you call home. Maybe together we can craft a solution. Something that will bring your wife back to you, if she is alive."

Rafe shoved a hand through his hair. Erin used to tease him about that. She said it supplied important information, though she refused to be more specific.

He tried not to show the hope those words brought. "Those things'll kill you," he said, indicating the cigarette. "Are they real?"

"The very item."

"Share one?"

Adam handed him the case. There was a beautiful and intricate Pictish etching on the top, much like the designs Rafe had seen at the stronghold of Sgathag Creag in the Early Middle Ages, when he lived as the monk, Taranis.

Rafe took one and Adam lit it for him.

Sitting back, Rafe drew in a satisfying lungful of smoke and struggled to regain his composure.

"Are you the leader of this country?"

"No." Rafe flicked ashes into the breeze. "I work for the leader. We call him president. Redmond Warwick."

"What do you do?"

"I advise. I help steer the country. I write most of his speeches."

Adam's lashes dropped briefly over those incredible eyes. "Is that all?"

Before Rafe could answer, a new revelation struck like a fist to the stomach. He pushed his chair backward, accidentally knocking the edge of the table with his knee. Coffee splattered.

Before his memories returned, he'd thought his eyes were playing tricks when he saw the aura around Brie.

No.

Brianne was Themiste.

Sweet holy Jesus.

Did she have any idea? He concentrated. Mostly, his granddaughter acted like a normal ten-year-old girl, but there was the disturbing "Sight," as McKenna called it. That had to be related to the lingering essence of Themiste.

What kind of cruel bitch would reincarnate Themiste as his granddaughter? Chrysaleon had made a child on Themiste, a child who became Aridela's heir. It was disgusting. Rafe didn't want to equate innocent Brianne with that sneaking, duplicitous Bronze Age oracle.

Just like that, the next puzzle piece fell into place.

Selene. She, too, was alive, or had been, in the body of Maya MacDonald, Erin's best friend. He had no idea about her current situation, whether she was dead, lived freely in another country, or was stuck in a cage farm.

How typical. Wherever Aridela was, Selene was sure to be close by.

Adam regarded him, his expression giving nothing away. He'd asked a question. Rafe sought to remember.

"I am also the leader of a men's group called Aquilo," he said as he brought his chair back to the table.

"Aquilo." Adam said. "The power of the North Wind."

Was there anything this young man didn't know?

What use is Aquilo anymore? It's nothing but a reminder of what men have lost.

Carnevale was just a few days away, and far more important than Aquilo.

"Will you tell me how these masks, leashes, and male protectors came about? What inspired them? How did it become necessary? Was that your idea?"

"It's a long story."

Adam lifted his shoulders in that purely European gesture. *C'est la vie.*

Chapter 11

"Maya. Where's Brianne?"

"Playing with Dharma. She's fine, and so are you, Erin. You're safe. Can you sit up?"

With Maya's arm supporting me, I could. "I feel weird."

As I dried my cheeks with a tissue, she pulled a thermos from her bag, poured steaming liquid into a cup, and handed it to me. It was fragrant, citrusy tea.

"Is there an umbrella in there?" I nodded at the bag.

She couldn't quite laugh, but managed a wry smile. I tried to read her face. It was hard. Maya knew how to keep her thoughts to herself.

"Do you remember what happened?" she asked.

"I think so." Real memories ran through my mind, no longer hidden. "Not sure I want to."

"Look at it this way. You can't be manipulated or lied to anymore. Knowledge is power, Erin."

"Yeah." I lifted the cup. The tea was wonderfully aromatic with a touch of garam masala. "This will change the way I look at Rafe, at my life with him, profoundly. Forever."

"Rafe isn't the man you married. He stopped being that man a long time ago, before you left him. I've never been with one guy long term like you, but I can imagine how awful this must feel. Like your whole being has been upended. I'm so sorry."

I should probably weep at my new reality, but I sat there, sipping tea, my eyes surprisingly dry.

Like a good psychiatrist, she changed the subject, giving me time to pull myself together. "Show me the scars you talked about under hypnosis. I remember them from when we were kids, but I don't remember you ever saying they hurt."

I set the cup down and pushed up my sleeves. "They're not usually swollen and red like this. It's like they get inflamed when I'm under stress. It's been happening more lately. Since Rafe found me, come to think of it. I almost forgot they were there when I was with Will."

Maya examined the scar on my right wrist then my left, where it floated atop the birthmark, before moving on to the carotids. Her concentration alarmed me. "You're giving yourself wrinkles."

Her expression relaxed and she crinkled her nose. "Did your parents ever come up with an explanation?"

"Nope. They went with birthmarks. I don't know, they look like scars to me."

"Me too."

"I can't believe it was that easy to bring back those memories. One hypnosis session, and boom. They're so clear."

"You have been trying to remember, quite diligently from what you've said. So perhaps all that was needed was a gentle push using a few tricks of the trade."

"No wonder I blocked it out. Rafe *is* an asshole. A Nazi. I remember him giving McKenna and me those pills. 'Gullible Erin.' They were laughing at me. Me and every other female who trusted them. I really am a traitor. I heard all this and just ran away. I left Rafe and Henry free to do what they wanted. I could have stopped them."

I drew in a sharp breath. "I could have killed him while he slept. I was lying there in bed next to him. I could have…stabbed him with a steak knife."

Maya chewed on her lip for a few seconds, then shrugged. "I'm not sure you could have done that, Erin."

Now the tears came. She was telling me, as kindly as she could, that I was weak, and she was right.

She handed me the box of tissues. "I doubt very much that you could have stopped anything. They're ruthless, Erin, and they would have treated you ruthlessly. Even Rafe's death wouldn't have affected much. The plot was bigger than one man."

I pulled a tissue from the box and tore it apart. My mind was racing. "Oh, no."

"What?"

"Those guards in the kennels. They were dosing us with something too. Before Rafe came in and shot them, I heard them talking about powder, and how it should have made me controllable."

"I'm not surprised to hear that."

"McKenna warned me about the pills before she ran away. She'd figured it out on her own. When she was sixteen, Rafe put her on pills with a lie about ovarian cysts. They messed her up, but Brie's father helped her get off them secretly. Those pills were designed to control both of us, but I'd bet a year's worth of coffee that the pills Rafe gave McKenna suppressed her sex drive while the ones he gave me increased it. Rafe tried to get me to take them again the very day after we left the hospital. I refused. I said I didn't need them, but several times, I felt dull, groggy, and all starry-eyed about my man, to use a euphemism. I thought I was drinking too much, but McKenna told me they were probably putting the pills, or some equivalent, in my food."

I reexamined the conversation in the sunroom. "I don't understand, though, why they would give McKenna the pills back when she was only two years old. Maybe hers really were for ear infections."

"You know what I think? I'd wager every one of those gold Krugerrands of yours that the real purpose of those pills was prophylactic."

"Against what?"

"Think about it, Erin. It's the only thing that makes sense. The only reason he would give them to both you and McKenna."

"Lunacy. My god. That's why we were never infected."

"Yep. There was something in them that attacked, destroyed, or shut down the nanobots."

"Then why…oh, shit. After there was no more lunacy, of course men wanted to go on using them for the other things. The increased sex drive. The foggy brain. All that mind control, right there in a simple, tiny, flavored pill."

"Under hypnosis, you remembered our dick of a president saying his wife 'got it bad.' That's what he was talking about. He refused to give her the antidote. The other stuff the pills treated, like ear infections and anxiety, was to keep you from figuring out the truth so you wouldn't scream to the heavens that there was a cure."

I blew my nose. "McKenna fooled them for years. She pretended to take them but got rid of them on the sly. She was smart, but in the end, it didn't help her."

"I am so glad you reconnected with her, boo."

"I should have been with her the whole time. She was never out of my thoughts when I was with Will, but it wasn't enough to make me go home. I told myself lie after lie, how I was doing what was best for her. Talk about brainwashing. She might be alive right now if I hadn't run away that night. If I hadn't abandoned her. She might never have got it into her head that a woman can be free if she's reckless enough."

Maya sighed and held my hands. "Erin, listen to me. You can't change the past. Maybe you're right. Maybe you're wrong, and if you'd stayed with Rafe or gone back to him, you still couldn't have stopped what happened. All you can do is make more informed choices from here on."

I'd felt like the stone goddess and McKenna both had tried to tell me this very thing.

She let me cry. When my sobbing turned to sniffling and then to quiet, heavy despair, she said, "I knew it was nanobots. I saw them. When I first realized I had lunacy and began dosing myself with *Moshe*, it did a fairly good job holding it off. That's when I started thinking there had to be a connection with the brain, because that drug was designed to interact with the limbic system. Others had studied the brain, sure, but they didn't find anything so they moved on to blood and DNA. I had access to instruments that provided images at the subatomic level. Holographic AFM and SEM microscopes."

I shook my head, clueless.

"Atomic force and scanning electron microscopes. They display incredibly detailed images of things too small to see with the naked eye. They can reveal every microscopic element inside a human cell. I saw my first nanobot the very night we were raided. If I'd had one more day, I could have blown the whole thing open. Instead, Pascal and I were attacked. He was shot and I was drugged. I woke up in a kennel, just like you."

A horrible chill ran over me like a ghostly breath. No wonder she understood me so well.

"Like you, my clothes were gone and I had on some kind of burlap sack. Unlike you, we were underground, in a salt mine. I was probably among the first to be rounded up after the government threw out all pretense of the quarantine being a benevolent venture. Part of the first wave. The cage farms were brand new. Groups of men in suits and hardhats regularly toured the place, laughing and joking and asking questions. The very first day I woke up in that kennel, a man told me I was too smart for my own good. He didn't say I was too smart to live, but that's what he meant. I was educated. I knew too much. I was not the type of female his budding dystopia wanted to keep around."

"Without a drug to hold it off, the lunacy must have overwhelmed you."

Maya shook her head, her mouth sliding into a sardonic smile. "Nope. It didn't, and I never heard that peculiar shrieking that was such a giveaway, so nobody else had it either. I never saw or heard any evidence of lunacy there. Once I woke up, I never felt it trying to overtake me again. I can surmise from your hypnosis that Novikov shut the nanobots down during that time period, to make us easier to control. Once we were locked up, they wouldn't want us acting like berserkers, would they? They switched out the nanos for the pills, or powder, or whatever, to make us amenable. I do wonder about you, though. Why didn't you contract the lunacy after you ran away? That happened at the beginning of May, right?"

"Yeah. The night of May second."

"You didn't take the pills with you?"

"I was so upset, I didn't even think about them."

"Women succumbed to lunacy that whole month. We received reports at the university every day listing new cases. But you didn't. Without any pill to hold it off, you didn't get sick."

I shrugged. "Because I was so far off the grid? That's all I can think of."

"Contracting lunacy didn't depend on being around other people. The nanobots were released in the air. They would have fallen everywhere, populated or not."

"The cabin was about 3600 meters. It was really cold when I got there, too. Maybe that's why."

She shrugged. "Or maybe Novikov gave orders that the drones only drop nanobots over cities and towns, but I don't think so. If that were true, they would miss a lot of rural people, and our research suggested otherwise."

"What happened to you? You're not dead. You must have escaped."

"In my area there were about ten cages. One by one, the other women were taken away and they never came back. I kept waiting for it to happen to me. I was going to fight like hell. If I was going to be raped or murdered, then I was going to leave a mark or two. Every now and then one of the guards would come along, squat, and look at me. I would think *This is it*, but it never was. I began having nightmares of the Jews being shot and gassed. I sat and rocked and had visions of smoke boiling out of brick chimneys."

"Oh, Maya." I didn't know what else to do, so I held her hand. She'd been holding mine a lot lately.

"The day finally came. My cage was unlocked and I was pulled out by the hair. I kicked, Erin, I kicked so hard, but it did no good. There were three men, and one of them slugged me in the jaw. They took me to a bunch of women, all of them tethered to each other at the wrists. They tied me to the last one. They were mostly older women, and there were about fifteen girls under ten. A few looked to be about three or four. They were crying. One of them had Downs. Another woman didn't have any hair. She looked really sick. The guards forced us to walk, single-file. That's when I found out there was a much bigger room and whole lot more cages full of women. We were taken up in an elevator and marched outside. Eventually we came to an abandoned wheat field."

She drew in a breath and stared at the wall. "We were pushed into a line in front of a deep, long ditch. There were men standing around with rifles and a backhoe at one end."

Sweat poured off me. I knew what she was going to say. How could she be sitting here so calm and in control?

"The ditch was about half full of rotting corpses. They were going to shoot us so we would fall backward into our own grave, on top of those they'd already killed, just like I'd been seeing in my imagination. Everybody else knew, too. They were crying and screaming, especially the little girls. Their screams were horrible. About ten men came up, raised their rifles, and started shooting."

"Maya!" I ran my sleeve across my forehead.

"I watched the closest two men and made a guess which one would get me. I dropped into the ditch just as the woman I was tethered to was shot. Two women fell on top of me. The one I was tied to was still breathing, but her wounds were fatal. There was blood and shit everywhere. I remember the stench to this day. I burrowed down, pulling her and anyone else I could on top of me, and worked the rope off my wrists, all the while watching the upper rim of the ditch. Men came up and shot anything that moved, so I didn't move."

It was all too easy to imagine. I was hyperventilating, and afraid I might vomit.

"I heard the backhoe start up. I was going to be buried alive. I shoved at the bodies and crawled towards the end, as far from the backhoe as possible, hoping none of the men would spot me. Then I heard it shut off. I hunkered down and looked. The shooters were walking away, back to the building. One man was talking to the driver. After a minute or two the driver got out and they left. It was my chance. I climbed over the bodies till I got to the end and pulled myself out. It was getting dark, but the sun hadn't quite set. I was afraid I might be seen, so I wriggled like a snake to some trees about ninety meters away."

It was like watching the suspenseful climax at the end of a movie. My lungs filled with air. It felt like the first breath I'd taken in a long while.

"I hid all night. I found some grass at the base of a tree and tried to sleep. I kept telling myself I was safe. Nobody would search for me. They thought I was dead. At sunset the next day, another group of women and girls were brought out and shot. This time, the backhoe did fill in the ditch. I was lucky. The driver must have been told to wait so they could add more bodies.

"I spent three days in that forest. I was so hungry. I'd been hungry since I was taken. They barely gave us anything to eat."

"I remember. That's when I understood how people could eat raw meat."

"Every time I saw a rabbit, my mouth watered, but I didn't have enough strength or cunning to catch one. There were plenty of wild mulberries, but they're not what you would call filling. I kept thinking about my books, and the art I'd collected. I wondered what had become of my apartment. And Pascal. He saw the nanobot too, and he was my friend. He was probably dead, but I had to know. I finally decided to go east. Eventually I should come to a sign or something that would tell me where the hell I was."

"Did you?"

Maya nodded. "Kansas."

"Kansas!"

"Yep. There was no way I could walk home, but I had to do something, so I kept going. Pretty soon the road intersected with Highway 50, which seemed to run pretty much due east. I was getting weaker by the hour. I needed help, but every time I heard a car coming, some instinct told me to hide. Wisely, as it turned out. I walked at night and hid during the day. I remember passing a couple of farms and seeing men and boys working, but no women, at least not outdoors. Once I saw a line at one of those food and drink stands. Every single person in line was a guy. I never saw a woman or girl anywhere. The guys seemed fine, not scared or angry. Now this was June or July, 2049, so the quarantine had been going strong for a little over a year. Maybe those men didn't know things had changed. Maybe they thought their wives, sisters, and girl-friends would get cured and come home. I wondered what they would do if they knew what was happening. And I wondered if the United States govern-ment was in the process of murdering every last female in the country. It didn't make sense. As hard as they try to convince themselves that women aren't important, *we kind of are.*"

"Yes."

"Then I thought about how, except for me, the women who were shot at the ditch were older, or children. Sick or disabled. I started putting it together. Value. Just like those assholes said that night at the chateau. They were keeping females with value and killing the rest."

I had come to exactly that conclusion the first time I attended Rafe's church. I'd seen no women over twenty-five or so, no babies, and only a few girls. My throat constricted, but I forced myself to speak. "Rafe hated how humans were destroying everything. He called us termites. In the beginning, he supported the ban on abortion and birth control, but having McKenna, seeing firsthand how helpless a baby is, changed him. He saw the evil of forcing a blanket law onto every woman, no matter her circumstances. He hated the outrageous number of humans that law was putting on the planet, but mostly, he hated how little kids suffered for the crime of being born."

I heard in my memory from hypnosis his buttery smooth voice saying, *Well-calculated gaps in births means recovery can get a solid foothold.* "He might not have known about children being shot in cold blood, but I bet he was behind the decision that included that trench. Damn him to hell."

Maya nodded.

"You were going east. You found food and water?"

"Yeah, and clothing. Farms are handy for stuff like that. I stole what I needed. As long as I kept clear of dogs, I was okay. Eventually I came to a town called Newton and decided to stay awhile. It seemed small, yet big enough I could hide and find things to eat. I hid in alleys, under bridges, or in clumps of bushes during the day and went through dumpsters and trash cans at night. I made my way north to a college. I guess I felt more at home there. More hopeful. Maybe a student would help me. There were parks and trees and shrubs, so good hiding, but that's where I got caught."

I waited, hoping what she was about to tell me wouldn't be as bad as I feared.

"I was going through a dumpster one night behind a bar. I was half in, half out, and didn't hear the men. There were three of them. It's pretty much the same story as yours. They were excited about finding a lone woman and had all kinds of plans, none of which involved my input. I won't say any more about it, Erin. Don't ask me."

I nodded. Hatred and the impossible need for revenge sent hot shivers running through me.

"I'm not sure how much time passed, maybe about a month, before they took me to the police. I understood from what they were saying that there was a fat reward for turning in females. They had their fun and at the end, were well paid. The policeman asked me my name. I didn't have any identification or any way to tie me to the Brown educated psychiatrist-turned-genetic researcher, so I adopted a southern accent and told them I was a waitress from Oklahoma City, just trying to get by. I knew I looked the part. Filthy, starved, my eyes swollen, cut and bruised from head to toe. This guy looked at me and I could tell he knew what I'd been through, but he didn't care. I was tossed in a cell with some other women. I never found out their stories because our guard wouldn't let us talk. You mentioned a carnival under hypnosis. Did Rafe ever say anything about that?"

I shook my head.

"Some men and a doctor came to the jail and looked us over. They asked me if I'd ever had a baby or an abortion, and my age. Thinking about those women who were shot, I said I was twenty. The doctor looked me over thoroughly, and when I say thoroughly, I mean vaginally. I was surprised to hear him say he didn't see anything wrong. After being at the mercy of those three guys and their friends I felt like the damage ought to be obvious, but if it was, he didn't see it, or he pretended not to, or he didn't care. I was taken to cages where women were kept for this carnival thing. They were nicer than the salt mines. Bigger. We were allowed to walk in a field every day. The women there were mostly teenagers. Some in their early twenties. We were fed a little better and kept cleaner. We could even brush our teeth. Doctors checked us out every few months. I remember the seasons changing, so I think I was there about a year. Then I was asked again how old I was, and if I was virgin. I said last I remembered, I was twenty, and no, I wasn't a virgin. I figured I couldn't get away with that, but I should have tried. Next thing you know, I'm dumped in a new prison, in my home state of Utah, as it turned out, in an old, abandoned building. The guards claimed it was haunted, and it actually was."

"Haunted? Really?"

"The nights were filled with noises I could not explain, and I saw things. I saw a woman surrounded in circles of light. She stared into my eyes and damn if that didn't creep me out. It felt like she was trying to tell me something, or get me to do something."

She took a moment, and I let her think. "I spent a long time in that prison. Even though this was a real building, with actual rooms, they kept us in kennels. It reminded me of an animal shelter, rows and rows of cages. Rooms full of cages. After I was free and could determine time, I added it up. I was there for seven years, in a cage, with just an hour of exercise every day, or every other day, and regular stints at the Glory Wall. It was just a flimsy wall, almost cardboard, erected for the sole purpose of us servicing without any part of us being seen. It added to the indoctrination that we were things, not people."

Somehow, I escaped that particular chore when I was caged, but had Rafe not intervened, I, too, would have been forced to serve there, a robed, anonymous sex slave.

"Men came through now and then. Well-dressed men. Happy men. Fat men. We were lined up and they would look us over. Sometimes a man would choose one of us. I saw a hell of a lot of women try to get chosen. Some of the things they did, you wouldn't believe if I told you. I didn't think badly of them. I was tempted to do the same. We were just human beings, trying to survive."

I nodded but said nothing, not wanting to disrupt her concentration.

"Sometimes, somebody got pregnant. No surprise there. The guards made free use of us just like they did where you were being held, and the contraceptive powder or pills didn't always work. Whenever it happened, the guards got really scared and mad. They took it out on all of us, like we were to blame. I'll bet the higher-ups knew what was going on and were happy to turn a blind eye, unless something forced them to deal with it, like a pregnancy." She shrugged. "If a woman thought she might be pregnant, she'd do anything to get rid of it without the guards knowing. Pregnant women were left alive, with no medical care, until the baby was born. They delivered in their cages, alone. Quite often both died. The guards would parade their bodies through every room so we could all know what to expect if we broke their rules. If the woman lived, she was murdered. If the child lived, it disappeared. Thrown to dogs, some said. Pregnancy is a cardinal sin in the Cages."

I couldn't help picturing those desperate women, impregnated through rape and punished for it, and the baby too.

"Anyway," Maya continued, "that's where you come into my story, sort of. I woke up one day hearing a voice I knew. I stared out the front of my cage and pretty soon there he was, Raphael Konstantinou, walking with a few guards and another man. I knew him, too. I'd seen him on the news. Grigory Novikov, the dictator of Ukrus. I started to call out. I thought here, at last, salvation. Surely, Rafe…but that other man, Novikov, spotted me. He grinned. Oh man, I cannot describe that grin. I felt like my blood froze solid in my veins. It must have been exactly like what happened to you, Erin. I shrank into the darkest reaches of the kennel and they went on. The chance was lost."

"What is it about that guy? How does he petrify us without saying a word?"

"I don't know," she said. "I can't explain it, but I'll never forget how it felt."

"Maya, Rafe would not have left you there. He would have saved you like he did me."

Maya's brows lifted. "The same Rafe you now remember was all for the Cages? I think there's an equal chance he would have been glad to see me like that. He would have enjoyed walking away and leaving me."

Thinking back to what I'd overheard the night I abandoned him, I couldn't argue, though my heart wanted to. My heart needed to believe there was some shred left of the man I'd loved, buried inside the monster he'd turned into. Shame made me lower my face and hunch into myself.

"After that, I decided I was done. I'd been screaming in the dark for years on end. I quit eating even the little bit they gave us. I kept to the rear of the kennel and it seemed like the guards forgot I was there. But then one day I was taken out and put in a line, and a man chose me. He bought me like a farm animal. He took me to his house and added me to his collection of women. His little harem. He liked to dress us up and have us dance, and other things. He called me his white-haired Negroid goddess. I was so miserable I didn't pay attention, but when I glimpsed myself in a mirror, I understood. My hair had turned white."

She wasn't dyeing her hair. It had literally turned white from what she'd suffered. "It surprised me when I first saw you," I said. "Now I understand."

"How I escaped is a story for another time. I've talked long enough and I'm sick of my voice." She lifted her hands and I saw they were shaking. "Wow, it's been so long, but telling it makes me feel like it was last week."

"I get that."

"There's something I've been meaning to say to you, Erin."

"Yeah?"

"I know you've been in a dark place, partly because of what those guards did to you when you were in the Cages."

I felt blindsided by the reminder. It was something I actively avoided remembering.

"Now you know my story, and how similar it is to yours. So, here's what I want you to think about, okay?"

"I'm listening."

"Rape. We all know it's about power, pain, and humiliation. What gets glossed over is that if we live through it, we have a choice. We can either allow the attack to destroy us, or make us stronger. We can give our attackers the power and humiliation they crave, or not. You, Erin, have the power in the end. Not those guards. Get up, live your life, and be the kind of proud woman who towers over those small, powerless men. If you can do that, then what they did will melt away, because you will dismiss it for what it was. A cowardly act against your body. They never touched you. Not *you*. Only your body. Think about prisoners of war. Many are tortured horribly, but if they survive, they're called heroes for the rest of their lives. I ask you. What's the difference between a rape victim and a prisoner of war?" She paused, frowning. "When you think about human interaction, from infancy to old age, it's easy to see that sex is one of the least important items on the list. It gets amplified into this all-encompassing thing, but in the scheme of the universe, sex is way down there with cleaning up a spill on your kitchen floor. Important acts may be more intangible, but they are far more powerful, and last far longer. Love. Kindness. Empathy. Rapport. Loyalty. Courage. Integrity."

"Damn it," I said, wiping my eyes. "You are amazing." I jumped off the bed. "Hug me, sister."

She laughed, got up, and hugged me. "I need a gin and tonic."

"You deserve one, baby."

"You want a glass of wine?"

I nodded. "That would be good, but Maya, how do we know if the stuff I said under hypnosis is real? How do we know I didn't imagine that entire scenario?"

"I was careful not to plant any suggestions in your mind, like about the nanobots. That's the only way I could be sure you would see and remember things that I hadn't prompted you to see and remember. It's wise to be skeptical, Erin, and I would be too, but for one thing."

"What?"

"Everything you saw and heard happened. The proof is our reality."

"There is that."

"Okay. Stay here. I'll get our drinks and I'll check on Brie. It's officially happy hour."

"Okay," I said, trying to smile. Maya had deftly broken through my despair by telling her story. She was a good friend.

Brie ran in as Maya was leaving. She looked at Maya then at me. Her brows lowered. She gave me the sweetest hug I'd ever had in my life, at least since McKenna was little.

This child. She made me glad to be alive, no matter what the circumstances.

"FOR ME, IT BEGAN WITH THE END OF LEGAL ABORTION. IT WAS A WAR HARD fought, for too long. I was just a kid. Fourteen, I think, not even out of middle school, but I was already political. My parents raised me that way. Prep school, church, conservative groups. They…molded me in their image."

Rafe's gaze followed two guards as they made a pass behind the chateau. Their German shepherd stopped to sniff at a line of shriveling hydrangeas. Petals covered the ground around the shrubs—shrubs he was sure had been blooming profusely days ago. They looked awful now, nearly dead. He must bring the gardeners in for a consult. "I'll never forget the first woman put on trial after the ban passed."

"Crucified in Times Square," Adam said.

Why was Adam asking questions about women and girls and who led countries? He obviously knew the answers.

He's testing me.

It didn't matter. Rafe wanted to say these things. Adam was giving him a chance to explain the importance of what they'd done.

Besides, every word he spoke pulverized a thin layer of guilt.

How many layers are there?

"She was made an example of," Rafe said firmly. "It was open to the public and televised across the world." He met Adam's impassive gaze. "It could have been worse. There were those who advocated for some pretty appalling things, like impalement. Crucifixion was chosen because of its link to Christ. It was considered a way for the woman, who had committed murder, to redeem herself before her death."

"Male murderers have never faced such punishment."

"True. There's just something about the murder of a baby in utero."

"Is that it?"

"You're probably more familiar than anyone else with the harsher kinds of punishment..."

His probing statement received no response but for the infinitesimal lift of an eyebrow. "The government hoped to make other women think twice before taking such a risk."

"She suffered a long time."

Rafe pictured Adam watching the woman without blinking for the entire week it took her to succumb. She began her sentence with defiance, even after her hands were nailed. He admired her courage. Later, she begged for death. Liberal news outlets maliciously suggested someone pierce her side with a sword so she could be even more like Jesus.

This conversation had become exceedingly grim, exceedingly quickly. "Since it did take a very long time for her to die, crucifixion was abandoned. Firing squads became the norm. Later, the birth control ban was passed. There was wild celebration. There had to be, to drown out the protests."

He picked up his coffee and sipped, giving himself a moment to construct what he wanted to say. The events had happened long ago, yet they remained painful to talk about or even think about. *Hindsight*, 20-20, *et cetera*.

"I truly believed it was about the babies. I'd seen the videos, the documentaries, all the horrible ways inconvenient fetuses were being slaughtered. It was preached every Sunday, every Wednesday. I was fourteen, but already deeply involved with Erin, my future wife. I knew if she were to get pregnant, it would be the most transcendent experience of my time on earth. I felt that way until I was older, much older. It wasn't until I joined the government that I saw the actual, day-to-day results of those bans. Miserable women compelled to carry and bear children they didn't want, had never wanted. Pregnancies that sometimes killed them. Pregnancies caused by rape. Pregnancies forced by fathers upon girls barely out of childhood. Men persecuting women for getting pregnant, acting like they played no part in it whatsoever. The worst was how the babies suffered. Abused in the most horrific ways by hopeless people taking out their resentment on the vulnerable. Tortured, sexually and in other ways I can't even describe, abandoned in dumpsters, creeks, on hillsides, murdered and tossed in shallow, unmarked graves, sold to sex traffickers, allowed to die from curable illness or injury.

"Activists worked hard to make sure every conception resulted in birth. But after the births, nobody helped with anything, oftentimes including the men who caused the pregnancies. They just walked away. As I gained a little real-world wisdom, I learned that there are worse things than quick death in the womb. Much worse. Torture that goes on and on for years, inflicting wounds that never heal. Not to mention what those successful births did to the world. The crowding. The starvation. Crime. This planet was no longer able to provide any kind of life worth living."

He glanced heavenward, struggling to reacquire the detachment he'd worked so hard to cultivate.

"The abortion haters saw things in simple black and white, and that's what I was taught. It took me years to understand. Real life is made of infinite shadows, some so gauzy you can see through them, others as deep and dark, as cold and impenetrable as the bottom of the ocean. Those shadows feasted on the innocents."

The woman had endured a long, nasty trial before she was nailed to a cross. He hadn't been there in person, being too young and in school, but his mother allowed him to watch on TV. Every day, she grew weaker, paler, but did not die. Some threw things at her. Others wept for her and called her a hero. That angered him. A hero, for killing her unborn child?

Years later, married and a father, with access to all kinds of things kept hidden from the public, he learned that the convicted woman had four other children she could not support. Her spouse abandoned his pregnant wife and family after years of eye-popping abuse. Seeing the grisly photos in her hospital file, Rafe investigated. He was shocked to find out the husband moved to another state, remarried, sired several more children, and started his abuse all over again. He'd paid no price at all.

"I was an abortion hater," he said. "Later, I became something else. I don't know what to call it."

Adam leaned forward, placing his elbows on the table. For the first time, Rafe detected hints of surprise in his expression, but he remained silent.

The old rationalizations mushroomed. *Caging females stopped unwanted pregnancies. At least our ideas accomplished that much.*

Rafe had never disclosed his change of heart to anyone but Erin. The pain of speaking it out loud now was visceral.

He quickly changed the subject. "I should start with President Montague. He was elected in the days when presidential terms were limited to either four or eight years. Henry Montague lost his re-election bid to a liberal Democrat. He and his Senate supporters demanded a recount. The recount changed nothing, but Henry and the Senate wouldn't accept the new administration. They argued about turmoil in Russia and America's struggling efforts in the Middle East. Some of their reasoning was more esoteric, like how the country would go bankrupt with a liberal in charge. The president-elect, a man by the name of Nicholas Caballeros, was a divisive force. Very far left, of Mexican descent. His heritage alone was an offense to many. Ten days before he was to take office, he was assassinated by one of Henry's supporters, and Henry was granted a second term. I don't mean to imply it was easy. America didn't just shrug and say, 'That's okay. We have Montague.' It was horrible. Chaos and violence for months. Henry promised to bring the country together again, and eventually, through a combination of implied threat and exhaustion on the part of the people, he won his case. During his second term, Henry revived the Republican Party. He renamed it the New American Nationalist Party, and they became very powerful. One by one, they ousted Democrats from nearly every seat in every state, and destroyed the free press. The Senate, with the help of the Supreme Court, abolished the eight-year presidential limit and Henry ended up keeping his job as president for thirty years. His nephew, Redmond Warwick, assumed the office after Henry's death, since Henry had no sons."

Adam's gaze remained intent.

"Henry passed the abortion ban during his third term. He and the Senate reworded the Fourteenth Amendment to the Constitution to make it work. He'd just appointed his fourth Supreme Court judge, so it was inevitable, as was the repeal of the Nineteenth Amendment much later, in June of 2049. He'd replaced all the justices by then. That was the amendment giving women the right to vote. The women on the Supreme Court were disbarred and replaced by men."

"This president cared about babies, like you?"

Rafe poured more coffee then realized what he really wanted. "Samson," he said.

"Yes, Mr. Konstantinou?"

"Ask Dale to bring martinis."

"Certainly, sir."

Dale appeared almost immediately with a dewy pitcher and two frosty glasses. He must have had it ready to go. Rafe was known to give generous bonuses for such foresight in his domestics, so most of them were adept at anticipating his desires.

Rafe sipped. Just how he liked it, cold, strong, with absinthe, brandy, and orange peel. What did it matter that the sun hadn't yet reached its apex? "I became good friends with Henry, but I can't answer that. He always spoke the right words."

"You had doubts."

Rafe knew he would reply, though he questioned why he'd lost his ability to keep his mouth shut. If Erin had possessed such power over him, she would have had him admitting about the Cages and worse. It felt like the words were burning through his larynx like fire through paper.

"When I joined President Montague's advisory team, I was briefed. You could say I was given the truth. The abortion ban was pushed through to force white women to give birth. We who believed in the sanctity of birth were a means to an end. By that time, whites were the minority, and it was the white women who were having most of the abortions. We couldn't come right out and say it so bluntly, of course. President Montague's agenda was to bring white Americans back to the majority. Whites were the ones who supported him but there weren't enough to make him feel secure. He and his supporters feared liberals would pull off a coup and the Nationalists would never get another chance. President Montague and his advisors set the country up to achieve certain, specific, unalterable outcomes. The outcomes we are living.

Some of what happened he didn't plan for and couldn't foresee, like the rise of Ukrus and the second moon. Others…yes. He knew."

Adam sat back in his chair and twisted the stem of his martini glass between his thumb and forefinger.

If this young man was not, in fact, his son, but something else, perhaps a spy for one of the Western Alliance countries, Rafe was spilling truths that could severely damage, if not destroy, Redmond Warwick's administration. Yet his tongue would not be stopped. "The way Henry and his team saw it, whites were going the way of elephants and ocean life. We needed white babies and this was the quickest, cleanest way to make it happen. The birth control ban was passed two years after the abortion ban, with the explanation that the majority of Americans wanted a more righteous, traditional way of life. That wasn't exactly true, but it was the oft-quoted line, and hard to dispute. Evangelicals had taken over politics. Even the president had to kowtow to them."

Rafe poured his second martini. His tongue was as loose by now as a prostitute's morals, and his mind no longer cared. Adam listened without any sign of judgment. It was heady. He'd never been able to speak to Erin like this, though he'd fantasized what it would be like. Her liberal psyche was deeply offended by everything he considered common sense.

He ran a fingertip through the condensation on the outside of his glass. "I say Henry and his advisors knew what they wanted to achieve, but looking back, I don't think they did. Maybe they just didn't care. By the time I joined his administration, it was far too late to choose another direction. You know, every living thing on this planet, plant and animal, regulates itself so that it doesn't exhaust its habitat. Except humans. We're indiscriminate, unapologetic reproducers. We go at it until there's nothing left, then we turn on each other. When I went to work for Henry, farmland was being compressed into tiny, arid plots. Low-lying areas and coastal cities were forever lost to rising seawater. All those people had to move inland, making everyplace that didn't flood even more crowded. Cities expanded like cancerous tumors. It was a mess. The air, the water, food. People routinely died of starvation in the richest country on earth. They died of weird new viruses. Crime was so bad people barricaded themselves in their homes, bankrupting themselves for locks, bars, and alarms. There was no safe city. No safe area. The cruelty humans are capable of…" He crushed the cigarette beneath his shoe on the flagstones, surprised to see two others. He didn't remember smoking them, but Adam's silver case lay open and empty on the table. "Henry blinded himself to everything but his own schemes and ambitions."

Adam was a talker's dream. Rafe could see he was absorbing every word, and he never interrupted.

"White women had been making huge advances in the workplace. They were the most educated and the highest wage earners. Pregnancy could derail promotions and put jobs in jeopardy. That's why they were the ones having the abortions and using the most birth control. That's why whites were declining, that and the mixed marriages. After the abortion ban and birth control ban, women were trapped in a very efficient catch-22. They lost their jobs in droves or were passed over for the best promotions."

Adam took one sip of his martini. Rafe looked at the glass. *You're not much of a drinker, son.*

Son. This incredible young man was his son. As he lifted his glass, he indulged in a brief reverie of Adam accompanying him on his travels, attending his speeches, supporting his goals. An heir to his legacy, a loyal companion—the opposite of Erin.

In a lightbulb moment, he realized that was why he wanted to tell Adam everything. Because a rightful son, a trusted successor, could hear the real, unvarnished truth.

I want this. Give me this, Lord. A son. A man who will die before betraying me.

"About a year after McKenna was born, astronomers got their first glimpse of the second moon. It was a long way off and could only be seen by the most powerful telescopes, but the news was impossible to keep under wraps. People were either fascinated or terrified. Henry and I, and handpicked NASA scientists, went out and gave speeches to reassure everyone. Lies, mostly, because nobody knew what would happen. Some thought it would veer off before it entered the atmosphere, but others didn't. They couldn't even agree on what it was. It couldn't have been a true moon because it traveled independently, seemingly impervious to the pull of any planet. Was it an asteroid? It didn't seem to be in the orbit of any star. The damn thing defied our knowledge. Of course, the screwballs said it was an alien ship."

Adam gave his signature smile, so slight it could easily be missed if one wasn't attentive.

"The moon arrived about a year after it was first detected. It was definitely a moon at that point, because it fell neatly into orbit. No little green men ever came out of it, but I swear, to this day, a quarter-century later, there are those who continue to claim it has aliens inside."

Vita rose from her sprawl and placed her paw on Adam's thigh. "She needs to go for a walk. Will you come?"

"Sure." Floating on martini fumes, Rafe left his seat. Vita pranced alongside Adam as they entered the chateau and exited at the front.

The guards stood straighter at the sight of him. Conversation halted. They knew they hadn't earned his forgiveness for the night Erin stole the Lykan. The car was found within twenty minutes at the foot of the mountain, but ominously, the windows were shattered and there was no sign of Erin or Brie. The scent dogs hadn't picked up anything, nor had the special forces he'd brought in. It was like his wife and granddaughter rose out of the windows and flew off into the sky like birds.

Rafe led Adam under the porte-cochère and across the drive, past the flower beds and beyond, into aspen wilderness. Vita took off with a growl after scenting the air.

"I am still unclear about the women and girls," Adam said.

Rafe plucked a pebble from the ground and sent it flying into the heavens. "A lot of things happened that resulted in this, none anticipated, none planned."

Something was wrong with that statement. It wasn't true, not completely. Why was this boy forcing him to regurgitate memories he'd much rather forget?

"The moon didn't do any of the things we thought it might. It didn't veer away or cause natural disasters, at least not on the scale that our experts feared. Instead, it affected females, which nobody predicted. We speculated that it could be the blue light it reflects, or the extra gravitational tug of war. Instead of one moon, there were two, constantly pulling, influencing the way their cycles and hormones functioned. First there was the incredible violence. As the infection worked deeper into their tissues, victims pulled out their hair, dug at their scalps till they bled, and screamed like something was gnawing on them. Nobody could understand much of anything they said, but one word sounded like the French *ombre*. That's the true reason the second moon came to be called *L'ombre Moon*, though we didn't make that public. We were afraid it would cause panic. We said it was because it was bluish and hazy, like a shadow."

He heard the defensive inflection in his voice, but damn it, he was telling the truth, exactly as it happened. Scientists scrambled to understand what was turning women into homicidal monsters. Was it the blue light? The tide pull? Or something else?

"It started with an enormous uptick in protests, different from anything we'd ever seen. Huge, angry, screaming mobs. Hordes of women—millions—a few men, mostly gays and transgenders. Suddenly the abortion ban, which everyone thought was established law, was repugnant. They demanded an overturn and a reinstatement of birth control choices. When Senate members held town hall meetings, they were attacked. One was dismembered, for chrissakes. The streets of DC were overrun, businesses vandalized so badly they couldn't be salvaged. These women were raving. Part of the reason sending women into the Protective Quarantine was so easily accomplished was because men were petrified. They wanted women put away. They didn't care where it was, as long as they could feel safe."

The sheer savagery of those months left a permanent stain in Rafe's memories. "When two congressmen and another senator were murdered, Henry declared martial law. That means ordinary rule is tossed out and the military takes over. The first imprisonments of women began. They weren't released because they remained violent, even in prison. Nothing calmed them except the strongest narcotics, but the moment the drugs wore off, the women were violent again."

"What about your wife? Your daughter? Did they get this sickness?"

"Not McKenna. Erin always had anxiety, but when the moon came, it got worse. Panic attacks and hallucinations, neither of which happened before."

Hallucinations! Now that Rafe was in possession of his past life memories, he wondered if those visions had been unconnected to the events happening around them. Erin was Aridela. In every life, her memories fought to break through.

Even now, if she would come home, he would welcome her. She might have abandoned him and been blatantly unfaithful, but he knew she loved him, no matter how she tried to deny it. Will or Athene had used some kind of mind trick or drug on her. That was the only explanation.

I'm the one who can guide her through this. She needs to be with me.

"When the lunacy started, I confined them to the chateau. Erin wanted to go out and speak, try to reason with the protestors. Refusing her was hard and she was furious, but I was afraid she would be exposed to whatever it was, or that she would become a target of the lunatics because of my close relationship with Henry. I promised I would make her part of the solution if she would agree to stay at home till the scientists figured it out. Henry messed up that plan when he had his great idea of using her to help get women on board for the quarantine."

Should he admit that from the beginning there was a completely viable, one hundred percent effective antidote for lunacy? That it resided in those icosahedron pills, and that none of the Konstantinou females were ever at risk for the madness? He wanted to. He opened his mouth then forced it closed, clenching his jaw.

Adam watched him steadily. Invasively. No, damn it, there were a few secrets he would keep to himself.

Vita emerged from the forest, a rabbit hanging from her bloody jaws. She stretched out in the grass to nose and tear at the carcass.

Rafe caught himself driving a hand through his hair. He glanced at Adam, who squatted in front of the wolf and crooned to her in an unfamiliar language that ebbed and flowed with rounded vowels and soft r's. A language that twined into Rafe's brain like snorted *Mozart.*

"Henry ordered me to go to Moscow and meet with Grigory Novikov, the president of Ukrus. He said Novikov had called him claiming his scientists had developed a cure. I was intrigued. I'd never met him at that point. He was a man of mystery, unquestionably ruthless, and well on his way towards conquering every nation in the world that had anything of value, unless the fraying threads of the Western Alliance found a way to stop him."

Adam remained squatting near Vita, but he turned and regarded Rafe soberly, as if he knew the point had finally arrived.

Rafe shook his head to clear out the webbed effects of that quicksilver language. "It turned out, Novikov and his scientists...well...it turned out that he and his scientists..."

Damn those laser-like eyes. "They did it. They caused the lunacy. It wasn't the moon at all. Novikov was quite proud. He took me on a tour through his labs."

"This Novikov. He is very powerful?"

Rafe nodded. "He is, and he has brilliant scientists." *Why am I telling him this? What if he is not who he claims to be? What if he is my son, but also my enemy?*

Adam had compared them to Mordred and Arthur. Everyone knew how that turned out.

Rafe had managed to keep his mouth shut about these facts for twenty-five years, but with Adam, he blurted almost everything. He longed for commiseration. If he was convincing enough, Adam would understand that he'd never meant for any of this to happen. Events had surged across the world, sweeping him along in the tsunami.

"They created machines so tiny they couldn't be seen without a special microscope. As tiny as they were, they could take control of anyone, anywhere. These were the psychotronic weapons our government had feared since long before I was born. Novikov showed them to me, explained how they worked, and let me see a map of all the places they had been deployed. His scientists had been perfecting them for years with other goals in mind, but when the second moon was spotted, they saw the opportunity it offered and the work was accelerated. By the time the moon entered orbit, they had trillions upon trillions of sophisticated computer-driven devices invisible to the naked eye, and so light, they floated. All Novikov had to do was load them into drones and drop them over the cities he wanted to infect. Once in the air, they were inhaled."

"They affected no men?"

"Only a few of what we call intersex. Males with female chromosomes. It was one of their directives. The nanobots read the chromosomes when they entered the body and were programmed to go inert if the host was male. If female, they swam through the bloodstream to the brain and embedded in the amygdala, where they initiated their programming."

He flexed his tense muscles and pressed his palms against his forehead. Seeming to sense his turmoil, Adam rose and placed his hand on Rafe's shoulder. "Don't worry, Father," he said quietly.

Rafe was oddly reassured. "Novikov took me into a room with a couple of his scientists and laid out his terms. He said the nanobots would continue to keep females violent. There was nothing anyone could do to stop it short of murder. To which he added that if he wanted to, he could program the nanobots to drive their hosts to suicide. He let that sink in then he proposed the solution. A quarantine, that would put infected females under the jurisdiction of men. We would reassure everyone that it was temporary, and once the women were contained, simply never release them. Take back authority, education, jobs, and power. It was a bold idea, and, I admit, I was attracted, not because I hate women. For me, it was a way to gain control over births, to slow the nightmare of overpopulation that was close to destroying us, that *would* destroy us if left unchecked, as it was in America, and many other places as well."

Rafe stopped. Again, he sounded defensive. He'd always revered America's wild, open spaces, hated that they had become smaller and fewer, some vanishing completely because of the sheer numbers of human beings, people swarming like cockroaches, leaving rot and trash and ruin behind. He took a moment to clear his throat and calm his voice. "I refused at first. I said it wasn't possible. Men would swarm the Capitol, the Pentagon, the White House, and we would be murdered. Novikov just laughed. He reminded me how term after term came and went and Henry was allowed to go on as president in a so-called democracy. His supporters were loud and violent, and Henry was who they wanted. Nobody could stand up to them. 'You will take the women,' Novikov told me. 'You can do anything you want, like I do.' I'll never forget those words, and the way he said them, like he was talking about a baseball game. We started hammering out the details. Novikov agreed to deactivate the nanobots if we helped set up the quarantine in America, left the Western Alliance, and openly joined with Ukrus. We had no choice. Not only did he have a hold over us with the nanobots, he'd also taken control of every orbiting space station and satellite. He packed a few strategically placed satellites with thermonuclear bombs, and implied he had them pointed at New York, DC, and our other most important cities. He did bomb Pyongyang in 2049, murdering North Korea's president, then Rio de Janeiro, and Athens, in 2051, after Greece refused, for the third time, to join him. He killed hundreds of thousands." He paused. "Even then, they refused."

He closed his eyes as the past washed over him. He hated Grigory Novikov for what he'd done. He hated the man's indifferent evil. Most of all, he hated how Novikov and Henry had taken his ideas and warped them, leaving Rafe to be blamed. He'd been out of his depth for so long he had no inkling how to recover, or if it was possible.

"The moon came a little too early to suit Novikov. Even though he'd had his people working around the clock for years, they didn't have enough nanobots to cover the entire world. That's why there are some places, like Greece, where women were never infected. Independent Territories, we call them. The remains of the Western Alliance. America wasn't so lucky. In fact, America was his first target. He considered us his biggest triumph.

"I contacted Henry from Moscow and told him to keep martial law in force, and that I would explain when I was home and we could speak freely. I knew we had to do something to prevent more women from leaving the country. We'd already lost more white females than we could spare, those savvy enough and wealthy enough to realize America was no longer the place they wanted to be. They abandoned us before martial law was enacted. Some got out after, one way or another, before we fully secured the borders."

"So," Adam said. "That is why your women need leashes, masks, and guards. Because they are demented. Lunatic. Because they have tiny machines in their brains."

"No." This was the hardest part to confess. "They aren't psychotic anymore. They haven't been for over twenty years. Novikov kept his word and disarmed the nanobots a month after he met with Henry and me here at the chateau. I suspect the program was bankrupting him, but of course he made it sound like he was doing us a huge favor, making the women calm again so they could be controlled."

Morosely, he added, "Erin left me that night. When I got her back, twenty-three years later, she claimed she couldn't remember why she left."

"You don't believe her."

"I don't know. She did lie to me about some things, but I think maybe she was telling the truth about that part."

"What are these countries that escaped the lunacy?"

"There are four in what used to be the New European Confederation. Germany, Greece, Norway, and Sweden. In the UK, it's Scotland. Greenland is another. To our south is Mexico. In the US, we lost five states after the nanobots were disabled. California and Oregon illegally seceded early on. Three more followed. Vermont, Connecticut, and Illinois. They call themselves the Unified Free States. Their women were infected and quarantined, but were released after. For them, life eventually went back to something close to normal, or what used to be normal."

He swept out his arm. "When I was a boy, you could see forever. Mountain ranges so far away they looked like they were floating. I remember driving down to southern Utah and nearly running off the road because I couldn't take my eyes off the scenery. One set of mountains, then another, then another. I remember a pretty range by Yuba. I was disgusted when it was destroyed in search of more copper. Vast, empty spaces, our American heritage. Gone. Choked. Filled in. It got so you couldn't see more than fifty, sixty meters, thanks to haze and pollution. Less than that in the cities. Our future was destined to get worse and worse. But look, Adam. Paradise is returning. That wouldn't have happened if we hadn't taken control. The air would be poison. The water undrinkable. There would not be a single centimeter of unpolluted land. I came back from Moscow and convinced Henry to give in to Novikov's demands. I knew Novikov didn't give a shit about the world or overpopulation. All he cared about was power. I saw the value for the future, for our children's future. By controlling women and births, I saw a way to make almost everybody happy. Henry wanted white babies? Now he would be able to dictate who could get women pregnant, and which women. Those who wanted the birth rate to drop so we wouldn't all die would also get their wish, and the disgruntled men who'd been complaining about women stealing their jobs? They'd be happy too, along with the men who turned against women during the lunacy. So yes, I did it, using Novikov, the nanobots, the lunacy, and the second moon. All of it is intertwined, and if even one detail hadn't been

there, the human race would probably be well on the way to its own annihilation."

Adam's gaze remained steady. "Look again, Father."

"What? What do you mean?"

"Look around you."

Rafe did, at first impatiently. Slowly, irritation cycled into shock.

Many of the aspens appeared to be dead or dormant, which was not possible for the middle of July. The grass around his feet was a withered sort of brownish yellow. He turned in a circle then looked up at the sky, expecting to see clear blue, but it was dingy, similar to the air in the city. He paid attention to his next breath and smelled something vaguely unpleasant, like industrial chemicals.

He hadn't been out here since Erin and Brie went missing, but he was sure it hadn't been like this a month ago. He remembered one of the gardeners proudly declaring this the best year for healthy vegetation he could remember. The chateau had been bursting with fragrant flowers in vases.

He and Adam had passed the gardens on their way out here. He hadn't paid attention, but now that he was thinking about it, the flowers had been wilted.

"What happened?"

"It doesn't seem to be the way you imagine."

"No."

He'd brought Erin home from the hospital the last day of April. April was early at Deer Valley, too early for much of anything, but that very same gardener had exclaimed over the flowers that were budding, and wildflowers were abloom in fantastic numbers across the mountain slopes. He feared a hard frost would come along and kill off everything, but that didn't happen.

They started walking back to the chateau. Vita followed, the rabbit dangling from her mouth. The sun was setting. How had the entire day passed? Rafe's stomach was growling. He hadn't had anything to eat since a slice of toast before he went out to the terrace. No wonder he felt sick and exhausted, with only coffee and martinis to sustain him. Adam, though, appeared alert. Unaffected.

"Are you hungry?" he asked. "Dale probably has something fixed."

"I am always hungry," Adam said with a smile that made Rafe think of Vita scenting prey.

The only thing Rafe knew for certain by now was that whatever Adam said, it could have multiple interpretations.

"You succeeded," Adam said. "You have what you wanted. Only white men and white women reproducing. The rebuilding of the white race."

"No." Rafe spoke vehemently but he wasn't sure why. He'd given Adam the notion that white was all that mattered. He couldn't really blame him for his conclusions. "Henry did actually want the abortion ban to apply only to white women. He kept trying to figure out a way to do that, but he never could. His advisors convinced him before I came on board that America needed black and brown children too, for many reasons. Mostly so whites would be free to pursue higher ambitions."

Should I tell him about Carnevale? No, no, keep your goddamned mouth shut. Not yet.

"I'm happy you're here, Adam. It means a lot—"

Adam stopped abruptly and stared into the sky. Both moons were visible in the east, like pearls chasing each other through a dusky, blue-violet ocean. "*L'ombre,*" he said softly.

Vita dropped the rabbit and whined.

"What is it?" Rafe asked.

"I have to go."

"What? Why?" *Is he abandoning me already? Betraying me?* "You just came. Dale has made…"

Adam turned his gaze from the moons and looked into Rafe's eyes.

The compassion Rafe saw unnerved him. He was accustomed to respect, to fear, to adulation. Even hate. Not compassion. Never pity.

"I will be with you for Carnevale. I promise, Father."

He knows! Who told him?

It was too late to ask, because he was lying in the grass near the aspen grove, waking from a dream, alone but for a cold sighing wind that breathed, again and again…

Mist turned to flesh. Mist…turned…to…flesh.

Chapter 13

"Did you ever get married or have a serious relationship before you were taken? I'm scared to ask, but what about children?"

We were sitting in a corner of the playroom, watching Brie interact with four new friends, ranging in age from three to eleven. I was flipping through the book I'd stolen from Rafe, not really giving it much attention. The happiness on Brie's face was too distracting. That's what got me thinking about children and love affairs.

"Not married, no kids, but it may surprise you to know I am actively involved." Maya lifted her chin in a *so there!* manner, which made me laugh. "As if my bloodline isn't mixed enough, he's Diné. Our kids will never figure out how to answer the heritage question, assuming there are heritage questions ever again."

"You're going to have children?" The book nearly slipped off my lap as I straightened. "At forty-nine? Why haven't you told me this? You're getting married? I want to meet him. Is he here? Diné. Navajo, you mean?"

"All in good time, boo. The Diné officially dropped the Navajo moniker years ago. We haven't set a date, but we have talked about having a child. We go back and forth. What if we had a girl? I want a daughter so much, but in this world? No way, and how would a son turn out? No. Not as things stand."

"Yeah, for the first time I'm glad I'm sterilized. Forgive my crassness, I know you can do many things, but surely forty-nine is too old to have a baby."

"I know it's a long shot, but I've never even had a hot flash, much less gone into menopause. Don't you remember those fertility breakthroughs from the thirties? I'm not sure how we could avail ourselves of that option, living in a freaking gulag, but we've talked about getting across the border and living elsewhere. Maybe the Independent Territories have kept up the program."

"What's his name?"

"Nash."

"Nash," I repeated, trying to picture him.

"His grandmother calls me At'ééd Nééz. It means 'Tall Girl', I think. Nash has a nickname for me too. Ádeezbaa'. He says it means 'She Leads the Raid,' which I kind of like, if it's true. For all I know, it could really mean 'She Who Drives Me Batty.'"

"Well," I said, "you are tall, you do lead, and you have been known to drive some of us batty."

She huffed. "Isn't that a fine thank you for all I've done."

"I'm only kidding. I love you, A-dez-baa."

"Nash left the reservation when he was eighteen on a scholarship to the University of Washington, and became a software developer. He made a good living working independently and didn't worry too much about his granny, because there were plenty of relatives on the rez to watch out for her. He tried for years to get her to come to Washington, but she refused. She's old, traditional, and stubborn as hell. You'll see. Anyway, one day he gets this call from the trading post. His grandmother is shouting at him to come home, that everyone's being murdered. The connection cuts out and he can't reach anybody. This happened around the same time I was taken, when communications went dead and everything was just starting to cluster. All flights were cancelled, but a friend of his with a propeller plane flew him directly to the rez. Kai—that's his granny—told me there's a story about how he came off that plane swinging a machete, ready to slaughter anybody threatening her or keeping her from him, and that's how he got his real name. Hashké Shash. I think it means 'Angry Bear,' but don't use it or even let on that I've told you, all right?"

"Okay." I knew about secret names and their power from fairy tales. "I'm sure I'd mangle it anyway. What was going on?"

"Remember what I told you about the military rounding up women and killing anybody who challenged them?"

"Yeah."

"By the time Nash got there, they'd swarmed across the reservation. It was illegal for anyone on the rez to possess deadly weapons, but some people had them anyway, and those were the ones getting targeted. They seemed to know who to go after."

"And those who didn't have weapons were sitting ducks."

"Right. The Diné, for the most part, had refused the whole idea of quarantine, so there were women. I'm unclear as to whether they were affected with lunacy or not, but if the military wanted to roust out women, they hit the jackpot on the rez. That slowed them up, plus many dwellings were so remote they had a hard time finding them, even with all their fancy toys. Nash's cousins drove him to Kai's hooghan. That's what they call their traditional dwellings. Hers was very remote and the military hadn't found her. He was torn between standing and fighting with his brothers and sisters and cousins, or staying with Kai. In the end, he chose to protect Kai. He disguised her as an old man and they rushed back to the landing strip only to find smoking wreckage and the body of his pilot friend, something he blames himself for to this day. I'm skipping a lot because I need to get to the classroom. I'll be taking Brie, just so you know. I teach science."

"That's fantastic. You guys have thought of everything."

"We have some creative people down here, and we definitely need these kids to be educated. Anyway, one of Nash's cousins got them to Albuquerque, and from there, Nash and his grandmother became well-funded homeless wanderers. Nash had wisely brought along a lot of untraceable currency." She rose, motioning to Brianne and the other children. They trotted to her, chattering and laughing. Brianne held the three-year-old's hand.

I reached out to Maya. "Just tell me. Is he nice? Really nice? Do you love him?"

"Of course. I waited till things were right instead of settling for the first guy who came along." Her squint was expressive.

"You know what I'd say if we didn't have innocent ears listening."

She laughed. "I'll tell you the rest later, okay?"

"Sure. Have fun, Ms. MacDonald. Brie owes you a shiny apple."

HAD I SETTLED FOR THE FIRST GUY WHO CAME ALONG? I COULD DENY IT ALL DAY, but that twisty sensation in my gut told a different story. In high school, Maya tried to talk me into breaking it off with Rafe so I could date somebody else. Even as a teenager, she didn't think what Rafe and I were doing was romantic or healthy. Neither did my parents. Neither did Rafe's. Typically, the opposition made us cling harder to each other. Our logic ran something like *What we have must be out of this world if so many want to break it up.*

Looking back, I could see how our detractors, not including Rafe's parents, had our best interests at heart. I couldn't blame myself, having been all of nine when Rafe starting courting me. Some would call it "grooming." It was extremely difficult to look at our relationship objectively. We'd been married now for somewhere around thirty-two years. We'd conceived two children. We had made love countless times and gone to bed angry too. Our fights had run the gamut from sulky silence to throwing things and punching walls.

Now we'd endured the death of our only living child. There were layers upon layers of history between us, the kind of established intimacy that made it possible to finish each other's sentences and sometimes, read each other's minds. I wished I could read his mind now. I'd like to know what he truly thought of this world he'd helped create.

I wasn't brave enough to venture beyond the Navajo blanket and perhaps come face to face with someone who thought I should be turned over to the government. I chose to hole up in the bed cave with the doorway closed off.

It seemed as though I'd just settled in with the Ramsay book when Maya and Brie returned. Maya had a tray loaded with plates of hot spaghetti and meatballs, breadsticks, salads, a bottle of red wine, and a glass of milk for Brie. We spread the feast across the beds and ate from our laps. It reminded me of the all-female slumber parties Maya and I attended nearly every weekend when we were kids.

Brianne relayed some of what she'd learned. She was obviously taken with Maya's chosen field of expertise. Thirty years ago, she could have expanded this interest and made it a career. Instead, her choices were two: hiding in these carved underground caverns or living with her grandfather, doing her part to create the next generation of girls who would also be forced to bow in servitude.

Thinking such thoughts killed my appetite. I set aside my plate. "The author of this book talks a lot about her visions. She says they mostly came after she and her co-authors ate a certain mushroom. It must have been raw psilocybin."

"Didn't you say she was from Scotland? Magic mushrooms grow wild over there, or used to." She grinned at Brianne. "On cow poop."

Brianne laughed. "Eww."

"She claims to have seen in one of her visions that an eruption caused major damage on Crete." I flipped the pages, trying to find that part. "What's really interesting is that she wrote this book long before archaeologists figured that out. She says it didn't destroy the civilization, more than a century before scientists and archaeologists had the technology to determine that for themselves. There's a forward, written in 2016 by a Pulitzer Prize winning historian named Helen Kathleen Fitzgerald. She calls the author prescient."

"Uh huh," Maya said, between a bite of garlic bread and a sip of wine.

I found the section. "Here it is. She says the eruption weakened the society and destroyed its naval fleet, which was its main strength. According to her, the city-states on the mainland took advantage and the island was overthrown. The forward backs all this up. It says that after the eruption, there's evidence of Mycenaean influence. The writing changed, and—"

"Brie and I just got out of school ten minutes ago, boo. Do you mind?"

My cheeks heated. "Sorry. It's just so interesting. The historian has added a series of photographs." I held up the book and pointed. "Look. They really did leap the bulls. This is a fresco Arthur Evans dug up. See the two women at either end?"

"How can you tell they're women?"

"It says Cretans painted women white and men red. That's a boy leaping the bull. Look at this." I flipped two pages forward.

"Hmm. A hunk, if you like that sort of naked barbarian, which I do."

I gazed at the color reproduction of a statuesque man with long black hair, a narrow waist, and feathered crown, walking in a field of flowers. "It's called 'Prince of the Lilies.'" I stared at the portrait, frowning. "I could swear I've seen this before, somewhere."

"Aren't you going to finish your dinner? I'm trying my best to put weight on you, but you're fighting me every step of the way."

I closed the book. "Okay, okay." Picking up my plate, I nibbled. "Brie, don't you want your salad? That's the healthiest part."

She made a face. "I don't like the dressing. It stings my tongue."

We heard a commotion. People talking, steps ringing, laughter. Maya perked up. "There's my surprise." She put aside her plate, wiped her mouth, stood, and smoothed her hair. Why was she doing that? She almost looked nervous.

Someone knocked on the wall next to the blanket. Maya ran over and pulled it to one side, revealing two men. One was about our age. The other was quite old, his face so wrinkled and weather-beaten it was hard to see his eyes. Both were dressed in faded jeans, dusty cowboy boots, and threadbare button-down shirts. The older man wore quite a lot of turquoise and silver jewelry.

"Ma'am." The younger man inclined his head. "Was told you might be in here." His steely appearance was transformed by an amiable smile.

"Nash!" Maya reached for him but at the last second, she stopped and put her hands behind her back, reminding me of a little girl being chastised for stealing a cookie. His smile twitched at the edges.

He and his companion removed their black felt hats. The older man's gray hair was pulled back out of sight but Nash's fell in two braids over his shoulders. His face reminded me of Old Man Sneffels. The hawk nose and high cheekbones were reminiscent of the mountain summit. It had gazed, unblinking, into the starry heavens for longer than could be imagined. We called the mountain "old man," because we knew he'd been there for millions of years, but the profile wasn't particularly aged. Just stern and wise. The face of a god, caught in a never-ending dream.

"Please come in," I said, rising and gesturing to Brianne to join me.

They stepped inside and Maya let the blanket fall, closing out the people in the corridor. I hoped they wouldn't blame me for the snub.

"I'm Erin," I said. "Erin Aragon. This is Brianne, my granddaughter."

"Pleased to meet you," the younger man replied. "Yá'át'ééh, we say in Diné. I am Nash Descheeni. This is Kai, mother of my mother."

"It's good to meet you," I said. I should have known this was no old man. "Have you been up above?"

"Yeah," Nash said. "We went to my granny's old hooghan on the rez. Granny had a dream and so we had to obey."

His tone held a hint of weary indulgence.

She spoke then. I didn't understand a word, not even slightly, like one sometimes can with French or Spanish. Maya leaned close. "She speaks

English, but generally chooses not to. Nash will translate. I only know a few words."

Kai stopped abruptly and I felt Maya stiffen. The old woman laughed. "Why go out for hamburger when you have steak at home?" she said.

"Paul Newman?" Maya's voice was faint.

I couldn't suppress an amused smirk. Anyone who could intimidate Maya had my respect.

Kai made an interesting gesture with her lips. Her grandson seemed to take this as a signal and nodded. "Granny says hello and welcome. She is glad you are here and safe. She wants you to know that she, Kai Descheeni, is of the Kinyaa'áanii, the Towering House Clan, that she was born for the Todích'íi'nii, the Bitter Water Clan, that her mother's grandfathers were from Ma'iideeshgiizhinii, the Coyote Pass People, and her father's grandfathers were from Tó'aheedliinii, the Water-Flows-Together Clan. In this way, she is a woman of the Diné."

"Oh." I was pretty sure my own voice had gone faint. This had the feel of a traditional, formal greeting, but I had no idea how to reply. Following Maya's lead, I smiled. "Thank you." I glanced from Nash to Maya, wondering if I should say something else as Kai kept her glimmering gaze focused upon me.

"She wants to know your clans," Nash said.

Thanks to the popularity of ancestry kits thirty or forty years ago, almost everyone knew their bloodlines, but it had been a long time since I'd researched them. "I'm Erin, daughter of Irene and Javier Aragon, who are deceased. My grandparents were Diogo Aragon and Emilia Diaz, and my great-grandparents were Tamala and her husband, Haruto. I researched this when I was a teenager, but I'm afraid I've forgotten their last names."

Nash translated what Kai said next as, "You are of many and far-flung clans."

"Yes," I said. "A real mix."

Kai turned her attention to Maya. "Sisters of widespread clans," Nash translated. "This gives you far-reaching sight. Those of few clans, or only one, see narrowly, as through a ravine, and some cannot even see the walls of the ravine."

Kai offered her hands to Brianne. At a nod from me, Brianne took them. Kai grinned, her smile showing a couple of gaps where teeth used to be, then she spoke.

"A serpent can see through flesh to the beating heart," Nash told us. "She says here is one who augurs with the eyes of the serpent." Listening and nodding as Kai said something else, he added, "The soul of the serpent is strong in this child's blood. Strong with lightning. She says this child's blood is serpent blood." He shrugged. "That's what she's saying."

Kai released one of Brianne's hands and took mine, drawing me closer and placing my hand over Brianne's.

"She says your blood is serpent blood too." Nash repeated his shrug. "I don't know what that means. She's been acting strangely ever since Noah and Levi left. In all honesty, she's put me through the wringer. I'm exhausted. To think I would ever have to admit that my ninety-two-year-old granny has more stamina than me."

Kai turned sideways towards Nash. I saw that her hair was arranged in a thick bun, tied with white yarn. It looked like it would reach her waist or even farther if it was unbound. There was not a single loose strand. I wondered if Nash fixed it for her every day.

Lifting my hands, she pushed at my sleeves and bared my wrists. The crescent scars were bright red, though I hadn't noticed them burning like I usually did when they were inflamed.

She traced first the scar on my right wrist then the left. She traced the bull's head birthmark with the tip of her index finger. It tickled. I wanted to pull away but I was afraid she would be offended, so I didn't.

When she spoke, her voice was calm, quiet, and somehow reassuring.

Nash frowned and asked her something. She replied.

"She says you are a new daughter for the new age, for the sixth world. She calls you daughter of Asdzáán Nádleehé. The Woman who Changes. Changing Woman."

His gaze was serious. "Who is that?" I asked.

"What?" This was Maya. She stared at Nash then said to me, "Changing Woman is *the* primary deity of the Diné. She created the people who later became the Diné, from her own skin."

Kai released me and spoke to Nash. When she was finished, her grandson nodded. He said to us, "I made a mistake. She says you are *foster*-daughter of Changing Woman."

His grandmother shook his forearm and he placed his hand over hers. "Calm down, Granny." Turning to us, he said, "My granny wants you to particularly understand. Changing Woman changes but does not die. She grows old with the coming of winter, then young again when spring arrives. She changes. But she does not die."

I felt like Kai was trying to make me understand something important, but I was missing the message. It was embarrassing. If I went on smiling and nodding like a bobble-head, they would think me simple-minded.

Kai studied me, then Brianne, then Maya, and spoke rapidly.

Nash dipped his head and laughed. "She says that Maya will form me like the water for which she is named, and settle me down. She's always thought me too flighty, leaving the rez and all, but she says Maya must first help her friend. She says her dream was true. It stands before her and she is happy to witness the three coming together at last. She says united, your power is limitless. Changing Woman draws disorder to a close. Yet one is missing. The sacred fourth."

Kai smiled and nodded.

Nash sighed as she made another gesture with her lips and her chin towards the corridor.

"She says this one—" he nodded at me— "needs a singer. A healing. I have tried to explain that it's impossible. We could not repair Granny's hooghan. It was demolished. There is no hataałii any longer, either. He died and there was no one to take his place. Nobody knows the songs."

"What's a hataałii?" I asked.

"A holy man, what we would call a shaman," Maya said, frowning. "What can be done?" she asked Nash as though she fully accepted the idea.

"I will keep looking," Nash said, rather wearily, I thought. "There are intact hooghans, a few anyway. They're further in, dangerous to drive to. We will figure something out."

Kai spoke to Nash and rubbed her stomach.

"She's hungry," Nash said. "I will take her to eat. Later, we will talk. We will find a way."

"I'm not sick," I said. "I'm not injured. You don't need to go to this trouble."

"Are you content? Do you have peace? Do you understand your purpose? Is your soul in harmony with your body and the earth?"

"If those are the requirements, I suppose I'm not quite well. I'm much better though, since I found Maya."

"You need a healing, Erin." He took his granny's arm and led her from the room.

"Not a lot of public displays between you, are there?" I said, once they were gone.

"He's more affectionate when we're alone."

"What's all this about healing?"

"The Diné have ceremonies for many things. Healing is one of them. I don't know all that much myself. I went to a ceremony once, in college. A Blessing Way. I'm not sure what's involved in a healing ceremony. I'll sit with them while they're eating. Maybe I can find out more. One thing is certain. Kai wants us to see or do something, and Nash told me a long time ago that when his granny has a hankering, she gets what she wants, one way or another. Truth is, he would move heaven and earth to make her happy."

I grabbed her hand as she was leaving. "He's cute, Maya."

"He is!" Brie piped in, nodding.

Maya grinned and fluttered her lashes.

Chapter 14

Brianne fell into unusual silence after Maya left. "We're really having experiences now, aren't we?" I asked, with what I hoped was a reassuring smile.

She nodded but said nothing.

"Don't be afraid. They're Maya's friends. I like them."

"Everything is going to change. I'm not afraid, but I am."

"You've seen something?"

She met my gaze. "Some of it is good. But some of it is bad."

I didn't know what to do, so I hugged her. "I'm here, okay?"

She nodded.

We stacked the dishes and set them on the trunk. I would help Maya take them to the kitchen and wash them later. While we waited, we took turns reading from *Secrets of Bronze Age Goddess Cults*.

I had barely succeeded in sparking her interest when they all came back, bringing Brie a cup of mulled cider and small glasses of tequila for the rest of us.

"Yá'át'ééh," Nash and Kai said as they entered.

I tried repeating it, and the way Nash smiled made me think I did all right.

Nash and Kai wanted to sit cross-legged on the floor, rather than on the beds. Maya and I shoved the beds against the walls so we could join them. There was barely enough room, and we had to sit very close. Brie's eyelids were starting to droop, so I hoped this second get-together wouldn't last long.

"There are problems we can't overcome at this time," Nash said. "We do not have a hataałii or a hooghan or a sand painting or peyote. We do have corn pollen and my granny knows some of the songs. While she ate, she talked about us going above to the buttes and holding a ceremony under the stars. They are sacred places."

I saw myself sitting on the summit of one of the flat-topped buttes under cloudless heavens, gazing up at the Milky Way and watching shooting stars. I wanted to go. If there was any place I could feel at one with the universe, it would be there.

Kai, who watched Nash intently as he talked, shook her head and said something.

"Now she's changed her mind. It doesn't sit well with her."

I tried to hide my disappointment. "It's all right. Thank you for your concern." I made a point of meeting Kai's gaze. "It's very kind, but I'm not sick."

Kai nodded then spoke to Nash.

"Okay," Nash said. "There are things she wants to say. I'll translate, because it's easier for her to talk in her own language. She doesn't have to stop and find the words. The first thing is that the three of you have been sisters in many lives."

I exchanged a glance with Maya and Brianne. It was a nice thought. Maya, especially, felt like a sister, and Brianne was as necessary to me as my right arm.

The room seemed to be getting warmer. I fought the urge to fan myself. A hot flash, perhaps. I hated those. I sensed Brianne watching me and tried to show nothing but calm.

All the while, Kai spoke. Sometimes she regarded us. Sometimes she kept her eyes closed.

When she paused and nodded to her grandson, he turned to us. "In the year 2049, the bilagáana swarmed the reservation with their big guns and bombs. Any who fought were killed. Diné girls and women were stolen. It did not matter if they were wives or grandmothers, small girls not even to puberty, or suckling babes. We do not know what was done to these women and girls. No messages ever reached us. They were never seen again."

Maya and I glanced at each other, discerning in each other's eyes the same dismal thought.

"Any of our women who successfully hid, now live in secrecy and fear, or as men. Our Nation is splintered and we roam as refugees. Our ways are lost, our people dead or scattered, our women dead or slaves, our hooghans smashed or burned, and only bones are left of our sheep. In the old days, a healing ceremony would be attended by five hundred or more. These days we are fortunate to have ten or twenty. Now is the time for imagination and dreams. Now is the time for courage."

Kai placed her hand on Nash's forearm. He remained silent. We sat, saying nothing. I watched Kai, who watched Nash. I pictured that time of violence and despair on the reservation. My eyes blurred. I wept, especially for the little ones. The little girls, so frightened, torn from their mothers.

Then I remembered that McKenna had said the same thing in Rafe's office. *Now is the time for courage.* It was odd. I shivered.

After some time, Nash addressed himself to me. "Granny says your hózhó is buried beneath doubt and fear, beneath self-condemnation, buried so deeply you can no longer hear it, feel it, or see it. She understands. This world is a bad place for females, and some will bury their hózhó in self-preservation. Beauty is the simplest way to translate hózhó, but the word beauty is often misunderstood. Hózhó is more. It is a state of harmony, both inner and outer. My granny says she sees strength in you, if you will allow it to wake, if you will set it free. She says it is as big as the night sky."

Kai's tone softened.

"Changing Woman gave the Diné what they needed to survive and flourish," Nash said. "Pottery, brooms, millstones, and stirring sticks."

"Like Athene," I said.

"What?" Maya blinked as she faced me. Her pupils obliterated her sea-colored irises, and I wondered if mine were the same. There was something about Kai's voice. It wove into my brain like a spell.

The pages of the book floated through my mind's eye. "Athene showed the Cretans how to create bronze and how to graft the olive tree. With that knowledge they grew rich and powerful. She also taught them how to weave, how to dye cloth, and how to form clay."

Kai nodded. For the first time, she spoke to me directly, in English.

"Changing Woman and your Athene, maybe they know each other. Woman is the middle of the clan, like the center of a wheel, with spokes fanning out. This is the way the Holy People, Diyin Dine'é, set up our world. Woman is the base of life, the soul in touch with beginnings and endings. In the beginning, your people were the same. Yours abandoned the sacred ways. Now your men are violent, your women afraid. The sacred has been hijacked, and there is blackness on the horizon. Erin Aragon. Your name is *Er-in-ys*, avenging warrior. Changing Woman and your Athene strive to wake you. Will you listen?"

I didn't know how to answer. That night in Rafe's office, McKenna had also told me to wake. I shivered again, sensing a mystical connection between my daughter and this woman.

Her words sank into my heart like round stones, heavy and hard. I was afraid it was too late. I could no longer hear the primordial voice. I had lost it somewhere along the way.

Kai seemed able to tune in to mystical things. Emotional things. Earth things. Divinity. Had we all been like that once? Did we lose the ability in our progression from ancient to modern times? Could we get it back? Could I get it back?

There was another time of silence. I could not tell how long it lasted. I sat, cross-legged on the floor, knowing that on one side I had Brie and on the other I had Maya, but I could not turn my head to look at them.

I came out of my trance, feeling like I was swimming to the surface of an ocean made of rainbows. Kai, Nash, and Maya had all risen to their feet. I stood hastily, sensing the end of our gathering had come.

Kai extended her hand and shook mine.

"She says sleep well," Nash said.

"Thank you," I said weakly. "You too."

They left, taking Maya with them. The blanket closed. I helped Brianne change into pajamas and get into bed. Everything felt like it was happening in another place, to another person. I did my best to make everything seem normal.

"Night, Meemah," Brie said.

I kissed her forehead. "Night, babe."

A ROUND, CLOSE PLACE. AN OLD MAN SITTING ON THE GROUND, EYES CLOSED, singing.

Kai lifts her hand, palm up, and blows. A yellow cloud, drifting.

A crimson-yellow circle of embers on the ground.

Mother, someone calls.

I leave the close place. I hear the stars whispering. There is no other sound. No wind, no birdsong, no coyotes yipping, no soft thump of leaping jackrabbits or squeak of mice.

I stand on the top of a flat butte high above the desert, halfway to the sky. The ridge goes on and on, as far as I can see.

I walk. The rocks become milky grass, twining around my ankles, rustling like voices of ghosts.

A girl in a white dress is dancing in the distance, twirling in a shower of blue-white light.

See the truth. Hear the truth. You have prepared through the ages for this.

A meteor soars, intensely blue.

I fall to my knees before the Lily Prince.

For longer than you can imagine, I will be with you, in you, of you. Together we will bring forth a new world, and nothing can ever part us.

Stars glimmer through him. He dissipates.

Until you see truly, this world my Mother loves will plummet deeper, ever deeper, into tragedy and suffering.

I weep, alone and desolate on the summit of a high butte.

Another takes my arm and lifts me. I keep my face turned down. I am ashamed.

Pebbles are round. Whirlpools are round. Robins make round nests. Stars are round, the moons are round, and so is the earth. Even the seasons are round, coming full circle from summer to summer, harvest to harvest. Round is universal. Redraw the circle, which has been severed and forced into a straight line.

This is not the Lily Prince. He is real. I jump away.

His voice sinks into my skin like the rumbling that comes with the earthquake. "In my home I heard the call. My grandmother heard. Every living thing who listens to the earth heard the call. *Go to my daughter.*"

He places something on my palm, something heavy and circular. A ring. He closes my hand, signaling that the ring is now mine. I finally look up. It is the young man with flowing copper hair. I last saw him at Dallas Creek, reaching for me just before the men attacked.

A wolf stands beside him.

"Go to Crete," he says.

I hear McKenna. *Where it began. You will remember. I am waiting for you.*

I search for her, but I don't see her. Where did the dancing girl go? That might have been her.

The copper-haired youth wavers. He turns his face up. He lifts off the ground.

My father will come. You will be reunited.

I watch him ascend, he and his wolf. They vanish somewhere in the endless starry abyss.

My knees buckle. The ring falls from my hand, drawing in the light of the stars.

Together we came, mist turned to flesh, from our Mother's imaginings.

I wake. I am in the Catacombs. It was a dream.

I feel something on my face. In my lashes. On my pillow. I light a candle.

Yellow powder.

And in my hand a silver ring.

Chapter 15

"MAYA, I HAD THE MOST EXTRAORDINARY DREAM."

She winked at Brie and sipped coffee. "Tell me about it. I'll interpret it for you."

"I was in a small structure. Kind of like a den. It wasn't round. It was hexagonal or octagonal. There was an old man sitting next to a beautiful design made from colored sand. He was singing."

"A hooghan," Maya said. "You were in a hooghan. The old man was a hataałii. The design was a sand painting. This dream is too easy."

"There was yellow dust. Kai blew it over me."

"Corn pollen. Sounds like you managed to get yourself to a healing ceremony, at least in a dream."

"When I woke up, it was on my cheeks, in my eyelashes. On my pillow. In my hair." I ran my hand through my hair and displayed my fingers, dusted with fine yellow grains. "See?"

Her brow crinkled. She poured me a cup of coffee. "Go on."

"I heard someone calling. I left the hooghan and found myself on top of one of the buttes, the biggest one we saw when we went hiking. What's it called?"

"Citadel Butte."

"Right. It was night and there were stars like you would not believe. I *heard* them talking among themselves. I walked and walked, it seemed like forever. I saw a girl, dancing, lit somehow, though there were no moons. Then I saw the Lily Prince. Remember?"

"Yeah. The fresco from the book."

"He spoke to me. Something about creating a new world. Then I saw the weirdest thing, Maya. A vision I've had for years and years. Even before I left Rafe. A man. Nobody else ever saw him, which made me think I was losing my mind. Anyway, he's a young guy, very handsome, and this time there was a wolf with him. I've never seen the wolf before. He told me to go to Crete."

"The wolf said this? Or the young man?"

"The young man, of course."

"You never know with dreams."

"The dancing girl said she would wait for me there. I felt like she was McKenna, but I never saw her up close, so I'm not positive."

Maya nodded and smiled sadly, which made tears sting my eyes.

"The guy said that if I went, I would be reunited with his father."

"I hope he wasn't talking about Rafe."

"Me too. Rafe and I don't have a living son, but he was referring to *his* father. He didn't say I was his mother."

"Like I said, you never know with dreams. Is that all?"

"Not quite." I held out my hand. "Here."

She opened her hand and I dropped the ring onto her palm.

"I dreamed the young guy gave this to me."

Her gaze catapulted from the ring to my eyes. "You didn't already have this?"

"Nope. I've never seen it before. When I woke up, it was in my hand."

"What we have here is a dream breaking through into reality." She examined the ring, frowning.

"How is that possible?"

She shrugged. "I have no effing idea. You're not messing with me, are you?"

"I'm not."

"This looks Pictish. I wonder how old it is?"

Brie pushed her plate away and lifted herself onto her knees in her chair. "Can I see it?"

Maya handed her the ring. A long moment passed. When she looked up, her eyes had that blank stare. "The ribbons will hide you. Your mother is the fulcrum and you are the force."

"Brie?"

Maya shook her head. *Don't*, she mouthed.

"The knife cut her and allowed her to live," Brie said softly.

I was getting alarmed, but before I could intervene, she blinked and her eyes cleared. "I think I've seen this before."

"You know," Maya said, "I feel the same way, boo-child. I've seen this ring before, too."

"Me too," I said.

After a moment where Maya's frown grew ever deeper, she said, "We could go there."

"Where?"

"Crete. Crete is part of Greece, and there are rumors that Greece was never overthrown by Ukrus. If it's free, and if we can get there, we'd be free, too. Free to walk around, have jobs, live our lives like regular people. Like the old days, if their economy hasn't collapsed. We'd be a long way from Rafe, too. I know that's a lot of 'ifs.'"

I had to take a moment. Maya was willing—no, she *expected*—to leave the safety of this shelter that had been her home for years, and her friends, to go off with me into the unknown, into real danger. It meant everything.

"We've heard that California and Oregon are free too," she said. "They seceded from the US."

I nodded, though I didn't understand why she'd veered off onto this. "The first night at the chateau, after I was released from the hospital, Rafe told me that California, Oregon, Vermont, Connecticut, and Illinois all seceded from the old US. They're called the Unified Free States, and their borders are closed. He told me the countries that never joined Ukrus, too. Greece was one of them."

"Okay. I hadn't heard that about the eastern states. Good on them. Tough to get into, I bet. Anyway, Canada's out. I remember when it caved to Ukrus. It's too far away anyway. Mexico, Erin." She smiled. "Unless something has changed that we don't know about, Mexico is an Independent Territory."

"Rafe said it was," I confirmed. "If we can believe anything he says."

"Once we get across the border, we can walk into any airport and board a plane. I'll bet everyone here would chip in to help us get airline tickets, passports, and visas." Her eyes gleamed. She was getting into this whole idea, working out the details in her analytical mind. "In fact, we won't even need to worry about that. We have a guy, Sanjay, right here in the Catacombs, who's an expert forger. He can set us up with aliases and papers in a couple of days."

The familiar, serpentine fears rose from the depths of hope. "It's impossible," I heard myself say. "There's probably a thousand alarms and detectors set up at the border to catch anyone foolish enough to try getting across. Have you ever heard of anyone getting out?"

"No, but it's not like they would print that kind of news for everyone to read. They would want to squelch reports of escapes."

I shook my head. "I can't put Brianne in such danger." I was picturing the cliché. Uniformed guards in helmets with slavering German shepherds on short leashes. Towers with spotlights. Barbed wire fencing. And those were old-school. Who knew what kind of technology there was now? Something that marked the exact location of a single footstep, maybe? Bottomless pits with holographic covers, making you think you were walking on solid ground just before you fell and broke any number of bones? Dying that way might be better than being captured by the US of U's military police, especially if you were female.

"Don't yell at me, okay?" I pleaded. "I've been wondering if maybe I should send Brianne home to her grandfather. I've brought her so far from everything she's ever known. We're hiding in the ground like worms. Is she going to have to spend the rest of her life down here? How is that better than the chateau?" I rolled the silver ring between my palms. Somehow it had defied the dream. It was real, solid, a heavy ring made for a man's finger, woven in a complex knot. I couldn't understand how this had happened. There was simply no logical explanation.

"Really? You think she would be better off with him than here, where she has friends, and is learning stuff she would never learn there? Better off there than here, where she won't be sold like a cow to someone Rafe owes a favor to? Maybe if you go to Crete, you can take off the blinders and put the past behind you. I've tried everything I can think of. If that hypnosis session didn't do it, I don't know what would. Maybe Crete has the magic key."

I shrugged. I wished I could explain. I was willing to try anything, take any risks for myself, but not with Brianne. I knew Maya would feel differently if she had children or grandchildren. I contented myself with saying, "I'm just trying to look at every angle with objectivity," and left unsaid that I could never believe Rafe would sell his beloved granddaughter to anyone.

Brianne looked from Maya to me and said nothing.

We took her to a watercolor class the next morning, taught by a woman everyone called "CeeBee." I tried to paint the Lily Prince.

When the class ended, Brianne tugged on my sleeve. "Meemah."

"Yes, baby?"

Brianne held out the painting she'd created. It was crude, but easy to decipher. A woman, her arms outstretched. Snakes wound around them. She wore a long robe, which Brianne had painted in horizontal stripes, and on her forehead was a blue crescent moon. Beneath this image she had painted her own name, "Brianne," in big black letters.

The book I'd stolen had a photo of a recovered Bronze Age statuette that looked remarkably like this drawing. The similarity sent a thin little chill fingering over the back of my neck, down my spine, then sharply through my stomach like a stabbing blade.

As I met my granddaughter's solemn brown eyes, my fear evaporated. "We're going to Crete, aren't we?"

She smiled. "I love you, Meemah."

I knew nothing would ever be the same.

And maybe that was a good thing.

THE END

When the Moon Whispers, First Chronicle
Continued in When the Moon Whispers, Second Chronicle

If you are enjoying *When the Moon Whispers* and would like to see what happens next, please look for the second installment, told in its own volume.
When the Moon Whispers, Second Chronicle

Ageless, changeless Athene deems her child ready to fight for the future of humanity. The year-god's daughter has reached *the seventh labyrinth*, the final circle promised by Athene 4000 years ago.
All her past incarnations return to her consciousness.

The Erinys Archives

Contributors:
Maya MacDonald
William Konstantinou
Raphael Konstantinou

Notes

If you have made it this far, I thank you!

But the story isn't finished.
The end of *When the Moon Whispers* is told in the Second Chronicle. I broke the
book into two parts because of its size.

After the Second Chronicle, the entire series concludes with Book Nine,
Swimming in the Rainbow.
For me, *the Child of the Erinyes* series revolves around *Swimming.*
It was the one I was most inspired to write and the only one that flowed as if
by magic from my heart through my fingertips as if Someone Else was
directing things.

In real life, I'm actually more of a Wall-e kind of person than Fight Club. But
this book insisted on being written in the style presented. Some readers will
find it tame, but others may be disturbed, and for that I apologize.

In Case You Wondered:

The image on the title page at the beginning of this book represents
Adamantinus. I mention it because a couple of beta readers thought the image
was female.

Adam is androgynous and *aes sídhe,* ("The People of the Mounds," a supernatural race in Celtic mythology, variously called faeries or elves) as pointed

315

out in the narrative, so this didn't bother me a bit, but I thought I ought to make it clear.

I developed this series (in fits and starts) more than thirty years ago, and wrote it during the eighties and nineties, but I'm glad it took this long to get published, because it took that long for the ideas, fears, and feelings in this book to mature inside me. I rewrote much of it because I changed so much.

I think it's inevitable that my story, as most any dystopian feminist story, will be compared to *The Handmaid's Tale*. I can't think of a dystopian feminist novel that hasn't been, just as any Bronze Age Cretan tale is compared to Mary Renault's *The King Must Die*.

This happened to *Native Tongue*, by Suzette Haden Elgin, I couldn't help noticing, but I have read *Native Tongue* and the similarities are superficial. The only similarity, in my opinion, is that it, too, is a feminist story.

As *Native Tongue* is its own story, so is mine, and I hope mine will be taken on its own merits. Margaret Atwood's is rightfully the most famous and successful, but there are other feminists, and their voices deserve to be heard as well. If you peruse the bibliographies on my website, you'll see that I was inspired by many, many voices. *Moon, Moon*, by Anne Kent Rush, was my first adult inspiration; therefore, it remains in my mind the most influential.

The Navajo scenes are from Erin's point of view. She is seeing and hearing all of it as a white person who is unfamiliar with the culture.

Did you know that you can help Indigenous women by donating to the "National Indigenous Women's Resource Center?"

From the website:

"Providing national leadership to end violence against American Indian, Alaska Native and Native Hawaiian women by lifting up the collective voices of grassroots advocates and offering culturally grounded resources, technical assistance and training, and policy development to strengthen tribal sovereignty."

"Each gift made to the National Indigenous Women's Resource Center strengthens our mission to end violence against Native women and vision of restoring sovereignty for tribes to hold perpetrators accountable. We are committed to providing national leadership in this work by lifting up the collective voices of grassroots advocates in tribal communities."
https://www.niwrc.org/donate

Wherever I could, I used tribal names. Otherwise, I used the term American Indian. I researched it, and found the terminology in flux, with many differing opinions. It became evident that whatever term I chose, it would annoy some. So I went with the one I thought would be clearest for readers.

Reviews help readers decide what to invest their time and money on. Please consider leaving one.

- Sign up for my newsletter if you'd like to hear about my writing news.
- The full link is: http://eepurl.com/hSrs6P
- Follow me on BookBub. You'll be informed whenever there's a special deal.
- Full link: bookbub.com/authors/rebecca-lochlann
- Instagram: https://www.instagram.com/rebeccalochlann/
- Connect with me and read lots of extras at my website. I have bibliographies, maps, histories, character details, epilogues, author's notes, and links. Someday I might even have stories there. You can find me at rebeccalochlann.com, or simply scan this handy QR code:

Titles in the Child of the Erinyes, by Rebecca Lochlann

About the Author

While growing up, Rebecca Lochlann began envisioning an epic story, a new kind of myth, one built upon the foundation of the Greek classics and continuing through the centuries right up into the present and future.

This has become her life's work, though she didn't exactly intend it to be that way when she started.

The Child of the Erinyes series is mythic fantasy, inspired by the Greek tale of Ariadne, Theseus, and the Minotaur. As one reader put it, "Loads of testosterone, slaughter, and crazy magic," with a love story, of course.

Though the story is fiction-fantasy, it still took about fifteen years to research the Bronze Age segments of the series, and encompassed rare historical documents, mythology, archaeology, ancient religions, and volcanology.

The Year-god's Daughter is her debut novel: Book One of *The Child of the Erinyes* series. It has been utilized as a study guide in an American university, named a B.R.A.G. Medallion honoree, and was a finalist in the Chaucer Historical Fiction awards. Book Two, *The Thinara King*, a First Place winner in the Ancient History category of the Chaucer Historical Fiction awards and a Next Generation Indie Book Awards finalist, continues the saga. Book Three, *In the Moon of Asterion*, wraps up the Bronze Age segment of the series and leads into the middle trilogy, set in Scotland. These are: Book Four, *The Moon Casts a Spell*, Book Five, *The Sixth Labyrinth*, and Book Six, *Falcon Blue*, which jumps backward in time to the Early Medieval Era.

The denouement comes in the final three books: *When the Moon Whispers, First and Second Chronicles*, and *Swimming in the Rainbow*.

Rebecca has always believed that certain rare individuals, either blessed or tortured, voluntarily or involuntarily, are woven by fate or the Immortals into the labyrinth of time, and that deities sometimes speak to us through dreams and visions, gently prompting us to tell their lost stories. Who knows? It could make a difference.

Connect with Rebecca at her website, BookBub, or in a review at your point of purchase.

<hr>

Attributions

<hr>

Girl stone bridge full moon: Tongsai, Shutterstock
Stars in space or night sky: Clearviewstock, Depositphotos
Abstract digital human face: Pinkeyes, Shutterstock
3D Rendered Space Art: Alien Planets, brita_seifert, Depositphotos
Kingfisher: Foster_Soul, Shutterstock
Title Page "Adam": Anna Ismagilova, Shutterstock

Labrys Axe graphic © "Labrys-symbol" Licensed under Public domain via Wikimedia Commons http://commons.wikimedia.org/wiki/File:Labrys-symbol.svg#mediaviewer/File:Labrys-symbol.svg

Crescent moons, necklace, & Erinyes Press logo: Lance Ganey: freelanceganey.com

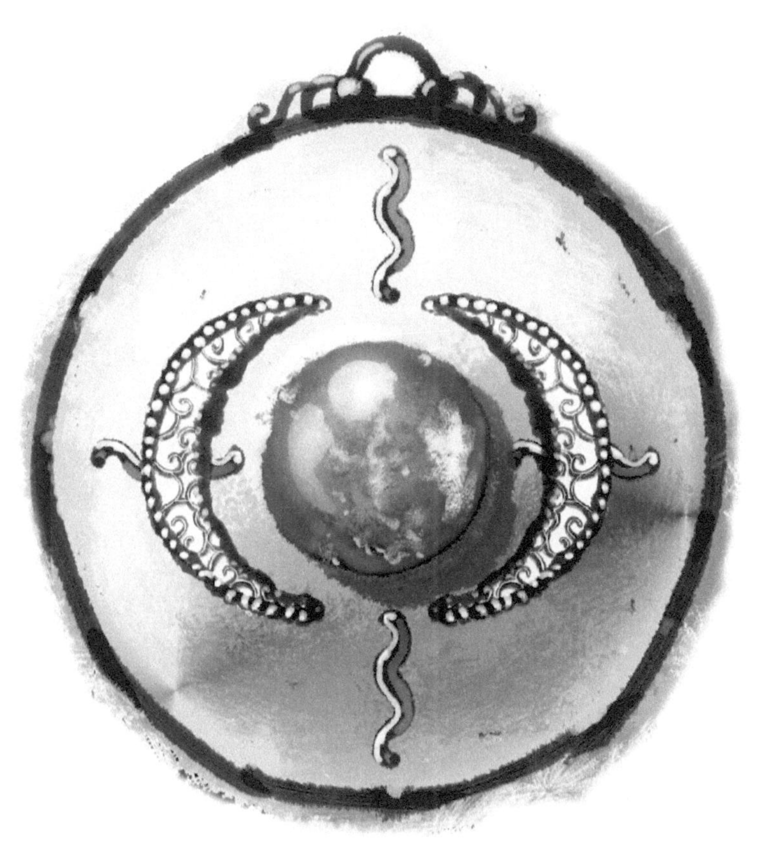